Praise for R. ... .ORTHAM
and his SONNY HAWKE *thrillers*

"If you look for the voice of authenticity in your books like I do, you'll swoon over Reavis Wortham. He's Texas true, and that's a fine thing to be."
—C. J. Box

"There's a term we use in the West, *the genuine article*, and those words fit Reavis Wortham to a Texas T."
—Craig Johnson

"Think: Elmore Leonard meets James Lee Burke."
—Jeffery Deaver

"The most riveting thriller all year!"
—John Gilstrap

"Reavis Z. Wortham had us all night. *Hawke's Target* is his best work yet, filled up with some of the finest quirkily entertaining characters we've read to date. Entertaining isn't the half of it. Think shades of Edward Abbey mixed with McMurtry."
—Michael and Kathleen Gear, #1 New York Times bestselling authors

"Wortham writes well in describing the forbidding landscape and the difficulties of those trying to survive in it, not easy even when people aren't trying to kill you. Readers who like action-packed thrillers that leave a lot of bodies should find *Hawke's War* to their liking."
—PCA Mystery & Detective Fiction Reading List

"This is one of those books, settings, and characters that make you want to cheer for the U.S. of A. In addition, this is also a brand-new character to star in his own brand-new series, so there's a lot more of Hawke to go around. Add in humor, a great cast of characters, both good and bad, along with a terrific ending, and *Hawke's Prey* becomes a must-read for everybody."
—*Suspense Magazine*

"An intuitive, creative synthesis of contemporary politics and policy into an original plot . . . Wortham writes excellent action sequences and knows how to ratchet tension. With pitch-perfect West-Texas flavor, Wortham paints a complex picture of Ballard, providing good backstories for his large cast of characters."
—*Lone Star Literary Life* on *Hawke's Prey*

HAWKE'S FURY

A SONNY HAWKE THRILLER

REAVIS Z. WORTHAM

PINNACLE BOOKS
Kensington Publishing Corp.
www.kensingtonbooks.com

PINNACLE BOOKS are published by

Kensington Publishing Corp.
119 West 40th Street
New York, NY 10018

All Kensington titles, imprints, and distributed lines are available at special quantity discounts for bulk purchases for sales promotions, premiums, fund-raising, educational, or institutional use. Special book excerpts or customized printings can also be created to fit specific needs. For details, write or phone the office of the Kensington sales manager: Kensington Publishing Corp., 119 West 40th Street, New York, NY 10018, attn: Sales Department; phone 1-800-221-2647.

ISBN-13: 978-0-7860-4625-6
ISBN-10: 0-7860-4625-2

First printing: June 2020

10 9 8 7 6 5 4 3 2 1

Printed in the United States of America

Electronic edition:

ISBN-13: 978-0-7860-4626-3 (e-book)
ISBN-10: 0-7860-4626-0 (e-book)

This one is for all the law enforcement officers,
in every branch, who put their lives
on the line each day
across this great country of ours.
Many thanks.

Chapter 1

My position overlooking a two-track pasture road cutting through the rough West Texas rangeland gave me a clear view of three late model charcoal-gray Expeditions speeding in my direction across the hot Chihuahuan desert. Thick rooster-tails of dust boiled behind the vehicles that looked like matchbox cars from where I sat.

The late evening sun stretched across the sage and ocotillo-covered pasture in the Big Bend region of the state, fifty miles north of where we live in Ballard, Texas. Harsh and dry, the claw cactus, sage, and creosote-dotted landscape stretched into the distance.

Buzzards rode the thermals, winding high above the landscape in endless spirals. It was wide-open country, once home to the Jumano Indians until around 1700 when the Apaches pushed them out and held the area until they too were finally driven almost to extinction.

White thunderheads towered to 50,000 feet, supported by dark gray foundations almost resting on the ragged, thin line of the blue Davis Mountains to the northwest. I was hoping the closest storm would collapse, pushing welcoming waves of blessedly cool air across the flat valley floor.

It was hot, harsh country as addictive as cocaine to those who found beauty in the rocky, thorn-covered landscape.

Beside me, my runnin' buddy since high school, Presidio County Sheriff Ethan Armstrong adjusted his straw hat and used a thumb to wipe a trickle of sweat from his temple. With two fingers, he smoothed a brush-pile mustache big enough to cover a good piece of his lower face and watched the rooster-tails of dust rise behind the vehicles. "Those two behind the lead car can't be seeing a stinkin' thing in all that dust."

We spoke barely above a whisper. "I'd be following a little farther behind, that's for sure."

Directly in front of us, I could see the backs of two dark Suburbans parked facing a wide clearing where the pasture road split to flow around the rocky little ridge to our rear. Eight men dressed in baggy clothes with white bandanas around their heads were spread out in a skirmish line with their backs to us. All held automatic weapons.

"I'd be standing closer to those cars." Ethan cut his eyes toward me and absently pulled at the tender gray leaves of a West Texas sage in full bloom. "When the shooting starts, everybody hunts a hole and I doubt thornbrush and cactus'll be much cover."

Trying not to move too much and attract attention, I used my hat brim to nod toward the scenario unfolding only sixty feet away. "*El Norte* there'll be the first to go. Why's he standing right out in front of the car? He'd just as well have a big red target painted on that blazer he's wearing. *I'm* burning up, and the least he could do is take it off and roll up his sleeves."

Ethan snorted. "*El Norte*. What kinda name is that for a cartel leader?"

"How do I know? I didn't name the guy." The SUVs approaching from the distance grew closer, but my attention went back to the parked Suburbans. The three *more* large SUVs parked off to our right sped up and raced past a dozen Angus-Hereford steers licking up soy hulls scattered on the hardpan. The dusty vehicles shot past two horses not far from the cattle, heads drooping in the heat.

When they reached the waiting vehicles, they split up, and slid to a stop like gunfighters spreading out in a dirt street. The men inside waited as the boils of dust caught up and billowed around the cars.

"Dumb move."

Ethan nodded. "I was thinking the same thing. I'd've parked sideways to those guys for more cover and to get away if things go bad."

"Bad guys aren't usually the sharpest crayons in the box."

The worst of the dust was gone when the doors on the new arrivals flew open. The men waiting with their backs to us tensed as armed gangsters poured out with a variety of military-style weapons in their hands.

I watched the men face off. "I still think they should be using the SUVs for cover."

"Amateurs." Ethan cut his eyes at me from under the brim of his hat. "I wish I had the SUV concession for all this. Somebody's making money somewhere. Which one's Gabe?"

I pointed at one of the men facing in our general direction. All but Gabe wore white T-shirts under unbuttoned plaid shirts. "That's him in the priest collar who just got out of the Expedition, beside Tortuga."

"What's with that?"

I shrugged. "He's getting paid."

"Which one's Tortuga?"

"The only guy who doesn't have a gun in his hand."

"He looks like somebody's grandpa."

Hollywood's version of a Mexican bad guy, the squatty man with thick rolled shoulders wore a gray mustache, a loose-fitting off-white *frontera guayabera* shirt, and baggy khakis.

Beside him was Gabe Nakai, my dad's ranch manager and a close friend. The hair rose on the back of my neck, watching an old buddy in the company of armed gangsters from Ojinaga, across the Rio Grande.

Ethan must have sensed how I felt. "It ain't right, seeing him down there, is it?"

"That and the priest collar around his neck."

"I'm still working on that one, too." He tilted his head like a dog, as if looking at the scene from a different angle would help evaluate the situation. "That's something else that doesn't make sense in all this."

"Ours is not to reason why." Even I was surprised at my quote.

"Tennyson."

"You *did* listen in Miss Adams' English class."

"Naw, just memorized those lines for a test, and for some reason they stuck with me."

El Norte still had his back to us, but his voice came loud and clear, a trick of the acoustics from the horseshoe bowl of rocks surrounding our position. His hair was so black and slicked back that it looked to be oiled. The side of his whisker-stubbled face looked to be chiseled granite. "*Tortuga!* Did you bring my money?"

The Mexican national standing beside Gabe spread his hands. "My coke?"

El Norte flicked a command with his fingers. A gangster holding an AK-47 reached inside the open door of his SUV and withdrew a leather briefcase. He flipped the latches and dumped a pile of taped packets onto the hood. The cartel leader waved his hand toward the drugs. "As promised."

"Who uses brand-new English leather briefcases these days? It's backpacks, mostly, from what *I've* seen." Ethan sighed. "This is making my head hurt."

I pointed at the dust clouds roaring down the dirt track, directly toward the scenario unfolding at an achingly slow pace. "Who are *those* guys? I've been watching 'em coming for a good long while."

"Don't know. I've been wondering the same thing, but they're about to make somebody down there pretty mad."

Tortuga snapped his fingers, and one of his men appeared with still another briefcase. Holding it awkwardly in one hand, he clicked the latches and it opened, revealing the interior packed with hundred-dollar bills.

"They must have gotten a deal on briefcases at Costco." Ethan cut his eyes to see if I'd take the bait and continue our evaluation, but I concentrated on their conversation to hear what the gangsters were saying.

"Bueno," El Norte waved. "Make the deal."

Trouble started when the gangster tried to close the

briefcase. Losing his grip, it flipped out of his hand, dumping the contents onto the ground. White paper cut to the size of U.S. currency exploded in a cloud, fluttering like snow and revealing that the authentic bills were only a thin layer on top.

El Norte shouted and retreated for cover behind an open car door. *"Mátalos!"*

Kill them!

The clear crack of a single gunshot opened the ball. To a man, the cartel soldiers on both sides raised their weapons, and the world filled with automatic gunfire. I found myself looking down the muzzle of a rifle pointed at one of the gangsters standing in front of me. My skin crawled at the flashes.

The three vehicles racing toward us grew larger, and the sound of rocks and gravel under the tires became clearly audible even over the exchange of gunfire.

Reacting to the situation, Gabe grabbed Tortuga by his collar and threw him into the back seat of their SUV.

The gangster who fumbled the briefcase struggled with the rifle slung over his shoulder, fighting to bring it to bear. Half a dozen bloody explosions erupted from his light gray and blue silk shirt. He wilted to the ground, face contorted in agony.

Men on both sides dropped like falling leaves while those who survived the initial exchange scrambled for cover. The hammering sounds of battle filled the air, echoing off the rocks and boulders behind our position.

The approaching vehicles we'd been watching rolled into the scene, sliding to a stop in one wide boil of dust. The lead car angled toward Tortuga's parked SUV and sheared off the open driver's door, crushing a gangster who'd taken cover there.

His yelp of terror and pain rose high and shrill, cutting through the air like a knife. Screams of shock and terror rose from dozens of men and women.

"Shit!" I charged toward the car, waving my arms. "Stop! Everybody stop!"

Ethan matched my pace, rushing past one of several movie cameras filming the scene.

"Cut!" The director James Madigan rose from under the umbrella beside his canvas chair. "Cut!" He turned to a woman holding a sheaf of papers. "Who the hell *are* these guys?"

Hard-looking, heavily armed Hispanic men poured from the newly arrived vehicles. Dressed in everything from torn jeans, T-shirts, track pants, and even an Adidas pullover, each one had the cold, rigid look of cartel members who killed for a living. Some faces were covered from their eyes down by tangles of tattoos; others wore bandanas like old west outlaws.

An individual stepped out of the lead Expedition's front passenger seat and pointed at the director. The red number 1518 centered in a web of tattoos on his bare chest, he was the only one without a bandana or facial tattoos. *"Eso es Madigan. Mátalo!"*

Those words for "kill him" sent an icy knife through my stomach. They'd targeted the movie director by name. It was a cartel hit.

"Ethan! No! This is real!" The smooth Sweetheart Grips of my 1911 Colt .45 filled my hand. I waved at the confused production team and uncertain actors. "Down! Down! Everyone down!"

You've heard of that old saw that in times of stress time slows down. People say it seems they're moving through molasses, and they're right. Even more frustrating, the people I was warning simply looked at me without understanding. It wasn't their fault. Most civilians go through life without experiencing trauma and aren't trained to deal with life-threatening situations. They also expect nothing bad to happen and aren't prepared.

Most law enforcement officers are on the *other* end of that spectrum. We're constantly evaluating the world around us, thinking, "what if?" and planning for any and every event that might occur. But there was no training for what was unfolding on that hot desert floor.

Even Gabe, who'd been in more than his share of fights and gunfights was startled at the sudden change from make-believe to reality. I could tell he was bumfuzzled for a couple of seconds before he made sense of what was happening around us and shifted from a guy trying to earn a few bucks as a movie extra, to a potential victim.

I waved him back and drew my Colt, the .45's Sweetheart Grip smooth in my hand. "Gabe, get down! It's real!"

A *real* gangster leveled an AK-47 and held the trigger down, shredding the director who went backward to land in the dust. The *cuerno de chivo,* or goat's horn, as they nicknamed the rifle because of the distinctive curved magazine, sprayed a stream of hot lead that punched holes in anything and everyone around Madigan as he died.

Ethan and I were on the set of *The Mexican Pipeline,*

a controversial movie targeted by the Coahuila Hidalgo Cartel who threatened to kill everyone involved in filming a fictionalized version of their illegal activities.

They were also known as 1518, or Quience Die-chiocho, the numbers signifying the year before Cortes landed on the shores of Mexico to conquer the Aztecs. It was the last year of their power before the destruction of an entire civilization.

Even though we'd been hired to provide security for the movie, there wasn't a damned thing I could do right then to stop the well-organized assault. A hard-looking tattooed gangster squeezed the trigger of what I took to be a Bushmaster, spraying indiscriminate .223 rounds left and right.

More men than I could have imagined streamed from the dusty, newly arrived SUVs and strolled casually through the movie set, firing indiscriminately at the terrified actors who scattered like quail. The guns in their hands belched fire, and the assistant director tangled his feet and went down as rounds blew out his chest.

Actors and crew members screamed, scrambling for cover in the chaos. Ethan and I charged into the melee, not by design, but because the only cover in the area was behind all the equipment used to film the movie. Ethan dropped to one knee behind a stack of thick blue metal cases, using the only concealment he could find.

The words "thank God, thank God" repeated over and over in my mind, a chant of relief that my wife Kelly and our teenage twins Mary and Jerry weren't on the set. Since high school was out for the summer, they'd been pestering me to come out and watch one day's shoot. I'd almost relented that morning.

Sharing the same cover with Ethan didn't sound like a good idea, and I was headed for one of the movie SUVs when I saw one of the real masked gangsters pointing his weapon at me. My .45 came up and the guy holding a Bushmaster disappeared behind the front sight. I squeezed the trigger and he went straight down.

Before I could swing the muzzle to a second guy crouched not far away, he dropped from a round that didn't come from either me or Ethan. We weren't the only ones fighting back. My dad, Herman Hawke was thirty feet away, making a few extra bucks acting as the set's wrangler of two dozen head of cattle and horses he brought in as backdrop stock.

A retired Texas Ranger, he was always armed. The Old Man sighted from behind his pickup parked just off camera. His own Colt .45 barked. It bucked in his hand, and he shifted targets, firing again and again as if he were on a live-fire range.

His presence and demeanor in the suddenly real shootout was as calming to me as a Xanax. Cameras exploded from the impact of high-velocity bullets, bodies fell, and the roar of gunfire filled my ears.

I squeezed the trigger, heeling a gangster when the bullet's impact knocked one foot out from under him. I never said I was a good shot. A firm believer in the anchor shot, the Old Man drilled the wounded gangster twice more to keep him down.

The cartel members continued to hose the area, spraying at random. Everything snapped back into real time as I juked behind a large metal box full of electronics, using the shoulder-high container as cover.

Panicked movie people ran for cover in all directions. One of the only things on our side was that most of the bad guys weren't certain *who* was sending in return gunfire. Incongruously, I saw two of the actors return fire with their weapons loaded with blanks. Maybe they thought the new arrivals were also actors. In shock, they might have thought it was some ad lib scene thought up by the director. Their response caused some of the cartel gangsters to take cover behind their own vehicles, but others zoned in and murdered the terrified extras.

A hard-edged young gangster swung his *cuerno de chivo* in my direction. He was standing in the open, probably the way he'd seen it done on television or in movies. I shot him twice and he crumpled. I caught a glimpse of Ethan dropping the empty magazine on his Glock and slapping in a fresh one.

A string of explosions stitched the dirt around me. The guy who popped up slightly behind me would've had us both had his own mag not run dry. He was close enough for me to see the surprise and fear in his eyes as he fumbled to reload.

Together, Ethan and I shot him bone dead.

As his surviving men continued to hose the area, their tattooed leader struck a pose beside the car, fists on his hips, and shouted above the gunfire. "*La Mujer del Diablo de Coahuila,* the Devil Woman of Coahuila says that this movie will not be completed. Next time we will kill everyone here! I am Incincio, and I am not afraid to tell you my name, because I am protected by *La Jefa,* who owns Coahuila and all *this* land as far as we can see." He waved. *"Vamos chicos!"*

Doors slammed seconds later, and the three SUVs filled with their surviving gangsters spun in tight circles, speeding away back down the same dry pasture road they rolled in on. I rose and punched holes in the windows and sheet metal of every car I could hit until they were out of range.

As soon as they were gone, the air was filled with dust, cries, and screams. In the chaos that followed, I slapped in a fresh magazine as shocked crew members rushed in all directions. Ethan and the Old Man moved through the chaos, kicking weapons away from the real cartel members on the ground, just in case they weren't as dead as they looked.

Ethan joined me beside the first young man I'd shot, the one aiming his rifle at me. "I think I'm gonna go back to smoking again."

Before I could answer, the wounded man's arm rose, beckoned, then fell.

"This guy's still alive." I knelt beside him, patting the kid down to make sure he didn't have any other weapons. Finding none, I pulled the bandana with a skeleton's face down to reveal a smooth, unlined face.

Gabe slid to a stop on one knee and ripped the boy's blood-soaked shirt open to reveal a dark puckered hole in his upper chest. He covered the wound with the palm of his hand. "This looks bad."

The Old Man's voice came from behind me. "It is. There's two more holes down lower."

Blood welled from between Gabe's fingers, his eyes filled with sadness. "He looks like he's not much older than Angie."

I understood how he felt. Angie was his high school-age daughter, and my twins were the same age. I swallowed the lump rising in my throat. "Those wrinkles at the corners of his eyes tell me he'd older than he looks."

The man's eyes flicked open. He raised one hand in a faint plea of agony and whispered. "*Padre.*" It took a second to realize he was looking at the priest collar on Gabe's costume. *"Quiero confesion."*

Gabe shook his head and answered in Spanish. *"No soy un sacerdote."*

I'm not a priest.

"Confesion." The man turned his pleading gaze to me. He must have recognized the cinco peso Ranger badge on my shirt. *"Guardebosque, to lo ruego. Pidele que me confesion."*

Guardebosque is what some Mexicans call us Texas Rangers, when they're trying to be nice, while some of the really old folks remember the past and call us *rinches*, a derogatory term that arose way back around 1916.

"It won't hurt to hear him, Gabe." The Old Man's voice was soft.

Just as I'd hoped, a blast of air pushed across the valley floor from a collapsed thunderhead, much like the pressure-wave from an explosion. Sage and grease-wood bent when the massive wave finally reached us. Hot only moments earlier, I turned my face to the wind, letting the dry coolness wash my face clean of the evil I couldn't see.

My eyes burned at the thought of this young man dying from my gunshots. I know, he'd been trying to kill me, but I also saw an older version of my son Jerry lying there, asking for absolution.

Blood trickled from the dying man's mouth. He

coughed, deep and wet as his lungs hemorrhaged, then switched to unaccented English. "I need to say something. I need to tell you something important."

The back of my neck prickled.

Gabe met my eyes, then leaned down to better hear. *"Adelante."*

The young man held Gabe's hand and whispered in his ear for a moment, as the ranch hand, cum actor, cum priest, listened intently. The mere breath of a voice weakened then drifted off. The gangster's eyes lost focus and drifted off to the side as he gasped, convulsed, and went limp.

His death brought me completely back into the noisy world of panicked victims, crying men and women, and unheard orders issued to people who simply wandered among the bloody carnage with vacant expressions.

Licking his dry lips, Gabe straightened. "Oh my god."

I saw fear in his eyes and leaned in. "What'd he say?"

"He's a federal agent, undercover, and says there's another agent that's, *come se dice infiltrado*, with this cartel, too."

"Infiltrated," I translated. "Undercover."

Stomach clenched, my head reeled at the thought of shooting a brother in arms. He was firing his weapon. I'd looked directly down the muzzle of the rifle when it was aimed at me and remembered the bright muzzle flashes. But I hadn't seen anyone fall. Was he shooting over my head? I struggled to recall if I heard the crack of rounds passing close, but there was so much rolling gunfire I couldn't pin down a specific sound.

"Is that what he confessed?"

"No. Worse. He says the 1518 is sending more hit teams between here and Van Horn. They plan to clear a path through the Border Patrol for the traffickers coming across the river. He said something else to watch out for, but I couldn't understand him. His last words were 'more people are going to die.'"

My blood went cold. An organized cartel hit team targeting the Border Patrol was in my country, and I wasn't going to stand for it.

Chapter 2

Highway 1776 just south of the West Texas community of Coyanosa isn't much on scenery. It's a harsh, sunburned landscape full of scrub, tumbleweeds, mesquite, and low-growing cactus. The two-lane divides desolate rangeland so poor it takes a hundred acres to feed one cow. Visitors are mystified to think cattle can live in the desert. Even in the wintertime, the sunbaked landscape looks dry as a gourd.

The scenic quality doesn't get any better at night. When the headlights and the soft glow from the heavens light the lonesome road linking the east and westbound Interstates 10 and I-20, it's worse . . . stark.

Cattle ranching wasn't always the primary source of income. In the 1950s, farmers drilled deep water wells to irrigate cotton, but by the 1970s, the price of fuel made cotton farming unprofitable. Times changed when drilling technology finally found a way to bring oil to the surface, and most ranchers immediately shifted to a much more lucrative income.

Once they signed on the bottom line, a vast network of caliche roads cut through the ranches, allowing an army of white company trucks to prowl the dusty roads between bobbing pump jacks and back out onto the two-lane highway.

No matter what the land produced, it was still wide and lonesome country.

The highway traffic was never heavy, mostly pickups and oil tankers driven by pipeline and oil company workers, with a few tourists and locals thrown in for good measure.

It was a beautifully sharp night lit by a full moon bright enough to read by, when Incencio Aguierre and Geronimo Manzano cruised northward on the empty ribbon of concrete in a four-year-old black Mercedes C-Class sedan. Incencio, the Hidalgo cartel soldier responsible for the massacre on the set of *The Mexican Pipeline,* chose the high-end automobile for the pair in the hopes that it wouldn't attract the attention of law enforcement officers or the highway patrol. Expensive cars driving a couple of miles over the speed limit usually weren't the targets for law enforcement officers.

Incencio was a *Regio*, short for *Regionales,* which means regal or royal in the Spanish language, a regional officer overseeing his specific drug and trafficking route into what he considered *his* territory, the Big Bend region of the Lone Star state.

The two men in the Mercedes who looked like tourists were in fact mid-level soldiers who'd proven their loyalty across the Rio Grande over and over again to *la Mujer del Diablo de Coahuila,* the Devil Woman of Coahuila. At first to encompass most of the Mexican state of Coahuila, they murdered anyone she targeted to expand her drug and human trafficking cartel.

It didn't matter who they were, people scratching

out a living in small communities, travelers, police, military, and especially rival gangs, or anyone she deemed a threat. Sometimes they died clean, with nothing more than a bullet through the head.

Other murders sent a message with beheadings, mutilations, or worse. A favorite calling card for the Devil Woman was the presentation of an individual's hands or feet to family members, rival *regios,* or law enforcement officials.

Once they had Coahuila under their thumb, her dream expanded.

Born of dirt-poor parents in the poorest section of El Paso, Chihuahuita, she hit the ground running as Tish Villarreal. Now confident in her abilities and people, she was pushing long fingers from across the border back into her home state of Texas.

The Mercedes' tires clacked on the highways expansion joints as *mariache* static hissed from the Burmester sound system. A cheap, plastic walkie-talkie on the console between the men squawked to life. Brake lights flashed in the darkness as Incencio steered the car onto the shoulder and turned the radio down.

Startled by the sudden appearance of the sedan, a jackrabbit darted across the highway in the headlights as Geronimo picked up the low-tech communication device and thumbed the talk button on the side. *"Que?"*

The voice on the other end spoke in faint Spanish. *"La patrulla frontier iza* is on the way."

Instead of utilizing modern technology and basic drop phones, they used old school walkie-talkies that had baffled law enforcement techs for months. The crackling low-tech signals between the hand-held units bounced through a vast covert network of signal repeaters on existing microwave towers, the tops of mountains, and even a medium-size high-rise hotel in Ft. Stockton. It was a shadow communications infrastructure created and installed by a Hidalgo tech specialist. The relays were impossible to intercept because the innovative tech used commercially available software to scramble their radio chatter into garbled nonsense.

At the device's squawk, Geronimo and Incencio exchanged glances in the dim light glowing in the dashboard. He answered in the same language. "How long before they get here?"

"Fifteen minutes. Their names are Manual Trevino and Frank Nelson. We want Trevino this time. Nelson has betrayed us. You know what the Devil Woman requires."

"We'll be ready."

Incencio activated the emergency flashers before he felt under the dash and popped the hood. They stepped out into the warm night air. He'd pulled onto the gravel shoulder beside a barbed wire fence clotted with a thick drift of tumbleweeds. Caressed by a light breeze, he pointed at the mass of dried bushes. *"Ahi."*

Geronimo snapped a flashlight to life and lit the tangle. "This will work."

Though they were alone, Incencio's voice was soft. "Yes. They are close, but you will need to move fast."

Keeping one eye on the empty horizon to their south, Incencio probed the drift of dried vegetation with his own flashlight. "You'll have to stay low when they first get here. They will probably check like this first, then you can come out."

Geronimo shouldered into waist-high drift and kicked

a clear path in the sandy dirt between the tangle and the tight bobwire fence. Satisfied that he could reemerge without much noise, he dropped to his belly, pulling a couple more of the dead tumbleweeds in place for camouflage.

Incencio brushed his light across the makeshift blind that appeared undisturbed. He couldn't see his partner. *"Bueno."*

The farm road was quiet as they waited. Minutes later, the glow from distant headlights on the horizon rose like a weak southern sun before the twin beams finally popped into view.

Leaving the driver's door open, Incencio leaned under the hood and waited for the whine of tires to get closer. The tone of the approaching vehicle changed as it slowed, then pulled up behind the Mercedes. He flicked the beam past the raised hood a couple of times, giving the impression that he was looking at the engine, then leaned around the car and gave a friendly wave.

The SUVs headlights illuminated the empty interior at the same time lights on top of the vehicle came alive, flashing in the darkness. After a moment, doors opened and two Border Patrol agents cautiously bracketed the car as they approached. One stayed on the highway. The other's footsteps crunched on the rough shoulder.

Incencio rose from under the hood to find what he expected. He directed the flashlight beam toward the officer's waist to avoid shining it directly into his face. "Good to see you guys." He spoke perfect English.

The Hispanic Border Patrol agent walking on the

highway turned on his flashlight and glanced inside the car. Finding it empty, he directed the beam onto Incencio, lighting the gangster's black slacks and white T-shirt covered with a light sport coat, perfectly appropriate for the weather.

The agent in the familiar green uniform stopped when he reached the front tire and spoke in accented English. "Good evening, sir. Car troubles?"

Incencio couldn't see the other agent on the other side of the raised hood, but the man's flashlight briefly skipped over the drift of tumbleweeds before coming back to the front of the car. Incencio's beam rose to the first man's chest and flickered across Agent Trevio's nametag. "It just quit."

"Would you please lower your flashlight?"

"Sure." He directed the light back onto the exposed engine. "You'd think a car that cost this much wouldn't just die for no reason."

The other officer Incencio figured to be Agent Nelson faced the car, peering at the technology under the hood. He whistled at the engine packed under the hood. "Man, what a car, but they're not made to work on, are they?"

"No." Incencio spread his hands. "All I can do is put gas in the tank." He aimed the beam at the engine. "It took me half an hour to find where to put the washer fluid when I first bought it. I almost added it to the oil."

"You live around here?" Agent Trevino's question wasn't a surprise.

"No. El Paso."

"Where you headed?" The question came from Nelson, who now had his back to the blackness of the fence and pasture beyond. His flashlight beam swept across the tangle of hoses, wires, and parts.

"Midland."

The agents alternated questions. It was Trevino's turn. "Taking the scenic route?"

"You can say that. I was down in Alpine for a couple of days."

"Business?"

"Yes."

"I love that town. Where'd you eat?"

Incencio's eyes widened slightly. He hadn't expected such a specific question.

Agent Nelson noticed. His demeanor changed. He rested his hand on the butt of the Glock on his hip.

Suddenly charged with tension, both agents had their attention on Incencio when a shadow materialized from the darkness. Sensing the sudden presence, Nelson whirled to face the threat. Before he could draw the weapon on his belt, the razor-sharp edge of a twelve-inch machete blade sank into the side of the border agent's bare neck, biting deep enough to nearly sever the man's spine.

At the same time, Incencio lurched forward and wrapped Agent Trevino in a bear hug, pinning both arms against his body and preventing the agent from drawing his weapon. They went over like toppled trees. Flashlights skittered across the hard pavement and onto the gravel shoulder, splashing beams of spinning yellow light across the pavement.

The flashing lights on the agent's SUV added to the surreal, horrifying sight of a bloody geyser spurting into the air as Geronimo yanked the blade free of Nelson's neck and struck again. The second swing was unnecessary. Nelson's forehead slammed the edge of the raised hood and the dead agent fell hard.

Geronimo rounded the car and knelt over the fighting men. Trevino shrieked in terror, then pain when the *sicario* grabbed a fist-sized rock and slammed it into the agent's head and face over and over.

The addled man quit fighting and held up one weak hand to ward off the blows. "Don't. Please don't hit me anymore."

Breathing hard, the cartel members gained their feet to stand over Trevino's writhing body. Incencio glanced up and down the dark highway. Satisfied no one was coming, he retrieved his flashlight and kicked the moaning agent in the side. "Can you hear me?" His strong Spanish accent was back. He kicked him again in the same place, harder.

Agent Trevino grunted at the pain. Squinting, one trembling hand shaded his eyes from the intense beam. Blood flowed from half a dozen deep facial and head wounds and his answer was liquid from the river of blood running down from the back of his throat from a badly broken nose. "Yes."

"Your partner is dead. Repeat that."

"What?"

"Repeat what I just said."

"Don't kill me."

"I won't. What did I just tell you to say?"

"That my partner's dead."

"That's right. Nelson is dead. But we wanted you to live. Do you know why?"

Trevino shook his head. Giving up on keeping the light out of his face, he wiped at the eye that wasn't swollen shut. "No."

"Because he failed us. That is why he's dead and you now work for us."

"No."

"Yes, you do. Listen to me."

Standing nearby and still holding the fist-size rock, Geronimo checked the highway for the glow of headlights. "We need to hurry."

"I know." Incencio nudged Officer Trevino with the toe of his shoe. "Do you still understand me?"

"Yes."

"Good. You hold the life of your entire family in your hands at this moment. We know where you live, your wife's name, the names of your children and where they go to school. We know your relatives, and *their* names, and where *they* live. We know if you have a dog, and where you buy your groceries. *Comprende*?"

"Yes."

"Repeat what I said."

"You know everything about me and my family."

"Bueno! Come se dice destilado?"

"Distilled?"

"Sí. You have distilled everything I told you, so you will remember everything about this night. We owned Frank Nelson, and knew everything about him, also. He did not give us the information we needed to move some of our product through here and has paid the price. He knew the cost, just as you do. His family will soon join him, because we told him the same thing you just heard. Only he didn't listen.

"We own *you* now. When they find you here, you will tell them that you don't remember what happened tonight. You don't know how your *compadre* died. It is all a complete blank. You will *not* provide the *policia* with any information at all. When they let you get back to work, you will be one of us. If you do that, you and your *familia* will live."

"Amigo." Geronimo's voice was full of concern. "Faster, before someone comes."

Blinded by the light, and the blood in his eyes, Agent Trevino couldn't see the men standing over him. He closed his eyes and laid back.

"You will be contacted again soon by one of us." Incencio wasn't finished. "That is when you get instructions on the cars and trucks you will not stop. They may have product or people inside them. If you do pull them over by mistake, you will let them go. Every time. If you do not, we will kill your entire family and turn them over to *los sanguinarios*. We will skin their bodies and use their faces for the *dia de los muertos*, the Day of the Dead. *Comprende*?"

Even through his pain and terror, Trevino understood the term for the "blood thirsty ones," or "blood-drinkers," low ranking members of the cartels who butchered their victims.

"Please. Don't hurt my family."

"Do not beg. They will not see the *sanguinarios* if you do what I tell you."

Trevino swallowed blood draining down the back of his throat and gagged. "I won't."

"Bueno. And look on the bright side, we are going to pay you also. A token of our friendship. The money

will help you keep everything quiet. You are now a rich man."

Using a bandana from his pocket, Geronimo took Trevino's duty weapon from his holster. He pitched it over the tumbleweeds and bobwire fence along with the radio. After he patted the agent down, he rose. "No *camaras* on him, or in the *automovil*."

Incencio pointed to Nelson's body. "Him, too?"

"*Sí*."

Incencio flashed a dazzling smile, one that attracted the ladies wherever he went. "Then we are done here. Trevino, you stay where you are until someone finds you. *Escucha*, listen to me, you do not remember what happened this night."

Trevino nodded. "I'm still listening."

"Say it."

"I don't remember what happened."

"*Bueno*. That is what you will tell everyone."

Trevino's arm dropped as the Devil Woman's *sicarios* returned to the car, slammed the doors, and steered around the agent's body. The flickering emergency lights shrank into the distance as Incencio drove exactly two miles over the speed limit to look as normal as possible.

In the passenger seat, Geronimo lit a cigarette. "Do we take care of the other agent's family tonight?"

"Yes. I sent Esteban. He is taking three *hombres* with him who want to prove themselves to be *sicarios*."

"Esteban is *muy malo*." Geronimo smoked the cigarette down to the filter, then flicked it out the window. "If that *pendejo* back there talks, I want to do his wife.

I have seen her in photographs. She is one of the most beautiful *anglo*s I have ever seen."

Incencio grunted. "Sure. I do not care, but I think you will wait a long time. This one will not fail us, I think. He is of our blood. He understands and believes."

Chapter 3

It was dark, and I was grilling steaks under our patio lights. Country music came through the screen door, along with the sounds of my wife Kelly rattling dishes. The comfortable smells of supper cooking on the stove reminded me of when I was a kid at my grandparents' house.

I wasn't really hungry, and my nerves were still jangling like old-style telephone ringers, but Kelly had already invited Perry Hale and Yolanda over for dinner that night. It was probably good to take my mind off what had happened earlier that day.

Approved by the governor, although in a closed room with the admonishment that we were never to disclose the conversation in public, they were military veterans who I called my Shadow Response Team, or SRT. We'd worked and trained together over the past several months, and they were both tough as nails.

They aren't sworn officers of the law, even though they carry badges authorized by the governor. They are my backup and operate on the dark edge of right and wrong, which means under my direction they occasionally step over the line, like when they shoot bad guys as dead as a T-Rex and simply walk away. The three of us are throwbacks to the Rangers of old, those who were assigned a job and handled it without politics or outside interference.

We'd grown closer to the couple than I would have imagined, and our high school twins loved having them over. We all knew Mary had a crush on Perry Hale by the way she acted when he was around, waiting on him hand and foot. It was funny to me, and Kelly called it sweet, but kinda pitiful. On the other hand, I watched how Jerry acted when Yolanda showed up. He laughed loud, and a lot, whenever she was talking.

Teenagers.

I didn't hear them come in, but Yolanda opened the back door and waved from the porch. In jeans, untucked fitted shirt and ball cap, she looked not much older than Mary. "Hey buddy!"

"Howdy gal. Steaks'll be ready in a little bit."

"Don't burn 'em up."

"Who's milking this duck?"

She laughed and disappeared back inside at the same time Perry Hale came through the back door. He thumped a bottle of Bombay Sapphire on the picnic table and began mixing a gin and tonic. "Thought you might be running low."

"Appreciate the thought."

"Nice shirt by the way."

I was casual, wearing a yellow Aloha shirt Mary gave me for my birthday. She said that I needed to relax every now and then, and that I didn't need to always look like a Ranger. I was growing to like the blousy, palm frond-covered shirts that hid my .45 when I wasn't working. "Thanks. They're comfortable."

"That's what my old aunts said about those ugly house dresses they wore when I was a kid."

"This isn't a house dress. It's a Hawaiian shirt, and Mary gave it to me. You can take it up with her."

"Nope. I'm afraid of teenage girls."

"You're smarter'n you look. How do y'all like your steaks?"

"Just the hot side of mooing."

I sprinkled the T-bones with salt and pepper.

Putting one of the drinks beside me, he opened a bottle of cabernet and poured two glasses. "I'll be back in a minute."

I leveled the coals while he was inside delivering the drinks to the girls. He was back out by the time I forked the steaks onto the grill.

He settled into a lawn chair and tilted back his gimme cap. "Hey, I meant to tell you. Yolanda's cousin Suzette is house-sitting in that new addition just south of town. You know, the old Rogers Ranch."

"Vista Ridge."

"Yeah, have you been in there?"

"Not yet." A drop of fat hit the coals with a smoky sizzle.

"They broke it up in different size lots. Some are a half acre. I think one's something like twenty acres. They're calling it an innovative community approach."

"You guys thinking of buying a house?"

"Nope. Not the point. Yoli and I went out there to have drinks the other evening and watch the sun go down."

"She'll kick your butt if she hears you calling her that."

"I'm not *that* afraid of her. Anyway, the house is on top of a little ridge, and they have a helluva wraparound porch on that place. You can see Ballard from there. I didn't realize what kind of bowl it sits in. We all know there're mountains around us, but it sure looks different from so high up. Anyway, about sundown I heard something in a deep draw behind the house. Suzette calls it a valley, but anyway, it's a pretty good-sized cut down the east side of the house. I looked over and saw movement at the bottom and thought it was javelinas, but I'll be damned if wasn't people."

"Hikers?"

"Illegals, I think. Yoli's cousin says she's seen quite a few people trailing down through there, on their way down to the highway. She says vans are showing up at that little picnic area on Highway 90, where 67 cuts in."

"Their pick-up point. Then they're taking them to a drop house after that."

"I imagine."

"I'll tell Ethan and he can holler at the Border P."

"Already did. They called Border Patrol, but the thing is, there's a lot of illegals moving through here these days."

"They're tightening the border downriver. That's forcing the illegals to find different routes. The National Park Service is arresting more and more coming through Big Bend. They're the lucky ones. They're finding a lot of bodies in the park, and on some of the ranches down around Chalk Canyon, a few miles west of Langry. It's not as rugged as the park, but they are seeing an increase of illegals and smugglers coming across."

The Big Bend sector is the largest sector of the U.S. southern border and is composed of seventy-seven Texas counties and all of Oklahoma. The operational area is a mind-boggling 165,154 square miles. The Sector is responsible for patrolling 510 miles of river front along the Rio Grande

The Big Bend National Park is 1,252 square miles. It includes the Sierra Blanca sector that has one particular highway checkpoint that's notorious for large drug busts. Unfortunately, the sector where we live has the smallest staff of Border Patrol agents in all of the nine national sectors that stretch all the way to California.

"It's everywhere." I didn't like the idea of illegals running the canyons and arroyos so close to my house. I didn't want to go too far down *that* rabbit hole after what had happened, so I changed the subject. "We need to go out and do some target practice. I need to take the kids."

"That sounds great. We're getting tired of just going to the range, let's go out to the ranch. I got this new rifle and need to sight it in. A friend gave me a bolt action 7mm mag that I fell in love with."

"Dang. That thing'll kill anything on the North American continent."

"Yep, and it doesn't scare people as much when they see it. I know a lot of snipers who have these tricked-out rifles, but I still like the simple things."

"I didn't know you were that much of a long-distance guy."

He dead-eyed me. "I wasn't, until we tangled with that freak out in East Texas here while back." Perry

Hale looked at his boots as if he'd scuffed the toe. "Fightin' that guy made me decide that I'd rather reach out and touch them from a distance, if I can."

"Bothers you, huh?"

"Man, he came out of nowhere." He rubbed his chest where a .38 caliber bullet had impacted his tactical vest that night. "I even have nightmares about that face of his. How do you handle it?"

I fended the question, my thoughts immediately back to the slaughter on the movie set earlier that day. I took a long swallow of icy Bombay to settle my stomach. Killing so many men in such a short period of time was taking its toll on me. For the past few months, it felt like every time I turned around, someone was shooting at me, and I was putting people in the ground. "Does Yolanda have the same issues?"

"No. She's hardcore, man."

I knew better, but wasn't going to get into a psychological discussion with him. I drained the glass and poked at the steaks with a pair of long tongs.

He took the opportunity to press the question again. "How *are* you handling it?"

"Not well." I squinted into the darkness, half expecting to see someone slip past.

Chapter 4

Frank Nelson, the sixty-year-old murdered Border Patrol agent, didn't have much family. Widowed ten years earlier, he had only one estranged daughter who lived in Hawaii with her husband and their two kids.

The traceable bloodline ended there, because Agent Nelson's mother found herself pregnant with Frank after a one-night stand with a man she never saw afterward. Unwilling to be saddled with a child that would cut into her time cruising the Houston night clubs, she left the baby at the front door of the Jacinto City fire station.

Freed from a lifetime of living with a sorry-assed mother who lived for men and liquor and not necessarily in that order, he grew up in foster homes. For five years he passed from one household to another without ever bonding with the families that took him in.

A middle-aged couple named Ruby and Edward Nelson adopted him on his fifth birthday. He lived with them until Ed passed away from a heart attack. An island unto himself, he drifted away right after graduation. He married once, divorced two years later.

Now, with the exception of his now eighty-eight-year-old widowed foster mother and her eighty-five-year-old spinster sister, Harriet, who lived with her, Frank had no one. He hadn't seen the old women in nearly twenty years, receiving only an annual Christmas card that arrived like clockwork on December twenty-fourth.

That made it easy for the cartel to bend him to their will after forcing the half-drunk agent into a guard rail on a remote West Texas road one night six months earlier. Agent Nelson had some of his birth-mother's same failings, and fought a near-continuous battle with alcohol, keeping it under control for the most part until he sometimes found himself driving home when he should have called for a ride.

On the night in question, Nelson was driving five miles under the limit to stay out of the local police department's radar when a car appeared from nowhere and caught up with him in less than sixty seconds. The sedan driven by Incencio and Geronimo cut in front of Nelson's sedan, forcing him to yank the wheel in an effort to miss their rear bumper. Reactions slow and erratic from four hours in The Spot, a club on the outskirts of Midland that catered to roughnecks just in from the oil fields, the rattled off-duty Border Patrol agent overcompensated, hitting the guard rail and coming to a stop just off the bridge over a dry wash.

Dragging the stunned man from behind the wheel, Incencio and Geronimo went through their familiar routine, beating him and threatening the officer and his family with death if he didn't cooperate. Slightly disoriented from the booze, shock, and pain, Nelson fought to regain his wits that starry night. As the minutes passed, his mind cleared and he understood what Incencio was telling him.

Nelson felt his now-grown daughter was safe, with half the Pacific Ocean between them and the mainland cartel, so he agreed to their demands to save his life that night . . . and found that a large payment of cash every six weeks made it easier to swallow his pride after he'd chewed it long enough.

He even came to grips with the odd rationalization that even if the cartel's *sicarios,* or hitmen, decided to take his adopted mother and her sister out for some unanticipated misdeed, the old gals had lived full lives. They might even see it as a blessing, if such things were considered up in Heaven.

Growing up hard had given him a dark sense of right and wrong, which had ultimately put him in place for the cartel's brief use.

That is until one night when he failed to intercede on a routine violation stop on Highway 67, with Agent Trevino driving. Inside the vehicle, they found a kilo of cocaine and one well-known gangster who'd been deported four times for illegal entry into the United States. That man, Hugo Nunez, was on his way to Dallas with a personal message and delivery from the Devil Woman. Because the mule wound up being arrested and deported, the *Mujer Malvada* lost nearly a million dollars in an interrupted transaction.

With Nelson dead, *Mujer Malvada* was making good on her promise to wipe out his entire family. She had the name of Frank's mother in Del Rio. It was nothing to find the address of Miss Harriet's tiny bungalow where she lived with her sister Ruby, not four hours from Frank's house in Midland.

Under orders from the Devil Woman, the *sicarios* meant what they said when they told Frank, and then Trevino, that their families would be exterminated. At approximately the same time Geronimo nearly severed agent Nelson's head from his shoulders, four heavily tatted Mexican soldiers drove down a dark, quiet street in a 1972 Barracuda, looking for the address.

Chapter 5

Miss Ruby Nelson and her spinster sister sat in matching floral Sharan rocking chairs in their Del Rio bungalow, facing an old tube television perched on top of an even older console Admiral TV. The television housed in a Mediterranean cabinet died only two days after Walter Cronkite signed off the air for the final time as the most trusted newsman in the country.

The newer "portable" TV that was heavier than a heifer calf was tuned to *Little House on the Prairie* on COZI TV, because that was their favorite television program outside of the more recent *Big Bang Theory* that both old women absolutely adored. They both wanted a Sheldon for themselves, a genius, OCD narcissist who was both quirky and loveable . . . in their view.

The house was furnished with hand-me-down furniture they'd owned for decades. Hardwood floors clean enough to eat from were smooth under their fuzzy pink house shoes Miss Ruby still called mules.

Both blue-haired ladies suffered from bad feet. Miss Ruby struggled for breath twenty-four hours a day after smoking for more than six decades, while Miss Harriet suffered from congestive heart failure kept at bay with half a dozen pills a day. Because of their inactivity, the television and crocheting occupied most of their time, after cleaning house each morning, of course.

Content with each other's company, the elderly ladies mostly talked during the commercials in the evenings while turning out a startling number of brightly colored chemo caps they donated to a variety of charitable organizations that provided the headwear to cancer victims.

After dark, the only lights on in the house were two floor lamps, carefully positioned beside their rockers, though neither really had to see what they were doing most of the time. Two small night lights, one in the kitchen and the other underneath the telephone niche in the short hallway leading to the only bathroom, provided enough illumination for safe shuffling.

At nine o'clock that evening, they were already in their nightgowns after hand washing and drying the supper dishes, feeding their four cats, and locking up for the evening. Cold natured due to their age, they didn't use the window unit air conditioners during the day or evenings. The windows gaped wide to capture the dry eighty-five-degree breeze coming across the river from Mexico.

Being the elder, and the sole owner of the 850-square-foot bungalow, Miss Ruby sat closest to the front door. A Viagra commercial came on and she stopped crocheting to drop both hands into her lap, disgusted. "My lands. How can they put something like that on the air this time of the night? It's indecent. You never saw this kind of thing back when *I Love Lucy* and *The Dick Van Dyke* shows first came on."

Miss Harriet paused in her rocking. "I wish *I* knew a man who took it."

"Harriet!"

"I wonder if old Dick takes 'em ever now and then. He's gettin' on up there."

"*Harriet!!!*"

"Well, I just wonder. It's been so long since I been to the well, I'd like to see how that stuff works."

Miss Ruby burst into laughter. "Honey, you beat all I ever seen."

"Well, I like to keep things spiced up." Miss Harriet set her jaw, either from laugher or mild irritation.

Miss Ruby couldn't tell. "I reckon."

Their calico cat, Miss Cooney, shot from the kitchen and froze in the middle of the living room rug.

"I swear." Miss Ruby stared into the dark kitchen. "What's got into that old cat tonight?"

"Maybe she likes our conversation."

"Honey, I can't believe you think these cats understand what we say."

Miss Harriet tugged at the dangling blue strand leading from her twisted fingers down to a skein resting on top of a basket full of yarn. Getting a comfortable amount of slack, she went back to the Bella Knotted cap she was working on. "Well, don't they come whenever I call?"

"Of course they do, because the tone in your voice tells them they're gonna get fed."

"Well, they sure pay attention whenever I'm talking to them, instead of *you*."

"That's because you're looking right at 'em."

The cat sat up straight on top of the oval rag rug

covering most of the living room floor, her ears cocked toward the kitchen door.

"You think there's another rat in the house again?" Miss Ruby glanced over her shoulder at the open window between them. "I told you we need to get them screens back on."

"I don't like to look through 'em. My eyes are bad enough as it is, and looking through that wire makes it hard to tell what I'm looking at."

"They aren't wire anymore, honey. They use aluminum or vinyl mesh. And them open windows just invite rats inside."

"That's why we have cats, and besides, you're watching way too much of that HGTV these days."

"Yeah, but them twins on that show are cute as bugs." Miss Harriet closed her eyes for a moment. "They are something else, I wonder what twins would be like . . ."

"Harriet!"

On the dark street outside, a Barracuda's throaty engine echoed down the street lined with simple bungalow houses. A mix of cedars, palms, and cottonwood trees provided shade and texture in the elderly neighborhood that was now almost all Hispanic.

The driver with Hollywood good looks, Esteban Barrera, pulled to the curb and pointed at the house half a block away. Yellow light spilled through half-open windows. "There. The one with the *palmeras*."

The three future *sicarios* riding with him leaned forward, as if it would help them peer through the darkness. All had been involved in shootings against other gang members when they were teenagers and recently against rival cartels. They were gunmen in the Movie Lot Murders, and now it was time for them to break into the world of targeted individuals, executing the victims on their own. The success of this night would take them from high-level *soldados* to a position equal to Esteban.

"I will wait there for you to come out." Esteban pointed to the crumbling concrete walkway leading from the curb, across the dark sidewalk and up one step. Few of the houses on that street were lit, and even fewer had porch lights. Another car approached, its headlights bright on the dark street. Esteban turned his engine off and they sat still, hoping it wasn't the police. "Be cool."

The voice came from a man who went by only Lopez, sitting behind Esteban. "What do we do if they stop?"

"Whatever I do."

The distinctive front end of a vintage Cadillac Eldorado made all four of the cartel members tense at the same time. A rival gang, but then again, anyone outside of the *Hidalgo* were rivals.

They knew what would happen if those inside the Eldorado saw strangers on their turf. It was the one thing the hit team wanted to avoid that night, though the young men toughened by a lifetime of struggles south of the Rio Grande would welcome a confrontation any other time to prove their *machismo*.

Puffing up and posturing had no place in their culture. They simply shot when it became necessary and went on their way without another thought.

Luck and a few more months of life was riding with those in the vintage Cadillac that turned left at the intersection only half a block away, the headlights in front of the long hood sweeping across the parked Barracuda. Maybe they weren't paying attention to the car, maybe there was just enough dusty haze in the air to interfere with seeing through the windshield, or maybe they were all stoned, but the Caddy continued at a moderate speed until they passed out of sight.

A collective sigh drained the tension from the car and the three hitmen exited the vehicle and disappeared around back of the little bungalow and into the night.

Esteban watched them go and thumbed a drop phone to life. It was one thing to snuff out two old women who had lived long and full lives. But there was no way his conscience would allow the murder of Nelson's daughter and family in Honolulu. He dialed a Texas number.

The phone rang twice before a woman's voice came on the line. "Hello?"

"It is Esteban. There has been a hit ordered in Hawaii. Go to this address in Honolulu." He recited it from memory. "Remove the family as quickly as possible."

"You want them taken to the safe house?"

"Yes. And tell the Alpha I've finally learned about a system engineered by the Devil Woman and others to clear the way for a new drug pipeline. Make sure they're safe and wait for my call."

Chapter 6

Almost indistinguishable from each other, the three heavily tatted *sicarios* slipped around to the back of the sisters' house. Of similar heights, near twins Lopez and Martinez were lean and ropy. Razor sharp features born of a lifetime of hardship, constant violence, and murder more horrible than any American could imagine could have been a genetically shared trait.

Slightly heavier, the third, Mejia, was the elder by only one year.

All were mean as rattlesnakes and had no compunction against killing anyone of any size, age, or sex. Mejia, the odd one out, had recently used a fully automatic AK-47 to machine-gun an entire family down in Nueva Del Rio, right across the river from the sisters' bungalow. The innocents were simply sitting in a car, waiting for an opportunity to turn onto a side street when he walked up to them in the intersection, stuck the muzzle into the open passenger-side window, and hosed them all down. Two men, three women, a toddler, and an infant all died in the bloody squeeze of a trigger on the order of *Mujer Malvada*.

Because of his experience, Mejia led the way onto the house's small, concrete five- by five-foot back porch. Using the thick blade of a honed lockback knife, he cut through the screen door and reached in with two fingers to flip the simple hook and eye latch.

"Abierto, lentamente." He gently opened the wooden screen door while Lopez reached under his elbow and removed the rusty spring that creaked once, preventing it from slamming behind them, and to eliminate any squall.

Behind it, the solid wooden door had seen better days. Mejia handed Martinez the knife and grabbed the worn aluminum knob with both hands and lifted the peeling door while at the same time pushing it back toward the hinges. There was enough play for Martinez to slide the blade into the gap and twist. The latch gave and the door swung inside.

A cat shot through the opening, startling the men and causing them to curse under their breaths. The cat disappeared into the night without a sound, and the men exchanged white smiles all around. It was time to go to work, and they looked forward to all the blood they would spill with the blades in their hands.

Inside the kitchen, Lopez stepped on a board that creaked.

The scene on their television program ended and in that silent half second before a commercial, a familiar creak reached Miss Ruby's ears. Only one board in the pier and beam house squeaked, and it was in front of the kitchen sink. The commercial came on, and she reached down and pulled her basket of yarn closer to the chair.

Her heart pounded. Too old and slow to investigate the sound, she held her crocheting still in her lap. "Dear, do you remember when father told us about the story he heard when he worked on the King Ranch."

"Which story is that?"

"The one where those Mexican *seditionistas* came across the river to raid the Norias Ranch?" Miss Ruby cut her eyes toward the other chair, hoping Miss Harriet would get her drift.

It took Miss Harriet a moment to shift her attention from the television to the topic at hand. "Lands yes. He told that story a dozen times about when that band came across on a murder raid at the Norias Ranch and bypassed a house where two women were . . ."

Located about seventy miles north of Del Rio, the ranch was the headquarters for the southernmost portion of the legendary King Ranch that encompassed more than 825,000 acres. In 1915, Norias was more than a simple ranch house, it was a small rural community made up of several buildings, a section house, corrals, and a small country store. The Missouri Pacific Railroad used it as a water stop at the small train station.

A rogue wave that was part of the Mexican Revolution, the incursion across the border was specifically designed to kill any *anglo*s in the area. For some reason known only to the four dozen rebels, they bypassed a solitary ranch house containing two wives who were there by themselves and continued on to Norias to launch a surprise attack on the handful of residents. Unfortunately for the rebels, there were

seventeen heavily armed men, including a local sheriff, eight soldiers, three customs inspectors, four male
ranchers, and one railroad foreman who were there that
afternoon. Men who were all prepared for any kind of
trouble at any time.

Miss Harriet closed her eyes, as she did when they
were children and she had to recite a poem. "When the
smoke cleared, five Mexican bandits were dead and
the survivors made a bee-line for the border and whatever safety it offered from the Texas Rangers who
trailed them back down to the river. Daddy drilled it
into us for years to always be aware and armed, no
matter where we live . . ." She stopped and put a hand
to her mouth, suddenly realizing what Miss Ruby was
trying to say. "Oh."

Though Miss Harriet's hearing was failing, Miss Ruby
could hear as well as when she was a teenager. The board
creaked a second time.

Her heart was near about to burst. She reached into
the basket of yarn, pulled out her late husband's .38
caliber revolver loaded with six rounds of hollow-point
ammunition. As young women, they'd lived alone in the
harsh South Texas rangeland and became experts with
pistols, rifles, and shotguns. She thumb-cocked the revolver and waited.

Eyes wide in fear, Miss Harriet set her little jaw and
reached down to her own basket to pluck out the time-
worn 32.20 pistol their daddy had carried in the front
seat of his truck for years.

Miss Ruby put an arthritic finger to her lips and kept
her eyes on the open kitchen door. She had a clear view
of the short hallway to her left and the mostly dark
kitchen was directly in front of Miss Harriet. The stove

and cabinets were highlighted by the glow spilling from their floor lamps.

Miss Harriet gasped when a shadow flicked across the ghostly white stove. "Well, shit."

"Sister! Your language." Miss Ruby realized that she hadn't breathed in a good long while and inhaled at the same time a heavily tattooed man with a shaved head appeared in the hallway with a machete in his hand. An armed stranger in her house called for only one action. Shooting with both hands in her lap, the report of her .38 was startling and loud.

Miss Harriet's pistol thundered over and over, not four feet away, as fast as she could squeeze the well-oiled trigger.

The small living room was full of people as scrawny, tattooed men charged the sisters from across the room. The deafening concussion of gunshots filled the house.

Mejia didn't want to use firearms, wanting to keep the murder as quiet as possible and to have plenty of time to mutilate the corpses for maximum impact. They were there to make the point to anyone who failed the *Hidalgo* in any way would pay with the deaths of their entire family.

So what else would he need against two old *anglo mujeres*? He looked for the fear in their eyes as he leaped across the living room to slash with the razor-sharp blade in his hand.

What happened in the next second was something he could never have anticipated. The moment the soon-to-be-carrion gangster came into full view of the tiny, gray-haired *abuela* sitting beside the window, a hard object knocked the breath out of the *sicario*. His breath oofed from his lungs.

Mejia didn't feel the second round that punched through the upper lobe of his right lung from less than five feet away. His legs buckled and his face slammed into the oak floor at the same time his own gray-haired *abuela* and a family of recently dead Mexican children gathered in a shimmering glow to watch his soul slip from the man's body and seep through the floorboards.

The first gunshot startled Martinez, one of the near-twin gangsters, when he raced through the kitchen door, the razor-sharp knife still in his hand. Because the tiny old woman sitting in a rocker hesitated, he almost made it to her chair before her little pistol barked over and over. He hadn't noticed what she held in her hand until the last second, but strangely, he didn't feel the impact of the rounds.

Instead, he was suddenly tired beyond description. Everything in the man's body refused to respond to any of his brain's commands. His legs refused to cooperate any further and he sat heavily at the woman's feet, finding just enough energy to wave the blade like a soft flower.

He blinked twice, staring at the wicker basket full of brightly colored yarn before she shot again.

Head aching from a continuing roll of gunshots in their small living room, Miss Ruby barely registered the first Hispanic man lying on their oak floor. Another dropped at Miss Harriet's feet, slashing feebly with a big knife at the basket of yarn while she continued to pull the trigger on the double action revolver until the hammer clicked over and over on dead caps.

There was no time to wonder at the room full of gore, because still another tattooed man popped from the kitchen and charged forward with a three-foot machete raised like a baseball bat.

Instinct kicked in. Miss Harriet needed to protect her sister. The arthritis in her hands forgotten, her pistol bucked with each squeeze of the double-action trigger. The man deflated, and three men bled out on their polished and once clean floor.

Outside in the Barracuda, Esteban saw flashes strobe through the open windows like a string of firecrackers ripping off. Thunder from the house followed, and he waited with rising anxiety as lights flicked on in homes on both sides of the street.

His men didn't have firearms.

Neighbors in bath robes and a few shirtless men stepped out on their tiny porches, looking both ways to see what had caused the commotion.

Still he sat behind the wheel, expecting to see his blood-covered brothers rush from the house.

The dark muscle car idling in front of the house drew notice as the neighbors realized a strange car was in the neighborhood. Esteban finally decided it was time to flee the scene. He pulled to the corner and turned right as sirens wailed in the distance.

Half a mile away, he flashed past the Cadillac they'd seen earlier. It was parked outside of a local convenience store. The occupants were inside and never knew he was on their turf.

His men had failed, and the chances were good that the Devil Woman would have Incencio or Geronimo put a bullet in his brain for it. Choking down rising panic, he turned south to cross into *Ciudad Acuna* and drove to the *Mujer Malvada's rancho* in Coahuila.

Shaking with terror, and despite the grinding arthritis in her left shoulder, Miss Ruby twisted around, picked up the receiver from its cradle, and punched three numbers with a shaking finger.

"Nine-one-one, what's your emergency."

Her voice quavered. "My sister and I just shot three men who broke into our house."

"Is this a joke?"

"I hope not. All three of 'em are dead."

Miss Harriet laid the pistol in her lap and turned both corners of her mouth downward. "And they've bled all over our clean floor."

Chapter 7

I was back on desk duty once again, standard procedure after an officer involved in a shooting. It seemed like I spent most of my time on administrative leave.

I was getting pretty good at it.

The media circus was in full swing after the attack on the set of *The Mexican Pipeline* they were calling the Movie Lot Massacre, taking up considerable time on the news channels and filling several hours of radio talk shows. I was in a meeting with Major Chase Parker, my commander of the Texas Rangers Special Unit, just off the third floor Grand Jury Room in the Ballard Courthouse.

We asked the crew members and actors not to speak with the reporters who descended on the scene like vultures, shoving microphones in the traumatized victims' faces both there and at the hospital, asking absurd questions. It wasn't because we were trying to hide anything. Far from it. I simply wanted to steer the news crews toward the sheriff's office so all the information they heard was correct and accurate while investigators worked their way through the process of gathering facts and evidence.

Those traumatized individuals didn't need to hear idiotic questions such as "how do you feel," or "what were you thinking at the time?"

That idea lasted about fifteen minutes, until after one of the healthy crew members arrived at the Chisos Regional Hospital in Ballard. While waiting for his friend in surgery, the shocky crewmember found himself staring into the glass eye of a camera and told what he remembered in graphic detail.

It was a feeding frenzy after that, with reporter after reporter interviewing the crew member riding the crest of sudden popularity. His story expanded with more detail and suppositions until it took on a life of its own. Within minutes the interview went national, and then international, attracting even more stations and outlets.

So as that cyclone continued to gain strength, the commander of Company E., Major Parker called us together in the third-floor corner office of the Ballard Courthouse, instead of holding our debriefing at Company Headquarters in El Paso where reporters might be waiting to speak to the Texas Ranger who was on the scene.

We were gathered around a rectangular conference table in the same small office where I'd killed two terrorists in self-defense several months earlier. I couldn't help but look up at the freshly painted ceiling that had been destroyed that day, and out the window at the rooftops and scraggly trees in our little town that looked quiet and peaceful from such a height.

The Major and I weren't alone in the debriefing.

Sheriff Ethan Armstrong was there, along with my dad, retired Ranger Herman Hawke, and Gabe. He'd also invited our local FBI Agent, Landon McDowell. He was the only one in a suit and tie.

Agent McDowell was the Bureau's liaison with the Ballard County Sheriff's office. He'd worked with us in the past. Well, worked might be stretching it a little. He reluctantly helped during what came to be known as the Ballard Incident in our home town when terrorists took over the courthouse. He'd also been involved in a little border fracas a few months earlier. Completely out of his comfort zone, the FBI Agent who cut his teeth in the department in Washington, D.C., still hadn't acclimated to his West Texas assignment, but at least he now owned a pair of boots that went well with his suit and tie.

Five hats lay crown down in the center of the wooden table.

This time it wasn't a formal debriefing, since the others were in the room, but a relaxed discussion with Major Parker. We began by recounting our versions of the shooting. With the exception of Gabe, we were all professional observers, a part of our training that evolved into almost a sixth sense over time, so that we could be accurate in our assessments of situations or events in the field.

Our recollections were the same, and that helped put the increasingly breathless news reports to rest in Parker's mind. He leaned back in his chair when we were finished and smoothed his dark tie. "It's good to get the real story, instead of what they're saying on TV. I know, I've read your report, but I wanted to hear what happened straight from the horses' mouths. I haven't asked, but did any of y'all recognize any of the shooters that got away?"

Shrugs all around the table.

"Well, it looks to me like the Hidalgo cartel has now advertised they're operating on our side of the river."

"That ain't news to nobody. They've been in and out over here for years." My old man's voice was sharp. "Hell, they cross the river as easy as it is for me to go to the store, and most of 'em have more ink on 'em than that tattooed man at the circus."

"I know that, Herman, but this time they've crossed to operate a lot farther north, and don't mind advertising it. This wasn't anything we've seen in the past. It was a major operation to clear the way for future projects, and that tells me they aren't afraid anymore. Chief Fitch agrees with me."

Chief Marlon Fitch is head of the Texas Rangers Division of the DPS. He's over all six Ranger companies in the state, and the Special Operations Groups or SOG, that's charged to counter criminal organizations threats, terrorists, and drug trafficking organizations along the Rio Grande.

McDowell scribbled on a yellow pad. A man of few words, he was as out of place in our part of the world as a cat in a doghouse. He listened, nodding from time to time. Unlike how agents are portrayed on television, he was content to sit back and take notes.

Resting both elbows on the arms of the scarred wooden chair, Major Parker rocked back. The chair creaked. "They know something we don't, which they feel gives them the confidence to just drive up and down our highways, shooting folks without worrying about getting caught."

"They've always acted like that." The Old Man

frowned and laced his fingers on the table. "Bad guys don't care about laws. Them damned liberals oughta understand that, they're bad guys because they *break* the law."

"Acted is right, Herman. But you're not educating kids here. We're all lawmen."

"I know it, but I'm still mad about what happened. The thing is, now them people ain't afraid of a stinkin' thing, and that's what scares the pee-waddlin out of me."

"Given." Major Parker tapped the tabletop with a forefinger. "Here's a problem. I've made calls to all the alphabet government agencies I know of to find out who the dead undercover agent belonged to, and *nobody* fessed up."

He glanced over at Agent McDowell who shrugged. "All I can say is that he isn't . . . wasn't ours."

"Well, at this point, we have no idea who he might be, and that worries the piss out of me. Especially if there's another man out there they won't admit to. *That's* a problem."

At least he didn't refer to "the dead undercover agent" as the man I'd shot. I didn't need to hear that right then. His death weighted on my shoulders, even though we all knew it was justifiable.

There were deep scars in the tabletop, and it was everything I could do not to reach out and trace the nearest one with my finger. I helped put them there by strangling a terrorist to death on that exact spot after he dropped through the ceiling during their takeover of the courthouse. It was hard to concentrate on the conversation.

A wave of emotion washed over me, threatening to

take me down in a dark swirl. I was thinking those scars weren't nearly as deep as the ones in my soul.

From the corner of my eye, I saw the Old Man studying my posture. Just like when I was a kid, he could see straight into my heart. Keeping my expression blank, I took a deep breath and leaned forward with both forearms on the table, forcing my attention back on the issue at hand. "So what do you wanna do, Major?"

"I want to put an end to what I think's going on . . . what you heard on the movie set." Major Parker set his jaw. "I need you to arrest those responsible, if they'll agree to handcuffs, if not, clean this nest of snakes out of my state."

Ethan patted his shirt pocket and located a toothpick. Tucking it into the corner of his mouth under his thick mustache, he shifted into professional mode. "My deputies have increased their presence on the highways, and even though the Snowflakes in other parts of the world might get their panties in a wad, we're committing the sin of profiling."

Chuckles all around. Except for Gabe, we'd all been behind the wheel of a highway patrol car and understood what all cops know. We look for certain signs or "tells," that indicate a variety of potential criminal offenses. We also operate on instinct, or a sixth sense that reveals to us when and if a person or situation looks wrong.

It's an evolutionary holdover that rings a subconscious warning bell any time something looks or feels out of sorts. Law enforcement officers, or LEOs as we're sometimes known, tap into that sense after being on the streets and dealing with all kinds of people and dangerous situations. We notice things regular folks don't, like a certain look in a person's eye, body language, or responses.

No one will admit it these days, but any LEO in the country can follow a car for only a short period of time before the driver commits an infraction. After that, well, one thing leads to another, such as drugs in the car, weapons violations, or warrants.

It's usually warrants that get 'em back in the bracelets.

I don't know of one single Ranger who won't perk up at the mention of day-to-day police work. It's in our roots. "Catching anything in that net?"

Ethan frowned. "Not so's you'd notice. We've mostly caught the usual, with a couple of drug busts."

"Catch many illegals?"

"Always. That's near every day of every week, but right now most of those taken into custody come from the Border Patrol. The limited number of two-lanes leading out of here helps keep that down. It's not like up toward I-20 and all that mess around Midland or Odessa where you can bet one out of a hundred cars and trucks are carrying something illegal or someone's breaking the law."

Even though our part of the state is vast and remote, what most folks don't realize is that there's a spiderweb of dirt roads expanding through some of the biggest ranches in the country out in West Texas. Most are accessed through gates and cattle guards, but once you're on 'em, a person can drive for miles, oftentimes bypassing the highways and possible checkpoints by following the squiggly roads winding through the mountains and across some of the roughest terrain in the country.

You've got to know where you're going, or you'll meet yourself coming back around to where you started.

Ethan's been called out a number of times in the middle of the night, when ranchers or hands see headlights far out in the country. Drug runners and human traffickers use them from time to time to miss Border Patrol check stations or avoid patrol cars on the highways.

The smart ones only use those skinny routes on occasion so as not to establish a pattern, driving through the deep night darkness. But drug mules and human traffickers are human, and will stick with what's familiar, returning again and again to the same places for meets, as pick up points, or to exchange money for the drugs.

We drifted from one topic to another, all relating to the cartels and drug trafficking.

I was watching Major Parker. He was only half-listening, and I was getting the idea he was waiting for the right moment to tell us what was on his mind. He adjusted the dark tie knotted around his throat as if to ease the pressure before speaking.

He swiveled toward Agent McDowell. "You guys have any questions for us?"

"Not right now. We're looking into it through our own channels, but nothing has come up so far. I'll let you know what we find out."

"All right." The Major was done. "Here's what I want you to do, Sonny."

The tiny room grew silent.

"What's that?"

"Find the head of this cartel snake and cut it off, and I want it done yesterday."

The Old Man cleared his throat. "What I'm hearing you say is . . ."

"Don't need to be said."

Dad wouldn't quit. "This is like them old westerns where they hire a sheriff to come in and clean up a town, and don't care how he does it until the job's done. And then they realize they've hired the same kind of person as they was afraid of, only now he's wearing a badge and has authority. Y'all know how those stories always end."

A door slammed somewhere downstairs and a light female voice laughed.

"Well, it won't be like that. You're the right person for this job, and I'll handle the rest."

"That's what the Montana Cattleman's Association told Tom Horn, and you see where that got him."

"Horn was a murderer, not a lawman." Major Parker studied my dad. "Herman, you don't trust me?"

"I trust *you*. Not them who use their men the wrong way."

"I won't let that happen."

The Old Man nodded, and I could almost hear his thoughts. *You better not.*

The Major turned back to me. "But that's not all, Sonny. Peel back the layers of this onion and find out who these undercover agents work for, if you can."

I nodded. "That part's even more personal."

"I understand." The Major stood and picked up his hat. "Just don't cause another international incident."

"So you're telling me to stay on this side of the border."

"I didn't say that. Cross if you need to, but let the Mexican authorities know you're coming." He grinned. "But don't go roaring up on anybody without thinking about it. Know what I mean?"

He was talking about my impulsive side. I sometimes act first when things get tense, a tendency that works for me only about half of the time.

Setting the hat just right on his head, the Major left at the same time the air conditioning kicked on, the gust of dry, cold air as chilly as a blue norther.

Chapter 8

The hospital in Ft. Stockton smelled the same as every other medical facility I'd ever been in, the astringent odor of disinfectant, chemicals, and pharmaceuticals. From my most recent stay in just such a facility, a rough-edged old gal named Nurse Maggie told me that these days the odor comes from something called Lodoform. It doesn't really matter; it smells like misery.

Border Agent Manual Trevino was tethered to his hospital bed by a tangle of tubes and what looked like electrical lines. Flowers filled every available space except for the couch full of bags and the obligatory light brown recliner occupied by a tired but attractive blonde woman I assumed to be his wife.

Hat in hand, I entered the room. She looked up. In the elevated bed to my right, Trevino's swollen eyes were closed. His face a mass of purple and bluish bruises. His bottom lip was stitched, as were several lacerations. It looked like he'd been hit with a truck.

Her immensely sad, dark and moist eyes went to the badge on my shirt, then the Sweetheart Grips on the Colt 1911 on my belt. "Can I help you?"

Rangers are used to such an examination from those who seldom see us. I stepped closer to the foot of the bed. There was no way to tell if he was unconscious or asleep. Clicks and hums came from the equipment plugged into the wall above Trevino's head. A flat-panel TV on the opposite wall flickered, the tinny sound coming from a handset looped over the bed's side rail.

"I'm Sonny Hawke. Texas Ranger. I came to see if I could speak to Agent Trevino about what happened last night."

I'd gotten the call about the incident right after breakfast from Major Parker. The murder of one agent and Trevino's severe beating was the lead news story on the radio as I drove to Ft. Stockton.

"You're his wife?"

"Yes. He's asleep."

Relief washed through me. Sleep is better than unconscious. "That's good. He needs the rest. Has he been waking up very often?"

Her Texas accent was soft. She pulled a strand of hair behind one ear. "He's in and out." She glanced over at her battered husband, and her face softened either in love or sympathy. I couldn't tell which. "The doctors have him on some pretty heavy pain medication."

"I'm not surprised."

"I doubt he can tell you anything more than he's already told the other officers who've been here this morning."

"I bet there was a line. Was he awake long?"

"Long enough to answer the same questions over and over." Her voice sharpened, a wife defending her husband in any way she could.

"That's how we are." I tried not to give her what my wife calls my puppy-dog look. I knew she was hurting, but I didn't want to make her think I was being patronizing. "Who was here besides his commander?"

"How about Border Patrol, the sheriff's department, highway patrol, FBI, Homeland Security . . ."

"Everyone, huh?"

"Yep. Even another Ranger. You're the second. Why don't you read *his* report? I can boil it down for you. In a nutshell, Rosie says he doesn't remember anything after he and Frank went on duty."

We were skating on thin ice, and I could tell she was barely holding it together. "I'll probably read it, but I need to speak with him myself, if that's okay with you."

Her face softened and I could tell I'd scored one with her. I was probably the first guy who actually asked permission, instead of seeing it as their duty.

"I don't want to wake him up."

I realized I'd been fiddling with the brim of my straw hat and dropped my arm. "Look, I know you're give out. Why don't you take a break for a few minutes, go get some coffee, or go to the bathroom." I watched her unconsciously reach for her cell phone. "Or go call and check on the kids. I heard you had three. Get some air and talk to them outside. The sunshine'll make you feel a little better. If he wakes up, I'll talk to him. If he doesn't, then you get a break."

She hesitated, then came to a decision. Gathering her purse and the phone, she stood. She glanced at her husband lying still as death. "He's been asleep for a while. He *might* wake up."

"It won't be me that does it."

Agent Trevino's lips parted, but his eyes remained closed. His voice was weak, but you could tell he was the kind of man who had a sense of humor and was full of determination. "Who can sleep with you two yakking over there. Lucy, you go on out for a few minutes while I talk to this Ranger."

She gently took his hand. "Will that be okay?"

"Sure." A crease appeared at the corner of his mouth. "I'm fine right now, at least until the drugs wear off."

She gave his hand another squeeze and met my gaze with a determined look that spoke volumes before she left the room. I took her place on the vinyl recliner positioned at an angle beside Trevino's head and put my hat on the tray beside the bed. "Did you hear who I said I was?"

"Hawke." He licked his lips with a dry tongue.

Seeing a plastic mug the size of a water barrel beside my hat, I picked it up and angled the adjustable straw. "Here's some water. Can you turn your head? Or I can raise you up some."

He turned enough to take the straw between his lips and drank like a horse. "Thanks."

"I didn't think to ask. Are you supposed to have that much water?"

"We'll know in a little while."

I liked the guy. "Feel like talking?"

"It's about all I can do right now. I'm pretty light-headed, but ask your questions."

"Tell me what happened last night."

His story was simple, but the words came slow and hesitant. He recalled starting their shift and pulling onto the highway. The next thing he remembered was waking up in the emergency room and hearing that his partner Frank Nelson was dead.

"Do you remember which highway you were on?"

"Like I said, nothing."

"They found you laying on the shoulder of Highway 1776, not far from Coyanosa."

"That's what they tell me."

"How long were you and Frank partners?"

"About a year."

"Who usually drove?"

"Me."

"You were driving that night, then."

"Yep."

"You pulled out of the lot. Which way did you turn?"

"Right."

"Good. Where were you going? Do you remember any conversation y'all had? Anything as simple as the weather, sports, sick kids? Maybe you guys said you intended to patrol one particular stretch of road."

The wrinkles in the corners of his blackened and swollen eyes deepened for a microsecond, but enough to let me know there was something he remembered or didn't want to discuss.

"What?"

"Nothing. I don't remember what we talked about."

"You guys were found on the side of the road. There were fresh tire tracks in the sand in front of your vehicle. It looks as if y'all pulled somebody over."

Instead of answering, he gave a tiny shake of his head. "Don't remember it, if we did."

"Who usually called it in when you made a stop?"

He swallowed and didn't answer immediately. A prickle at the back of my neck told me something wasn't right. "Frank."

"S.O.P.?"

"Yes."

I wished I could see his eyes, but they remained closed. I wondered if he wasn't able to open them, if it was too painful. "So he would have called it in, if you'd stopped anyone."

"Yes."

I waited in the silence broken only by the sounds of the equipment monitoring his vitals, and the EID, or electronic infusion device that regulated the flow of liquids flowing into his arm.

The question finally came and it seemed like he was playing a role, doing what I should have expected. "Did he always make the call. Was there any time he didn't?"

I waited, not trying to give the poor guy grief, but to see what his reactions were. Something wasn't adding up, and I couldn't figure what it was. "No."

"He didn't this time."

I knew then that he was hiding something, because a single tear rolled from the least swollen eye and his chest hitched. Once.

Agent Frank Nelson committed a vital sin. Tracks in the sand told the story. They made a stop, but he didn't call it in. We always, always, call in a stop. It's ingrained. Frank had a reason not to follow procedure, and I wondered what it was.

The machine hummed again, dispensing a dose of clear liquid into his IV tube. I figured it was for pain, because Trevino sighed. His voice softened. "He should have, but he recognized . . ." His eyes rolled like a tired toddler and he slipped into a deep sleep.

Dammit!

The drugs almost caused him to slip and tell me what I needed to know. It was obvious that Frank didn't want anyone to know they'd stopped a vehicle that night. But for what reason, and why did Trevino look the other way?

Frustrated, I sat there beside the bed, thinking, until his wife came back. I hugged her neck and left, hoping Agents Trevino and Frank Nelson hadn't been playing some dangerous game that had already cost one man his life.

Before I had time to ponder that thought, I got a call that Frank Nelson's foster mom and her sister had been involved in an attempted murder at the same time Frank was killed. I knew where I was headed next.

Chapter 9

It's not a long way from Ballard down to Del Rio in Texas terms, a little over three hours. I headed down there as quick as I could to check out such an odd coincidence.

Travel in the Lone Star state is usually measured in hours instead of miles. For example, if I was telling someone how far it is between Ballard and Brownsville, on the southern tip of Texas, I'd say nearly twelve hours instead of 656 miles. It's our way of dealing with the vast distances Texans have to travel.

The time alone gave me time to figure out all the fancy technology in the new Dodge dually. The white truck replaced my old champagne-colored pickup after I was forced off the road a few months earlier into an East Texas bayou, not far from Jasper, way back behind the Pine Curtain.

I'm not a technology guy for sure. Even cell phones bumfuzzle me, and I have trouble enough with 'em when things get hot. Learning to use the radio and cruise control on the truck was aggravatin' enough, but there were bells and whistles I didn't know I had.

The Michelins whined on the empty highway as I finally got the radio to working. George Strait was singing about cowboys like us when the phone rang. The large screen on the dash showed it was Major Parker, and all kinds of things happened. The words "Accept," appeared on the touch screen, so I took my eyes off the road long enough to tap it with a fore-finger.

"Hello?"

"I didn't think the call was going through."

"Took me a second to figure out how to answer it." The dually punched a hole through the air in the barren South Texas landscape near Langtry. Best known for Judge Roy Bean and his Law West of the Pecos, I al-ways thought he was nothing but a con man of ques-tionable sense and quality.

I was running along the Rio Grande in a hardscrab-ble *caliche* world of heat, catclaw cactus, creosote, and a variety of armed desert plants I couldn't identify on a bet. In Mexico, across the river on my right and be-yond the bleached, crumbling cliffs cut by the river eons ago, it was even rougher and harder to live.

Papers rattled on the other end of the call and Major Parker cleared his throat. "I got some more info for you."

"Go ahead, but I can't write it down."

He grunted into the phone, knowing what I meant. Rolling along at eighty-five miles an hour, I couldn't chance taking my eyes off the shimmering two-lane.

"Nelson has no one else but a daughter in Hawaii. With her permission, our investigators searched his house and found two hundred thousand in cash. All hundred-dollar bills. The house had a high-end security system on it, too. This whole thing smells to high heaven, so I'm not going to tell you what I think. I need your assessment of the situation."

"What situation is that?"

"The one that's about to be your full-time job until you get to the bottom of it."

Crime scene tape was a flimsy barrier around a neat little frame and stucco house in Del Rio. Two police cars were parked on the street outside the scene. I killed the diesel engine and stepped out, adjusting the new O'Farrell hat that replaced *another* one I'd replaced months earlier.

It seemed like I was keeping that little Santa Fe hat shop in business.

The yellow tape was wrapped around whatever they could find to cordon off the area, trees, posts, and the radio antenna on a tired-looking Ford Pinto parked in front of the house. Police, sheriff's department, and DPS cars lined the street. I lifted the tape with one finger and ducked underneath. A uniformed police officer came out of the house at the same time and started to read me the riot act until he saw the *cinco peso* on my shirt.

He straightened a little as I walked up the short, cracked walk leading to the front door. A dry breeze rustled the tall palm in the yard. "I'm surprised to see a Ranger here."

I shook his hand. "Sonny Hawke. I just got the call a little while ago." That specific time frame is acceptable in Texas. "What's up?"

"I'm Ybarra." He was a good-looking kid. They all look like kids to me these days.

"What can you tell me?"

"Damnedest thing. Three individuals made entry through the back door and ran into something they didn't expect."

"What's that?"

"Two tough little old ladies with revolvers, and those old gals *won*. Forensics is through shooting pictures. C'mon in."

Banana trees grew up against the tiny porch, shading the entry. The interior was what I expected, a once neat house that now contained half a dozen cops trying not to step in congealing pools of blood. I took my hat off and paused just inside the door. The ladies were sitting in comfortable-looking chairs in front of the windows.

The one farthest away noticed me first and perked up. She wiped her eyes and it looked as if she'd been crying. "Ruby, looky here what just walked in."

The other saw me and grinned, but it wasn't as bright as I figured it should be. "Settle down, girl. I recognize that badge. You're a Texas Ranger."

I admired those two old gals. They'd been in a shootout the night before and had killed the intruders, but they didn't seem any the worse for wear.

"Yes, ma'am." I looked around for another chair, but there was nothing but an ottoman with a complex needlepoint top. It didn't look like it'd hold a toddler, so I stood. I'm glad I did, because a huge calico cat flowed onto the ottoman like a panther, glaring at me as if she knew I'd considered sitting down.

A detective in black slacks and a sport coat stepped

out of the kitchen with a notepad in his hand. I met his gaze. "I'm Sonny Hawke. I'd like to talk to these ladies and then visit with y'all outside, when you're finished."

He nodded. "Lieutenant Cordova. I'm supposed to meet with Sheriff Ortiz in a little bit. He should be here by the time you're finished." He gave the sisters a little wave. "Ladies."

"See you out there." I turned to the Nelson sisters who hadn't taken their attention off me for a minute. I knew one had a different last name, but the Nelson Sisters came to mind easy as pie. "Y'all want to tell me what happened?"

I took notes while Miss Ruby and Miss Harriet alternated like my twins do when telling a story. They'd been together so long I figured they could finish each other's sentences on any topic. Their routine was seamless, and I just listened.

"All right. You're telling me you've never seen these guys before."

"No."

"You sure they've never been to the house. You haven't seen them at the grocery store, maybe accidentally cut 'em off with your car?"

They shook their heads in unison.

An old-fashioned black push button phone rested on a telephone table not far from the television setup. "Have any calls come in from people you don't know?"

"Why, honey, that happens about three times a day. It's usually people trying to sell us something or get a donation."

"We don't give 'em a dime." Miss Harriet set her lips in a straight line.

"I need to ask this question just right. Y'all know about Frank."

Their eyes brimmed over at the same time. Miss Ruby nodded. "We know, hon. We got word this mornin'."

Relieved that I didn't have to give them the bad news, I plowed on. "When was the last time you heard from Frank, Miss Ruby?"

"Why, it's been years. We were hoping to see him this coming Christmas."

Miss Harriet dabbed at her eyes with a tissue she plucked from an embroidered holder on the table between them. "He was a good boy, but he always had an edge on him I didn't like."

Miss Ruby blinked away her tears. "He was a rascal when he was little."

"Like what kind?"

Miss Harriet wouldn't look at her sister. "Well, he'd tell a lie when the truth was easier."

"Lies about what?"

"It didn't matter." It was Miss Ruby again. "He wasn't always truthful. Me'n Ed didn't hold it against him. The boy probably took that from his mama or daddy, but he never knew who they were or what they were like." Pride brightened her eyes like the sunrise. "God love him, he turned out better than we expected, being a Border Patrol agent and all that."

Looking through the open window, I saw a sheriff's department SUV pull up to the curb. "Well thank you, ladies. Y'all did a fine job handling this situation."

Miss Ruby gave me a smile. "Daddy told us to always be ready, but son, there's a problem."

"What's that?"

"We don't know why these men came here. We don't have any money, and anyone who lives in this neighborhood knows that. They didn't come to rob. They came in here to kill us. You think it was one of them gang initiations? We've heard about them on the news."

"No, ma'am. These guys were too old from what I hear, and experienced. It was something else."

"Like what?"

"Well, I can't say right now. Let me work on it for a while, and I'll give y'all a call when I figure it out."

Miss Ruby rested both gnarled hands in her lap. A gray-and-white cat jumped onto the arm of her chair, and she went to petting it. "You must know *something*."

I shook my head. "I don't know, but I intend to find out."

Miss Ruby frowned. "Well, I need to ask you something."

"Yes, ma'am."

"The first police officers that got here took our pistols. Now we don't have any way to protect ourselves. Can you get them back for us or get us some more guns? You know, this neighborhood's not safe anymore."

I grinned. "Well, I don't have any pistols to leave with y'all, but I'll ask the officers to keep someone outside the house for a while."

"Well, we'll still be unarmed when they quit sitting out there. I've seen them television programs where they have to call the officers in because they don't have enough money to pay 'em no more."

"Can y'all put us in witness protection?" Miss Harriet looked hopeful. "I'd like to move somewhere else and start over."

"Well, the witness protection program is federal. It's for people who have special knowledge of a case. Those boys out there'll take care of you. I promise you that."

Miss Harriet cocked her head, and I could tell she wasn't finished.

"Is there something else you wanted to ask me, ma'am?"

"There sure is. Are you married?"

"Harriet!" Miss Ruby threw up her hands. "You ought not be asking the man that. And looky there. You can see as clear as day that he's wearing a wedding ring."

"I saw it, but it don't hurt to ask. I just needed to know how married he *really* is."

I couldn't help but grin, and backed out the door, holding my hat between us like a Spartan shield. "I'm as married as you can get. To a good gal, but thanks Miss Harriet for asking. I'm flattered."

"See?" She made a face at Miss Ruby. "He's flattered. I still got it."

"Why you don't have any such of a thing. You've never had a man in your life and . . ."

I fled the scene and went back outside where it was safe.

Chapter 10

In faded jeans and a bright white shirt with puffy sleeves, the light-skinned Devil Woman of Coahuila, known back in Texas when she was a high school student as Tish Villarreal, led a contingency of armed men across a flat valley floor more than a hundred miles from Del Rio. Fenced on one side by sheer rock cliffs that formed a semicircle around the valley, the area where they walked was dotted with mounds of varying sizes, heights, and age.

Several of her *soldados*, or soldiers, remained beside a line of black Lincoln SUVs to keep an eye on the two-track dirt road weaving across the landscape.

Black wings circled the sky and a weak voice called. *"Agua!"*

Slender, almost boyish in figure, the five-foot two-inch woman with shoulder-length raven black hair wove through mounds of dirt. As if shopping, she occasionally paused beside some of the older, weathered mounds, reading names and dates written on small plastic tags hanging from crude wire handles that disappeared into the ground.

Two men from Coahuila's *narco* government walked beside her, their heads covered from the burning hot sun with straw cowboy hats. The duo didn't carry themselves with the same wary bearing as the others, but sauntered across the hardpan as if there was nothing to fear within a thousand miles.

Villarreal pointed downward with a slender, manicured finger and spoke in Spanish. "That was Roberto Vega."

Esteban, the getaway driver and only survivor of the failed Nelson hit in Del Rio, followed a few steps behind her, bracketed by two men with dead eyes and hard sets to their jaws. He followed the point. *"Sí, señorita."*

She cut her dark eyes toward him and smiled. Deep dimples formed at the corners of her mouth. They gave her a mischievous look, one that once drove the boys crazy at Gomez High in El Paso. "He was one of my friends from the start. He helped make our organization what it is today."

The look would have been coy in a bar or a party. It was out of place in the hot valley baking in the sun. Instead of feeling any attraction to the pretty woman with blue-black hair, Esteban shivered. "I knew him."

"You know why his name is on that *etiqueta*?"

The weak voice beside the SUVs called again. *"Agua."*

Villarreal ignored the interruption as Esteban's eyes flicked to the man lying prone on the rocky ground, quickly sliding off and back to the little piece of orange plastic that looked like an ear tag for cattle. *"Señorita, lo siento.* I cannot read."

"Entiendo." She resumed their walk, the heels of her caiman-skin boots making tiny thumps that were almost lost in the shuffle of the other men's footsteps who followed without speaking.

It was safer that way.

"You're sorry I can't read?" Esteban frowned. The conversation wasn't following any path that it should have. "Many of us can't."

"That's not what I'm talking about." Villarreal's tone sharpened for only an instant. She softened the statement with a wan smile.

None of the armed men met the cartel leader's eyes. Instead, they studied the distance, the nearby cliffs, even their own feet, in an attempt not to look too hard at the graves.

She passed a fresh mound that looked to have been created only days earlier. "Do you know what Incencio would have done if I had sent him to Del Rio instead of you and those other three *idiotas* to wipe the rest of Frank Nelson's relatives from the face of the earth?"

He started to shrug again, but stopped in mid movement. "I don't know what to say to that."

The tiny crease at the corner of Trish's mouth deepened when she smiled on only one side. "It's probably best."

She stopped on a bare, flat piece of hardpan and nudged a rock with the toe of her boot. *"He* would have done what I asked." Holding out her hand, she stared into the shimmering distance. "Roberto."

One of her gangsters with 1518 tattooed across his forehead plucked a Beretta M9 from the waistband at the small of his back and held it out, butt first.

Tish Villarreal took the large pistol with her tiny hand and let it hang loose at her side. "Esteban. You understand how I run this organization."

Her men separated from Villarreal, circling around so as not to crowd her. Because she'd stopped, the gangsters carrying an assortment of automatic weapons scattered and faced outward to ensure complete coverage of the area. Safe in their own territory, they nevertheless kept their guard up and fingers close to the triggers, for to do otherwise would draw the wrath of the Devil Woman.

Mouth suddenly dry as the ground under their feet, Esteban stared at his shoes. *"Sí, señorita."*

"You know the men who serve under me."

"Sí."

"Do you know how I came to this position?"

"No." Esteban cut his eyes upward.

"I didn't sleep my way here, like you probably think." She presented him with a brilliant smile. "It didn't happen that way. Many thought I was a boy when I was younger. I wore T-shirts and kept my hair short." She flipped her head, throwing one side of her long black hair back over a shoulder. "I did what I needed to, so I could move up in the ranks.

"Because I looked like a boy, I was the perfect *sicario,* small and almost unnoticed. I learned from another boy who was my age, who killed up close for the *Sinacolas.* He taught me much. I liked him, but he disappeared one night and I never saw him again."

One hand on her hip, she studied the distant ridgeline, possibly seeing into the past. "No matter. He'd taught what he knew. After that, I killed when ordered to, and when the time came, I killed those who issued the orders and took their place." Her brilliant smile was like bright sunshine on that sunny day. "I *assassinated* my way to the top.

"I created this *cinsorcio*. Our world is simple. Move product and people. Obey without question, and never, ever cross me. Those who listen and do as I say profit with plenty of money and a good life. Those who fail to do their jobs weaken the cartel. You understand that, don't you?"

Esteban finally met her gaze with fearful eyes. *"Sí."*

Tish nodded solemnly, as if he'd given an answer full of thought.

"Agua, por favor, señorita!"

Villarreal turned her head toward the man lying on the ground nearly seventy-five yards away. "I'm tired of listening to that *pendejo*. Bring him over here." Two of her soldiers trotted in the man's direction. She addressed another *soldato* with an AK-47 slung muzzle down over his shoulder. He carried a shovel in his left hand. "Salazar."

He stepped forward. *"Sí, señorita."*

She pointed at the flat piece of ground. "There."

The man handed his weapon to another, took three steps away from where she stood, and punched the blade into the hard, dry ground, digging steadily. The two soldiers returned, half-carrying, half dragging a shirtless man across the rocky ground.

They held his sunburned, tattoo-covered body upright. Covered with sand from where he'd been laying, his ghost-white face was full of pain and terror. *"Por favor."*

"Do not speak." Villarreal flicked a dismissive hand. "Tell Esteban your name and why you are here."

He coughed, wet and deep. "I'm sorry, señorita."

"Tell him!"

He dropped his gaze. "I am Juan Sarmiento. I took some of the *cocaina* I was supposed to deliver."

She watched him, as if memorizing the scene at her feet. "Why?"

The Mexican's face twisted in pain. "To sell, and for my own use."

"You *know* my people don't use the product."

"*Sí.*"

"You know the punishment for stealing from me. Tell everyone the penalty."

"*Por favor.*" A steady trickle of blood leaked from his mouth. "Please. I will do anything you ask if you spare me."

"Get on your knees."

Moving with great pain, the prisoner dropped and bowed his head. *"Lo siento."*

Esteban almost gasped at the horrific sight of the man's bare back. He'd seen the final results many times in the Devil Woman's courtyard, but never men at this stage.

A loop of wire protruded from the puffy, lacerated skin between the man's bloody shoulder blades and curled up into the exact same braided handle as those rising up from the surrounding mounds. The other end disappeared into a similar fresh wound in the middle of his back. The wire looped around the man's spinal column at both ends, anchoring the "handle."

Esteban unconsciously crossed himself. *"Madre de dios."*

Villarreal pointed with her left hand at a wire handle protruding from a nearly flat mound only six feet away. "Roberto. It is time to pull that one."

Face devoid of emotion and eyes downcast, the appointed *soldato* nodded and approached the low mound. Straddling the wire handle, Roberto bent his knees, grasped it with both hands, and pulled slow and steady, as if tugging a particularly tough weed from the ground.

The dry soil rose and soft cracking sounds came from beneath the surface. Roberto continued the pressure, gently pulling the handle upward. From underground, muffled pops like the tearing of small roots reached those standing under the hot sun. The dry surface cracked and still he pulled slow and steady. He'd done this before.

He adjusted his grip, rocking the handle slightly to put more pressure on one end, then the other. More pops came clearer as the ground reluctantly gave up what it had held.

Esteban gasped and started to step back. One of Villarreal's soldiers put a hand against his back to hold the shocked man in place.

Her face impassive, Villarreal watched Roberto do his work with the attention of a farmer pulling potato vines. The foul smell of human decomposition filled the still air as the shallow grave finally gave up the remainder of the spine and skull that had been buried only inches below the surface. The popping sounds were the corpse's ribs ripping loose from the rotting cartilage. Held together by a few remaining ligaments, the skull and spinal column was dark with sticky clay and full of not-yet decomposed flesh.

Decaying flesh and hair curled off the skull. Dried ligaments prevented the cracked skull from falling off the spine. The entry hole from a bullet in the left temple was tiny compared to the size of the exit wound.

Grimacing at the stench, the usually unmoved narco government men turned away from the sight. Most of her *soldados* mimicked Esteban's sign of the cross at the sight of what Roberto held. Like a fisherman examining his catch, and breathing through his mouth to avoid the odor, he turned the grisly trophy sideways for Villarreal to see.

She blinked her long lashes. "That was Juan Duarte."

Throughout the process and only a few feet away, the *soldado* named Salazar had continued digging the shallow grave, keeping his full attention to the job at hand.

"Duarte worked for the Nueva Laredo cartel." The Devil Woman told the story as if they were sitting in a living room instead of standing in the middle of a field from hell. "He killed one of my people after joining them. The rest of his family sleeps beneath the ground in Parral where he came from, but Juan Duarte will never rest. He will hang in the mesquites at the *patio de huesos* with the others, so that everyone will know his fate."

Horrified, the man with the handle wired into his back groaned and held up one hand. *"Por favor, Dios."*

Villárreal tilted her head like a puppy examining a strange noise. Expressionless, her arm rose and her finger tightened on the trigger. She paused, as if listening to someone they couldn't see, then handed the pistol to Esteban.

"Shoot him and redeem yourself."

Without hesitation, he took the pistol. It bucked in his hand. The report was sharp and echoed off the cliff.

The pleading man's head snapped sideways when the bullet plowed through his skull and buried itself in the ground only feet away in an explosion of dry soil. The body folded forward to rest on its chest.

Esteban swallowed the lump in his throat and watched impassively as the body remained on its knees, the braided wire handle rising straight and true from his back. He handed the semi-automatic back to her, prepared for what might happen next.

Tish Villarreal passed the 9mm back to Roberto and met Esteban's gaze. "You didn't intentionally fail me. You made a bad decision in taking the younger *sicarios*. You got sloppy, but because you obeyed me just now and your past loyalty, I will let you live."

Overcome with relief, his knees almost buckled.

Villarreal took his upper arm as gently as a child. "You will never fail me again. If you do, you will join these flowers in my garden. *Comprende,* my handsome man?"

Weak with relief, Esteban's voice cracked. *"Sí, señorita."*

Flicking her fingers at the silent *tenientes*, or narco lieutenants, she fixed them with an icy regard. "Go back and tell your capos what you've seen and how I deal with treacherous *halcones*."

She let go and turned on one heel. Without looking back, the Devil Woman struck out back toward the Lincolns. *"Bien.* Roberto, let us go hang this one from the mesquites and have *alumerzo*. I'm starving."

Chapter 11

Detective Cordova from the Del Rio police department and Val Verde County Sheriff Ortiz were talking to a DPS officer beside a big Mexican palm in the Nelson sisters' front yard when I stepped outside and set my hat. They quit talking as I approached and weighed what they saw.

I weighed them back and decided they were safer than Miss Harriet.

Thick black hair buzzed short on the sides and probably in his forties, Detective Cordova was slender, but leaning toward a spare tire around the middle. He looked like a good, solid cop to me. I've known those kind of officers all my life, men who did their job well and worried at night when they couldn't figure a case out.

Sheriff Ortiz was an elected official. I could tell he was my kind of guy. Forced into politics by the nature of the job, he was at the core a good solid man and it showed. White shirt, jeans, and a new straw hat, he was the kind of lawman you'd expect in the Valley. The poor guy looked weathered, as if the sun had taken a particular dislike to him and redoubled its efforts every time he stepped outside.

Leaning against his cruiser, the highway patrol officer named Rene Rodriguez was a lean, muscular individual I'd met not long after moving from the DPS to the Rangers. He gave me a nod, attention focused on the *cinco peso* pinned to my shirt. "I plan to wear one of those someday."

"It's tough to get in. You'll need eight years under your belt as a state trooper."

"Already have them." He flashed a smile. "I'm older than I look."

"You've applied?"

"Yessir."

"It's a pretty competitive field, so stay sharp."

Sheriff Ortiz raised one eyebrow and flicked his eyes toward the little bungalow. "Get a date with Miss Harriet?"

"Came close." I laughed. "I guess I'm not the first guy she's interrogated."

"Nor the last." Detective Cordova reached under his jacket as if pulling a pistol to defend himself. "That's dangerous business in there."

Officer Rodriguez jerked into a quick stance, as if waiting for Miss Harriet to come charging out like a fullback. It was a little odd for Rodriguez to be there, but in small towns, even the highway patrol is looking for a little variety and excitement. This attempted murder filled both bills.

We laughed and quickly sobered in case someone with a cell phone was recording us. The whole world's a news crew these days, and none of us wanted to give the wrong impression about how we felt. Six seconds taken from context could present problems for all of us and our departments as well.

I posed the first question. "So what do y'all think?"

The mood shifted into business mode. They'd been there longer, and had more time to work out their theories. When a Texas Ranger shows up on a scene, the dynamics of an investigation shifts. All information funnels to us, even though the local departments handle the cases.

They took turns briefing me on what happened and their own suppositions. We traded information for a good long while, trying to understand why two elderly ladies were targeted by a cartel from across the river.

Sheriff Ortiz shook his head. "I've seen a lot of trouble come across that river, but never anything directed at *old* folks. It always involves people much younger, and mostly drugs, though there's a lot of human trafficking going on. But this beats all I've ever seen, even the drugs coming over on drones."

I'd heard about that. Cartels were using technology to fly packages across the river, and directly into the hands of those who quickly made it disappear into the fabric of the country.

"You seeing a lot of that?"

"More than you'd think. The last few months, I've seen a lot of them buzzing around on the other side, but they ain't carrying anything. Found one outside of town about two weeks ago that went down. Had about thirteen pounds of meth strapped to it. Street value around fifty grand. Now *that's* money."

I whistled. "You ain't a-woofin'. Won't be long before the air's thick with 'em."

"Yep. There's no technology to stop them yet. We're liable to be using shotguns to bring the damned things down. But this don't have nothing to do with that. Why do you think two little old ladies had to help us clean up the gene pool?"

I had the answer for them. "I'm sure y'all heard we lost a Border Patrol agent the other night. He was Miss Ruby's foster son. Now, this is all supposition on my part, but I believe the individuals who popped him didn't stop there. They intend to kill anyone related to him. A cleansing because Nelson was into something dirty."

They'd already heard what happened, but I gave them what the media didn't have. Law enforcement officers can't, and won't, tell reporters everything. The public information officers keep certain facts back for a variety of reasons, one being that withholding certain specifics might help determining whether captured suspects are guilty. If a suspect's knowledge of a crime is more detailed than what they release, then it's a good bet they have the right individual.

There's a lot of screwballs out there who'll fess up to anything, just for the attention.

Sheriff Ortiz tilted his hat back when I wrapped it up. A red line on his forehead from the headband almost glowed in the bright sunshine. "I've heard of that across the river when someone gets sideways with the cartels, but not around here, and not with Americans targeted."

"Vengeance murder?" Detective Cordova held his pen over the tiny pad in his hand. "Did the surviving agent have any information?"

I didn't want to tell them about my visit with Agent Manual Trevino in the hospital or how he acted when I pressed him on what happened. I danced around the truth. "Everybody with a badge interviewed him, but he doesn't remember anything."

They didn't get to know my other suppositions right then, neither. It wasn't the first time I had my suspicions about a strange incident involving an attack on Border Patrol agents in West Texas. Months earlier, two officers were ambushed on a similar dark highway. One died and the other could only tell investigators they were parked on a dark side road when someone opened fire on their vehicle.

The strange part was it seemed to be a targeted incident. Four rounds entered the passenger window, three of them hitting the officer sitting on that side. The terrified, quick thinking driver instinctively shifted into gear and sped away as rounds shattered the windshield on his side of the vehicle.

When investigators arrived at the crime scene, they found nothing but scuffs in the hardpan and a dozen brass .223 hulls.

"Call it what you want." Sheriff Ortiz chewed the inside of his lip, thinking. "What these people didn't figure on was a couple of armed ladies who're tough old hides."

Detective Cordova flipped his notebook closed and tucked it into the inside pocket of his sport coat. "They won't underestimate them next time."

I'd been thinking the same thing. "If they come back. I hope you plan to have someone watch the house for a while."

"It might be a short while." Sheriff Ortiz flicked one hand for emphasis. "We can't afford that forever."

"Miss Ruby's worried they can't protect themselves after y'all took their guns."

"We had to take them . . ."

I held up a hand. "I know. Not being accusatory, just telling y'all what they told me."

"Maybe they can go stay with someone else for a while?"

I tried not to argue against everything Ortiz said, but they needed all the facts I'd already gathered. "No other family, except a granddaughter in Hawaii. We've reached out to their local law to keep an eye on things. They're not going anywhere."

Sheriff Ortiz caught Detective Cordova's eye. Something passed between them, and I figured it was a personal thing regarding an out-of-town stranger getting into their business. The sheriff scuffed the pavement with his boot. "Well, that'll cost a lot and take one of my men off the street. Don't get me wrong, I'm not saying your idea isn't without merit, but I'm not convinced this is a vengeance attack like you're talking about. It might just be a gang initiation."

"Could be." I knew he was only trying to work through what had happened in his town. "But even though I haven't seen the DRT photos of the bad guys, I'd imagine they were full of prison gang tats, and they weren't kids."

In our language, DRT stands for "dead right there."

Another exchange of glances. Detective Cordova grinned, telling me I was right. "I haven't heard them called that in a long time."

"I'm an old soul."

Detective Cordova drew a deep breath. "We have a citizen's patrol program. Maybe they could come by."

"I'll come by ever' now and then." Arms and ankles crossed as he continued to lean against his car, Officer

Rodriguez looked like a young James Dean. All he needed was the cigarette.

"Won't hurt." I was facing south, toward Mexico. "I intend to stop this pretty quick."

Rodriguez tilted his head, and I'll be damned if he didn't flip a pack of Marlboros from his shirt pocket and fire one up with an old-fashioned Zippo. "How're you gonna do that?"

I shrugged. "I have no idea, yet." The phone in my pocket buzzed with a blocked number. Figuring it was a robocall, I thumbed it off.

The detective tilted his head. "Hope that wasn't important."

"Sales call, I think. Blocked number. Look, I know this isn't my town, but is there a chance you can assign someone to keep an eye on the place for a while longer than usual? I have a bad feeling about this one."

Rodriguez hooked both thumbs in his pockets. "You're really worried they might come back."

"I have no reason to think they won't." The phone buzzed again in my hand, annoying the piss out of me. I answered that time. *"What?"* Nothing was there and when I looked at the screen, it showed I had a voice mail. I punched the Play icon and listened.

Crackles filled my ear. ". . . hope . . . this . . . Ranger Hawke?" The static cleared for a moment. "I have to talk fast, so listen. I'm undercover. Calling from a drop phone in Ciudad Acuna. My partner was killed in the movie lot shooting. I know what's happening with the Border Patrol agents. I . . ."

More static.

". . . need to meet you . . . here. No place . . . safe,

but go to the *Caballo Diablo* bar in Ciudad Acuna and see Fosfora. Tell her Flaco sent you."

The look on my face must have told the two lawmen beside me something was going on. They watched as I hung up from the call, taking care not to delete the recording.

I pivoted to look south. "Someone on the other side has information we can use. Looks like I'm crossing."

Sheriff Ortiz nodded. "You know anyone over there? They don't take to *Americano* lawmen poking around on their side of the river."

"Yeah, I've worked with a captain in the police department in Ciudad Acuna before. Guy I've known for years."

"Well, be careful."

"Always am."

Chapter 12

A soft, warm wind pushed across the dry land around Tish Villarreal's ten-year-old sprawling Spanish Colonial *rancho* in Coahuila, Mexico. The scrub desert beyond the low courtyard walls was covered with yucca, agave, and creosote. Only one long dirt road led to the house, guarded by a dozen men bearing automatic weapons.

More *cholos* watched from the surrounding chest-high walls. Some loafed in outbuildings not far from the white stucco main house. Others, unseen, were close enough to call in the event of an emergency.

From under a wide umbrella, the Devil Woman of Coahuila sat at a red tile table on an elevated teak deck, allowing her to see the distant mountains and desert shadows growing long with the setting sun. Low-growing tarbush, the dominant shrub, competed with white-thorn acacia and leggy ocotillo. Up close to the stucco walls, transplanted yuccas and agaves mixed with desert grasses and creosote bushes provided the expected characteristics of a well-established *rancho*.

Despite the late afternoon heat, Villarreal enjoyed the lush courtyard created and landscaped under her exact specifications. Thick green grass watered three times a day was bright in the hot sun. Mature coconut palms trucked in at great expense stretched high above the structure, dwarfing a tree dahlia beside a cluster of juicy banana trees. Broadleaf plants and bromeliads mixed with flowering agave, aloe vera, hibiscus, and golden trumpet vines.

Incencio Aguierre and Geronimo Manzano were at the table with her. *Ranchera* music filled the air. Their shirts were open, exposing the rough tattoos that covered much of their upper torsos. Unlike many of her men, their necks and faces were free from ink, allowing them to move freely in the *Estados Unidos*.

It was a rare day when the bloodthirsty murderers were acting like the kids they had never been. Geronimo cocked a black and gray plastic Bug A Salt gun with orange barrels, aimed at a fly sitting on a bowl of sliced limes, and pulled the trigger. A shotgun spray of table salt blew the fly to bits. "I love this toy!"

Sitting alone at another table, her youngest *sicario,* Esteban, sat motionless, watching. He was still reeling from what had happened in the Devil Woman's "garden."

Drawn to the sugar in the limes they were using in their beer and tequila, the flies swarmed their table. One landed on Incencio's arm and Geronimo shot it off with a laugh.

Not a wrinkle creased Villarreal's forehead, and her cheeks were smooth except for two small indentations at the corners of her mouth that deepened when she smiled. At the moment, her face was blank. "I am still not pleased with what happened in Del Rio." Soft and low, her voice held more poison than a rattler.

Incencio nodded and laid the gun on the table, as if the statement was deep and thoughtful. The fun was over. "I know, and I apologized, *jefa*. I should have taken care of it myself."

"You failed. You should have taken the task I assigned to you."

This was dangerous. She'd absolved Esteban, and now her eyes were dark and smoky, as if a cancerous fire burned inside her brain. Incencio took the high road. "Yes. I sent men who had proven their worth in the past. This time they underestimated the people they were to eliminate."

Villarreal took a tiny sip and placed the sweating bottle exactly on the wet ring in the middle of a blue-and-white Talavera tile. "So how will you rectify this problem? I have to keep my . . . promises to those who work for me. If they fail, everyone who shares the same blood will die."

The men's eyes met. Neither looked over at Esteban. Incencio reached for the tequila, then stopped. "We have already sent a man to complete the job."

Her eyes flashed. "I said I wanted you to do it yourself."

"But you wanted me here today, so I sent *El Camaleon*." Incencio's eyes flicked to Esteban, then back to the Devil Woman.

The Chameleon had killed dozens of times in the past without fail.

The tension that was in the air dissolved when she smiled as if they'd offered her a rare treat. "That is what I wanted to hear. And your new border agent. He will do as required?"

"Yes. He has already repeated the story."

"So the road is now clear to move all of our products?"

"*Sí, señorita.* We already have one agent in place who is still clearing the way, and when Manual Trevino returns to work, we will have two northern pipelines open. That will double what we have in place now. Our men outside of Del Rio are working out very well. We moved one hundred kilos of cocaine over to San Antonio last week without a problem, now that the new man is in place."

Still cotton-mouthed from his near-death experience, Esteban filed that statement away for future use. He wanted to know the new man's name, and the others, but asking would raise eyebrows. It was none of his business.

"*Bueno.*" She tilted the bottle again, doing nothing more than wetting her lips. "There is still one life in Hawaii connected to Agent Nelson."

"Yes. We sent someone to the house, but they weren't there. He is looking for them now."

"Do you have more contacts in the islands than just one *hombre*?"

"We do."

"Assign them."

Geronimo's lips tightened. "*Con permiso,* as we just discussed. If they fail, it will be our fault, even if they are so far away."

Eyes narrowed, she inclined her head to study a wide mesquite near the far corner of *rancho* wall. The beauty of a lush stone-lined pond and cascading fountain beside two decorative wrought-iron gates was off-set by half a dozen spines and skulls dangling like horrific Christmas ornaments. Two more of what she considered *decoraciones,* or decorations, had fallen apart and dropped to the dusty ground beneath the mesquite, the vertebrae and skulls separate and scattered. When the wind was right, the smell of carrion from the newer additions wafted past. Lucky for them at that time, the south breeze took the odor over the wall and away from where they sat.

The corners of her eyes crinkled in soft amusement. "Then choose well. There is another concern. You know I have two computer technicians who monitor the security system here."

Incencio nodded. "*Sí.* Carlos and Hector. They are the ones who came up with the idea of low-tech walkie-talkies and repeaters."

"They are geniuses in the world of electronics. Carlos came to me recently and told me the computer here on the *ranchero* has been used to look for my name. He found the search for it in what he called a 'history' file."

"I know nothing about computers." Incencio spread his hands to prove his innocence. Eyes wide, Geronimo only shook his head to confirm the same.

Her eyes narrowed. "If I find someone is using my office for any reason, and especially for researching my name, they will be dealt with."

"*Sí, jefa.*"

"In fact, no one can use my office and television in the main house again. Understood?"

Up until that moment, her most trusted men availed themselves of the huge flat-panel on the wall. She often found them there, lounging on the leather sofas whenever they had a few minutes.

Villarreal twisted in her chair to catch Esteban's eyes. "No one. *Comprende?*"

Heart pounding, he lowered his chin slowly in acknowledgment.

She picked up the Bug A Salt gun and shot at a fly buzzing past. She missed, spraying Geronimo in the eyes. He howled at the sting of the salt as Incencio laughed and Villarreal's dimples deepened, her point well made.

Esteban worked up enough spit to swallow and joined with a smile.

Chapter 13

Sitting in my truck parked in a busy lot near the Texas side of the Del Rio-Piedras Negra International Bridge, the air conditioner fought to overcome the heat. I was talking with Perry Hale back in Ballard. He and Yolanda Rodriguez were the Shadow Response Team I'd put together after Major Parker gave me the new assignment as the only Texas Ranger in decades to cover the entire Lone Star State.

The other 166 Rangers are assigned to specific Companies, ranging from Company A through F. A memorized paragraph ran through my mind as perfectly as the Pledge of Allegiance, because I'd taught my wife's high school class one day and had memorized the details directly from the Texas Ranger website.

Rangers are supervised by a Division Director, Assistant Division Director, two Headquarters Majors, three Headquarters Captains, six field Majors and sixteen field Lieutenants. The force is organized through six companies. A Major, Lieutenant, and from two to five Rangers are located at each of the Company Headquarters. Additional Rangers are stationed in various towns and cities throughout the state, with each Ranger having responsibility for a minimum of two to three counties, with some even larger areas.

What I'd done, on the Major's orders, was step back in time to when Texas Rangers went where they were told, depending on where the trouble was. While not officially on the force themselves, Perry Hale and Yolanda backed me up whenever I needed them, moving in the gray area between right and wrong, but always supporting the law.

The truck's hands-free feature allowed me to talk with Perry Hale at the same time I was trying to fix a stubborn plastic lid on the coffee I'd bought from a vendor down the street. Styrofoam's never been my friend, and the rim was boogered up, allowing coffee to seep through every time I took a sip.

A military veteran, Perry Hale wasn't overly thrilled with me crossing the river into Mexico by myself. "You don't know who that guy on the phone was. They're probably gonna kill you as soon as you walk into that cantina. You know as well as I do it's a rough town, controlled by the cartels. They'd love to hang a Ranger's head on the wall like a trophy deer."

I watched a clot of slow-moving vehicles moving south across the bridge into the Mexican state of Coahuila. He was right, not about hanging heads on a wall, though I wouldn't put *anything* past the cartels.

Only a couple of years earlier, the mayor of Ciudad Acuna, Rico Dominguez, was shot in the back of the skull while he stood in the street taking a selfie with a supporter. That single shot made him the 112th candidate or politician to be killed in just one year.

No one was ever brought to justice for the man's murder.

It wasn't my first time to cross, though. I'd been in Mexico as a law enforcement officer a number of times, working cases in tandem with the Chiahuahuan *policia* south of our Big Bend towns of Lajitas and Ojinaga.

My contact in Coahuila was a tough captain named Alejandro Maldonado, who'd somehow survived for years as a policeman in that crummy border town full of danger and corruption.

"Well, Alejandro's gotten me in and out more than once."

"I don't like it." Perry Hale paused. "And neither does Yolanda. She's shaking her head. When are you crossing?"

"In a few minutes." I took a sip, and a drop of coffee fell on my light-colored shirt. "Dang it." I took a napkin from the console and blotted it.

"Hang on 'til we get there. We'll cross with you."

"No." I'd already told him about the Nelson attack. "I'm worried about those two old gals more than me. I talked with the local constabulary here, and they're capable of handling car wrecks and crimes of passion, but they're in over their heads with this one. I want y'all to come and move these gals out for a while until I can get 'em relocated somewhere else."

"You want us to babysit two little old ladies."

"Call it what you want. Tell them you're with me, show 'em those badges the Major gave you, and then move 'em somewhere. Hell, take 'em to my house for a little while. Kelly'll enjoy having them around for a few days. After I'm sure this is over, we'll get 'em back, or settled somewhere else." Another drop fell. "Dammit."

"What? Something wrong?"

I wiped at the growing stain. "Naw, I got coffee on my shirt."

"Sounds like a tragedy to me. On second thought, why don't you take that shirt to the cleaners and wait for us? We'll all go together."

"Because I've already told Alejandro I'm on the way. He's probably waiting at the bridge right now."

"Call and tell him you'll be there in the morning."

"Just so y'all can walk in with me."

"Well, no. I don't want to go in *with* you. I want to *follow* and keep an eye out."

I knew how he usually traveled, and that was armed to the teeth with a variety of weapons that could shoot or cut. "You'd be unarmed if you crossed at the bridge, which I would highly recommend instead of sneaking across like you did the last time. They catch you with weapons, you'll spend the rest of your life in prison, 'cause I doubt I'd be able to do anything about it. I really don't want you or Yolanda walking around down there and not be heeled, neither. So stay where you are."

"We can take care of ourselves."

It was like talking to a petulant teenager.

"And so can I." Using my thumb, I pressed the thin plastic lid down over the lip.

Perry Hale wouldn't give up. I figured Yolanda was listening in and pushing him to talk me out of my impetuous idea. They both know what gets me in trouble.

"You know the whole town's fallen, right. The cartels are in charge, and they kill anyone whenever the mood strikes, including officials. The place has been in the hands of animals since that big prison break back in 2012. It don't pay to be police or military down there, and I doubt there's any legit cops left. If your contact still has his job, he's probably on the take." He paused, and I could tell he was either whispering to Yolanda or thinking. He came back with an accusation. "You're not taking your pistol, are you? Hope not, because even though you have a badge, they'll throw you under the jail in a heartbeat. To me that means you don't go until we get there."

"You're right." I glanced down at my hip. "Already got it in the lockbox under the back seat. I feel like I'm talking to Kelly." I'd just finished the same discussion with my wife, and she wasn't happy about the situation, either. "I'll be with Alejandro, and I trust him. You don't need to worry."

"So you're gonna go over there, get in trouble, and then we'll have to sneak into a foreign country and try to find you, and hope we're not there looking for your body when we have to cross. I see it happening. Remember the last time you were in Mexico."

"That wasn't *my* idea *then*. This one is, and it'll be just fine." I took another sip of the hot liquid, feeling it dribble down my chin. "Argh!"

"Spill some more?"

I wiped it off with the palm of my hand. "I'm about to throw this cup out the window."

"Well, I don't like it."

"Me littering?"

"Funny guy. Thousands of comedians out of work and you're making really weak-ass jokes."

"I haven't heard that one since I was a kid." I glared

at the foam cup containing two dollars of coffee I couldn't drink. "I'll call you when I'm back across."

"What was the name of that cantina again?"

"The *Caballo Diablo*."

"Devil Horse. That's fitting. You know what street it's on?"

"You writing this down?"

"Damn right."

"Morelos Street. But go take care of those old ladies first." I punched the phone screen and peeled the lid off the coffee to drink like a human being instead of sipping through a tiny hole. Somehow it had sealed better than I thought, and when I flicked it off, the foam cup tore, dumping half the contents on my shirt.

"Dammit!"

Then I remembered I hadn't thrown in my little suitcase Kelly kept packed for me for just such emergencies. All I had was that flowerdy Aloha shirt in the back seat I'd meant to take to the cleaners.

"Dammit!"

Chapter 14

The Devil Woman's single-story stucco ranch house looked simple from the outside, rustic to match the surrounding desert full of scrub cactus and bushes. Inside, the appointments were also rustic, but expensive. Every architectural feature was imported at great cost. The massive beams overhead once held the roof of a centuries old Irish castle and were imported to Coahuila to satisfy the Devil Woman's whim. Art stolen during World War II and thought lost forever decorated two walls.

But in many cases, what looked old, wasn't. Bois d'arc floors seemed ancient, but each detail of antiquity was hand crafted. Despite the desert heat, a fire crackled in the fireplace built to the specifics matching one in a house once owned by Shakespeare. A specially designed air conditioning system kept the house's interior cool until the desert evenings allowed her to fold back an entire living room wall to catch the fresh breezes.

A shape appeared in the doorway to that same huge open living room. "You wanted to see me again?"

Barefoot and curled up like a kitten on a leather couch in her study, Tish Villarreal was changing channels with a high-tech remote control, looking like a teenager putting off the weekend's homework. A ninety-eight-inch flat-panel TV mounted on one wall was turned to a news channel. Half a glass of red wine rested on a round table beside the Hidalgo cartel's leader.

The slender woman barely glanced up at Esteban from the screens. "I have an . . . assignment for you, but you handle it on your own. You are not to tell anyone. Just leave."

"Sí, señorita."

She absently bit down on a red manicured fingernail, a habit she'd been trying to break. "Benito Oaxaca has been working on his own."

Esteban inclined his head in question.

"He and others are *traidores*. None of my people are going into business for themselves. You all know that."

"You want me to take care of the traitors, then?"

"Yes."

"Do you want me to bring the bodies to the garden?"

"No. Leave him where he lays. They need to see what happens when I am disobeyed." She gave him a cold smile. "I have another in mind for my garden."

"Bueno. I will do that."

"Make it messy, Esteban. I want his blood to run down the street."

"Sí."

"Do not fail. I'm tired of failure this day. Kill Oaxaca and your family will be safe."

He paused a beat. *"Gracias*, but if you will remember, I am a *huerfano,* I have no family."

She returned to the television and flicked her fingers, dismissing the man.

As Esteban faded from her doorway, she spoke to the blank-faced CNN reporter staring outward from the HD screen. "Yes, you do." She took the smallest sip of wine possible. "Everyone has family if you dig deeply enough, and my friend, if Oaxaca isn't dead by tomorrow morning, I'll find out."

The Devil Woman took a larger celebratory sip of her wine aged in bourbon barrels, savoring the taste. There were so many good things in life, when you were finally successful.

Chapter 15

Ciudad Acuna police Captain Alejandro Maldonado was waiting not far from the end of the bridge on the Coahuila side of the Rio Grande, just like I said. Folks expecting to cross and be right in town were often surprised to see a wide, pleasant plaza converge into one thoroughfare lined with palm trees and what looked to me like live oaks.

In a light linen sport coat, khakis, and a black T-shirt, Alejandro was leaning against a four-door black Dodge Ram pickup parked on the sunny curve across the street from the *Bienvenido a Ciudad Acuna* sign.

I'd walked across, so I was already hot and sweating. Trickles rolled from under my hat and tickled the sides of my cheeks. His pockmarked face broke into a wide grin. *"Hola amigo!"*

We gave each other one of those big, slapping hugs that men like. I hadn't seen him for almost a year, and in that time his once short black hair had become salt and pepper. Still black, and possibly from dye, his pencil mustache was as carefully tended as I remembered.

I stepped back. "Good to see you, my friend."

He gave me the once-over. "Even with your hat, you don't look like a Texas Ranger in that loud shirt."

I didn't really like to hear him say that in the open. Glancing around, I made sure there weren't people close enough to hear. "Incognito."

He plucked at the bright yellow, flowered Hawaiian shirt I'd slipped on back at the truck. It was all I had to replace my coffee-soaked Ariat western shirt. "Camouflage."

"You might say that."

"*Bien*. You wore the right shirt, then. You look like the rest of the gringo tourists who come down here in hats." He reached into the truck's open window and handed me a small but heavy nylon daypack. "You can tuck this in while we drive. Get in."

I hefted the bag, suspecting what was inside and wondering why he handed it to me in the open, instead of passing it over when we got in the cab. For an instant, my conversation with Perry Hale gave me a moment of paranoia. Was this a setup? Would the Mexican army come swooping around the corner to arrest me for having a firearm in their country? There was no way to prove he'd given it to me. If so, it was an immediate prison sentence that would become a death sentence in a matter of days, if not hours.

American lawmen had no place inside a Mexican prison.

He must have seen something in my eyes. "It is safe. I am not corrupted . . . yet." He rolled the word on his tongue, something I'd never been able to do.

I swallowed, glad to see I had enough spit to do the job. "I trust you."

"You shouldn't."

There was that thing in my eyes again, and he laughed. "Just teasing. But truthfully, don't trust anyone else here. It is very dangerous. If anyone asks, you are a tourist looking to buy some *botas*. We'll drop by a shop while you're here and get you a pair."

I never did like Mexican boots. The toes are always too long and sharp for my taste. I glanced down at the black Justin Ropers on my feet. I'd left what I still thought of as my Sunday boots back at the truck. Wearing expensive Luccheses on that side of the border could get you killed in a hurry.

We settled into his front seat. As usual in nearly all vehicles since 1968, the seatback bumped the brim of my hat. I took it off and pitched it up on the dash. Glancing back into the back seat, I was surprised to see a khaki-colored Scorpion 9mm submachine gun lying on the seat. "Nice hardware."

"It is sometimes necessary." He must have been waiting for me to notice the weapon, because he reached back and pulled a bright blanket over the gun.

I opened the daypack as he pulled into the street. Inside was a Beretta M9, a weapon I was intimately acquainted with. I liked the big pistol that holds fifteen rounds in the magazine. It looked brand new, and there were several more magazines besides the one in the handle.

"There's a lot of ammo in here."

"If shooting starts, you'll need every round." His eyes flicked from the street to the pistol, and then back again. "I know you like your Colt with the Sweetheart Grips, but I assume you left it on the other side."

"Sure did, and thanks for this."

"They *asesinar,* assassinate people with regularity

here in Coahuila now that the cartels are in charge. I don't want you killed under my watch, so don't bring notice to yourself beyond that shirt."

"Don't intend to." His warning on top of what I'd heard from Perry Hale had my nerves humming like tension wires. It hadn't been that way the last time I crossed there.

The clean look of the city that visitors saw at first was nothing than a thin façade once we turned onto a narrow side street well away from the tourist area. An overwhelming sense of poverty took over at the sight of dirty, cracked, and potholed streets lined with cinderblock buildings. The farther Alejandro drove, and it wasn't truly that far from the bridge, the more desperate the area became.

Every house had some kind of metal fence or masonry wall around it, and those made of stucco had a startling number of what I took to be bullet holes. Laundry hung on the metal fences, drying in the blistering sun. Scattered throughout the neighborhood, small businesses painted in startling colors brightened the somewhat drab area.

Some of the more ragged, dusty shops didn't have front doors or even front walls. They reminded me of three-sided cow sheds my relatives built from scrap wood back in East Texas.

Each building had a covey of hard-eyed men loafing in whatever shade was available. They watched us pass with dead expressions. I tucked the big Beretta into the waistband at the small of my back and slid two loaded magazines into the left front pocket of my Wranglers.

Alejandro showed his bright white teeth again. "So

you are here investigating the attempted murder of two Anglo *abuelas* in Del Rio."

"Yep. Somebody tried to kill a couple of little old ladies." I hadn't told him of the mysterious phone message, just that I needed to speak to someone on the Mexican side in the *Caballo Diablo* cantina. "We think that incident has something to do with other murders closer to the Big Bend region."

"All murders down here have tie-ins with other killings. It is the way of life now. Blood leads to blood."

"That's a hard way to live."

"Most of the time it's not living. It's survival."

"Like I said, that's a helluva way to live."

He laughed. "Helluva. I love the way you speak."

A shiny black Expedition suddenly shot from a side street, missing our front bumper by only inches. I grabbed the dash with one hand and reached for the pistol, expecting the SUV to stop, ejecting men with automatic weapons.

"Dammit!"

Alejandro slammed the brakes and the car passed, disappearing down the street. "*Pendejos!* They drive like they're the only ones in this whole *country*."

Nerves jangling, I took a deep breath and sat back. "It's the same way back home, except the drivers are probably texting."

He snorted and we continued down a paved street crumbling to dust. He soon pointed. "There it is."

He parked on the street, and I got out and set my hat. We went inside.

I didn't like the place one little bit. The *Caballo Di-*

ablo was the darkest, smokiest, most frightening gun and knife joint I'd ever been in, and I'd been in some Oklahoma honky tonks on the Red River back when they still had sawdust on the floors.

The old men I grew up around said gun and knife clubs were so mean and tough that when the owner asked you if you had a weapon when you came in, if you said no, they'd give you one to help even up the odds.

Alejandro led the way into the dim interior and stepped to the side to let his eyes adjust. I did the same with my heart in my chest, just waiting on some dark shape to come roaring up at us.

It wasn't that I was afraid. I was terrified. It reminded me of the time ten years earlier when I was on vacation with the family. One day we were snorkeling in a bay in Hanalei, Hawaii, when I swam alone to the far reef that stopped at the open ocean. The bay was clear and no more than twenty feet deep, but when I reached the outer edge, a current pulled me beyond the reef and the next thing I knew, I was suspended over the edge of deep, blue water. In my mind, all I could see was a behemoth shark coming up from the depths, all teeth and mouth wide open like that movie poster for *Jaws*.

It was the same in that loud Mexican bar. Breath caught in my chest as we stood in the shadows beside the door. It felt like some kind of electrical current was pulling me into the blades of a spinning propeller. Cursing the impulsiveness that led me there, I wondered if I should have worn body armor under my blousy Aloha shirt.

Colorful neon light from Mexican beer signs provided just enough light to see dark stains on the worn wooden floorboards that could have been blood, and there were a lot of them. *Corrido Norteno* music, local to the region, filled the air from speakers mounted right above our heads.

The air was thick with cigarette smoke. Cherries glowed in the dark as customers dragged on their toonies, adding even more to the cloud swirling only inches above my head. Finally adjusting to the light, I made out the shapes of nearly a dozen men sitting at raw wooden tables. A few more lined up at the bar like birds on a wire.

Alejandro nodded at the bartender whose face looked to have been beaten sideways and we made our way across the gritty floor. Two men were nursing drinks at one end of the bar, as far from the door as possible. A black-haired woman sat alone at the other.

The whoppy-jawed bartender took his time drifting down to take our orders. *"Que deseas?"*

Up close I wondered if he'd ever seen a toothbrush. From three feet away, his breath was harsh as a landfill. Alejandro answered for us. *"Dos cervezas, por favor."*

The bartender went for the beers and I angled myself. "Beer in the morning?"

"Would you prefer tequila?"

"I'd prefer to find this guy and get out of here."

"You nervous?"

"Sure am."

He angled his head toward the center of the room. "Don't let them know it."

"This ain't my first rodeo."

He frowned. "Rodeo."

"It's a country saying."

Alejandro kept frowning and I gave up. The pock-marked bartender came back with two dripping bottles of Corona. Slices of limes stuck up from the top. Knowing he'd used his bare fingers to pluck them from a plastic container of ice, and because of his horrific halitosis, I couldn't help but wonder if he'd ever heard of soap and water.

The beer signs produced a surprising amount of light once we adjusted to the gloom. Details appeared, and I really didn't want to see most of them. Dust was thick on what decorations were nailed to the walls. A dusty, spiderweb-laced coconut-head pirate hanging on a post behind the bar hadn't been touched since it was hung in front of the mirror forty years earlier, or longer.

Most of the glasses stacked on shelves looked dirty and water spotted. I was glad our beer came in bottles. Knowing what was in the water down there, it was probably best that Alejandro hadn't ordered mixed drinks with ice.

Feeling like a bird dog on point, I couldn't get comfortable enough to slump over the bar like the other customers. Sinuses full of cigarette smoke that seemed to get thicker by the moment, I pulled the rodeo-cool Corona close.

If necessary, it would make a pretty good weapon if things went south for any reason. "Do you recognize any of these guys?"

He shook his head. "No. *She* looks familiar, though."

The black-haired woman in a tight white blouse and red pants was looking at me as if I owed her money.

"You ever arrest her? She's giving me the hairy eye-ball."

"Maybe. *Prostitucion,* perhaps. Maybe she's really looking at *me*."

"I hope she is." Sensing motion on the floor, I glanced down. A skinny speckled dog walked up and sniffed my Justins. It looked up with hopeful eyes, but I didn't have anything to feed him. I considered offering him the lime, but there was no point in exposing the poor critter to the bartender's germs.

Ignored by the rest of the customers, we waited. Conversations were low and way too fast for my limited border Spanish. I leaned in to Alejandro. "So do you recognize the name Flaco?"

"Flaco Jiminez."

He'd thrown out the name of a famous Tejano musician from San Antonio. I grunted. "Anyone else?"

"There are lots of Flacos. It's a common nickname. It means skinny."

"That doesn't help us much."

"Why do you have that name?"

"I'm supposed to make contact with him."

The woman shook a cigarette from a pack lying on the bar, slid off her stool, and strolled toward us in ridiculously high heels. Alejandro must have seen that her cig was unlit. He lipped a smoke from the pack in his shirt pocket. Lighting it, he held the flame out for her when she came close. She stuck the toonie between her lips and leaned into the flame.

Up close, her eyes were dark and pretty. The rest of her was coarse and hard as nails. She spoke English, for my benefit. "Are you looking for a party?"

"Pretty early for that, ain't it?"

Alejandro shot me a glance, then turned back to her. "No. We're here to meet a friend."

"So am I."

The silence was thick for a long moment.

She inhaled and blew the smoke toward the bartender from the corner of her mouth, as if to spare us the additional carcinogens. "Who is it you're meeting?"

I inclined my head. "Flaco."

Alejandro watched us, like a spectator at a tennis match, but his full attention wasn't on us, though. He kept glancing at the other guys, keeping them in place in his mind. How'd I know that? I was doing the same thing. I didn't want a chess game to start up around us, with players moving in positions I didn't like.

To prove my point, one of the guys at a table in the shadows near the door stood. The pockmarked bartender saw him coming and they met and exchanged words I couldn't hear. Pockmark reached under the bar and I tensed, feeling like an idiot when he came up with a bottle of tequila and poured the man a shot.

The woman beside us took another drag, this time blowing the smoke straight down. It billowed in our direction and I wondered if it was some kind of statement. "I'm supposed to meet a *norteamericano*."

Alejandro stepped in. "Do you know his name?"

She shrugged. "No. What's yours?"

"My wife won't let me tell strangers."

"You're here without her." She smiled. I got the feeling she was having fun jerking me around. "So you *are* here for a party."

"Get lost."

The light in her eyes died. She spun on one heel and stalked back to her place at the end of the bar. Alejandro leaned on his elbows. "That ended abruptly."

"I'm not here to play games."

Two dark shadows in the corner rose. One went to the bar. The other had a different idea. He sauntered toward us and from the way he was walking I knew he was looking for trouble. I've seen that kind of nonsense all my life, from high school through adulthood.

Working as a highway patrol officer I learned to read body language, faces, and even the tone of an individual's voice. It's a skill all good LEOs acquire, and it serves us well in escalating situations.

Angling myself to face him, but keeping my head low so the hat brim partially covered my eyes, I picked up the beer bottle.

Alejandro was between us. He planted his feet and straightened. *"Necesitar algo?"*

The guy was wearing what we call back home a wifebeater shirt. Tattoos covered both arms and drawled up his neck. He spoke in English to make sure I understood. "This bar is not for tourists."

Alejandro pulled back his jacket to reveal his badge. "He is here with me."

"I don't care. You should not bring him here. It is dangerous."

"For who?"

"Both of you."

"Not me." Alejandro looked as casual as if they were talking at a church social. "I suggest you go back to your *compadres* and leave us alone."

One of the men slumped over the bar finished his drink and headed for the door, followed by another guy who took his beer with him. As they passed the table where the troublemaker had been sitting, another man stood and drifted in our direction. Chairs scraped the floor and two more rough-looking guys joined him. They'd been listening to the exchange and moved in like lions surrounding their prey.

Still leaning one elbow on the bar, Alejandro shook his head. "Don't do this."

"He is leaving now." The first guy puffed up, and we were suddenly in a schoolyard situation that every guy in the world recognizes. People keep swelling up and joining in, and before you know it, no one can back out and save face.

With the almost untouched beer in my hand, I sidestepped to get clear of Alejandro and face those who were crowding around. "Hey guys. Y'all just cool down and I'll leave. How about that?"

The man grinned. "You don't tell us what to do. You leave when we say."

It was a Catch-22 statement in the room full of tension as thick as the smoke swirling in the neon lights. Nothing I said was going to alleviate the situation that was about to spiral out of control. A stocky Mexican in a taco hat was the closest to me. I figured I'd lay him out with the bottle across the eyes and Alejandro could handle the first guy. Getting two of them out of the picture at the outset might break their courage.

It didn't look like a situation requiring firearms. Just a good old friendly fight in a Mexican honky tonk. That was until one of the men clicked open a switchblade and the dance opened in an instant. The guy beside me swung a roundhouse blow toward my head. I slapped it aside and backhanded the beer bottle at his eyes, just like I'd imagined.

The dark bottle exploded against his temple in a burst of foam and glass. He went down and the big M9 was in my fist as if by magic. You don't carry that double-action 9mm cocked and locked like my 1911, so the hammer was still down, but my thumb flicked the safety off as it was coming to bear. It leveled in the middle of another guy's chest, my finger on the trigger.

As fast as it happened, I was a little slow. Alejandro had a Glock in the compressed ready position, pointed at the man with the knife. I was glad to see he wasn't holding it straight out at the end of his arm. That's an amateur's move, and there are people who can strip it from your hand in the blink of an eye. Besides, aiming wasn't necessary in such close quarters. If people started shooting or cutting, it would be a mow 'em down scenario with the weapon held close to his body.

That's when the woman stepped in. Concentrating on the guy I was about to ventilate, I didn't see her until she was right between us and the home-town boys. For the next ten seconds, she gave them a dog cussing in Spanish. No one answered back, and when I glanced over at the barman, he was holding the stubbiest cut-down double-barrel shotgun I'd ever seen. It was pointed in the general direction of that crowd, though if he'd pulled the trigger some of those pellets would have gotten into the rest of us, too.

The men had seen him, also, and they stopped.

Seeing her words and the shotgun had taken the fire out of them, she turned to me and spoke one word. "Hawke."

Keeping his pistol at waist level and close into his body, Alejandro stepped back, and the line of men bracing us wavered, then backed away. I nodded. "Hawke."

She turned toward the semicircle of barflies and opened up with another firehose of Spanish that I couldn't even *begin* to comprehend. They backed off, and I don't blame them. After what seemed to be a blistering five minutes, they were done, all except for the original guy who kept eyeballing me. I wouldn't look down, so he finally helped his bloody friend up from the floor. They turned and headed for the door, throwing a sentence back toward her that I didn't understand.

When he was done, she snapped her head toward that same door. *"Ven conmigo ahora."*

I did what she said and followed, keeping my weapon leveled at the room. Alejandro fell in as a rear guard and when I stepped outside about half expecting to get shot, he backed out behind me.

Seeing the street was clear, I slipped the M9 into the small of my back and pulled the shirt down. She was standing hip-cocked about five feet away. There was no one else in sight. I got the idea that was how she always stood, from a lifetime of posturing on the corners and in bars. It seemed that everyone had cleared the street in anticipation of the three of us coming outside. In those old westerns it would have been an ambush.

She didn't hesitate. "Give me the name you have."

Turning so that my back was against the wall, I met her gaze. "Fosfora. Flaco sent me."

The corner of her mouth ticked. *"Sí.* Come with me." She led the way and turned at the corner.

Keeping one eye on the closed cantina door, Alejandro snickered. "Fosfora."

"That name's funny?"

"It isn't a real name. It's a nickname. *Fosfora* means a short-tempered girl who burns down quickly, like a match."

"Great. Someone just like me."

"I was thinking the same thing."

Chapter 16

Esteban's Toyota Tacoma shot down the two-lane desert highway. He drove with one hand hanging over the top of the wheel, worried sick about his recent conversation with *la Mujer del Diablo*. His whole world seemed to be coming unraveled, and he knew for certain why.

He knew as much, or more about her, as the Devil Woman did about him.

Ticking over the items that connected them, he kept an eye out for roadblocks. They were both U.S. citizens. They'd both worked their way up in the cartel, unlike 99.9 percent of those around them. Despite what he'd told her, both had family weaknesses, a chink that was easily manipulated, if she ever had cause to find them.

It was obvious she'd figured out that someone was investigating her background. He usually shut her computer down after using it without asking, but she'd appeared suddenly in the courtyard that day while he was researching her background and he had to hurry and log out.

It was those damned geeks who told her someone had searched her name.

His life had been dangerous up to that point, but now it was almost assuredly at what he considered Defcon 1. Angry at himself for taking so long to act, he worried that everything he'd set in place was too late. She'd acted first.

Now he was in catch-up mode.

Chapter 17

Despite the high heels on her feet, the girl I knew as Fosfora set a right smart pace down a dirt alley full of barking dogs shouted quiet from unseen people. Alejandro and I stayed with her, frequently checking our back trail. I kept expecting a car to come barreling down the alley to run us down.

We caught up to her just as she turned onto a street even grimier than the one we'd left. A man stepped out of a doorway, saw her with us following, and went back inside.

Despite my hat and jeans, I stuck out like a sore thumb in that dumb Aloha shirt that was quickly becoming a bad idea. It felt like hundreds of eyes were on me from the windows. I also didn't like being so far away from Alejandro's truck, and the look on his face said the same thing. He finally dug in his heels.

"Alto!"

She stopped and whirled. "Why?"

"Because I'm not following you any more on foot."

"So stay here."

"No. You stay here. Hawke and I are going back to

get my truck, and then we'll come back around to pick you up."

She puffed like a little banty rooster and cut loose with another river of Spanish. This time, without all the accordion music blaring in the background, I picked out a few words that I wouldn't repeat in mixed company.

Alejandro jumped right back at her and spun on his heel, waving a hand back as he stalked off down the street. I paused. "He's right. We need his truck."

She paced the cracked sidewalk, weighing her options. "I can get someone to drive us to the person you need to speak with."

I shook my head. "Nope. I'm not getting into a car down here with folks I don't know."

Angry, she flipped her hand with the cigarette in the air and followed us, jabbering away under her breath. I knew for sure then why they hung her with the nickname about her temper.

Behind her, a sledgehammered car pulled out of an intersecting street and paused, the driver giving us the once-over. An individual riding in the passenger seat leaned over to get a better look.

Even though it was her town, I figured we needed to get out of there. "You better come with us."

"You are making this very difficult."

Without being obvious, I pointed with my head. "Cool down. We just need to get gone, and I think letting Alejandro drive is smart. He's the law, remember?"

She glared at me, then the car that was still there, and back at me. "*Bueno*."

* * *

Alejandro's eyes flicked to his rearview mirror as he drove. "Where are we going?"

"A small *ejido* straight ahead." Fosfora's soft voice from the back seat belied her temperament. She curled up like a kitten in the corner and looked comfortable enough to take a nap.

I turned my head to see her behind Alejandro. "How far?"

"You'll know when we get there."

He didn't like that answer. "What is the name of this community?"

She shrugged. "It has no official *nombre. El Cruce.*"

I didn't like the sound of that. It could mean the crossroads or the cross.

Alejandro set his jaw and kept driving. The desert flashed past for half an hour until I couldn't stand the silence any longer. "You know where we're headed, bud?"

He'd cooled off a little "Yes. I have been there before."

"We getting close?"

Fosfora spoke up. "It will not be long now."

"Back home we'd say it was up the road a piece."

"What does that mean?"

"Up the road a ways."

A little furrow creased her brow. "I still don't understand."

"We'll get there in a little bit."

Knowing I was messing with him, Alejandro cut his eyes across the cab. "You Texans speak funny."

"Sure 'nuff."

We passed a number of cars going the opposite direction, but none were either in front or behind us, at least until we came upon a military blockade. I must have seriously tensed, because Alejandro held his hand out flat, about two inches above the seat. "Easy. This is common."

"Not to me."

He rolled to a slow stop as armed soldiers with slung AR-15s spread out and surrounded the truck. A youngster wearing camouflage and a floppy boonie hat looked no older than my seventeen-year-old son fixed on me sitting there in the passenger seat with the window down. A ranking officer swaggered up to the driver's side, his hand on the sidearm at his waist.

"Papers."

Alejandro flashed his badge.

"You are out of your jurisdiction."

They were speaking Spanish, but slow enough that I could work out the words, and if not the actual pronunciation, at least the meaning. Alejandro jerked a thumb over his shoulder at Fosfora. "I'm working on a case. She is a witness and we're heading for El Cruce for her to identify a suspect."

"You are still out of your jurisdiction." The officer pointed at me. "Who is this?"

"He is my friend from Texas. He came across to buy boots, but when I needed to come here, he wanted to ride along."

"I want to see his passport." He snapped his fingers to hurry me up. "Papers."

My pucker factor increased a thousand percent. It was back in the truck. Without papers, I was sure they'd yank me out of the cab and find the pistol tucked in the small of my back. I wondered if Mexican prisons were as bad as I'd heard.

It was about that time that I noticed the youngster on my right squinting beyond my shoulder and into the back seat. My heart dropped. Did he see the Scorpion back there? I'd forgotten about the little machine gun and prayed Alejandro'd moved it before Fosfora got in the back.

One more thing to worry about, an unknown woman within reaching distance of a weapon that could spray an entire magazine in about three seconds.

The young man stepped closer, and I followed his eyes. He was definitely interested in something back there. I twisted around to see Fosfora curled up behind Alejandro's seat.

Her top was tighter than I remembered, and much lower across her breasts. But it was the way she was sitting that had the boy's attention. Instead of keeping her knees together, she was sprawled back there like a guy, knees splayed. She gave the boy a wink

The official at the driver's window also noticed Fosfora. He and the youngster seemed to be stunned.

Alejandro gave them a few seconds to examine the back seat before speaking. "Is this yours? I think you dropped it." He held a folded bill between the ends of his index and middle fingers.

It disappeared as if by magic, and the officer slipped one hand into the front pocket of his pants. "Yes, I did. Thank you."

He straightened and waved at the men blocking the road. "Let them pass." They kept an eye on the back seat as we passed.

As soon as we were past the road block, Fosfora adjusted her top and closed her knees, sliding over to the middle. "El Cruce is up the road a piece."

Making fun of the way I speak broke the tension in the truck and it lasted almost twenty minutes, when we came up on another roadblock.

Chapter 18

The two-lane road cutting through the Coahuila desert made a bend and Alejandro and I spoke in stereo. "Shit."

A single four-door red Nissan parked perpendicularly across the road was manned by four armed men who were definitely not soldiers in the military sense. I took a quick inventory of their automatic weapons as Alejandro slowed. One of them standing at the open driver's door wore a hooded camouflage jacket zipped up to the middle of his chest. He held an automatic weapon at the patrol carry position, with the muzzle angled downward, but ready to quickly shoulder the weapon.

Beside him, leaning against the closed back door was a young man in a green T-shirt and a modular tactical vest bulging with magazines and a holstered semi-automatic handgun. Number Three with his rifle casually slung over one shoulder was talking to Number Four, who sat on the hood with the butt of an AK-47 resting on one thigh. He was cocky looking, and I immediately disliked him.

This was one of those scenarios I'd heard about and dreaded because so many things could go wrong in a drastically short amount of time. *"La mordida?"*

"Yes." Alejandro's eyes narrowed.

"Two stops in this short time takes away what little faith I still have in your country."

He snorted. "The *soldados* was not the bite, only the cost of living here. This is real, and much more dangerous."

"We're seriously outgunned."

"They won't be expecting us to be prepared."

These guys were gangsters. You never knew what those wingnuts were thinking or what they'd do in a town or city. Out where we were, miles from other people or law enforcement officers made them particularly dangerous. I pulled the M9 from behind my back and slipped it under my right thigh. "Does *everybody* in this country have machine guns?"

"Everyone but the common citizens." He flicked a finger toward my feet. "Fosfora, lean forward slowly and hand me the Scorpion. They are waiting on us. One of the soldiers called them. Because you're a *norteamericano*, he likely thinks you have much money. They may try to kidnap you."

"They use Sat phones?"

"I'm sure of it."

"So pull around them and keep going." Fosfora slipped him the weapon and pointed. "Maybe we can outrun them."

"No." Alejandro absently pushed the shades up on his nose. "We don't want to get into a running gun battle with these guys. We'll lose."

I was glad we were in a truck and sitting up higher

than if we'd been in a sedan. It gave us a slightly better angle and sight line. "So what's the plan?"

Alejandro's eyes hardened. "I'll offer them payment to pass. If they take it, good. If they don't, shoot them if they make any threatening moves."

"A threatening move in my country is when some-one points a weapon at you. Don't shoot unless we have no other choice."

Alejandro's jaw tightened. "I say we kill them all as soon as I stop. They won't be expecting that."

"Yeah, well, we're law enforcement. I can't shoot a man just because he *looks* like a threat."

"You see that weapon pointed at us. These are rattle-snakes. You'd kill one if you came across it in your house."

"That's right. We're not in my house."

He slowed. "Your morality might get us killed."

Keeping plenty of distance between us and the red car parked across the highway, Alejandro stopped in the middle of our lane, shifted into park, and opened his door. He put one foot outside, holding the Scorpion low behind the dash in his right hand. Designed for ex-actly this situation, the little six-pound weapon was perfect for maneuvering in small, tight spaces. "*Amigos.* Let us pass please."

"It will cost you." Camo Guy, the one I already didn't like, snickered and swept his arm towards the horizon. "We own this highway, and all this as far as you can see. And if I want, I can own your *camion*, too."

Alejandro nodded, as if the man had made some profound statement. "I understand. I prefer to keep my truck. We will pay to pass. How much?"

Confident in past shakedowns, the other gangsters relaxed.

"I am Oaxaca, the premier *soldado* for *la Mujer Malvada*." Camo Guy walked closer, showing us the gold in his front teeth. "How much do you have? A man who wears such a shirt as this *anglo* must have plenty of money and *machismo*."

His men laughed as if the guy were a comedian. I was wishing I hadn't worn such a bright shirt.

"He has very little money, and I am but a poor businessman. You mis-read him. He only wears such clothing because that is all he can afford." Alejandro reset his grip on the still hidden Scorpion. "We can give you forty dollars."

The guy who'd been sitting on the hood slid off like a snake and stepped to my right, getting an angle on the truck. Even though he still seemed relaxed, I didn't like that one bit, or the AK-47 still halfway pointed at us. Lots of Mexican gangsters like that weapon. They call it *cuerno de chivo,* the goat's horn, in reference to the long magazine curling from the bottom of the rifle.

At the same time I held up both hands so he'd relax, our car rocked ever so slightly. I figured Fosfora was wriggling down behind the seat. I wondered if they'd already seen her.

She spoke, her voice low. "I recognize that one. He is one of *Mujer Malvada's* most dangerous . . ."

"Who is *Mujer Malvada*, and which one are you talking about?"

"The most evil woman you have ever heard of. Kill him first. He is a very bad man."

Not knowing which one she was talking about, I pasted a dumb grin on my face and waited.

On Alejandro's side, Camo Guy threw out a larger figure that was probably close to the annual salary of most Mexicans. Alejandro shook his head. "Be reasonable. How about fifty American dollars from my friend here?"

The gangster didn't change expression. "If he has that much, he has more. Let me see your other hand."

The guy holding the AK tucked the stock into his shoulder, holding the rifle downward at a 45-degree angle. Here was that patrol-carry position again, and it made me even more nervous, needing nothing but a quick tuck against his shoulder to open the ball.

Heart pounding, my mouth went dry. Blood pounded in my temples and I wondered if I needed to be on blood-pressure medicine. AK Guy moved close enough that I could see his eyes were dead. There was no way to read him. I had no idea what he was thinking, but I've seen bad guys burn slow like that, following some kind of predatory instinct that most of us have never felt, then exploding into violence

I worked up a swallow. He was probably getting ready to shoot. "Alejandro." My voice was low.

Left hand holding the door open, Alejandro caught my drift and jerked his chin toward AK Guy who took another sidestep. "Tell your friend to make this guy un-shoulder his weapon. We mean no harm. We only want to pass. We're going to *El Cruce*."

"I want to see your other hand." Camo Guy took note of AK's stance and halfway shouldered the automatic weapon he was carrying. He called across the hood. "What is wrong?"

"There is someone in the back seat."

Dammit. I turned to look over my right shoulder.

Fosfora was sitting upright. Keeping my voice low, I slid my fingers around the butt on the pistol under my leg. "Alejandro. She says this guy's a threat."

Her voice was full of fear. "Not that one. That one."

"*Which* one?" We were in the middle of a vaudeville routine and I halfway expected her to say Who was on first.

Maintaining calm, Alejandro was still trying to talk our way through the incident. For me, I could see the train coming down the tunnel at full speed. Nerves jangling, a low humming sound filled my head.

"Amigo," Alejandro knew I had the pistol in my hand and held out his left hand like a traffic cop to keep the guy back so he wouldn't see either of us was armed. "Please lower your weapons."

"We will when you show me both of your hands!" Camo Guy squared his stance.

Like dogs sensing weakness, the other two brought their arms up.

AK Guy glared at me, his look challenging.

"Tell these guys to . . ." I searched my limited Spanish vocabulary for "back off." "*Apartate!*"

AK Guy's wingman, the one who'd been leaning against the car when we drove up, shifted three steps to my side, spreading out for a better field of fire and to make sure we couldn't take them all out with a full burst of automatic weapons.

He was directly in line with our car's right headlight. He raised his rifle.

I thumb-cocked the double action M9. It was about to go down.

Camo Guy's rifle came up. "Get out!"

I twisted to shoot through my open window at the

same time two loud bangs from a few inches behind my head started the dance.

In that same nanosecond, Alejandro's Scorpion opened up with a ripping sound.

Fosfora had fired through the open window, over my right shoulder. Heat roasted my numb right ear as AK's wingman twisted sideways and collapsed against our fender, grabbing at it for support as he slid down.

The AK-47 rose and the next thing I knew I had a sight picture down the M9. It bucked in my hand over and over until AK Guy was no longer a threat. The two on my side of the truck were down, but the guys on Alejandro's side could easily rake the Dodge until we were all dead as yesterday.

The air vibrated with machinegun fire as Alejandro's stream of bullets traveled only a few feet, nearly cutting Camo Guy half in two. The man deflated as he shifted his aim and emptied the rest of the magazine into the last stunned gangster who snapped his weapon to his shoulder.

I yanked at the door handle, rolling out. Using the door for cover, I emptied the M9's magazine into the same gunman. Glass behind him exploded as bullets chewed the man to pieces, popping puffs of powdered paint and dust from the car's sheet metal.

The corpse settled onto the highway and stilled. The desert was suddenly quiet except for that buzzing still in my head, and the sound of fresh magazines slapping into our weapons. I rose and put a hand to my ringing right ear. Feeling that it was still there, I looked into the back seat to see Fosfora holding a Glock 43 that must have been in her small purse the entire time.

She shrugged. "The one I shot raped me once, and he was about to shoot us. You were taking too long."

Not knowing what to say, I scanned the immediate area, then glanced upward at three buzzards already circling the sky. It's damned odd what you notice in times like that. A white contrail high overhead told me there was still normalcy in the world, but it was insane down on the desert hardpan where we stood.

A year earlier, shooting two men would have almost sent me into a rigor. But the Old Man once told me you do something enough times, it loses its thrill or threat or regret. I waited for the shock to hit me, but this time I felt nothing. No remorse. No let down.

Nothing. I feared I'd finally crossed some line into a world of numbness.

Before I could evaluate myself any further, the buzzing sound in my head made itself even more prevalent. I wondered if I was about to have a stroke before a flicker of movement in the sky caught my eye. A large, distant object receded into the distance toward a thin blue line of mountains. "Did y'all see that up there?"

Alejandro was still concentrating on the bodies around us. "No, what?"

The buzzing faded. "It was a drone."

Too late, he searched the sky. "That isn't good. The cartels are now using drones for a number of things, including carrying drugs across the river. I've also heard they use them for security around their territories."

I studied on it for a moment. "I hate this country."

Chapter 19

Yolanda knocked on Ruby Nelson's front door. On the way to Del Rio, she and Perry Hale decided that she should do the talking, feeling that the traumatized elderly ladies would relate to her more than a strange man.

Waiting at the bottom of the cracked concrete steps, Perry Hale slipped both hands into the pockets of his jeans. After what had happened at the house earlier, he was surprised that there were no police cars out front or news-crew vans for that matter.

The handle finally rattled and a soft voice came from the other side. "Who is it?"

"Miss Nelson? My name is Yolanda Rodriguez. You talked to a Texas Ranger this morning named Sonny Hawke. He sent us."

The door opened and Mrs. Ruby Nelson's wrinkled, smiling face appeared in the crack. "We sure did. He was a nice man." She paused when Perry Hale moved into view. "Who's that?"

"My partner, Perry Hale. He's friends with Ranger Hawke."

The door opened wider. "Okay. Y'all come in, hon." She moved out of the way as they stepped inside the neat little house.

In her chair, Miss Harriet put down her crocheting and leaned forward. "Who is it? Another reporter? I told you not to let them in."

"They're Texas Rangers, hon."

Neither Yolanda nor Perry Hale corrected her. They preferred not to use the *cinco peso* badges the governor issued. He ordered them to keep them in their pockets, only to be used as a last resort and only upon the arrival of law enforcement officers who demanded credentials.

Perry Hale paused in the short hallway when he saw a dark stain on the floor that he knew to be blood. Yolanda waited for Miss Nelson to settle slowly back into her chair.

The elderly woman picked up her crocheting from the basket beside her and rested the work in her lap. "Now, what can I do for you two?"

"Miss Nelson, Ranger Hawke is worried about your safety. He asked us to come by and escort the two of you to a secure location, where you can stay for the next few days."

"We'd feel better if he'd tell the police to bring our pistols back to us."

"I think we should get the car and go to the hardware store and get two more." Miss Harriet pointed toward the kitchen, and supposedly the garage beyond.

"I'm not sure they carry pistols in hardware stores anymore, dear." The sisters talked as if they'd forgotten Yolanda and Perry Hale were standing in their living room.

Yolanda gently broke in. "Ranger Hawke has a place for you to go. You might be there awhile until they figure out why those men broke in."

"Why, this is our home." Miss Ruby shook her head. "We need to stay *here*."

"Yes ma'am, it is. But those men were from a drug cartel, and you two were extremely lucky. Even though y'all took care of them, there might be more."

"But we don't want to leave."

"You aren't safe in this house right now. They underestimated you, but that won't happen again. Whatever the reason they were here, I'm afraid it'll bring them back. Ranger Hawke wants us to take you to another town."

Miss Harriet shook her head. "Who'll watch the cats while we're gone?"

"Don't you have a cat door?"

"Well, yes."

"We can put plenty of food and water out for them, and I'll arrange for someone to come in to check on them every day."

Perry Hale was listening and keeping an eye on the empty street. They'd parked around the corner. He stiffened when a police car pulled up in front and a Hispanic officer stepped out and glanced around. He strode toward the door with purpose, holding a box from a local donut shop, looking up and down the street a second time.

"Yoli. Police."

Yolanda frowned and bit her lip.

A knock came and Perry Hale thought for a moment. He decided to go on the offensive by yanking the door open. Startled, the Del Rio officer froze at the sight of a stranger who looked tough enough to eat nails. He seemed indecisive, something that made Perry Hale's neck prickle.

The officer who didn't have a name badge on his uniform shirt looked down at the box he was holding like he wasn't sure where it'd come from. "Who're you?"

"Friend of the family. I'm Perry Hale, officer . . . I think you've lost your name badge."

The policeman started to reach toward the empty spot on his shirt, but stopped. "Yeah. The name's Hernandez. I'm here to check on the ladies."

Perry Hale stepped back. "They're in here."

Quickly taking Perry Hale's measure, Hernandez moved past him and into the living room. Hernandez paid little attention to the sisters waiting for him to speak. "You a friend, too?"

"Yes." Standing in front of the kitchen door, Yolanda smiled, deepening the dimples in the corner of her mouth. "We're here checking on them."

Perry Hale's alarm system jangled so loud he expected someone to comment on the noise.

The officer hesitated, indecisive, shifting from foot to foot. He kept cutting his eyes around the room, at the same time balancing the flat donut box in his left hand as if it contained a cake or pie, instead of donuts. Hernandez finally addressed the ladies. "Is there anyone else here I should know about?"

Miss Ruby shook her head, the crochet needles in her hands stayed busy. "Nope. Just us."

Miss Harriet spoke up. "They're Texas Rangers. We haven't seen *you* since all this started. They send you to stay with us?"

The officer straightened. "Rangers? You don't look like Rangers." He held the box closer to his body.

Yolanda shrugged. "She misunderstood us. We told her Ranger Hawke sent us to take them somewhere for a couple of days . . . for safety sake."

"That won't be necessary. I'm here to watch out for them." He held the box slightly higher. "I brought donuts."

"Cops and donuts." As soon as it was out of his mouth, Perry Hale wondered if the officer would take offense. "That's funny."

Hernandez didn't smile. In fact, he looked nervous.

"I'll put them in the kitchen." Yolanda held out her hands and he backed up.

"No. I want the two of you to stand over there." He pointed with his free hand. "I need to check out your story. Why would a Ranger send civilians to take them somewhere?"

Perry Hale stayed where he was. "He's concerned for their safety, like she said."

Tension radiated off Hernandez. "That doesn't make sense. Show me some I.D."

"You being so nervous doesn't make sense." Perry Hale spread his hands. "We're just trying to do our job."

The officer licked his lips. "Do you ladies even know who these people are?" Now holding the donut box with two hands, Hernandez angled himself so he could see the entire room.

Miss Ruby shook her head. "Why no, we just met them, but I believe Ranger Hawke sent them, just like they said. He came by and was worried about us."

The way the man's eyes kept darting around caused

Perry Hale's stomach to clench. And the way Hernandez held that donut box was bothering him, too. He caught Yolanda's eye and volumes of information passed between them.

"Look, Hawke's out of pocket right now. Why don't you radio in and get your supervisor to call the Ranger headquarters in Austin and ask for Major Parker. He'll tell you about Ranger Hawke and *us*." Perry Hale was playing long odds with the suggestion.

His gamble paid off. Hernandez reached toward the Push to Talk radio in his ear, then hesitated. His thumb worried at the box lid, raising it slightly "No. I want you to do what I said and move over there right now." His voice quivered with tension, and Perry Hale knew why.

"Did you radio in you were here? We'll talk with your supervisor."

"Quit talking and move now." Right hand free again, the officer rested it on the butt of the Glock for half a second, then removed it like it was hot.

"You're awful indecisive." Perry Hale hung his thumb in his front pocket, only inches from the slender Colt 1911 in the IWB holster under his untucked shirt. "Look. We're taking these ladies with us in a minute so you don't have to worry about them. You can tell your C.O. that you don't need to stay. Why don't you call in right now and let's all relax."

Breathing hard, Hernandez's focus shifted back and forth between Perry Hale and Yolanda.

She crossed both arms under her breasts and spoke softly. "I know. You can't leave now, and you can't let us go, either, because we've seen you."

His thumb lifted the lid and while his attention was

on Yolanda, Perry Hale's voice rang out sharp in the room. "Don't!"

Hernandez's head snapped around to see the .45 in Perry Hale's hand, pointed at his abdomen. "Don't open that box or I'll shoot you deader'n hell."

"Young man!" Miss Ruby's voice was just as sharp. "This is a *police* officer."

"Yes ma'am, he is, but he's not here on official orders."

Yolanda drew her Glock and stepped forward, slapping the box from Hernandez's hand in an explosion of donuts. A worn revolver with a duct taped handle thumped on the handmade rag rug at his feet. She kicked it out of reach with her boot.

Hernandez's face quickly changed from stunned to frightened and then sadness. His demeanor crumbled, and he swayed as if in a high wind.

"Oh, my lord!" Miss Harriet put her hands to her cheeks.

Perry Hale remained rooted where he was. "Take the pistol from your holster with your left hand and give it to her."

"I can't do it with my left. The holster won't release."

Perry Hale hadn't thought of that. "Fine. Hands behind your back. Yolanda, cuff him."

Hernandez made no move to resist, and seconds later he was in his own cuffs and unarmed. Head low, he swayed like a tree in the wind before dropping to one knee. "You've killed me and my family."

Miss Ruby struggled to push herself to the edge of her seat. "What's happening?"

Tucking the Glock 43 back under her shirt, Yolanda

moved over to Miss Ruby and patted her shoulder. "He came to kill you."

"What? No. He's a policeman."

"Yes ma'am," Perry Hale said, tucking his own pistol back out of sight. "The cartel got to you, didn't they?"

The devastated police officer nodded. "A year ago."

"You aren't the first."

Hernandez blinked tears from his eyes. "Would you let me call my wife and tell her to get the kids? Maybe they can disappear if they get gone fast enough. It's the only thing I can do now."

"You did this to yourself." Perry Hale's voice crackled with disgust.

"I know. I messed up and needed money. They got to me and ordered me here."

"Who's they?"

"A man named Incencio. That's all I know. I thought I could do this to stay on their good side and not get us all killed, but believe me, I don't think I could have gone through with it."

"You could have fooled me." While Hernandez watched, Yolanda took out her cellphone and tapped at the screen. "I just contacted the sheriff in Ballard. We know we can trust him. He'll call back in a few minutes and we can get the ball rolling for you. I don't trust anyone else right now."

He nodded. "You shouldn't."

Perry Hale backed against a wall to keep an eye on the disgraced officer and punched at the screen on his own cell phone. Sonny's dad answered. "Herman?"

"Go ahead, Perry."

"We need you to come pick up a couple of ladies who need to get gone for a little while." He gave him the address and town.

"I'm on my way. Where do you want me to take 'em?"

"Someplace safe, that we don't know about."

"I'll be there directly."

"Fine." Perry Hale hung up and dialed again, listening to Sonny Hawke's number ringing, unanswered.

Chapter 20

The Devil Woman glanced up from the laptop computer angled on the end table beside the sofa and picked up her satellite phone. She quickly punched in a number and waited for the linkup.

Incencio Aguierre answered. *"Sí."*

"I just watched your drone feed."

"You saw what happened."

"Yes. They are very good. I'm sad that Esteban won't get to gut Oaxaca like a fish now, but I truly wanted that *esa espino y cranio*."

"Who would you like to pick up the bodies?"

"Leave them for the *aves carroneras*. Find those people and kill them all, but bring me the body of the *anglo* in the colorful shirt. He interests me. Kill Alejandro."

"You recognized him?"

"I've paid that *policia* plenty of money through the years, and now he betrays me."

"I think he has other business besides us. Maybe he's working a case outside of Ciudad Acuna."

"It doesn't matter. He killed one of ours."

"But señorita, you were going to have him killed anyway."

"Yes, but that was under *my* orders. No one kills my people but *me*. No one denies me pleasure."

"*Sí, señorita.* What about the woman?"

"*Ella no es mas que una puta.*" The Devil Woman had no compassion for women who didn't attempt to rise above their birth station in life and only survived by submitting to men. "She is nothing."

She ended the call and watched the video again, enjoying the way Alejandro and the *norteamericano* dropped some of her best men like they were amateurs. Those two were very good.

She hoped Incencio would send men equal to the task.

But it didn't matter. If those he sent were killed, well, it fulfilled what she'd learned at El Paso High School, survival of the fittest. If her weakest soldiers died, better men would rise to take their places.

Picking up a sweating glass of fresh squeezed lemonade, she padded barefoot across the cool deep red Mexican tiles and stopped at a wide picture window, studying the landscaped grounds. Living there was a huge step up from the tiny eight-hundred-square-foot frame house she'd grown up in back in El Paso.

Being a *pocho,* a slang term for a Mexican born in the U.S., still bothered her, and she was determined to overcome her past. She'd done that by working her way up until she could buy her way into the narco government of Coahuila. Now they depended on the pipeline of American cash that flowed through her hands and into their pockets.

It was good to be *La Jefa,* the boss.

Chapter 21

We passed acres of Coahuila blackberry fields before rolling into the surprisingly pretty little town of El Cruce late in the afternoon. Instead of the dusty little desert community I'd envisioned, it was green and cool with trees, palms, and a beautiful view of the distant mountains forming a semicircle around the flat valley floor.

The square full of manicured trees and a pale-yellow three-story bell tower rose over a butter-colored church. On the opposite side of the square, Fosfora pointed to a small, brick building standing alone at one corner. "There."

I squinted through the dirty windshield. "What's that?"

"Here you will meet the one who called you."

"He's in there?"

"No. You will wait until he comes."

"When will that be?"

"Who knows?"

That answer told me for sure that we were operating on Mexican time. Not living by the ticking of a clock, their culture operated at a more sedate pace. Businesses often opened whenever the owner unlocked the door, rather than at a posted time. If someone said they'd be there first thing in the morning, their "first thing" might be nearly noon.

Alejandro pulled up against a wall running the length of the street and ending at the corner of the building. He looked pained. "I had no idea we were going to be gone this long. I will have people questioning my whereabouts."

"We'll deadhead back after I talk with this guy. It shouldn't take more than a few minutes." From our angle at the curb, I translated a neat, hand-painted sign above the door. *Articulos para el hogar.* "Housewares?"

Fosfora shrugged and scanned the square. "That is what I was told."

In the square beside us, a handful of people milling under the cool shade trees paused to study our car. The air was filled with the fragrance of spices, cooking meat, and wood smoke from push cart vendors selling street food, or *antojitos*, until the vendors completed their transactions and everyone faded away.

The hair prickled on the back of my neck once again.

I nudged Alejandro. "They're gone."

"This is a cartel town. They don't recognize this truck. It is better to leave than to stay and be accused of association with strangers."

"I stick out like a sore thumb. I guess they don't take kindly to strangers."

"Huh?"

"An old western movie joke."

"I like John Wayne."

"So do I. A lady told me not too long ago that he was the source of all toxic masculinity."

"I don't know what that means."

"It means she didn't want men to be real men."

"Ah. That's one of the problems with your country. When it comes to *machismo,* it is no longer honored or desired as it is in my culture."

"My wife would disagree with that."

Alejandro opened his door. "I'll go in with you." He rounded the front of the pickup and joined me on the passenger side, opposite the square.

A head-high stone wall stretched the length of the sidewalk. Missing chunks at the top made it look as if an angry T-Rex had taken a bite here and there. Head high, the openings allowed me to peer over into a wide, manicured courtyard the size of a city block that looked like the parade ground in an old frontier fort. An ancient, roofless stone building squatted right out in the middle. Doors and windows long gone, the dark gray color reminded me of mausoleums I'd seen in old New England cemeteries.

"I'm staying here." Fosfora shifted over to the middle of the back seat and stretched out, resting what the Old Man would have called cotton patch feet on the console.

Leaving her behind, we pushed through the corner store's peeling front door that opened with a low squeal from the worn hinges. The doorknob and hardware looked to be as old as the church we'd just seen.

Throwing one last look at the empty square, I followed him inside. "Looks like they don't carry oil."

He didn't get it.

Inside, it was a far cry from a houseware store in the states. Bare bulbs dangled on frayed lines from the cracked ceiling, their low wattage barely supplementing the sunlight filtering through dirty windows overlooking the street corner.

Narrow aisles sagged with dusty boxes on bare wooden shelves. Still in their shipping containers, most of the writing and advertisements were in Spanish, but I recognized a surprising number of logos.

A short, nervous-looking man with big ears and thinning hair rose to his feet behind a plywood counter when we entered. His eyes went flat and skipped off my face to settle on Alejandro. *"Puedo ayudarte?"*

The guy probably couldn't speak any English at all. Alejandro answered and they took off again at warp speed in their native language. There were no other shoppers. Instead of standing there rocking back and forth on my toes and grinning like an idiot, I wandered away and strolled through the cluttered aisles, more to make sure we were alone than anything else.

Tall windows on two of the four cinderblock walls allowed me to keep an eye on the town. I crossed the store, not paying attention to what Alejandro and the owner were doing by the front door. The first set of windows looked down the street where we'd parked the Dodge. I checked out what I could see of the empty, shady plaza.

The owner ignored me, talking in earnest to Alejandro. I crossed to the opposite side of the store. The street was empty. Satisfied, I had one more place to check out. A single door leading out back into the courtyard was closed. Turning a metal knob, I peeked outside into the large, tree-lined lot.

Back home I'd'a said it was the biggest backyard I'd ever seen.

What I'd originally thought was the ruins of a mausoleum was actually a small mission or *convento,* probably part of the original Spanish settlement in that area. Hundreds of years old, it once had a pole and wood roof that was long gone. Crumbling arched walls defined what was left of a small plaza surrounding the tiny structure.

About to turn back inside, movement in the single entrance caught my attention.

Tensing, I scanned the big courtyard even closer than before. It offered little in the way of cover, except for what was provided by the small building's crumbling walls smack dab in the middle of the open space. A man stepped into view in the *convento*'s doorway. Once he was sure I'd seen him, he disappeared back inside.

Glancing over my shoulder, I saw Alejandro still talking to the owner. He noticed me. I pointed at my chest and then outside. He nodded.

The aromatic, recently mowed grass was soft as a carpet underfoot. I could have been walking into an ambush. It didn't matter. This was likely the guy I'd come to meet, the one who had called with the information I was looking for. I crossed the grass. The throaty rumble of a passing car engine was the only sound on the street.

With the 9mm in my hand, I stopped fifteen yards and to the side of the little chapel's gaping doorway. I spoke English. "Let me see you."

Hands splayed, a man reappeared, half in shadow. I expected him to whisper, or answer in a low tone. Instead, his voice was strong. "Come inside where we can talk."

"I'm pretty comfortable here."

"Yes, but there are eyes everywhere, Hawke."

Yep, this was my guy.

The man had backed all the way to the rear wall of the roofless building to where I figured the altar once stood. I didn't go straight in like someone stepping into a backyard shed, but checked the corners on either side of the doorway. Half of the room was filled with sunlight angling in from the west. It would be sunset soon, but right then there were no dark corners where someone could hide.

We were alone.

I repositioned myself to a side wall, so I could see him *and* the doorway. I sized him up. Dressed in jeans and a gold T-shirt, the young, muscular man stood somewhere around five foot eight or ten. His eyes flicked from me to the outside.

I was relieved that he kept both hands to his sides. "All right. I'm here. Who are you?"

"Call me Esteban. Some call me Flaco." He saw my eyebrow raise. "I was skinny when I first came here. My real name can get many people killed."

"You have information for me?"

"More than you can imagine." His eyes were never still. "You might find it hard to believe, but I'm an American agent. Don't ask me who I'm with, though."

"Nothing about this country surprises me. But how do I know you're telling me the truth? Name the capital of Texas."

"Austin. Satisfied?"

"Name the vice president."

He did, and I relaxed. "I only halfway believe you."

"I wouldn't expect anything else. There were two of us. One is dead. You know that."

"Cartels are careful about who they let in. There's no way an American can infiltrate."

He was a good-looking kid, and his face lit up when he smiled. "Several years ago we came in as young men working undercover for the El Paso police department in one of their public high schools."

He saw my eyebrows raise again.

"I wasn't as hard-edged back then. My partner and I didn't look our age. There was a huge flow of drugs in that area, and we heard they were moving it through the school. We passed for juniors. Our story was that we'd moved in from Arizona. Our paperwork was perfect and everyone bought it, all the way down to the girls and our teachers.

"It worked better than we expected and we were about to shut the operation down and make the arrests when we found something even bigger. The cartels were changing their tactics here . . . there in the U.S. Instead of staying south of the border, they created independent cells in Texas, recruiting kids directly from the school. We gained some of the 'older' kids' confidence, seniors, and our stories about moving to El Paso held up, and we were finally able to join."

My voice was harder than I intended, but I knew what they must have done to be completely accepted. "You don't get in these gangs without initiation."

For the first time, his eyes dropped, then met mine. "I won't talk about the things we had to do, but they were necessary to save lives then, and in the future. Once we were in, we moved up in the organization."

I knew what he meant but wanted him to say it. "You killed people."

He barely nodded.

"Keep talking." My stomach tensed, as if expecting a punch.

"As my grandfather would say, *hicimos nuestros hueses*. We made our bones, and got so deep we can never get out."

"You became them."

"Yes, in a sense. But we still kept our morality."

"Really?"

"The morality that binds us to the United States." His eyes hardened. "Okay, we crossed lines, but for the better good."

"Judges back home won't agree with that."

"Wouldn't expect them to."

"So you've been in for years."

"*Sí* . . . yes. Some associations in the states admit there might be deep cover assets on this side of the river, but only our handlers have our names. Not even our families know about us. We simply vanished, like kids do all the time on the border. They think we're dead."

Man, that was a tough one. This guy disappeared when he was pretending to be my son's age. I wondered what I'd have done to find him. "That's rough on the people who love you."

Pain flickered across his eyes. "Us, too. We've helped them, in many ways. What we did was to help keep them safe, or so we thought. Now I think all we've done is screw this country completely up, not that it was much better than when we arrived."

"You sound like those Washington spooks I've run into."

"Look, I'm not here to debate right or wrong with you. We were unique. There are no others doing what we do, but that all changed when you shot my partner."

My stomach flipped again, both from the recollection, and the information he had. No one but law enforcement investigators knew it was me who pulled the trigger. "The kid in the Movie Lot Massacre."

"That's right. We were both supposed to be there, but the day before it happened, I was sent to . . . well, I wasn't there."

"How did you know I shot him?" I couldn't bring myself to say "kill."

"My handler told me. Word filtered down."

I wondered what else "filtered down." "He was part of an attack that killed innocent people. All because they were making a movie."

He closed his eyes, nodded. The lids were tattooed with red eyeballs that seemed to stare straight through me. "Yes, he was, but the movie was based on the Devil Woman, and she prefers anonymity." He held up a hand. "She exists, and she's worse than any cartel leader you've ever heard of. Whoever wrote the script knew way too much about her operation, and the movie would have brought too much attention to her operation."

"It's gonna be made anyway."

"You and I know that, but she thinks she's stopped it."

"By killing innocent people. Your partner was there with an automatic weapon."

"He was, but we had a pact. On American soil, we

carried blanks. We won't kill our own people . . . innocent Americans." He was trying to cover himself regarding the blood work he'd participated in.

"You're lying about that part. You don't become
cartel soldiers without killing people. If they found out
you were loading blanks in your rifles, you'd be in a
ditch before you could whistle Dixie."

He gave a wan grin at the reference. "Rationalizing
what I do is the only way to stay sane. Once we started
crossing back and forth across the border, we agreed
we wouldn't kill civilians."

His rationalization struck me as bullshit. "But you
kill down here. You share the same DNA with these
folks."

"Again, you don't know what we do, and your
morality has no roots this side of the river. Here, there
are bigger fish to fry than you can imagine, and the information we've gathered is incredibly important."

That statement guaranteed who he was. No one but
Americans would know how to use that phrase about
frying fish. My stomach was still at my feet, though.
Grinding my teeth to choke it down, I took a deep
breath. "Why am I here? Why'd you call me?"

He checked the door again. "Because I don't want
those old women killed, the ones in Del Rio. And
there's another, bigger reason, but I need to start with
the fact that there are others on a list, also. Someone in
Hawaii, and a baby. This has to stop. I don't have much
more time, so listen to what I have to say."

For the next five minutes he told me how border
agents were *recruited* through threats and murder, how
their families were targeted if the agents lost their ef-
fectiveness or if they failed. I learned Frank Nelson's

daughter in Hawaii was about to be just as dead as if she was in Texas. He told me Ruby Nelson and her sister in Del Rio were still on the list, and then he described a cartel drug pipeline that flowed from the border, all the way up to Interstate 10 in Texas, all protected by men who were betraying their departments, the state, and our country, but only to protect their families.

He filled in a dozen holes in what I knew, but he wasn't finished.

"The person in charge of all this is the most evil woman I've ever met or even heard of. The Devil Woman of Coahuila is also from El Paso, and she's behind all this. She's about to start moving more than drugs or humans across the border. She is more horrible than you can ever imagine.

"It's going to get worse, and more people will be hurt, on both sides of the border. In fact, tomorrow night she's sending a group across to test a new pipeline she's put into place, and it won't be just people from Central America. Everyone thinks it's just people from Guatemala or Honduras, but I know for a fact some are from China and Iraq. This time there are five Syrians. These guys are bad dudes, and I think they have something planned, and all this is coming up through that system she's put in place. Even more, this is all a feint, to draw attention away from the drones she's using to move drugs. In a year or two, Amazon is going to start delivering packages with drones. Her plan is to mix her own drones in with them and drop the drugs right down in her people's back yards. No one will know which drones are legal."

From where I stood, I had a good view of the open

lot behind the housewares store. It was quiet out there, so I figured we had at least a little more time.

"So where is this . . . Devil Woman's ranch?"

He described the area less than a hundred miles away. "She's going to be running more operations through your region, because they're tightening security in the traditional crossing places. There are too many border agents these days, and now the coyotes are funneling these people through rougher country where it's easier to use the land to avoid detection. They'll arrest the people on the ground and the drones will fly over without notice."

"I have to get the word to my people."

"Yes, I knew you were the only person I could trust, who would believe my story, and would keep me out of it."

"How'd you find me?"

"We can read, you know. You've been in the papers more than once in the last year or so. You're a legend down here, and Señor Mendez in there who owns the housewares store was talking about you at the cantina here in town. I was here with my compadres, and heard him. After you killed my partner, I decided to call you."

That one hurt. "How'd you get away to meet me here?"

He gave me a sad smile. "I am a *sicario*. I had a job to do here, but you finished it for me."

"What was it?"

"I was sent to shoot someone who betrayed the Devil Woman when she had faith in him."

"Find him?"

"You did, before you came here."

"Well, hell. Those guys who stopped us."

"*Sí.*"

"I did your work for you."

"*Sí,* and you did it well. We're putting the finishing touches on my assignment, and I will soon be gone."

"We?"

He shrugged. The guy had a lot more info he wasn't giving up. The corner of his mouth twitched in a tiny smile. "*Bien.* One more thing. You have to be careful. There is someone who is loyal to a rival cartel here in Coahuila. *They* want the Devil Woman's pipeline. His name is Incencio, and he is very dangerous to everyone but himself."

That name rang a bell, but I couldn't put my finger on where I'd heard it before. "Don't you have any *good* news?"

"Yes. This meeting is over. I've told you all I can. Now, we have to get out of here."

"You keep my number handy, just in case you need it."

"*Sí,* but there is no cell service here."

"I noticed that. There'll be other times and places. Oh, I need one more piece of information from you."

"What's that?"

"What's the name of the agent I killed? His real name."

"Ricky Delgado."

That was the best bona fide I could come up with. With that name, I could call Yolanda once I got cell service and have her check it out. But I wasn't through. Yeah, I know he'd said they disappeared when they were "kids," but the El Paso PD would have their names on file. As a Texas Ranger, I could get the information fairly easily. "I need to inform his family. No organization'll admit to having him on their payroll. He should have benefits coming. What was his name here?"

"You have too many questions. You're going to get on the bad side of my handlers."

"I need a lot of answers, and I'm not afraid of them. I might need to talk to you again in a day or so."

He licked his lips, thinking. "Since my work here is done, by you, I will return to the Devil Woman's *ranchero* down in Coahuila. There is a cantina there in town called *El Fuste*. I'll be there at night for about a week."

"That'll work." Tucking the pistol back under my shirt, I stuck out my hand. "Thanks, Esteban."

His grip was strong, like any good Texan who'd been taught to shake. We both came from where a handshake still meant something, and any doubts completely faded away. Without looking back, I stepped out of the little chapel.

"Hey, Hawke."

I turned.

"His name was Pollito on this side of the river, because he looked so little and young."

His offhand comment hurt my heart, so I shifted my position to study the area, and so he couldn't see my suddenly watery eyes.

Late evening shadows from the town square's trees stretched across the courtyard. I've always said it was my favorite time of day, when the heat dissipates and the shade is cool and welcoming. Wanting to look like a tourist, I strolled around the plaza's crumbling walls, taking it all in, even shooting a couple of pictures with my cell phone, just in case someone had eyes on me.

Like any good visitor, I snapped a few of the surrounding area, then went back inside the store. From the moment I stepped through the doorway, I knew something was wrong. Alejandro wasn't waiting for me, and it was too quiet. There were no voices.

"Anyone here?"

Silence.

Walking as lightly as possible, I approached the counter.

A stream of blood flowed around a pony wall blocking the public from the register side of the counter. I peered over and saw Alejandro and the owner were lying side by side, their throats cut from ear to ear.

Chapter 22

The sky was rich with color from the setting sun. Dusk was the best thing about Morelos Street. It wasn't the worst paved street Perry Hale had ever seen, but it ran a close fifth. Narrow and dirty, drivers had to thread their way through cars parked at the curb. Volkswagen beetles, beaten up Ford Rangers, and a variety of broken-down sedans lined both sides of the street.

He unconsciously rubbed the week's growth of whiskers on his chin. "I hate coming over here."

Yolanda Rodriguez walked beside him, fingers tucked into the front pockets of her jeans. Her boots clumped on the gritty sidewalk. The black ponytail sticking through the adjustment hole of her coral-colored Life is Good cap flipped with every move of her head. "It could be worse."

"How?"

"We could be on our side of the river and find this. We saw a lot worse in Afghanistan."

"Yeah, but we were walking around armed. I feel nekked as a jaybird out here."

Knowing Mexico's convoluted gun laws, neither he

nor Yolanda carried firearms. He didn't even have his fixed-blade Tac II knife that always rode in a specially designed sheath on his belt. When revealed, the sight of that little instrument scared more people than a handgun.

Not far from the Disney-like clean tourist section of Ciudad Acuna, the buildings around them were dingy and weather-worn despite the bright paint that was supposed to provide a cheery, inviting feel. After cracking in the desert heat, the paint job simply looked seedy. The crumbling, dirty sidewalks were busy with people of all ages. Dozens of highline wires crisscrossed overhead, giving the illusion of an open ceiling.

Yolanda pointed at an unimpressive building on the corner. "This is it."

Built to provide a homey touch, a useless, peeling picket fence sagged in the narrow two-foot span between the sidewalk and a cinderblock building once the color of clay flower pots. Now faded to a light earth tone, someone tried to brighten it up with a sweeping strip of blue evolving into a stylized horse head, which contained the hand-painted words, *Caballo Diablo*.

"This is the definition of a gun and knife club. Stay frosty." Perry Hale gave the street a quick glance before pushing the door open and stepping inside the neon-lit, smoke-filled cantina.

"Always am." Yolanda followed him in.

Grupero music enveloped them with a wall of accordion and guitar runs. Perry Hale waited for his eyes to adjust, feeling Yolanda's shoulder against his back as she did the same. Confident that she was covering their rear, he watched several of the bar's patrons turn to peer at the new arrivals through the dimness.

A drawn-out comment from an unseen source told them someone appreciated Yolanda's appearance. *"Orale!"*

Choosing to ignore him, Perry Hale tilted back the bill of his green "Come and Take It" gimme cap and wound through a minefield of scattered wooden tables and chairs until he reached the bar. He hoped none of the men in the cantina were history buffs and wondered if he'd made a mistake wearing it south of the border.

The cannon logo on his cap was a symbol of defiance from the Texas Revolution, when the Mexican government demanded that the Texans return a small brass cannon they had supplied to help protect the colony of Gonzales. The Texans refused and the Mexican military tried to take it by force and lost.

It was just the type of spark to provoke an explosion in what looked like the roughest joint Perry Hale had been in in years. Watching from the corners of his eyes, he saw most of the patrons were watching Yolanda.

That was both good and bad.

Instead of sitting on one of the empty seats at the bar, he leaned his elbows on the scarred wooden surface. Yolanda moved up beside him and half-sat on a stool, angled toward Perry Hale so she could keep an eye on the room.

A bartender with unruly hair and an offset jaw took his time coming to take his order. "You got some *cojones* wearing that cap in here." He spoke English with a heavy accent. "You lost?"

It was just his luck to find an educated bartender. "Is that a philosophical question or religious?"

The pockmarked barman frowned. "This is a *local*

cantina." He flicked his hand toward the tables. "For *Mexicans*. Tourists need to stay where they belong. We don't need your money."

"How do you know what my ancestry might be?" He jerked a thumb at Yolanda. "If DNA's the case, then she's my ticket."

The man's grin held no humor. His eyes went flat. "You already talk too much."

Perry Hale had seen that grin a number of times in his life, usually preceding a fight. He also wondered if the guy owned a toothbrush. "Hey, we just came in for a beer."

The barman dismissed Perry Hale and spoke to Yolanda in their native language. "Why are you with this *gringo*?"

She flat-eyed him and responded in border Spanish. "None of your business, and you talk to him, not me. Just because I look like you doesn't mean we are the same."

Perry Hale returned the man's dead grin and also spoke in border Spanish. "Don't mess with her. She'll bust you up. So now that we understand each other in more ways than one, give us a couple of beers, please."

Taken aback by the *anglo*'s grasp of his language, the bartender took a moment to sort things out. "You can have one, on the house, then get out."

"We'll leave faster if you'll answer a question for me."

The barman placed both hands flat on the bar. This time he spoke English. "Be quick about it."

Annoyed by the whirl of languages and irritated by the man's demeanor, Perry Hale had to concentrate. The song on the jukebox ended, only to be replaced by another that was so similar he couldn't tell the difference. "You promised me a beer."

Without taking his eyes off Perry Hale, the bartender reached down and plucked a dripping bottle from the cooler directly in front of him. Snapping the cap off a Sol with an old-fashioned church key, he thumped it on the bar in a gout of foam. He made no move to open another.

Not trusting the ice, or the barman's hands, Perry Hale scooped it close and wiped the top with his shirt sleeve. He slid it across to Yolanda, who took a sip, keeping an eye on the bar's patrons.

Perry Hale dead-eyed the man to make his point. "I'm looking for a guy who might have been in here this morning. Not much to describe, just an *anglo* looking to meet someone."

"You said you only wanted a couple of beers."

"Yeah, and I see only one. To fill in the time while you get another one, let's talk."

"Lots of people come in here. I don't want to talk to any of them if they're *anglo*."

Yolanda leaned forward on her elbows. "You just told me this is a bar for Mexicans only. You don't get too many *norteamericanos*. How about you cut the shit and tell me if my friend was here. Then we can go."

The barman scanned the room as if someone might come help him handle the uncomfortable three-way exchange. He shrugged and dried his hands with a damp, filthy rag. "There was an *anglo* early this morning. He came to meet someone."

"Who?"

There was that flat grin again, this time directed at Yolanda, as if she would understand. "My sister."

"What's her name?"

"Fosfora."

"Did he see her?"

"Yes, and they left together after one of my friends beat him to the ground."

Perry Hale snorted. "*That* didn't happen."

"It's easy when it comes to an *hombre marqueta* in *camisas hawaiianas*."

"Hawaiian shirts? Not this guy. Looks like a cowboy, and I can tell you, he ain't no sissy man."

"Cabello rojo?"

"Yep. Redheaded."

"It was him."

Perry Hale and Yolanda exchanged looks. She thought for a moment. "I remember seeing an Aloha shirt in his truck the other day. Mary gave it to him for his birthday, and he kinda liked it. He kept it there just in case he wanted to look casual."

Only Sonny Hawke's teenage daughter would think to give her daddy a Hawaiian Aloha shirt. More than once she said she liked seeing him out of his Texas Ranger "uniform" every now and then. Not a uniform at all, Rangers wear khaki pants, legendary tooled leather gunbelts and badges, light shirts, and their ever-present western hats. In any crowd, anywhere in Texas, Rangers are immediately recognizable.

But Sonny sometimes liked what he called "dressing down," wearing oversize untucked shirts, because the blousy material hid his .45 when he wanted to be casual.

"That's our man." Perry Hale watched Yolanda take another drink. Behind her, two young locals made of rope and wire walked up and stopped, one on each side.

One sported a thick drooping mustache and a fresh, blood-stained bandage over one eye. The other dressed like a *vaquero* with gold teeth, a taco hat, and a dangerous smile was holding a beer bottle by the neck, thumb hooked in his hand tooled belt. Voice low, he leaned in and spoke Spanish. "*Chica*, I'd like to stuff your *piñata*. Can I buy you a *cerveza*?"

She batted her dark eyes at him. "Does that rude pickup line really work for you?" His buddy snickered as she held up her Sol. "I have one, and my husband bought it for me."

That sounded funny to Perry Hale, because they'd never talked about getting married. Preferring to let her handle herself, he turned back to the bartender. "Was Flaco here, too?"

Something flickered behind the lopsided bartender's dull eyes.

Taco Hat wouldn't quit. "He doesn't look like much. Come join me and my friend and leave that Sol. We order only Coronas, because they are colder. Juan, open two for this *chica*."

"I'm sure they come out of the same ice bucket," Perry Hale answered Taco Hat without taking his eyes from the bartender's face. He wanted to be sure the man understood that he was listening. "Anyway, did Flaco show up, too?"

"There was no Flaco." Juan shrugged. "My sister left with your friend, and she hasn't been back."

"Do you know where they went?"

The side action continued when Taco Hat moved closer to Yolanda. "Come drink with *men*."

Perry Hale sighed. Cutting his eyes toward the pair, he pointed with his cap. "You don't want to mess with that little gal, buddy. She'll eat your lunch."

"*Que*? *Chinga tu madre*. I'm talking to her, not you."

Turning back to Juan behind the bar, Perry Hale kept himself angled just enough to keep the two men in his peripheral vision. "Look, I'm kinda worried about my friend, and that goes for your sister if she's with him. He tends to attract trouble," he jerked a thumb at Yolanda, "like her."

Yolanda turned away from Taco Hat. "Just minding my own business here, buster. Go back over there and play with your friends."

Taco Hat ran his fingertips down Yolanda's arm. "*Mira*. I can show you a good . . ."

"Hey, Taco Hat. You're about to draw back a nub." Perry Hale switched his attention back and forth, watching Juan's eyes. "My friend hasn't called in. Have you heard from your sister?"

Ignoring Perry Hale's warning, Taco Hat cupped Yolanda's chin. Her hand snapped up as fast as a rattlesnake strike. He shrieked when his finger suddenly turned at a horrific angle away from his hand. She held on and twisted. In an effort to relieve the excruciating pain of muscles and ligaments stretched almost to their breaking points, his knees bowed backward.

"There you go," Perry Hale said, trying not to laugh.

Taco Hat's mustached friend reached for Yolanda's thick ponytail. The edge of her free hand scythed through the air like an axe blade, catching him on the tip of his nose that exploded in a burst of blood. The lackey's boots left the floor and he crashed backward onto a table full of empty bottles and dirty glasses. The men who'd been sitting there leaped from their chairs and backed against the wall.

Effortlessly pushing Taco Hat's hand up and backward even more, she bent the finger to an impossible angle. Screaming like a little girl, he curled backward and she followed his momentum, exerting even more force until his back slammed onto the filthy floor.

Not taking his eyes from the barman's face, Perry Hale waited for the scream to change pitch. He knew what was coming. No one touched Yolanda. He'd gone too far.

A sharp snap told him Taco Hat's finger broke, just as he expected. The man shrieked.

The bartender moved to pick up something from behind the bar, and Perry Hale shook his head. "Nope. You could have stopped this."

Yolanda kicked Taco Hat in his *huevos* and he shrieked again. "I don't want your beer. I don't want you touching me. *Comprende*?" She finally turned loose of his broken finger and blistered the air with a string of Spanish curses that went on for thirty seconds.

Blood pouring into his mustache from his busted nose, the lackey rolled off the table and staggered backward, wanting no more of the slender woman who fought like a *gato montes,* a wildcat. Eyes flashing, Yolanda spun toward Juan the bartender, planted her feet while at the same time pointing an index finger at his face, and unleashed another torrent of border Spanish that had the man blinking in stunned silence.

Breathing hard, she grabbed the bottle of Sol and drained half in two swallows. She slammed it onto the bar and threatened the rest of the patrons with a hot glare that was almost luminous.

"Now." Perry Hale smiled at Juan. "Do you know where your sister and my friend went?"

Stunned, Juan answered. "El Cruce. She told me she'd be back by dark."

"What else did she tell you?"

As Taco Hat's bloody, groggy friend half-drug him toward the door, Juan told Perry Hale and Yolanda what he knew.

When he was finished, Perry Hale nodded. "Now, one more thing. If anyone follows us from here, if anyone from this cantina causes any trouble for me, her, or the friend I'm looking for, or if you're lying to me and any of us gets hurt, I'm coming back here and burn this place to the ground, with your corpse in it. *Comprende*?"

The bartender could only blink.

"Yolanda, would you repeat that so he can understand what I said, please? I don't want to figure out how to say it in Spanish."

Giving him a dimpled smile, she repeated Perry Hale's statement in a soft, even voice. *"Ahora, una cosa más. Si alguien nos sigue desde aquí, si alguien de esta cantina causa algún problema para mí, para ella o para mi amiga, o si ella me miente y uno de nosotros se lastima, volveré aquí y quemaré este lugar para El suelo, con tu cadáver en él. Entiendes, mi amigo?"*

He understood *that,* and nodded as they left without further molestation.

Outside, they hurried down the street, glancing over

their shoulders from time to time to be sure they weren't followed.

"Did you *have* to break the guy's finger and bust his balls?"

"He was lucky it wasn't his arm, and I only kicked him once. You know I don't like for people to touch me."

He intentionally poked her with his index finger, like a little kid prodding his sister to make her mad. "How about me?"

Her laugh was high from adrenaline. She reached for his hand, slowly, so he could jerk it away and they hurried back toward the border.

Chapter 23

The houseware store was silent, but it was one of those quiets that parents recognize when a toddler hasn't been heard from in a while, and they know something's up. Well, something was. A black-haired man came out of nowhere. One minute I was standing there beside the counter all by myself, and the next thing I knew, a mean-looking guy with enough tats on his arms and neck to work in a circus rushed at me from around the end of an aisle.

The knife in his hand looked to be the size of a machete. You talk to any hand-to-hand self-defense instructor about knife fighting and they say there are no real winners when it comes to sharp edges. The first person to bleed out loses, while the other guy is simply the survivor.

I've taught those classes, and instruct my students no matter what the age or experience, to turn and run like a striped-ass baboon if anyone comes at you with a knife. I'd've listened to my own advice if I could.

The guy was so close by the time I saw him that running wasn't an option. There was a ragged, shoulder-high display of some kind of candy and cookies I couldn't pronounce. I slapped the wire rack into him with one hand, just to get something between us and give me time.

It worked better than I expected. Tangled in falling sweets and rattling metal that swarmed him like a closet full of wire hangers, my assailant went down.

The Beretta was back in my hand, but before I could shoot, I sensed another someone rushing at me from behind. Keeping the weapon close to my body, I whirled just in time to see a skinny little guy charging at me like a linebacker. Funny thing was, he didn't have a knife in his hand, but a pistol.

Maybe he got all excited and wanted to see the fear in my eyes as he killed me, or he could have been a bad shot and needed to get closer so he wouldn't miss. Either way, it was a mistake. Pistol close to my body at waist level, I shot three times at center mass, and his knees buckled. Limp, he landed backward on his butt and slumped against a dusty shelf of metal rods.

That threat down for good, I spun back to the first guy who'd kicked and cursed himself from the display rack. He rose at the same time a boil of crushed sweets and baked goods reached my nose. With no time or inclination to tell him to put his hands up, I shot him twice, again center mass, and he fell backward onto those wire shelves. He gurgled for a moment and then stilled.

I might have felt bad, until I saw a wet, perpendicular stripe on his pants where he'd wiped the blood from his knife after killing Alejandro and the counterman.

"Hawke!"

In fighting mode, my finger was on the Beretta's trigger when I crouched and twisted toward the shadow standing in the back door. It wasn't a third attacker, but Esteban holding what looked like Alejandro's Scorpion. I still almost shot him, but it was pointed down.

"What the hell!!!???"

"We have to go." The steel in his voice completely covered his accent. "Follow me now!"

Voices rose outside and tires squalled on the pavement out front. Esteban disappeared from the rear doorway. Someone on the street was issuing orders, and, with no other options, I left my friend's body where it lay and charged after the man I didn't know.

Chapter 24

As a scattering of sharp gunshots echoed from the square, I followed Esteban through the long shadows stretching across the huge courtyard. A round pocked the stucco five feet in front of me. I ducked at the same time Esteban disappeared through an arched opening, shouldering the metal gate out of the way with a squawk of rusty hinges.

Movement in my peripheral vision gave me just enough warning to juke sideways as a guy holding an M4 leaned into a section of crumbling wall twenty feet from the houseware store I'd just left. I was still forty yards behind Esteban when the guy led me too far. Pops of light in the gathering dusk flashed at the same time a line of bullet holes ripped the stucco a couple of feet ahead.

Cursing my Aloha shirt for being so bright, I spun, dropped to one knee, and brought the Beretta to bear. Squeezing the pistol's trigger as fast as possible, I really had no hope of hitting anything at that distance. It was suppression fire that worked when the sheer volume of firepower from the double-stack magazine did its job, and the shooter ducked back out of the way.

The Beretta's slide locked back and I thumbed the empty magazine free. Slapping in a fresh one from my pocket, and wishing I had the daypack full of loaded mags back in the car, I sprinted for the metal gate up ahead. More shots hammered the courtyard, and I figured the best thing to do was get out of the open.

Esteban leaned back around the arch and added his own touch to the fight, sending a string of automatic weapon fire from the Scorpion toward the people popping up like Whack-a-Moles in the openings across the courtyard. His bullets chewed up the crumbling wall and someone cried out.

An odd thing happened inside my head, and for an instant I had an inkling of what it was like for those boys back in the Alamo in 1836. Here I was in a courtyard too large to defend, with people shooting from all directions. I knew good and well that Crockett would have hauled ass just like I was doing, if he'd gotten the opportunity.

Esteban's weapon ran dry, and he waved. "Come on!" He vanished from sight, and I raced toward his arched opening, struggling to see in the fading light.

Dusk and a line of tall trees and fat palms in the poor neighborhood beyond the courtyard added a darker element to all the fun we were having. Because of all the vegetation, light was almost gone on the street beyond the arch. The guns were momentarily silent.

Esteban said the way was clear, but I just couldn't run blind into the unknown. I skidded to a stop under the arch and peeked around the corner to see him high-tailin' it across the empty street and into an alley. I wanted to holler for him to slow down, but decided that probably wouldn't be smart, even though those guys already knew where I was.

Tires squalled around the corner and a truck running without headlights came into view. The Beretta rose in my hands and I almost put holes in the windshield before a woman's hand waved through the open driver's window. Fosfora pumped her arm up and down as she braked Alejandro's pickup to a shrieking stop.

She stuck her head through the open window. "Get in!"

Instead of heading toward the passenger side like she ordered, I hoofed it to the driver's side. "Move over!"

She didn't argue, or put the pickup in park. It was rolling when I grabbed the handle and yanked the door open. She'd already thrown herself over the console and into the passenger seat when I slammed the transmission into reverse. Three men rounded the end of the block at a run, all carrying weapons. It was time to get gone.

There was barely enough light to see when I squinted into the side mirror. The tires threw up a cloud of white smoke until there was enough room to turn into the alley where Esteban disappeared. A gangster with a machine pistol appeared in the arched opening. Muzzle flashes strobed the area as the weapon raked left to right spraying a little house several feet away. I hoped there was no one home and threw the transmission into drive.

"Buckle up!" I hit the foot-feed. We shot forward

into what I thought was an alley, but turned out to be a narrow dirt street. Tall earth-tone colored stucco walls flashed past on either side, broken only by gated openings into the tiny patios. I hoped no one stepped out to see what all the fuss was about, because the truck's side mirrors had only inches to spare on each side.

The block wasn't long, and when I slowed at the next street, a set of headlights came on. It was still light enough to make out Esteban standing half in and out of a Toyota Tacoma pickup. I partially opened the big Dodge's door to he could see who was behind the wheel.

He nodded and dropped down into the seat, gunning the truck's engine and waving at us to follow. After half a dozen turns, some down similar alleys, we were soon out of town. I followed right on his bumper as we shot west down a two-lane road. I glanced in the rearview mirror. No one was following, yet.

I had to force my hands to relax on the wheel as we trailed Esteban's taillights down the highway. "What'n hell just happened back there?"

Fosfora pulled several strands of thick black hair from her face and tied a thick ponytail with a strip of leather to keep it from whipping in the slipstream. "*Mira wey*. I don't know."

I let her sarcasm pass. "What did you see?"

"One of the food carts opened back up after you went inside, and I went over to get something to eat. I was finishing my tortilla under one of the trees and saw some *cholos* coming down the street, walking. They were carrying guns, but that's not unusual. They always have guns out to scare everyone.

"A nice man I didn't know came up to me and told me to talk to him. He said that if he was with me, the *cholos* might not notice me. He hates the gangsters that have taken over his town. So I acted like we were together while two went inside the store where you were. I was going to stay there until they came back outside, but the next thing I know people are shooting."

"The ones you saw?"

"No. Others. People I hadn't seen. They were suddenly everywhere. I ran to the truck and jumped in it when neither one of you came back outside. I thought you two might have gone out the back, so I drove around to find you and that's when the shooting started. Where's Alejandro?"

"He's dead."

Her face went blank. *"Neta? No manches?"*

"Yeah, for real."

She licked her lips and turned to look back over her shoulder, as if I wouldn't have let her know if someone was coming up behind us. "We need to get back to Ciudad Acuna."

"The only way is back through town, and I'm not interested in doing that right now."

She jerked her head toward the windshield. "So we're following who?"

"My contact. Name's Esteban."

"Where are we going?"

"Wherever he takes us."

"Let me out at the next *ejido*."

"I don't know when that'll be, and it's probably not safe for you to be in some strange one-horse town by yourself."

"Horses?"

"It's an old saying. You don't need to be alone any-place around here, especially little . . . *como se dice* . . . community?"

"*Comunidad.* As for your one-horse town, we would say *pueblo pequeno,* but it isn't as descriptive."

"Well, no matter what you call it, I don't feel right dropping you off in the middle of nowhere."

"I have my *pistola.*" She laid it on the seat between us, and I wondered why I hadn't noticed it in her hand. Her eyes widened, and a second later she was on her knees, leaning over the console and digging around in the back. "Where's that little *ametralladora*?"

I wondered that myself. "I have a good idea Esteban has the Scorpion now. Is that Cordura bag still back there?"

"Cordura?"

"Tough material. The gray backpack."

"Yes."

"Hand it up here."

Snagging it by the straps and passing it over, she flipped back around like a pensive child. "How'd he get Scorpion? *When* did he get it?"

"That's a good question."

I unzipped the pack with one hand and felt around inside. The Beretta's magazines were still there. Main-taining a light touch on the steering wheel, I ejected the almost empty mag from the pistol's butt and snapped another in its place. Releasing the slide, I tucked it under my leg and put the bag on the floorboard.

The blazing orange and yellow horizon ahead would have been something to admire in any other situation. It lost its appeal half an hour earlier when people were shooting at us.

She settled down without putting her seatbelt back on. Someone must have monkeyed with the electronics under the dash, because that annoying warning bell didn't go off. "Don't worry about me. My brother will come get me tomorrow, since I haven't called in."

"Do I have to point out that we're on our way to somewhere else?"

"He does not look too smart, but he is. I told him about the houseware store in El Cruce. He will call when he gets there and sees what happened."

"Call where?"

She dug in her purse and held up a battered cell phone.

I snorted. "Yeah, well, mine didn't get a signal there in town." Realizing I hadn't checked my own phone since before we went into the store, I dug it from my back pocket. As I figured, there was no service. "And it sure as hell ain't gonna ring right now."

"You don't live here. We have learned to communicate when we have to. He will find some place in town with a signal and will call tomorrow at noon. If I don't answer, or call him five minutes after that time, we will try again at six." She watched the depressing landscape flash past. "I will find a signal somewhere. They are stronger when we get closer to the border."

"Y'all work the system."

She gave me a grin. "*Sí.* It is how my people have survived revolution after revolution, by working the system." She intentionally emphasized her accent, making it sound like *see-stem.*

I didn't take the bait. "But we're not going to the border, I don't think."

"Yes, we are. I know this road."

"Where does it come out?"

"Cuenca Seco."

"Dry Basin. What a name for a town."

"It's what you call a one-horse town."

Chapter 25

The moon was full and bright enough that we drove without headlights, plowing a hole in the darkness as cool desert wind whipped through the open windows. The dim glow from a distant pair of headlights popped up over the horizon far behind us. We hadn't seen more than a couple of vehicles since we left.

Back home, we'd have been passing the flickering posts of bobwire fences, along with brush and mesquite trees and a steady string of cars destined to places unknown. Here it was nothing but scrub brush alternately growing close to the two-lane, then an expanse of open ground.

Once, well off to the right, we saw dozens of flickering campfires. Silhouettes of cars and other unidentifiable vehicles flashed between us and the fires. Out close to the highway, a dozen men squatted in the darkness beside a pickup, watching us pass.

When we neared with our headlights off, two rose, as if in challenge.

Esteban's little Toyota truck didn't slow and neither did I.

The fires disappeared into the distance. I twisted the light switch, turning on the dash lights enough to check the gas gauge. There was still a quarter of a tank left, and I wondered what kind of mileage the old Dodge was getting these days. I flicked it back off. "Who are those people?"

"*Inmigrantes*, probably from Guatemala. They are walking to Texas."

For every mile we traveled, the headlights came closer. When they reached a distance of about one hundred yards, the car slowed and paced us. The moonlight was bright enough for them to see our vehicle, and I was sure the reflectors warned them that we were ahead. I flicked on my own lights and kept going, waiting for them to pass. They didn't. Taking my foot off the gas, I slowed. They slowed also. I didn't like that one damn bit. "Keep that pistol handy."

Noticing that I kept looking behind us, Fosfora glanced in the mirror on her side. "What's wrong?"

I tilted my head. "Guy back there's pacing us."

She didn't like it any better than I did. I didn't want Esteban to get too far ahead, so I gave it the gas and we caught back up with him.

We plowed on through the darkness until Esteban's brake lights flickered. He slowed and drifted off the road, onto the shoulder. I thought he was dozing off, or stopping to deal with the car behind us, but my headlights picked up a two-lane track angling off toward a ridgeline to the north. He hit the dirt with a rooster tail of dust and kept going at a slightly slower pace than when we were on the highway.

I let off the gas and followed, rocks rattling against the undercarriage. Growing up on dirt roads, I knew to back off from the plume of dust rising from beneath his Toyota. "Roll your windows up."

She did and my stomach knotted with the question of what was going on. Nothing made sense at that point. Was Esteban leading us into an ambush? And who was in that car behind us. If he wanted to kill us, he could have let that happen back in town.

He rounded a bend and slowed even more. An SUV was waiting in the darkness, facing our direction. The headlights flashed on and Esteban stopped.

Squinting into the brightness, I slammed on the brakes and slid to a stop. "Dammit. Is this another shakedown, in the middle of the night?"

I saw Fosfora's head shake in the lights of the dash. "No. It might be smugglers or coyotes, or even the road leading up to a cartel ranch house."

The whole thing was a mess, and I wanted out. Shifting the transmission into reverse, I twisted to see over my shoulder and back up. Old habits die hard, and I wasn't going to trust the mirrors. The car that had been following caught up to us and slid to a stop. I figured they had us.

Before I could stomp the gas, the night behind us exploded with the flash and roar of automatic weapons fire directed at the sedan. There was an ambush all right, but it was directed on the car that had been following us. I had the Beretta in my hand as the light show flickered through the truck's back glass, the sounds of gunfire muffled by the closed windows. The yellow bursts of at least three weapons on both sides of the dirt track looked like sparklers in the darkness.

It was surreal, sitting in a settling dust cloud while

chaos ensued in the rearview mirror, and calm reigned thirty feet ahead. There was no return gunfire from the car that slowly drifted at idle speed off the track and into the desert.

Blocked in from the danger behind, I threw the gearshift lever into drive and almost stomped the gas, but Esteban stayed where he was, blocking any escape attempt I had in mind. Driving across the desert was impossible. In our headlights, boulders that had rolled down the ridge were scattered everywhere, along with thick stands of banana yucca, lechuguilla, and a buttload of tree cholla rising up toward the sky.

The light show ended, and the desert was once again silent. Esteban opened the door and stepped out, waving for me to follow. "It's all right. These are friends." Without waiting for an answer, he dropped back in the truck and crept forward past the waiting vehicle.

Still not sure of what was happening, I hesitated, thinking. A man stepped into the open between us and the parked SUV, backlighting himself. He waved. I accelerated gently, holding the Beretta on my right thigh. "Keep that pistol of yours ready."

We drew close to the car and my eyebrows rose. The guy in the headlights was an *anglo* dressed in desert camo and loaded with battle gear. He would have been right at home in Iraq. I slowed and he twirled his finger, ordering me to roll down my window. I did and pulled forward.

"No more lights, sir." The hard-looking young man with a high and tight haircut exuded military testosterone. He wore an expensive set of night vision goggles up on his forehead and leaned forward to peer inside before giving me a big smile and speaking with a distinctly southern accent. "Nice shirt. Your last name's Hawke?"

Surprised, I sat there with my mouth open. It was a good thing there were no flies swirling around my head. One sentence I'd memorized in high school Spanish popped into my head. *En boca serrada, no entran moscas*, or loosely translated, Flies cannot enter a closed mouth.

What an odd thing to remember at such a strange time. My mouth closed with a pop.

"Lights, please."

I snapped them off. "Funny meeting you here in the middle of nowhere."

The guy frowned and threw out another question. "I need confirmation. What LEO agency are you with, sir?"

"Why?"

"Just wanted to make sure who I was talking to. I'm Judge." He didn't offer his hand. It rested on the grip of the battle rifle slung over his chest.

"Pleased to meet you, Judge. Sonny Hawke, Texas Ranger."

"How long you been on the job, sir?"

Those two questions told me a lot about those guys. "Been with them for ten years. Before that, I was highway patrol. It's really me."

His grin returned. "Right answer. Come on in, sir. You're safe now."

I threw a thumb over my shoulder. "Those guys in the car back there?"

"Neutralized. They were the bad guys. Hidalgo Cartel. The car and the occupants will be gone in fifteen minutes."

"Hard country."

"They made it that way, sir. Not us."

"My turn with the questions."

His grin widened even further, but cut me off. "Can't say much, sir, but we've been working with Esteban for a good long while now. We're the good guys." Still grinning, his eyes flicked to Fosfora. "Ma'am, you can point that weapon somewhere else now."

I realized she had the muzzle pointed more in my direction than toward the undercover agent. I pushed it away with a fingertip. "Yeah, I've been shot enough this year."

"Yessir. Left trapezius. See? We know who you are." Judge pointed north. "Follow Esteban around that copse of brush. We have people and rations there."

"How'd you know it was me?"

"Besides Esteban's call, we got another one from higher up. Voice told us a friend of yours code name Perry Rodriguez said you might be coming this way."

Good old Yolanda Rodriguez and Perry Hale.

But then again, I was frustrated that Esteban had a Sat phone and I didn't. I made myself a promise that I'd get one as soon as I got back to the states, and damn the cost.

Chapter 26

The Special Operations unit was making a cold camp against the sloping wall of the high ridge I'd seen from the highway. Another SUV was parked nearby, all four doors and the rear cargo hatch standing wide open. They'd either removed the light bulbs, or had rewired the vehicle so the dome lights didn't come on when someone opened the door.

We didn't need the lights once the moon came up, washing the desert in pale, cold light. Esteban's Toyota pickup wasn't there. Instead of stopping at the camp, he'd driven on past and was gone. I didn't like that one little bit, because I couldn't figure out why he'd led us there in the first place.

At first, Judge didn't seem inclined to talk. Other than to tell us there were other guys in the group, but they were busy dealing with the ventilated sedan full of cartel bodies.

He leaned into the Dodge and knocked the dome light out with the butt of a large knife. "Sorry sir. We can't have lights coming on and off out here tonight."

"It's not my truck, but I doubt that little dome light'll

make much more of an impact on the night than your ambush back there."

"You're right about that." He slid the knife back into its sheath on his chest. "But it's protocol." He led us over to the rear of the SUV backed against a cluster of large boulders. "Sorry we don't have spare NVGs for you guys, but your night vision will sharpen with the lights off."

Some kind of desert bush I didn't recognize created a natural screen around the vehicle. The cargo section was packed with a variety of boxes and bags. A collapsible table set up at the rear was filled with packets of Meals Ready to Eat, also known as MREs.

He dropped the NVGs into place. "I wouldn't be using these, except it's damn dark in here." While Fosfora took in our surroundings, he rustled around in the back of the SUV, fiddled with a plastic bag for a few minutes before reaching into a pocket and pulling out a small plastic collapsible cup. He filled it with coffee. Half-sitting on the rear of the SUV, he held it out. "MRE coffee. Only comes in packets that make six ounces, which ain't much, but's hot and has caffeine. That's all I can say."

I took it and offered the cup to Fosfora. She shook her head, holding up a hand. "I don't like coffee."

Shrugging, I sipped at the steaming liquid and coughed. "Don't worry. This ain't coffee."

"I'm surprised you didn't spit it out." One of the other guys in full battle gear materialized from the darkness. He was also looking through goggles. "Worst coffee in the world, but I like the caffeine jolt. Nice shirt, by the way."

I glanced down at my Aloha shirt that seemed to

glow in the moonlight. Staring into the blackness of the cup, I remembered that coffee was the reason I was in that bright shirt in the first place.

"Let me show you how to do it, so you don't have to *drink* that shit, sir." The new arrival rummaged through the MREs and located another packet. He ripped it open and poured the powdered coffee into his bottom lip like he was dipping snuff. Then he added a packet of sugar, puffing the lip out even further. Packing the whole mess with his tongue for a minute, he swallowed what had already dissolved. "Tastes pretty bad even like this, but I've learned to like it." He held out a small pack. "Cream?"

"No thanks, and you don't have to call me sir." Shifting to sit on a chair-high boulder, I sipped the dark liquid, thinking it might at least *look* like coffee in the light, but it sure didn't taste that way. "I never was in the military."

"We know who you are. You're one of us." He reached out a hand. "Call me Jury."

I returned his shake. The guy's hand was like a vise. "Jury . . . and Judge, not your first name like I thought. Code names."

Judge nodded at the other members of his group who drifted in to join us. "That's Executioner . . . but we call him Ex for short."

They all looked like strange bugs with the NVGs over their eyes and carried tricked out AR-style rifles muzzle down on their chests. They were walking armories, with more guns and knives strapped to their bodies than most people have in their closets. I figured they were the ones who ventilated the cartel members behind us. I wondered what they'd done with the corpses and the car.

The guy beside him picked up a loaded magazine from those stacked in back of the SUV and slid it into the empty pocket on his vest. He had a strong Hispanic accent. "That's really because of all his ex-wives."

Soft chuckles in the cold desert air. We were hunkered up beside a rocky ridgeline. The other three directions were wide open to the flat landscape, and the waxing moonlight revealed everything, even the shapes of boulders lining the rim far above. I felt the desert chill for the first time that night, and shivered as a meteorite streaked overhead.

They didn't take off the goggles, and I realized that they were keeping watch on our surroundings. One always faced outward while the others replaced used magazines, and they switched out, taking turns as if through some mental communication process.

"This smartass is the Prosecutor. You can't tell it, but he's a redhead like yourself."

"We gotta stick together." I sipped the coffee again and wished I hadn't.

"Yessir. Then there's Defender there that popped off about ex-wives. He hated the name Defense." He pronounced it Dee-fence.

Defender grinned, teeth white in the darkness. "It sounds like a football term, and I'm the only guy in the world who hates football." His accent told me English was his second language.

Prosecutor turned to scan the area. I liked that. Seeing no movement, he swung back around. "Tell 'em what you *do* like."

"Planting cartel members." Defender's voice was flat. His Spanish accent deepened. "They killed my grandparents down in *Camargo*. Every one of those *pendejos* I catch will pay with their lives."

"And he's in a *good* mood today." Judge jerked a thumb to his left. "The last guy is Victim."

"Victim?" Fosfora was obviously confused, but I almost wanted to laugh at the courtroom nicknames.

"He comes by it naturally. If something happens, it happens to him first. Hell, he even got stung by a scorpion today, and we haven't had that happen before."

Victim pointed to his neck. I could see a small bandage over his left jugular. "Little bastard crawled up on my shoulder and hit me before I even knew it was there. It still hurts like a bitch!"

More chuckles.

"Interesting names. Y'all come up with 'em?"

"Nossir. They came from the Governor, and I suspect I know what you're angling at. Don't ask who he is or who he works for. This country down here is twisted like a nest of rattlers, and that kinks things up on both sides of the border so much you don't know who's who." Judge dug into an open pack beside him, feeling in one of the cargo pockets. "Now we're mixed up with them."

"You're here to deal with the cartels, though."

"You don't *deal* with cartels. I can tell you we're here on a special assignment." He handed a small packet to me, and offered one to Fosfora. "Energy bars. It'll make that nasty witch's brew taste a little better. I'd offer you an MRE, but we've already eaten the good stuff, though I think there's one beef stew left."

I suddenly realized I was starving and hadn't eaten since early that morning. "This will be fine." I peeled the packet open and bit into something that tasted like peanut butter flavored sawdust. I saw Fosfora wolfing her bar like she was starving, though she'd eaten earlier while I was meeting with Esteban.

That reminded me. "Well, guys, thanks for taking us in." I chewed for a moment. "Where's Esteban?"

Judge answered. "He's gone already. He's like a ghost."

"He didn't drive out the way we came in."

Judge jerked a thumb. "Back way. Winds through a gap in this ridge and comes out a little farther down the road."

"He already knew you guys were here."

Judge nodded. "He stopped by on his way to meet you."

"Y'all're working together then."

He shrugged. "More or less."

"He coming back?"

"You never know."

"Well, that kinda leaves us hanging."

"It won't. You're just lucky we happened to be where we are. We're leaving you two right here while we go do a little work tonight, then we'll be back by sunup and stick around here all day tomorrow, then we all head for the border when the sun goes down. We leave your truck where it is and you two ride with us."

"It'll be crowded."

He shrugged. "We'll make it work. You'll be back across by daylight after that."

"I'm not staying here all day tomorrow," Fosfora snapped. "I need to get back."

I almost heard Judge's eyes harden. "You'll do what I say . . . ma'am. You two are secondary to our mission. If this man wasn't a Ranger, I'd leave you right where you're sitting, come daylight."

"You guys get caught over here in that gear, it could spark an international incident. Invading army and all that." I sipped the coffee again. It tasted worse as it cooled.

"Yessir. That's why we won't *get* caught. Sir, why are you here, if I can ask? All we know is that Esteban said he needed to drop off two packages under our care. And then that call from your people of course that verified your I.D."

"I came across on a murder and attempted murder investigation. Two elderly sisters in Del Rio were attacked by cartel members, but we didn't have any idea why. I believe they're possibly connected to the murder of a Border Patrol agent, and a female cartel leader's running the whole shebang."

"Yeah, that nest of snakes thing." Judge and Jury exchanged looks. Judge sighed. "We know about that."

"What?"

Jury took his turn at scanning the area while Judge paused, weighing something in his mind. Coming to a decision, he scratched his scalp under the helmet. "You didn't hear this from me, but now I think you need to know. Have you ever heard of the Devil Woman of Coahuila or the Hidalgo cartel?"

I nodded "I heard a guy mention it once."

"The narco government down here's allowing a female cartel member to run the country and she's getting *wayyyy* too much power. They won't arrest her, because she's pouring money into their pockets, more than all the other cartel leaders combined. We keep hearing about raids on different safe houses and ranches, but they always say she wasn't there when the police or military arrives."

"That's pretty standard."

"Yessir. So now *we* know where she is."

He left the conversation hanging.

"You guys are going after her."

"I didn't say that, sir."

"I've heard of her. I'm going with you."

"Nossir. You're not."

I told them about the Movie Lot Massacre and my part in the attack. When I got to the part about shooting the undercover agent, they shifted and swayed like grass in the wind, uncomfortable with the thought. I told him everything I knew about what happened to the sisters in Del Rio.

"That makes no difference, sir." Judge sniffed through dry sinuses, the sound loud in the night. "Our job is to take you back with us when we return, and to put you in the hands of Perry Rodriguez."

"Well, that's actually two people. Perry Hale and Yolanda Rodriguez. They're my team."

"So you understand what we're supposed to do."

"Yeah, but I'm going with you."

Adjusting the goggles in front of his eyes, Victim sorted through a box of MREs, probably so he wouldn't have to pay attention to our argument.

My phone buzzed with an incoming text message that was loud in the quiet night. I had a signal. "I'll be damned. I bet it's from my wife. Hold that thought."

"Don't take that phone from your pocket." Judge scanned the area. "Get in the back seat and cover your head with this blanket. Two minutes, and I better not see so much as a glow in there."

Feeling like a scolded teenager, I climbed into the SUV and sent three quick texts.

Chapter 27

Fosfora bucked and snorted when I told her she was going to wait there or take Alejandro's truck and drive her butt on back to Ciudad Acuna by herself. She didn't want to get caught driving a dead man's pickup, but she didn't like the idea of staying all alone at the camp by herself.

"What if all of you get killed?"

"Then you can drive yourself to whatever little *ejido* is closest and ditch the truck. You said yourself you could ride your thumb back home. And besides, didn't you tell me that brother of yours was coming to pick you up?"

A look passed over her face, but I couldn't figure out what it meant. "At some point."

"So there you go."

She frowned into the darkness, watching the team gear up.

Judge and Ex pulled several cartons from the SUV and stacked them against the rocks to make room. Judge waved me over. "Changed my mind. You can go as far as the jumping off point. We can use you to wait with the vehicle, but you don't go in with us."

I wanted to argue, but thankful for the small victory, I for once remained quiet.

Judge nudged one with his toe. "We're leaving the extra ammo here. All six of us in this Expedition will be crowded, but that's the way it'll have to be."

Defender came up and handed me an AK-47 and several loaded magazines. They all carried modernized rifles, and it was a surprise to see it in his hands. "I don't like these things, but they're reliable." His soft voice didn't fit with a man who loved planting cartel members. When he wasn't irritated, his accent was light. "You familiar with this *cuerno de chivo?*"

I took the Russian-made rifle and popped the goat's horn–shaped magazine to see that it was fully loaded, then made sure a round was chambered. My palm came away slightly sticky. "I've shot 'em."

He handed me the Cordura backpack loaded with magazines for the Beretta. "There were some 9mm empty mags in your truck. I reloaded them with our stock, then threw in a couple more boxes, along with rounds for the AK. The bad guy only had one other mag, so you'll have to hand load it if you have to use this thing. Other than that, you should be good to go. Sorry I couldn't offer you a better rifle, but this was all those guys had in that car we took out."

So that's what was sticky on the pistol grip. The previous owner's drying blood.

I tried not to think about it as I wiped my hand on my jeans. "This'll do just fine."

Judge came around. "You do what we tell you, when we tell you, sir. You're to stay with the vehicle as we deal with our business. It'll likely be hot when we leave, so you're the designated driver."

"You taking her or killing her?"

"Does it matter?"

"To me. I'd like to talk to her as part of that investigation, and I'm not a fan of assassination teams."

The guys around us shifted back and forth in the shadows of the setting moon. It was a much different pattern of movement than their deliberate process of loading up for battle. This time they were fidgeting around to stay close and listen to our conversation. Not that I could blame them. They had orders and I was the wild card, changing their mission.

Judge adjusted the rifle hanging over his chest. "You know I don't have to take you at all. You're what I guess we'll call the secondary interest. You can stay here. In fact, I'd prefer that."

"My CO, the Major, ordered me to find out what's going on with these hits back home. If they originate here, she'll be the prime suspect and we can extradite her." That even sounded stupid to me, but I had to make my case. "I can't talk to her if she's dead."

"Sir." Judge's voice hardened. "As one redhead to another, I can understand how you feel. I'm feeling it right now." He paused to let that sink in, telling me he was getting irritated, but I was, too, though it shouldn't have been directed toward a man who'd saved my bacon earlier that evening. "But I have my orders and you know as well as I do, we're operating in a dangerous place. I need to concentrate on my job. You might think about doing yours *north* of the river. Remember, it's you who's insisting on going with us, not the other way around."

It was time to quit arguing. I shut up and shouldered the AK. "Fine, but I need to talk with her if I can."

"I haven't said she was our mission, sir."

"You haven't said she isn't either. So while we're out driving this evening, and if you know where this Devil Woman lives, would you mind if we stop by her house so I can knock on the door?"

They laughed and the tension was broken.

We loaded up in the Expedition, and I saw Fosfora through the side mirror, watching us drive away.

Chapter 28

squeezed in the back seat between Ex and Victim, two guys big as mountains. Prosecutor rode in the rear cargo area, saying he preferred to spread out rather than to be stuck in the middle between those guys. I wish I'd thought of it before everyone loaded up.

Though the Expedition had a lot of room, it was crowded in there between two professional shooters covered in battle gear and firearms. I added a little to the constriction because of the tactical vest they gave me. I'm sure I looked ridiculous with it strapped over my flowery yellow Aloha shirt, but it was better than getting shot again.

The desert camo vest helped hide some of the shirt's glare, and I was thankful for that. No one had brought extra clothing, or I would have borrowed at least a T-shirt. They were dressed for the mission, and spare shirts for visitors weren't included.

Judge spoke over his shoulder. "We're making entrance into the compound at three. That's all you get to know. When we come back, it may be hot, so I need you behind this wheel, waiting. Just be ready to drive us the hell out of there when we exfil. That's your job."

He paused, thinking. "I oughta have my head examined, bringing you along though."

"It's not your fault. I'm impulsive."

"What's that mean?"

"It means I'm giving you an out. This is my idea, but I don't like staying behind."

"Roger that. But you keep your ass right here in this vehicle, Ranger. You may be able to throw some weight around north of the river, but down here, I'm the stud duck."

I have no idea what Defender was using to guide him along the dark desert, but we'd long since left the paved road and were zigzagging westward along a web of dirt roads. I lit up my phone, but the No Service sign was up.

Victim grunted. "Technology, huh. Nothing works down here in hell."

"It probably wouldn't work right for me if we were in the middle of a city."

Ex coughed a laugh. "I was in Honolulu a couple of years ago and the damn map application wouldn't load. I walked fourteen miles that day to a place that was three miles from where I started."

Judge glanced back over his shoulder, but didn't chime in. I'm sure he'd seen his men prepare for a mission a thousand times before, and much of it was banter and cross talk to bleed off nerves.

I've rolled with SWAT many times in the past, and have always been a little surprised at the conversations between the officers as they rode into danger. It's their way of calming themselves before the storm.

As we rolled through the night, I checked the contents of my vest, making sure none of the magazines I'd inserted into the pockets had fallen out. It was impossible that they had, because they were designed to keep the magazines in until I needed them.

Ex watched me pat the pockets. He nodded. "I do the same thing."

"Nerves."

"Nerves and habit," Victim said. He placed his hand over a pocket on his vest. "First aid. Compression bandages. Everything I need in case I get hurt. It's an obsession with me."

I saw he'd changed the dressing on his neck to one that wasn't as bright. "I don't think I like sitting next to you."

"You shouldn't like sitting in the *car* with him," Prosecutor said from the back where he was folded in with Jury. "I don't. Hey, are you *trying* to hit every bump and hole in this damned desert? You're bouncing me around back here like a pinball."

Defender slowed, checked the device in his hand, and steered around a tall yucca. The two-track lane we'd been following vanished at the edge of a shallow arroyo. The steep, rugged ground made it possible to continue downward and across to the other side. He steered right and from there we followed the wash through the untracked landscape until he found a place he liked. After making a three-point turn, facing us back the way we came, he killed the engine. "Time to go to work."

We detrucked into the chilly air. The team quickly checked their equipment for the umpteenth time, mostly by feel, and dropped their NVGs into place. Judge nodded. "We'll be back in two hours at the most. You wait for three hours. That'll be around daylight. If we're not here, follow our tracks back to the highway. Turn right. One point five miles from that turn is a dry wash. That's our secondary exfil. Pick us up there."

"If you don't show up then?"

"Drive as far as you can to the border and dump the SUV. Don't get caught in it. There's enough armament in this thing to put you *under* a Mexican prison until the second coming. We have a third option, but you're not included in it."

"I'll need to get Fosfora."

He eyed me for a long moment. "She won't be there."

I was confused. "That's where you ordered her to be."

"She doesn't follow my orders, or yours, or anyone else's. She has her own job to do."

"What?"

"I told you. This country is twisted like a nest of snakes. She's already on the move, under a different name."

"What'n hell are you talking about?"

"She sometimes goes by Flaco, because she's a he, and he's working with us, though about half the time I'm not sure about that, either."

"But." I held both hands toward my chest, the way we did when we were kids describing the most recent sex symbol on television. "She has…"

"Yes. He does, and they're real. Now we have to go.

Trust no one." Judge paused as the guys faded into the darkness. "If I bring a prisoner back with me, you'll have the drive time between here and the border to question that individual. That's all I can offer."

They disappeared into the night, and I leaned back against the Expedition, trying to sort out what I'd just heard.

Chapter 29

The team was gone, and I waited in the desert beneath a canopy of stars.

Yeah, I should have done what they told me, but I didn't answer to Judge, or any of his team members. And I'd already explained that I was impulsive. They were after someone I had to find. She was ultimately the reason I was in this mess in the first place, and I was afraid they intended to kill her, and I needed the Devil Woman alive.

See, if they killed her, then maybe the murders and attempted murders on my side of the river would stop. But I wanted *justice,* not retribution or a reckoning. I wanted to know exactly who had ordered the hits on my fellow officers, who were destroying their lives and those of their families, and who would send an assassination team to kill two little old ladies.

If Judge's dark cover team killed her, who would say that the drug pipeline she'd been putting into place wouldn't remain, expanding and involving more officers. I chewed my lip for a little while longer, fighting the urge to do what I shouldn't have been doing in the first place.

I lost the argument with myself.

Leaving the keys in the ignition, I trotted through the pale moonlight in a dim arroyo lined with scrub brush and a few dejected cottonwood trees. Along the way, a lot of dominos fell into place, at least they seemed to.

Earlier that evening, when Defender was telling me about planting cartel members, he had a look in his eye that was familiar. It was at that moment that I remembered it was the same look in Border Agent Manual Trevino's eyes, lying the hospital bed back in Ft. Stockton when we talked.

Back there, Trevino was afraid of something, and wouldn't give me the whole truth. Now I knew that the cartel had gotten to him, threatening his family. And good lord, that's why they came after Miss Ruby and Miss Harriet. Agent Nelson had failed in some way, and they made him pay with his life and the lives of others. I remembered reading his file and seeing that beside his foster mother, the agent had only the grown daughter in Hawaii.

Ol' Davy Crockett said, "Be sure you're right, then go ahead." That's the way I've always operated, but there's nothing concrete in making sure you're right. There's always somebody who'll question right and wrong. But that's how I've always operated. Once I'm sure of what needs to be done, I'll do it. Sometimes there's an easier way, but by god I'll make a decision and do whatever's necessary to get the job done.

I trudged on, the little daypack full of ammo riding

comfortably on my shoulders, mentally flipping info cards in my head.

More dominos fell, like when I was a kid, lining them on end on my grandmother's smooth linoleum floor while warm breezes blew through the rusty window screens in their little farm in Northeast Texas. Once I'd placed the last one just so, I tipped it with a fingertip, watching the curved line of dominos standing on end fall in clicking rhythm.

Curved. Snakelike. A nest of snakes.

That's what Judge had told me, and that image had been writhing in my brain. It's odd how a man's mind works, allowing him to concentrate on the job at hand, twisting through desert cactus and scrub without getting a leg full of needles, while at the same time working on a mental problem. Sub-levels of consciousness are even in play, working behind the scenes, trying to sort out details I wasn't even aware of.

There was still enough moonlight above the arroyo that I could see their distinct tracks in the sand washed into soft white drifts from the last rain. The deep footprints stepped over a half-buried, sun-bleached log before angling up a slope leading to the top.

I followed, trying to put my feet in their tracks whenever possible. They'd taken what appeared to be a game trail angling up the opposite bank. When my head popped above the rim and halfway under a greasewood bush, the glow of lights from a nearby ranch told me I'd found their destination.

And mine.

The familiar, insect-like buzzing I'd heard several hours earlier cut through the still night air. This time I recognized it for what it was. Someone was piloting a drone, probably as security. I stayed where I was, trying to locate the source, until I saw a dark shape flickering across the stars nearly fifty yards away.

The drone was traveling in my direction, slow and steady. I slowly sank back down below the arroyo's rim and waited, tracking the irritating little machine by its sound, until the tone changed.

That wasn't good.

I knew it hadn't spotted me, it was too far away, and if it had, they'd've likely shot up overhead to check me out. I eased up to find the drone hovering thirty feet away. It remained in place for a few seconds, then made a quick turn and accelerated.

I rose and cursed myself for not waiting, praying the damned thing didn't have a camera in the rear. My mama had eyes in the back of her head, but I hoped the technology hadn't caught up to *her* uncanny natural abilities.

Give 'em five minutes, then follow.

The luminous hands on my wristwatch told me I only made it three minutes before I couldn't stand waiting any longer. The moon was low over a faraway ridgeline and I was about to take off when the night sounds ceased and the distinctive rattle of an AK-47 reached me as soft pops, like distant fireworks. I knew in an instant what it was. None of the team members carried the Russian-made rifles. I didn't have to wonder who was doing the shooting.

That firearm was joined by several others, and the battle rose in pitch that told me everything up ahead had gone south. The team's rifles were equipped with sound suppressors, so the loudest reports came from the bad guys.

That doesn't mean their rifles were silent. People think that putting what they call "silencers" on a rifle will eliminate all sound. They still make reports each time they fire, only softer. Listening to the battle, and that's what it was, was like picking out different instruments in an orchestra.

The bad guys liked to fire their weapons on full automatic. One or two seemed to run on forever until it stopped when the magazine ran out of ammo. Others ripped long and steady for maybe half a mag before stopping.

Judge's team was better trained. They fired quick three-round bursts most of the time, soft, like a baby's cough. They were surgical in their responses, both through training and to save ammo.

I checked my watch, wondering how long it would take running men to make the trip back to my position. There was no way they could proceed with their operation. All surprise was gone, and without knowing how many men they were up against, and how well armed, I doubted they'd press forward. By the time they arrived at the ranch, The Devil Woman would be gone.

Judge and his team probably *couldn't* try to fight their way into the house to find her. Or would they. Dammit! I didn't know enough about those guys, or their mission. Most of the Special Forces I'd ever encountered were outstanding fighters and crack shots. So maybe they were advancing, taking out every cartel member they encountered. Hell, maybe their whole plan was to shoot their way in and back out.

No matter, they were going to eventually come back my way. My initial half-baked plan was to follow them inside the compound, and once they'd neutralized all the bad guys, I could get a crack at deposing the Devil Woman.

But now things had changed. I'd just hunker right here and wait for them to come back. If they didn't shoot me on sight, maybe I could lend another gun to what I figured would be an organized retreat.

Since I had no idea how far away their objective was, I had no accurate unit of measurement on how long it would take them to reach my position. And that's if they retraced their own steps. Men in their situation might take any clear trail that would allow them to move fast. I knelt on one knee, thinking.

"I'd stay right there if I was you, Ranger."

The voice was soft, but firm. My heart stuttered and I almost jumped straight up. The smart thing to do was to stay still and hope I didn't get shot.

The voice came again. It was Victim. "I saw you coming a mile away in that neon shirt, sir. You've been wandering around like a lost calf. Judge's gonna be pissed when he sees you here."

My head about twisted off my neck, and it took several moments to find him, kneeling in a natural divot in the hardpan not far from where I'd climbed out of the arroyo. I couldn't believe I'd missed him. "Rear guard?"

"Yessir."

"I almost walked right past you and didn't see a thing in the shadows. You were gonna let me go."

"Yessir. My orders were to cover their exfil, not babysit you, but they've run into a problem and I can't have you wandering around right here. They're coming."

Squinting into the dimming light, I couldn't see any movement. "They close?"

"Roger that."

"There's a drone . . ."

"Yessir. It's come by twice on patrol."

The distant battle was moving. I figured it had become a runaway scrape headed our direction. Wishing I had a pair of NVGs, I stepped back to my greasewood bush and dropped down chest deep into the wash. "Tell me what you see."

"Nothing yet. Hang on." I heard him speaking softly. He was talking into a radio. It couldn't have been VOX, or voice activated, because they would have heard him talking to me and breaking protocol. "Shit! Ex is down!"

Tucking the AK's stock against my shoulder, I held the rifle pointed halfway to the ground, squinting toward the direction of the ranch. The glow from their lights looked almost pleasant against the star-filled sky, kinda like the promise of a cool oasis of civilization in the desert.

There it was again, that buzzing sound telling me the drone was close. It vibrated the air, coming in our direction twenty feet above the brush, glittering in the moonlight.

The gunfire picked up again, soft, but closer pops rattling the night. Sometimes it was one weapon, other times what sounded like three or four joined in.

The drone moved a few feet at a time, flying like a dragonfly, or what the Old Man called snake-doctors, zooming a few feet in my direction and pausing. The only thing it didn't do was rest on a stick or branch from time to time. It was positioning itself to pick up the retreat and send images back to the cartel members. They might even be able to swing around and flank the retreating team.

When that annoying little hummer came close enough and I could see it hovering still and steady against the stars, I drew a tight bead and pulled the trigger. It exploded in a spray of plastic parts.

"Just like target shooting, only different." I scanned the ground, looking for the team, and explaining to Victim why I'd fired. I wanted to be proactive. "I don't like being spied on. Besides, I bet you wanted to do the same. They're looking for the guys."

My night vision was momentarily shot from the muzzle flare, so I couldn't see Victim on my right. His voice came through loud and clear, though. "Good thinking, but against orders."

"I don't have 'em."

"You're gonna get us killed."

"Nah. If you believe my wife, she say's our time is already written in the Book when we're born, so there's nothing I can do to change that."

I could feel him studying me through the NVGs covering his eyes and I wondered what he was thinking. A bright light flickered to my left. Headlights. Someone was barreling in our direction and they had to have been on some kind of open ranch road to move at that speed.

My sight had returned enough for me to see him turn his head away to avoid the intense glare.

"Is that your team coming this way in a vehicle?" My voice was louder than I wanted it to be, but then again, things were getting tense.

Victim spoke into his microphone again for a second before answering. "No. Targets."

"You do your job." I rose from the arroyo. "I'll stop 'em."

"Wait!"

I've heard people holler that at me in the past, and it usually didn't work. I had no intention of waiting. Like those on my grandmother's linoleum floor, these dominos were falling faster, and I knew that vehicle was headed our way to intercept the team. I wasn't operating under orders from a man who didn't know what was going on around us.

With experience in running through the desert, I popped out of the arroyo, keeping an eye on the ground to avoid cactus or anything else that might cut, trip, or stab me. The headlights headed in my general direction bounced on the uneven ground. Doing the geometry in my head, I angled to intercept them. The engine roared and the lights steadied. They'd reached smoother ground.

Dammit! I couldn't get as far ahead of them as I wanted.

Those guys were intent on cutting the retreating team off, probably figuring to flank Judge's team and catch them in a crossfire with the others who were chasing him. I ran several more yards and finally saw the ranch road the vehicle was following. Dropping to one knee that landed on the sharpest rock in Mexico, I shouldered the Russian rifle and led the speeding SUV.

For a brief moment, the thought that it might be a car load of innocents fleeing the gunfire crossed my mind. Nope. There was enough light from the lowering moon to see the windows were down and the barrel of a weapon protruded into the night. Thankful for the AK's open sights, I settled them on the driver's side of the windshield and held the trigger down, letting the car's momentum pull them through the string of hot lead.

It was like leading a flying dove with a shotgun, letting the bird fly into the pattern of pellets.

The 5.56 rounds punched across the windshield, raking down the side and through the open windows as it passed, stitching holes in tempered glass, metal, and finally flesh. Holding the trigger down on full-automatic, I twisted, following the moving vehicle and keeping the sights on the open passenger window. A couple of rounds ricocheted off and whined into the distance as I swung the muzzle again into the back seat. The driver, wounded or dead, lost control of the vehicle that left the narrow dirt road and punched out with a loud bang into the thick trunk of a gnarled cottonwood tree that had been struggling for decades to live in the harsh desert.

Dropping the empty mag, I jammed a fresh one from my pocket into the empty well. It clicked into place. Advancing on the wrecked Suburban, I reached the driver side at the same time the rear passenger door popped opened and a shape stumbled outside, backlit by the dome lights and of all things, blue accent lights on the floor and in the doors.

A weapon in the man's hands came up and muzzle flashes froze him into my mind. Rounds whizzed by several feet away as he held the trigger down and sprayed in the hopes of hitting *something*.

I shouldered the rifle and took my time hammering him dead as a day-old stogie.

He was nothing but a dark, bleeding mass on the ground and beyond his still shape, I could see four very still bodies slumped in the seats like rag dolls. Or at least I thought they were all still. One guy in the middle of the back seat wasn't through. Whatever machine pistol he had in his hand went off, stitching the darkness.

I was pissed and tired of being shot at. I held the trigger down on the AK, anchoring him and the other two as well, just to be on the safe side. It's hard to hold the muzzle still on a fully automatic rifle, but I didn't mind the overspray in that situation.

Despite ears deadened by the gunfire, I reacquired the sounds of the running gun battle headed my way. "Coming back!" At that point, yelling didn't make any difference and I wanted to make sure Victim didn't mistake me for a surviving bad guy.

"I got eyes on you."

"Oh." I'd forgotten in all the excitement that he was peeking through NVGs.

"Good work, but get your butt back over here. What I can see of that damn shirt's glowing like a campfire."

"This is the last time I'm gonna come to Mexico in a tropical state of mind."

Chapter 30

The gunfire had been over for several minutes before Esteban, Incencio Aguierre, and Geronimo Manzano crept down the two-track lane, weapons ready and pointed at the silent, wrecked Suburban filled with their dead friends. It never paid to ride with the others. Most of the time the *soldados* were too impulsive, and felt they were invincible.

Incencio and Geronimo preferred their own vehicle, and because they spent so much time together on the road for their leader, no one ever questioned their actions. It looked as if habit and caution paid off once again when they killed the engine on a Suburban farther back and came forward on foot to intercept the retreating invaders, whoever they were.

Esteban wanted to cross himself in thanks. He'd almost gotten into the shot-up SUV, but because the seats were already full, decided to join the engagement with those he considered more professional.

* * *

Back at the ranch, things had already gone south when the drone operator, Carlos Tamayo, saw movement on his computer screen. The young man who'd been flying security drones for the past five years worked the controls and zoomed the camera in to pick out a man half-hidden under a bush. Half a second later the drone would have missed him, but the man tucked a leg into the shadows, giving away his position.

Watching the screen, he gently pushed the toggle with his thumb, moving the little aircraft forward a few feet, recording footage to be viewed later. Now that he knew what to look for, he picked up another human-shaped shadow, then another.

Carlos had orders to capture video but not engage, so he piloted the drone past the bush and continued on as if he hadn't seen a thing. At the same time, he radioed Incencio, telling him that several men were creeping up on the ranch.

In response, Incencio alerted the guards that a team was advancing through the darkness and word spread among the *soldados.* Always loyal to their boss, and constantly ready for a fight of any kind, the heavily armed men boiled out of their *barracon,* or bunkhouse, like fire ants.

Many of the *soldados* were former Mexican soldiers and quickly formed up into two ambush teams that moved through the *rancho*'s gate and melted on foot into the darkness between the *rancho* and intruders. Minutes later, they moved into place and waited to ambush the intruders who dared to enter their territory.

Unfortunately for the U.S. team, NVGs work great

in most situations, but against fighting men who lived in the desert and used the terrain to their advantage, the technology wasn't enough. Had they been using thermal imaging, the results would have been dramatically different.

Through intel supplied by the drone, the *soldados* had the team's position, and that's all they needed. Assuming anyone moving on them in the darkness was using night vision, they dropped into depressions in the ground or used the low vegetation for cover and became as still as rocks, waiting for the men to pass.

The U.S. team advanced quickly, much too confident in technology, passing through the impromptu ambush zone. Fixed on the ranch compound only a hundred yards ahead, they completely missed the armed men scattered around them.

When the intruders took a knee, concentrating on their target, the *soldados* opened up on them. The fight was brief and vicious, and the only thing at the outset that saved the infiltration team was their body armor.

Many of the cartel members thought they were shooting at spirits, ghosts that bullets passed through without damage. But ghosts didn't shoot back, and their incredibly accurate fire cut through the cartel gangsters like a scythe through green hay. But instead of standing and fighting, or pushing through, the huge camouflaged men fell back, covering their retreat in a manner none of the *soldados* had ever seen.

They kept up heavy fire even as the *Americanos* retreated. Their shouts in English cut through the darkness. "Moving!"

"Move!"

Their crescendo of gunfire increased, then decreased in a strange rhythm as the Americans fell back in increments, keeping up a steady stream of fire to pin the cartel members to the ground.

That was fifteen minutes ago, and now Geronimo knelt in the moonlight not far from the vehicle full of corpses, casting around for any sign of a second ambush. The other two followed his lead, heads almost touching.

Incencio dug a small walkie-talkie from his pants pocket and keyed the button. "They are close." He spoke so softly it was almost a whisper. "We are near where the drone went down. They are moving in our direction, but someone killed Ricardo and four others."

The radio clicked twice, indicating he was heard and understood.

Incencio pointed. "We go back to that game trail that drops into the arroyo. I know where it is, because this is close to where we used to practice with our weapons when Mapache was the head of our cartel, before you joined us, Esteban. They will be coming this way and will have to cross. We will wait until they get to the bottom of the arroyo and catch them in a crossfire."

Fully immersed in his identity as a cartel soldier, Esteban peered into the surrounding shadows. After so long, he easily slipped back and forth between two worlds, one as an undercover agent in a world of violence and death, the other as a loyal cartel soldier without any moral conscience.

Right now, he was that *soldado*, wondering who had the *huevos* to try an assault on the Devil Woman's *rancho*. It could be a rival cartel in the darkness, or Mexican soldiers working for the government or for themselves.

In a world of changing alliances, you never knew who was planning a takeover.

For that reason, Esteban was ready to kill anyone who crossed him. He'd long ago released himself from any guilt associated with what he had to do in the crime-ridden country of Mexico. He'd pay for it some day when he finally returned home, finished with the business of drug and human trafficking, and ready to live a normal life that he'd looked forward to way back in high school, before the El Paso police recruited him.

Then again, late into the night, when he was unable to sleep, he lay awake wondering if he'd ever be able to return to a normal life in the U.S.

But now he knew what he had to do to stay alive. Esteban and Geronimo retreated back the way they came. Fifty yards away, a game trail angled down into the deep arroyo. In line like the deer that had created the narrow pathway, they filed to the bottom and hurried in what would have been downstream, if there'd been water.

Geronimo stopped and pointed. "What is that?"

They froze, looking for movement and to let their eyes pick out any irregularities in the terrain. Esteban felt his breath catch. There was still just enough moonlight to register the neon yellow of a Hawaiian shirt. It was the Ranger he'd dropped off with the black ops team.

Maldito! Dammit! Why was that man here? He was supposed to have left for the border and should have been out of harm's way. Now Esteban was caught between a rock and a hard place, in that dangerous area between his two worlds.

"A man, standing just below the edge."

Incencio raised his weapon and Esteban grasped the barrel, pulling it downward. "No. Shots will reveal our position. I will kill him." He drew a sharp knife from the sheath on his belt and crept forward.

Knowing from experience how quickly Esteban could do the job, Incencio and Geronimo continued down the arroyo without looking back.

That bright shirt the man wore was like a beacon in the night. When Esteban got close, he saw the Ranger peering ahead. He was wearing a ballistic vest and had a daypack over his shoulders.

He was also armed with an AK-47. Esteban looked down at the Scorpion hanging from the sling over his shoulder, the one he'd taken from Alejandro's truck back in El Cruce, and wondered where the *anglo* had picked up such a weapon.

Never mind. The knife in his hand would go through the vest, or he could slide the blade in under the bottom edge, taking out the man's kidneys. It would be a painful death.

Each step was steady and deliberate.

Risking a quick glance over his shoulder, he saw the dark shapes of Incencio and Geronimo picking their silent way down the sandy wash. Replacing the knife, he selected a fist-sized rock. Breathing as shallow as possible through his open mouth, he followed the slope leading upward to the Ranger he couldn't kill.

But now that no one was watching, he could knock him in the head.

Gunfire exploded both up on the rim, and in the arroyo, covering his advance.

Chapter 31

Hurrying back to my arroyo, I slid down the slope until the edge was once again chest high. Some of my view was hindered by bushes and cactus, but anyone approaching would be silhouetted against the starry night sky. It wasn't perfect, but it'd do.

"Two minutes out." Victim's voice was strong, tense. "Someone else is down. The whole thing's a cluster. They've aborted the mission and left the Devil Woman behind. Didn't even make the ranch. Going silent."

Good thing the guns on both teams were now quiet or I'd have missed his loud whisper. My ears felt as if they were full of cotton from the gunshots. At least it helped muffle the steady ringing from tinnitus that reminds me each day that I should carry ear plugs everywhere I go.

Hooves coming my way told me the combatants had likely spooked a deer. I heard it pass and cut to my left, following the arroyo's lip.

"People on foot. Coming from your left. Shit!" Victim opened up on to his right with a quick three-round burst.

I wished I had a set of NVGs.

Wish in one hand and piss in the other and see which one fills up the fastest.

The Old Man's voice in my head was clear as a bell. I'd heard that old saw all my life. Mumbling under my breath, I shouldered the rifle and waited for those Victim'd warned me about to step into view.

Gunfire came from the arroyo behind us. Someone'd heard Victim's gunfire. I couldn't see the approaching running fight, but people shooting from slightly below would be easy to find. Cracks and snaps swarmed in his direction, whanging off limbs and whining away.

Pops and flashes filled the arroyo. My sixth sense told me someone was way too close and there shouldn't have been anyone over my left shoulder at all. A single crunch reached my ears. Gut tightening, I spun a second before stars brighter than those above us exploded from a blow over my left ear, and I felt the earth go out from under my feet.

Chapter 32

The dark night was quiet when I opened my eyes to see the world turned sideways. Lying on my stomach, I was at the bottom of the arroyo with a headache as big as the sky above. Instead of getting up, I stayed right there, taking stock of everything around me.

If anyone had been watching during that time, they'd've thought I was still out, though I ran through a quick list to check out my fine motor skills. Wiggling my toes, I was pleased to find that everything worked. My fingers twitched, so all the electronic wires were in place.

Though it was sandy under my cheek, sharp rocks told me that I'd have a few indentions there when I finally stood up.

Two soft pops in the distance proved Judge and his team were still in the fight, and I hadn't been out that long, but they came from the wrong direction. I figured that once he realized their original exfil had gone south, and they were cut off from their SUV, they'd moved toward the second escape plan.

No engines roared through the desert, and I didn't

hear any more drones over the roar of blood in my ears from the pounding ache that was about to split my skull. It felt like those old cartoons I'd watched when I was a kid. It wouldn't have surprised me if happy little bluebirds and stars were whirling overhead as my eyes rattled around in their sockets.

I couldn't lay there relaxing all night. Hoping no one was watching, I slowly sat up.

The world spun for a moment, and my stomach clenched. I had to hold down that rotten coffee and the energy bar I'd choked down earlier. My head was loose on my shoulders, and nausea came and went like rhythmic ocean waves. The good thing was that each wave was less intense than the previous one.

Hoping I wouldn't find any fresh bullet holes with my shaking fingers, I probed my scalp with light fingers, dreading the discovery of a new orifice proving someone shot me. I was as pleased as possible under the circumstances to find that my skull was reasonably intact, but a knot big enough to have its own zip code stuck out behind one ear. While I lay on my side, blood from a wide gash in my scalp matted my hair. When I finally sat up, a small trickle went down my neck.

What'n hell are they doing hitting me in the noggin instead of shooting me?

Someone wanted you taken out of commission, son. The Old Man's voice made my head ache even worse. *But they want you alive for some reason.*

His ever-present voice in my mind was right. Bullets do more damage and are likely to be permanent. Someone wanted me out of action for a while.

The AK was lying in the sand beside me, the stock shattered.

The vertigo-like symptoms were already fading, and I remembered the firefight that broke out around me just before everything went blank. Still seated, I cast around, looking through the fading moonlight for Victim. He was nowhere in sight.

I creaked to my feet at the same time a skinny coyote came loping along the arroyo's lip. Seeing me standing there, it whirled and disappeared toward the ranch. "Vic?"

My whisper faded into the silence.

A quick scattering of shots came to me as soft as popping corn. I wasn't sure they sounded that way because the shooting was so far away, or because of the cotton that was in my heard from the recent gunfight, or the bonk on my noggin.

Vic must have followed orders after I was hit and covered for his men as they passed through. All I had to do was follow our original tracks back to the Suburban and drive off, hoping they'd made their escape as planned.

But then another thought popped into my aching head.

Judge and his team hadn't reached the *rancho*. The operation was aborted. That meant the *Mujer Malvado,* the Devil Woman was still there, and likely with minimal protection. With the majority of her *soldados* off chasing the black ops team, it was the perfect time to do something completely stupid.

You're being impulsive again, son.

The Old Man is always talking, no matter where I am. I'm probably the only guy in the world who argues with the ghost of a man who's still living.

I prefer to think of it as being innovative, though

somewhat impulsive. Miss Russell always said "use your time wisely."

Of course, that same seventh-grade teacher always told me that every bad thing I did in class would go on my permanent record, too.

I climbed back up that game trail one more time and knelt beside the greasewood bush, listening. The moon was resting on the mountain ridge to the west and not providing as near as much light as it did. Just to make sure Victim was gone, I crept across the hardpan toward where he'd been hiding. Maybe he'd left a message of some kind.

A dark shape lay on the ground. The bottom of my stomach fell out, because he was way too big to be Mexican.

"Vic?"

He didn't answer, because he couldn't. Kneeling beside the body, I found him lying in a black puddle of blood still soaking into the ground. "Dammit, Vic. You still with me?"

I rolled him onto his back and half his skull was gone. Still not believing what I was seeing in the faint light, I felt his carotid, but there was no pulse. There was nothing to do for the man.

Though I hated to, I tugged his AR's sling free and slipped it over my shoulder. I thought about swapping shirts with the dead man, but that was a little too much.

His NVGs were around his neck like a loose tie. I needed them, badly. Gritting my teeth at the gruesome job at hand, I worked them over what was left of his head as gently as possible, even though he was way beyond feeling anything at all.

The bullet that killed him missed the glasses, and

they seemed to be in good shape. Choking down that coffee and energy bar again, I pulled the strap through my thumb and forefinger to strip off the blood, then wiped my hand on the leg of his pants.

Swallowing, I settled the NVGs over my eyes to reveal a bright, green world. Everything stood out in sharp relief and I found myself acting like a kid, examining my hands in the strange light.

Sonny, you're gonna get yourself laid out beside this man if you don't straighten up and fly right.

I said "yessir" to the Old Man in my head and got back to business. I left the daypack on the ground and pulled Victim's pack off. It wasn't as heavy as I thought it would be, but I was sure it had more of what I'd need before the night was over.

Settling the straps over my tactical vest, I took off toward the nearby glow made much brighter by technology borrowed from a dead man.

To avoid a potential ambush on the team's trail, I looped around through the countryside and quickly drew close to the *ranchero*. There was enough vegetation growing close to the compound's low walls I wouldn't stand out like a sore thumb. Had I owned the place glowing like a jewel in the desert, and been in the business of running drugs, I would have cut everything within a hundred yards down to the ground for a clear sight line.

Even from that distance and in the dark, I could tell the place had been there for a long time. It was likely a real working cattle ranch, but decades under a corrupt government probably drove the business into the ground.

Even through the green world, I could tell a lot of renovation had taken it from a simple ranch house and likely bunkhouses and barns, to an upscale villa, if that's the right word. Palm trees rose over thirty feet in height over the walls, and I guarantee some struggling rancher didn't plant *those*. Landscape lighting both within the compound and outside the walls had two functions, aesthetics and security.

The whole thing was built up against the steep slope of a ridge, probably for protection from south winds. The one-story main house rose up against that ridge. I scanned the elevated area as best as I could but saw nothing. If it were my place, I'd put security cameras up there, looking down in the courtyard, and a couple of guards, too, but I didn't see any human movement, up there at least.

Other than one guard standing near the open gate leading into the courtyard, smoking and staring into the glow of his phone, there was little else happening at the ranch. Kneeling in the darkness well beyond the spill of light coming from the compound, I studied my surroundings and watched the moon wink out over the ridge of low mountains.

As throbbing pain over my ear faded, second thoughts crept in. Here I was alone, on foot, planning to put the *phantom sneak* on the home of one of the most dangerous cartel leaders I'd ever heard about. Being impulsive sometimes worked out, but I wondered if this was truly a bad idea.

I wasn't trained in military tactics. The only ones I'd learned were from Perry Hale and Yolanda, and I'd never put them into practice. This was the time to cut and run, make my way back to the highway and maybe hook up with that caravan of immigrants headed north. I could dump the artillery, shuck the vest, and in my casual Aloha shirt, maybe blend in as a reporter or hanger on.

But that's when my stomach growled so loud that I was afraid I'd wake the neighbors. At the same time Stupid Guard over there with cell phone laughed and lightly swatted at a drone that buzzed up close and circled his head.

Even murderers played around.

Who was guiding the drones? Where was *that* guy? And how many of the damned things did he have? This bad idea was getting worse.

A stick snapped behind me and I swung around, rifle to my shoulder. One guy had already snuck up on me that night and dented my skull. I wasn't going to allow that to happen again. I'd already threaded my finger through the trigger guard when I saw a doe stop at my movement. We looked at each other for several seconds, me through lenses, her through what nature had provided. Deciding I might want to eat her, she stomped her foot once to make me move, and when I remained still, she bounded away.

I thought about doing the same thing, cutting to run, but Stupid laughed again at something he was looking at on his phone. If they'd been on high alert, he and others would be watching.

I put a couple of pieces together in that puzzle. Judge and his team had failed. Everyone chased after them, leaving a skeleton crew to man the compound. Those guys weren't worried, so they were getting updates from those who were dealing with the remainder of Judge's team.

It was time to go.

I decided to leave Stupid to his social media, if that's what he was intent on, and circled around, looking for another way in. They might have surveillance, but I was hoping they'd be standing down now that the initial assault had failed and everyone was chasing the intruders like hounds after a rabbit.

I slipped through the darkness, circling the compound and doing my best to look for cameras mounted on the walls. The drone buzzed around the *ranchero*'s circumference and disappeared around back, moving toward the steep rise to the south. I made it to the wall without being seen and paused to let the butterflies in my stomach settle down.

My mouth was dry as cotton. I remembered seeing the team members load several bottles into their packs. Victim said he was always prepared and I figured he'd have plenty in there. Good lord, I really wanted to suck down a bottle of water from my pack, but those plastic containers are like door alarms. It would crackle loud enough to wake the dead, and I didn't want to join those guys right then.

Four doors slammed on an unseen vehicle in the courtyard. An engine started.

Dammit! Everything I'd put together was wrong. There were more than a couple of guys in the *ranchero*. Back against the stucco wall, I waited to see what would happen next. Voices shouted back and forth. A minute later, extremely bright tail lights of a retreating SUV appeared from the front side and shrank as they sped down a dirt road.

At least four more people were off my field, if only for a short period of time.

The slight breeze from the compound brought the smell of rotting carrion. I wondered if I was close to trash cans. Garbage pickup in the desert was a stretch, and it was entirely possible that they were using a nearby wash or arroyo as a dump.

Climbing over the wall near the dump sounded like a good idea. Most folks wouldn't think about keeping watch in that direction or posting a guard there to breathe the stench all night.

A huge, waist-high boulder sticking from the base of the wall gave me an idea. It looked as if it had been there for centuries. Instead of designing the compound wall a few feet one way or the other, the builders had simply built over it, making the chunk of rock part of the architecture itself.

That's great from an aesthetic point of view, but it defeated the point of a wall, if its purpose was to keep people out. Standing on the boulder, I slowly peeked over and into a well-groomed and empty courtyard. There were no kind of anti-climb measures on top. I'd have expected something as common as broken glass set in the stucco, or spikes, or even concertina wire.

The smooth, flat surface made it easy to roll over the top and into the courtyard. The night-vision goggles strapped to my aching head gave me a clear view of my carefully landscaped surroundings and the sight of an oddly decorated mesquite tree several yards away.

Large crooked objects dangled from the limbs and I couldn't figure out what I was looking at through the green lenses. After studying it several moments the strange forms came clear and my breath caught at the horror of what I'd found. Hanging from wire handles were the gruesome remains of stained human spines and barely attached skulls. Grisly ornaments on a common mesquite tree.

She was truly a Devil Woman.

Chapter 33

The gunfire beyond the courtyard walls caused Carlos Tamayo to lock the door of what he called the Control Room. Oftentimes the portly technician saw himself as a pilot, one who operated his drones from as far as eight miles away. His expertise was technology and drones. He was far from being classed as a soldier.

An hour earlier, while making a routine security sweep, he'd located at least two people moving near the deep arroyo just east of the ranch. Then another. Anyone out there that time of the night was bad news.

He alerted Incencio who told him his men would handle the situation. Having done his duty and identified exactly where the intruders were, he toggled the drone and reversed its position to make a sweep along the arroyo, just in case there might be others skulking in the darkness.

He was right. A human shape caught his attention and then, as he swung the tiny aircraft around to get a better look, the live feed went black. When that happened, he second-guessed himself, wondering if what he'd seen was real or a camera malfunction.

He'd never lost a drone before, and it confused him. Fingers flew over the keyboard as he attempted to contact the missing aircraft. Annoyed that he was blind, Carlos was also frustrated that Hector Tejada was sitting a few feet away, watching porn.

The second technician's job was to man the security system with the cameras scattered throughout the ranch, but that wasn't happening. Usually conscientious, Hector was in the process of updating all the software in the windowless room that night, and to do that, he had to take the entire system down and bring it back up again.

He'd shut it down at midnight, not expecting trouble.

Chapter 34

Knowing for sure now that I was in the right place, I licked my dry lips and breathed through my mouth to avoid the stink. Turning away from the tree full of death, I scanned the tropical courtyard. There were no guards. No one patrolling the area. Dark windows in the surrounding buildings stood open, probably for air circulation. A few doors yawned wide, left open by those who split in a hurry to kill people.

Directly across the courtyard from where I crouched was what I assumed to be the main ranch house. The facing wall was one of those bi-folding glass walls designed to bring the outside in and gape open to the lush courtyard. The large room full of lights was way too bright for the NVGs, so I pushed them up on my forehead.

An agitated small person walked from one side of a bright room to the other, talking on a cell phone and waving a glass in the other hand. By the stride, and certain physical characteristics, it was obviously a woman.

I was about to move across the courtyard when a blow that felt like a Sammy Sosa homerun swing punched me in the upper left side of my chest. The impact and my own contracting muscles knocked me backward at the same time a dry buzz like an angry wasp hissed upward under my right ear.

The blow was followed by the crisp sound of a gunshot, and I realized the wasp was really the ricocheting bullet deflecting off the steel plate in my tactical vest. I landed with a hard thud, gasping for air.

Twisting in the general direction the shot came from, and still on the ground, I brought Victim's AR to bear on Stupid, the guy who'd been on his cell phone instead of guarding the gate. He'd apparently decided to do his job and check the grounds, finding me crouched there like a peeping tom. The shooter's mistake was that he expected that one round to take me out, and it would have if I hadn't been wearing a tactical vest.

There was an Expedition parked between me and the arched gate, and he'd used the SUV for cover until I stepped out into the open. He should have used all the firepower in his hands like his buddies, and the swarm of bullets would have likely hit something to take me and keep me there. Thinking I was down and out, he straightened to check the results when a three-round burst from my rifle killed the man who'd just shot *me*.

His mouth opened at the impact of at least one of the 5.56 caliber bullets. The cigarette in his lips tumbled down past the glow from a cell phone tucked screen outward in his shirt pocket. He staggered sideways, reaching out with one hand to steady himself against the Expedition. I took a bead on that glowing screen through the material and pulled the AR's trigger twice more, killing the guard and the phone at the same time.

He slid down to sit on the ground like he was tired, shoulder leaning against the fender. His head drooped against the side of the vehicle, and he stilled.

Gasping at a sharp pain in my chest, I rose to one knee, and swept the muzzle across the courtyard, looking for more targets. A door opened on the plain building to my right, and a man stepped outside with a rifle in his hand. Uncertain where the shots were coming from, he hesitated, probing the shadows that the landscaper's accent lights didn't reach.

The AR in my hands cracked again and the backlit *soldado* went down on his rear. As he fell backward, the door slowly swung open, revealing a now empty room bathed in dim yellow light.

The thought flashed through my mind that I was shooting unknown individuals on private property, in a foreign country, and that put me on dangerous ground at the very least. Once again, I was in a gray area, as far as the law was concerned.

None of that mattered right then. That odd thought vanished as quickly as it came. These people were part of a cruel cartel, and they made their living by breaking laws, those in Mexico, and across the river in my country. As far as I was concerned, Davy Crockett was dead-on when he said be sure you're right. I was. The evidence was hanging in the mesquite tree behind me.

Lucky for me, Stupid was trained to aim for center mass. His round caught me in the plate on the upper left side of my chest. Sticking my hand in between my Aloha shirt and the vest, I felt around for a hole or blood. There was neither, though it hurt like hell, and I figured there might be a cracked rib or two I'd have to deal with later.

Dammit! That was only a few inches from where I'd been shot a few months back. The big trapezius muscle and scar tissue under my left arm was *still* sore in the mornings and now this.

With the wall to my back and satisfied I was going to live a little while longer, I stayed on one knee and swept the area again. No one else appeared from any direction. I was right. Most everyone was off after Judge and his team, mostly leaving the henhouse unguarded.

The now familiar buzz of a drone came from the opposite side of the wall. Someone, somewhere, was looking for the action. Luck had been with me. I'd crossed the wall after it had passed on one of its many rounds, but sooner or later the operator was going to bring it inside the courtyard.

That thought had no more than entered my head when the drone appeared over the main house and slowly drifted my way. I lined up on it and emptied the magazine. It was like bird hunting, except this time I didn't have to lead it. One of the rounds hit it dead center, and the machine pitched over and thrashed itself to death on the ground.

Chapter 35

Despite his irritation, Carlos was distracted by the high definition images on Hector's screen. Naked women did things he'd never thought of, and their actions made it hard to concentrate on his job securing the area.

Focusing on his own screens, Carlos piloted the replacement drone around the exterior of the *rancheria*. He made a mental note to tell *La Jefa* that he needed more sophisticated aircraft that would give him clearer images at night. In his mind, he played out a scene in which he stood beside her with a glass of wine in one hand, rubbing his other hand up and down her side, explaining how only *he* could keep her safe, using technology.

Then his hand rose higher, like those images on Hector's screen and . . .

The system still wasn't up when time gunfire erupted just outside their building. Both men reacted by almost jumping out of their chairs Who would have thought someone would attack at four in the morning? Certainly not the two young men who'd never been physi-

cally involved in any violent act. Neither were *soldados.* They were *technicos,* or technicians. The original
intruders had been repelled, and likely dead by now.

It was probably those *idiotas* out there, celebrating
their victory by shooting into the air.

Hector had been watching with his mouth open.
Shocked back from the world of skin and moans, his
teeth clicked shut. "Who is it?"

Carlos swung the upgraded DJI Phantom 3's over
the wall and instead of a celebration, saw a lone figure
on one knee, exchanging gunfire with someone else.
He zoomed in to find the man was no one he'd ever
seen. Carlos flinched when the unknown individual
aimed directly at the drone and fired. His screen went
blank and he knew the man had killed his aircraft.

"Turn that shit off! We're under attack."

"Another one? What do we do?"

Carlos nodded toward two H&K machine pistols
laying on the table beside them. "We kill anyone who
comes through the door."

Like twins, they picked up the weapons and laid
them in their laps, watching and waiting in silence,
surrounded by a room full of flickering screens, terrified that the door was going to open or worse, explode
inward.

After a moment, when no one kicked in the door,
Carlos turned toward the screens showing animated
sand drizzling through an hourglass. "Hector, when will
your security system be up and running?"

His eyes flicked from the door to the flickering
screens. "When we are already dead."

Eyes wide with fright, Hector ran his hands over the

submachine gun as if it were a woman. "You should have sent out an alert when your first drone disappeared."

"You could have suggested that earlier, instead of watching *pornografia*!"

"Cameras are my job."

"Your job is security and you've failed. If the *Mujer Malvada* finds out, she will decorate her *arbol cadaver* with your backbone and I'll tie a ribbon on it."

"Be quiet. Someone might be listening at the door."

Chapter 36

I slapped a fresh mag into the AR and studied the courtyard. With two guys on their way to the hereafter, and the drone operator probably holed up somewhere inside one of the handful of buildings built around the courtyard, it looked like it was just me.

All except for that small individual I'd seen in the bright room across the way. The large windows and open bi-fold glass wall gave me a clear view of a bright, grand room.

Weapon at the ready, I crossed the landscaped space, feeling the hair on my neck prickle at the thought of the shot I wouldn't hear. Would the drone operator come out blasting? Good lord. Did they have *weaponized* drones? I wondered if he was one of those geeky tech guys that could shoot me down like a stray dog.

I've got to quit being so impulsive.

Heart pounding and twisted tight as a mainspring, I closed on the ranch house, one slow step at a time, following the muzzle of the rifle in my trembling hands. After one last swing to make sure no one was behind me, I edged into the bright room.

The smallish person I'd seen wasn't there, and I wouldn't have been either in their situation.

Thick hand-hewn beams supported the ceiling of a wide, open-concept room decorated in the traditional, brightly colored Spanish style they love down in Mexico. A leather couch sat with its back to me, along with a couple of fat, comfortable-looking chairs facing a huge flat panel television mounted on the far wall. Tuned to the History Channel, the irony was that the night's program was about drugs and cartels.

In plain sight to the left was an office with a massive desk holding three computer screens facing an empty chair.

A wide granite island on the right separated the combination grand living/media room and office from a fully appointed kitchen. A lot of money had been spent on upgrading everything with high-end stainless-steel appliances. It was a hundred-thousand-dollar kitchen that looked as if it had never been used.

Rifle at my shoulder, I waited for someone to pop up and start shooting.

Nothing.

The island was a good place to hide. Two closed doors on the back wall in the kitchen indicated there was more house beyond. I held the AR steady toward the upper edge of the granite island where I expected someone to pop up and start cranking off rounds at me.

"All right. Name's Sonny Hawke." My voice sounded high and reedy. I cleared it and brought it down a notch. "Texas Ranger. I'm here with a warrant for your arrest."

That was the best I could do without knowing the Devil Woman's name. "I saw you a minute ago, and if you're hiding back there with a weapon, I'll kill you just like I killed the rest of those punks out there."

I eased around the left side, hoping to see a foot or a leg, while at the same time keeping an eye on the rest of the room and the courtyard beyond.

"Step out and put your hands up."

It was hard to concentrate on that small section of the house when an entire wall was open to lord knows what. Kelly and I had talked about installing one of those folding glass walls in our house, but the one only yards away seemed like an invitation for a whole battalion of bad guys to come marching in. Might have to re-think that.

Another step brought me near the left side of the island, providing a view of the red Mexican tiled floor and a petite blue-jeaned knee. I drew a fine bead on that knee and stopped, twisted tight as a watch's mainspring. "I hope you speak English, 'cause my Spanish ain't that good. You need to know I could shoot that knee I'm looking at and you'd walk with a limp for the rest of your life. You can tell I'm a pretty decent guy, or I'd have already shot. If you have a weapon, put it on top of the island and stand up."

Just to be sure she got my drift, I switched to Spanish. *"Manos arriba y salgo, o te desparare en . . . esa parte del cuerpo."* At least I hoped I told her to come out with her hands up or I'd shoot her in the knee.

One way or the other, the knee disappeared. A hand rose, holding a Glock, and gently placed the weapon on the polished surface.

"Good. Now stand up with both hands where I can see them."

"You just said to stand up or you'd shoot me in that

body part." It was a woman's voice and she was using English.

"My Spanish isn't great."

"I'll stand up. Don't shoot me."

"Hands!"

She stood, what there was of her, in an untucked white shirt and jeans. She couldn't have been more than five foot three, with thick, black hair. "Don't shoot. I'm only the maid."

I'd never seen such an attractive and well-constructed maid, except in movies. "Maids don't usually come equipped with Glocks. Come around to this side."

She padded around on bare feet. I couldn't help but notice her toenails were painted red. "They're all gone."

"Who?"

"The Devil Woman and her men. They left me behind."

Movement in my peripheral vision told me someone was easing the nearest door into the kitchen open a centimeter at a time. The smart thing would have been to empty the AR's mag through the door, but I couldn't take the chance. There could be innocents or children on the other side.

The maid moved around the opposite end of the island, then edged toward the center of the room. That's what I would have done if I'd wanted to keep someone's attention away from the door. She spoke English, but her accent had that soft, musky tone that makes Spanish sound wonderful in the right, intimate circumstances. I knew, because I'd dated a few Spanish girls before I met Kelly.

"There's no one else in here. Please lower your weapon."

I let her go on with the charade until the door opened wider and the muzzle of a gun peeked through. That's when my AR came level. I sent three rounds just above the other weapon's barrel, still maintaining control of the rifle.

The weapon dropped in the doorway and the sound of a falling body told me I'd done some damage. I spun back to the maid, but she stood rooted to the spot with her hands still in the air. Glad I wasn't having to struggle for the right words in Spanish, I reached for the wall switch and flicked off the lights. Half of the room went dark.

"Where are the other switches?"

One slender hand waved toward a narrow strip of wall at the closest end of the folding glass panels.

I pointed with my head. "Back toward them and turn the lights off."

She did, and just before the lights went out, I saw her nails were also painted red. Dropping the NVGs into place, I gave the courtyard the once-over. It was still empty.

Back to the room and situation at hand. "You're the only one, huh?"

"I didn't know he was in there. I promise. Can you see through those in the dark?"

"Yep. Name?"

"Lucinda Diaz."

"Well, Lucy. I'm not sure I believe you."

"It's the truth, mister."

"The truth is that you're a little too put together and

intentionally casual to wash dishes and scrub floors at this time of a morning, but you can convince me somewhere else. Right now, we're headed out of here."

"Who are you? You said something about a warrant."

"I'm the law. That's all you need to know."

"You're not wearing a badge, and that shirt . . ."

"The shirt's not important, and the badge is in my pocket for now."

"You're American."

"Right."

"I don't want to be a hostage."

"No one *wants* to be a hostage, but you're going as a temporary prisoner, if there is such a thing."

"Where?"

"Away from here. Where are the keys for that SUV sitting out there?"

A beat.

Her voice had been slightly nervous, but now it was steady as a rock. "It belongs to the owner of the house."

"Keeping up with the charade, huh? Good for you. Where's the keys?"

She jerked her head toward the office. The TV was still on, but the blue light didn't give me any problems with the night-vision goggles, as long as I didn't look directly at it. "They're in a wooden box on the desk."

That's when I was pretty sure I had my girl. Most Mexicans who learn to use English south of the border don't usually use contractions.

Keeping the weapon trained on her, I edged over to the desk and flipped the lid on a carved wooden box. Sure 'nough, a key fob was in there, along with two thick packets of hundred-dollar bills in American currency. I dropped the fob in my pocket and left the money.

"Hands on top of your head and turn around."

"Why?"

I shrugged. "Well, because I said so and I have the gun. I need to pat you down." There wouldn't be much patting. She'd almost painted the jeans on, but that untucked shirt was a little too blousy for me. Even if she didn't have a gun under there, she could still have a knife. "Do it."

Interlocking her fingers like I said, she turned around and waited. Letting the AR drop across my chest, I quickly patted her down, fully expecting her to try and fight or squirm around to get away. She did neither, simply standing there and looking out into the night. The pat down was almost as thorough as if it was a guy, but there were certain places I wouldn't explore. She wasn't wearing a bra, so that simplified things in that general area.

"Lay down on the floor." I yanked a lamp cord free from the wall and cut it with my pocketknife. "On your belly." She settled to the polished tiles and rolled onto her stomach like a cat stretching. I tied both hands behind her back, not tight enough to cut off the circulation. "Sorry about this, but I'm not convinced you're who you say you are."

"This is how you *gringos* treat women?"

"It's how *this* gringo is gonna stay alive."

I scooped her feet together and threw a loop around them drawing them tight with a half hitch, like tying a calf, then connected them to her hands so she couldn't wiggle out, or away. The level of detail through the NVGs surprised me and the knots pulled snug.

Time was running out, making me nervous, wondering when the rest of the *soldatos* were coming back.

With her cheek on the tiles, she tested the limits of her movement. "How do you expect me to walk like this?"

"I don't. I expect you to stay still and quiet while I check the house." Even though I was 99 percent sure I had the right person, I wanted to be sure there were no other women hiding in any of the other rooms. I had no intention of trying to clear the rest of the buildings. If anyone was there, they were laying low and out of the fight.

A satellite phone was charging on its base at one end of the island. It was the one she'd been using when I first saw her. I plucked it off.

Dammit. That knock on the head must have scrambled my brains more than I'd thought. She was on the phone when I shot those two guys outside. Whoever she'd been talking to probably knew someone was on their property. If they were close, they'd be in my back pocket within the next minute or two.

I still had to be sure I was taking the right gal with me. The second door in the kitchen was closed. Weapon ready, I pushed it open to find an empty pantry.

Dark blood leaked out from under the other door I'd shot through. I pushed it open to find the fanciest master bedroom I'd ever seen and the bad guy lying there deader'n nickel coffee. He looked to be about eighteen. The sight of someone so young made my breath catch, because even though he was far from the first, he was near the same age as my own kids.

In the past several months I'd taken more lives than I cared to admit, and the weight of that crushing responsibility once again got to me. My chest hitched, and tiny whimpering sounds came with each contraction, but I clamped my teeth together and fought through it, looking for something to take my mind off that cooling body.

I turned to clear the ostentatious bedroom. That's the word I was looking for. The whole room was designed by someone who probably didn't have anything when they were young and made up for it as soon as they had enough money. Even I could tell the artwork on the walls was expensive and probably should have been in a museum rather than a cartel leader's ranch house in Coahuila, Mexico.

Overdone and way too flashy for my taste, I wondered if the Devil Woman hired someone to design it, or if deep down inside the dangerous person I'd heard about was nothing more than an insecure woman.

I hoped Kelly wouldn't ever want a room like the one I was in. It'd take a year's worth of work to earn enough to pay for it. The bathroom was just as ostentatious, with a Jacuzzi tub big enough to swim in and gold fixtures that almost glowed in the greenish light. Sitting side by side, and more out in the room that I would have wanted, was the toilet and a bidet.

The whole layout was spectacular through the goggles, and I kinda wanted to flick on the lights for a minute to take it all in, but the clock was ticking.

Following the muzzle of my rifle, I returned to the kitchen, relieved to find the "maid" still lying on the floor, staring into the courtyard. Probably waiting on that help she'd called. "All right, Miss Ma'am." I used my pocket knife to cut the wire around her ankles. "We're going on a road trip."

"To where?"

"The states." I grabbed her elbow and yanked her up.

"You're a fool. You can't come in here and think you're simply going to drive back to your country. Every officer and soldier within a hundred miles will be after you."

Miles instead of kilometers. Another domino fell.

"Why would soldiers care about me and a maid?" I pressed one section of the key fob and the engine started. "How will they know?"

A look crossed her face. "My employer is very rich. They'll know soon enough."

"Outside and into that Expedition. You're pretty confident to be a simple housekeeper."

"I grew up here. It's a harsh country."

"No, you didn't. You're from the states."

There was that look again, and this time she knew she'd given it away.

Still holding her elbow and holding the AR in my right, I shoved her toward the open wall. "We have no choice. I've always bulled my way through china shops, so we're heading north."

No one shot at me when she stepped out into the open, so I followed close enough to smell the coconut shampoo she'd used on her hair. Staying right up against her might make a sniper think twice about shooting and harming their boss.

My stomach against her back, I yanked the passenger door open. She threw her head backward, hoping to head-butt me in the nose. I grabbed a handful of soft hair and banged her forehead against the top of the open door. It wasn't hard enough to knock her out, just enough to keep her from trying again, but my skin crawled with the thought of crosshairs finding me.

She dropped into the seat, blood welling from the strawberry on her forehead. "You bastard!"

"Language." I gave the courtyard one last look and slammed the door behind her. If there was a sniper, now was the time he'd pull the trigger.

Circling the Expedition's hood as fast as my feet would move, I yanked the door open and dropped in behind the wheel. She was trying to lock the automatic door with her chin to keep me out. I grabbed her hair again and yanked her back against the seatback. "Sit still!"

I reached across and pulled her seatbelt across and locked it into place.

"You'll die before we get to the river!" Her once-attractive face was contorted in fury. In the eerie light through the NVG lenses, the growing knot on her forehead made her look like a demon.

"That's possible. I could have a heart attack, too, but it don't matter. We're going."

"Why don't you just throw me in the back like a *cuerpo*?"

"Thanks for the suggestion. It sounds like you've had practice at that, but no. I want you where I can keep an eye on your little lyin' ass."

Angling the AR across my chest with the muzzle partially out the open window, I shifted into gear and pulled out of the open gate and onto the dirt road. A sudden splash of light in the rearview mirror told me there was still someone back there, but they either hadn't wanted to engage, or hid long enough to tell someone we were leaving.

My passenger saw it too, and her face relaxed into a smile bracketed with deep dimples.

Chapter 37

In their buttoned-up control room, the technicians Carlos and Hector sat in terrified silence. The percussive gunfire in the courtyard wasn't random, as it sounded when the *soldados* went beyond the walls for target practice with a variety of automatic weapons. The military occasionally came by in their Humvees and pickup trucks carrying 50-caliber machine guns in the back, and practiced with the *soldados*. Those times, the sound was a steady roar that continued until they ran out of ammunition, or tired of standing in the hot sun.

On occasion, and if they were in a good mood, the Devil Woman's soldiers executed rival cartel members, or traitors to their cause, just outside the walls with single shots to their heads, or a quick burst from one or two weapons.

What was going on in the darkness outside their walls was surgical in nature. One or two shots, then a quick, controlled burst. The first exchange was only feet from their door. The next was farther away, and somewhat muffled.

Carlos's eyes widened in the dim light from their computer screens. They'd turned out the fluorescent overheads, just in case someone saw light around the door that never completely sealed when it was closed. He swallowed and exchanged glances with Hector. "They are in the house."

"How many? Can you tell?"

"We would know if you could get that damned security system back up and working so we can use the cameras."

Holding a machine gun in his lap, Hector spun in his chair and tapped at the keys. "The update will be complete in five minutes."

"We may not have that long."

A single controlled burst reached their ears, sounding somewhat muffled.

Again, they waited. It seemed like a lifetime to the young men before two car doors slammed, and an engine started, the sound loud in the still night air. Silence reigned long enough for Carlos to finally muster the courage to crack the door and peek outside.

An armed man threw a backpack into the Expedition's open rear window and slid behind the wheel. Gravel crunched when the vehicle rolled out of the courtyard without headlights.

Shaking with fear, Hector stood behind Carlos. "Do you see anything?"

"Yes. *La Jefa*'s Expedition is driving away." Carlos saw the barrel of Hector's submachine gun in his peripheral vision. He used one finger to push it to the side.

They took another long moment before Carlos opened the door all the way and stepped outside. Soft breezes swayed the palm leaves and grasses in the night air. A body lay close to the main ranch house's open glass wall. "He has killed Eusebio, and I can promise there was another soldier in the main house. He is dead, too, or the Expedition would not be leaving so slowly."

Carlos studied the now peaceful *ranchero*. "It could have been that man who pulled everyone away, too. We would have known if you had not been watching *la gente folla*."

"What else was I going to do while the security system was rebooting? Stop bothering me with that. You have your stupid drones that are useless when the *baterias* run down. What are we going to do?"

"We need to check on *La Jefa*."

"I will stay here and cover you." Hector held the weapon as if it were a snake. His voice betrayed the seriousness of the words. He glanced over his shoulder at the computer screen that reported the update was 98 percent complete.

"Point that *ametralladora* somewhere else. I do not want to be shot in the back by *you*." Carlos stepped into the night. All the lights were off in the main house, and that had never happened before. Shaking in fear, he crossed the courtyard, wheeling dramatically every few feet to check behind them. *"Jefa?"*

No sound came from the big house.

"Señorita? Are you there? You can come out now. I will protect you." Carlos squared his shoulders, hoping it would make him look tough and capable in her eyes.

Still no sound. He stepped into the main room through the open glass doors and snapped on the light that nullified the glow coming from the television on the wall. The office was obviously empty, as was the living room. He rounded the island and stopped in shock at a stream of dark blood on the tiles. It was coming from *La Jefa*'s bedroom.

Dreading that he would find her body, he snugged the compact H&K to his shoulder. Finger curled around the trigger, he shouldered the door open and stopped in shock at the sight of Ignacio Lavaca lying in a pool of blood. The Devil Woman's personal body-guard had taken two bullets to the face. Carlos frowned at the sight of the man's undone trousers and then almost laughed at the realization that Ignacio had been taking a *mierda* at the moment an assassin had come calling.

"Señorita?"

There was no answer. He searched the house without finding anyone else. She was gone, and he knew that she hadn't been killed, but taken by men who'd killed her soldiers with professional ease.

"Hector!" Carlos bolted from the house and charged across the courtyard. "They have taken *La Jefa*! We have to follow them!"

The door swung open at the same time Carlos reached the control room. He charged past the startled technician and closed his laptop, noticing that the security system was finally up and running.

"Get in the van. You drive and I'll use this to keep the SUV in sight. We can radio Incencio and tell him we are following. He'll know what to do."

"We can stay right here and you can follow with your toy."

"They'll be out of range soon. The ones I have left are not as strong as the first two. We have to go!"

"You will not tell them the cameras were down, will you?"

Carlos stuffed the laptop and a walkie-talkie in a small blue daypack. He slung it over his shoulder and grabbed another, larger drone off a shelf. "Not if they don't ask me." His voice softened. "If they do, I'll tell them you were doing maintenance."

"You will not mention what I was doing while it was rebooting?"

"No."

Outside, Carlos dropped to one knee and launched his drone. It rose with a familiar buzz and shot off toward the east. Minutes later, Hector steered around Eusebio's body and raced through the darkness. The van's bright headlights picked up fine dust still hanging in the air from the Expedition's passage.

"If they are driving fast, we might not catch them." Hector leaned forward as if that position closer to the windshield would help him see better. "They could take any of the intersecting roads and we might miss where they turned off."

"That is why I brought this." In the passenger seat, Carlos's face was lit by the glow of the computer in his lap. His fingers raced across the keys until he stopped and pointed at the screen. "There! I have them five kilometers ahead."

Hector momentarily took his eyes from the road to see where Carlos was pointing on the screen. There was nothing but a cloud until a quick flicker of brake lights flashed on, then off as quickly as they'd come on.

"What is that?"

"Dust from their vehicle."

"How fast can the *zumbido* fly? They are driving pretty fast."

Carlos moved the toggle switches in his lap with experienced thumbs. "The drone might catch them. I learned to upgrade it when I was in the military. It will fly over fifty miles an hour. He cannot drive that fast on these roads, and pretty soon Incencio can intercept them."

"What if you lose the signal?"

"That will not happen if you stay this close." Carlos fished the walkie-talkie from the backpack at his feet and pressed the talk key. "Incencio."

The voice came back startlingly clear and sharp with irritation. "Who is this?"

"Carlos."

A beat.

"What?"

"Someone came into the ranch and kidnapped *La Jefa*."

"*Qué? Se llevaron La Jefa!?* How? How did they get in?"

Carlos and Hector exchanged glances. "We do not know, but they have her, and we are behind them in the van."

"*You* two are chasing them!? Where are the others? Where's Ignacio?"

"Dead. Everyone is dead, and we're following in the van, a few kilometers behind the drone."

"How many?"

Carlos swallowed and looked across at Hector. His face was expressionless as he concentrated on the road. "One, I think. Somehow they took out the security system before he got in. Hector got it back up and running, but it was too late. They were already gone."

Hector visibly relaxed, and he nodded.

Silence for nearly thirty seconds. Carlos was about to key the radio again when Incencio came back on. "You have them in sight?"

"Yes."

"Where are they?"

He relayed their location.

"Good. Stay behind them, and we will catch up. Do not let them get away, or your *cráneo y columna vertebral* will decorate her tree."

Carlos shivered at the thought and prayed that the chase wouldn't take more than twenty minutes, the life of the drone's battery at that speed. *"Sí, jefe."*

Chapter 38

Once we were away from the *rancho*, I sped up as fast as I could safely drive on the dirt road. I grew up running just those kinds of roads and they were as familiar as the back of my hand. Since it was night, I wasn't worried about the plume of dust rising behind the Expedition and giving our position away.

At first I was leery about driving fast with the NVGs, but though the world was stock pond green, it was still clear. One thing I had to worry about, other than the bad guys popping up, was a deer running out in front of the SUV.

It was that flash of light in my rearview mirror back at the compound that worried me, too. I'd left someone back there and hoped they weren't organizing a chase.

I was like a horse going to the barn with the wind in his nose, but no idea where we were going other than away from that ranch. We crossed other intersecting dirt roads a couple of times. Once we came to a Y, and I took the left fork only because it angled toward the states and hopefully a highway.

For once technology was on my side. At that particular moment, the compass in the dash told me we were pointed northwest, the general direction I wanted to go. That technological cooperation went away as soon as I punched my cell phone alive. The familiar No Service alert was what I expected, but I had an ace in the hole from the ranch.

The "maid" watched as I reached between the seats and dug her satellite phone from Victim's backpack. One eye on the green road, and the other on the phone, I punched in Sheriff Ethan Armstrong's number. SAT phones are glorious inventions as long as there are no obstructions overhead. We were good there, because the only thing above us was stars. Off to the right, a dark ridgeline of mountains was far enough in the distance that they wouldn't interfere with the signal.

A two-track road angled off, but I suspected it was nothing more than a ranch road, or one leading to an unseen house. I wanted pavement and with it, the speed we needed to put some distance between us and the bad guys.

The phone rang seven times on the other end before a gruff voice answered. "This is Ethan. Something better be on fire."

"It is, in a sense. This is Sonny."

"Sonny!" I could imagine him starting upright in the bed, shaking Marilyn awake. "Where are you? People are looking . . ."

"Save it. I'm in trouble."

"I almost didn't answer. Your number didn't come up."

"That's because I'm calling from a SAT phone that belongs to a cartel leader."

"You don't hear that every day." He processed that

bit of information for several seconds. "Where *are* you?"

"Somewhere in Coahuila, heading north with a prisoner."

"Prisoner! You can't take . . ."

"You gonna talk about jurisdiction, or listen?"

"Fine."

"I think I have the Hidalgo cartel leader in custody. I intend to cross at Langtry, but I need extradition papers ready and signed by the time I get there. And by the way, I'm probably only thirty minutes ahead of her people. I'm moving pretty fast here."

"Sonny, you know the Mexican government won't extradite on a *phone* call. The papers on our end take days at best. And you know there's no crossing at Langtry. There isn't even a bridge."

"I'll deal with that little detail when I get there. I know you can get things done when other people can't. I need those papers."

"It's going to be next to impossible. The judge is gonna ask for evidence. Do you have that?"

"I have a verbal confession from that other undercover agent we heard about."

"You found him? How?"

"We'll talk about that later, when I have time, but he told me about the whole operation and that's all I need to know."

"It still won't fly with a judge."

"It'll have to. Look, I'm crossing at Langtry one way or another. If I can't wade the river, I'm gonna float this gal across like everyone else."

"Wait, what? You said *gal*? That rumor of the Devil Woman is legit?"

"I have her in here with me."

"Not voluntarily, I imagine."

"Took a little persuading."

"That's probably an understatement. You know they call it kidnapping on this side of the river."

Her glare from the other side of the Expedition was hot as coals.

"We'll hammer out the details when I get to the border, but I can't show up at any bridge crossing with her all trussed up, in a stolen Expedition. The border guards on this side'll stop me for sure. That's why I'm headed to Langtry, but I don't know these highways down here and they're dangerous as hell, especially with a prisoner most people don't want me to bring back. The navigation system in the dash shows me a dirt road that leads almost to the river. I think I can find it. Why don't you contact agent McDowell and get him to help? A request from both you and the FBI might kick things into high gear."

Ethan's voice was even, telling me he was thinking hard. "He might, after he bucks and snorts for a while. You haven't told me what she's under arrest *for*?"

"She ordered the execution of Border Patrol agent Frank Nelson for a start, and for the order resulting in the attempted murder of the Nelson sisters in Del Rio. Then there's drug trafficking and if we dig a little, I bet we can find that she's ordered the murders of American citizens down here."

"You're a damned liar!" She thrashed in the seat. "He's lying! I'm being kidnapped!" Her voice went up to a shriek.

"She's pretty loud." Her outburst didn't faze Ethan

one bit. "I bet she has anger issues, too. Look, I'm tellin' you, they're gonna ask for *evidence*."

"See if you can get Agent McDowell and Major Parker to the hospital in Ft. Stockton and have them tell Agent Manual Trevino that we know what happened to them on the highway that night. This gal here is blackmailing agents by threatening their families if they tell that they've been turned and paying off these agents who are afraid to talk. Tell Trevino we have her in custody, so she can't issue any more orders for murder raids."

"You bastard! You're making all of that up! I own a ranch. I have businesses, but I am not a murderer!"

Ethan's voice was loud in my ear. "Son of a bitch! That all makes sense now. How do you know all that?"

"A little bird told me."

"I'm gonna need a name for the extradition papers, if we ever get to that stage."

I turned enough to see her face. "Tish Villarreal." Her head snapped around and her eyes widened when I spoke her name. Bingo! I'd gotten all that from Esteban back in El Cruce. The undercover agent's stock went up with her reaction.

"Look, there's no number that comes up on this phone."

"I don't have the time to figure this out to get you a number, so I'll call back around noon."

"We can't get all that done by then. You know as well as I do how long it takes to get to Ft. Stockton."

Back when we were kids, he and I referred to distances by six packs of beer. Ft. Stockton was two six packs away from Ballard.

"They'll have to bring the papers later. I know they

won't be there when we show up, but like you always said . . ."

"The wheels of justice turn slowly. Fine then. I'm on it."

The phone went silent, and I punched in another number.

A familiar voice answered. "Perry Hale."

"It's me."

We went through the where are you, how are you discussion. I again explained where I was, and what was happening. This time my passenger was quiet, stewing with rage.

"I'm gonna need some help here." The relief I felt at having Perry Hale on the line caused my voice to shake. He was calm and competent in any situation, and simply talking to him brought my emotions to the surface once again. "Where are you guys?"

"Ciudad Acuna."

"You're a little over an hour from Langtry. I plan to cross there, but I have bad guys on my tail. I may be an hour or more south, maybe two, depending on how these roads are." I gave him the best description of my location. "I know there's no crossing there, but I can't follow a main highway up to the border. It'll be too easy to intercept us, and I figure I have an ass-load of bad guys trying to find me."

"You have an exfil point in mind?"

"Yeah, a place called Chalk Canyon."

"Hold on. Yolanda's bringing up a map now."

"I'll probably get there before y'all do."

His voice was full of enthusiasm. "Maybe not. I have an ace up my sleeve."

"I hope you have all four. We're gonna need 'em."

Chapter 39

The dirt road twisted a couple of times, and then the next thing I knew, I was on a paved highway. I figured it was the same one I'd come in on with Judge's team, but in the nighttime desert, most everything looks the same. I palmed the wheel onto the two-lane and headed north. The Expedition's big engine roared, pressing us back into the seats.

I glanced at the navigation system in the dash, seeing the hardtop I was on, and a spiderweb of dirt roads branching off. After punching at the screen for a few seconds, I magnified the map and identified narrow trails leading toward the rough country on both sides of the river.

I knew the area a few miles west of Langtry pretty well. I'd worked a human trafficking case there a couple of years earlier and learned how illegals and smugglers came across using Chalk Canyon. Though not as long or rugged as the canyon south of Big Bend, the deep, winding cut's as isolated now as it was back when Black Jack Ketchum robbed a train there back in 1897 and got away with $6,000 in gold and silver.

It worked for him back then, and in that part of the world, little had changed on this side of the Rio Grande. I planned on using that same terrain to evade those guys who were after us.

When I glanced at the Devil Woman, a.k.a. Tish Villarreal, she was looking into the side mirror, likely hoping for a glimpse of headlights. It was still dark back there, but I could've sworn I'd seen another flicker of lights back behind me at one point while I was dialing Perry Hale.

She finally spoke. "You're going the wrong way." Tied up and strapped in the seatbelt, she could only use her nose to point at the dash. "You can see there are no towns there, only a few isolated ranches."

"Last time I looked, the states were north, and that's the direction we're going."

"Turn up here. It is a house I own. We can stop there and negotiate."

"Negotiate?"

"I have lots of money. You said you have information on me. You already know who I am. I bet it came from one of my people. Tell me who he is and I can make you a very rich man, and in your position, we can make millions more. I have a magnificent house in Texas. I can set you up in it." Those dimples of hers appeared, and she gave me a smile that would melt the heart of any single man in the world. "You can have me, too."

"Not even remotely interested."

The dimples disappeared, and her face hardened. "Then you will die, and I will hang your remains from my tree."

I stifled a shudder, recalling the sickly sweet smell

of carrion that suddenly seemed to waft from her side of the SUV. "Pipe down. That's not happening."

"I heard you Rangers were smart, so show some intelligence. This is the only way you or your family will live after this night."

That was the last thing she should have said to me.

A fury I've rarely felt in my life washed over me like a tsunami and to control my hands, I gripped the wheel so hard I was afraid I'd break it off. It was all I could do not to backslap her through the door glass. The last person that laid a hand on one of my family members was on the wrong side of the grass back in the Ballard Cemetery.

"Lady, you have seriously underestimated me. Do *not* threaten my family or even *think* of it. If anyone comes around my people on your orders, I'll hunt down everyone you know. I'll find a way to kill you, even in prison, and I'll personally burn your damned ranch to the ground."

"You won't do that. You're an American. You're a Texas Ranger."

Words poured from me in a demonic voice I didn't recognize. "I'll do *anything* to protect my family. I'll get down and roll around in the gutter with you and be worse than the scum you live with. If anything happens to me, I have people you don't even know about who'll pick up where I left off. I'm your worst nightmare." I gave her a good, long look, "I'm a damned ghost from over a hundred years ago."

Chapter 40

Fifteen minutes after he called Incencio, Carlos sucked in a frightened breath. He'd done that half a dozen times since the chase began. His body was wracked with fear, filling his stomach with acid that intensified as the chase wore on.

Once he thought he'd lost the black vehicle running wide open through the night when they came to intersecting dirt roads. They had to slow while he scanned one particularly wide dirt road to see if they'd taken it.

Another time he was fooled when he thought they'd turned on a ranch road that led to a dark house sitting by itself in the desert. He wasted valuable minutes while Hector stopped the van and they followed the road with the drone to the house, and then flew around the structure to be sure the Expedition wasn't parked behind it.

Lucky for him, unlike their van or the gringo's vehicle, the drone didn't have to stick to ribbons winding across the land, so once he was sure they weren't there, he flew the drone cross-country back to their road and finally picked them up.

Carlos's stomach knotted again in fear. "This speed is draining the drone's battery. It won't last more than a couple of minutes more."

Hector didn't take his eyes off the road. "I thought you said we had more time."

"I know what I said." Carlos tapped at the keyboard and stopped. He clapped his hands in joy. "There! He turned on the *autopista*!"

Betting the fleeing vehicle would race for the border on the smooth hardtop, he piloted the drone in that direction and sent it into the air over the two-lane highway. It took another minute, but he saw a glint that could have been moonlight reflecting off a windshield, or chrome. A clear flash of red taillights told him the driver slowed to take a curve.

He keyed the walkie-talkie again. "Incencio."

"What." The sounds of gunshots came through the walkie-talkie's tiny speaker.

Hector and Carlos exchanged looks. "We have followed them to the *autopista*. They're going to the *Estados Unidos*."

"Bien."

"The battery on my drone is almost dead."

"We don't need you anymore. Return to the *rancho*. We have killed all the *soldados* here, but there may be more."

"But the *Mujer Malvada* is not there."

"Don't let *La Jefa* hear you speak those words, or you'll wind up in her garden. Others may come for the money, *idiota*."

Carlos and the rest of those at the ranch knew that millions were stashed in a variety of safes set in walls, sunk in the floors, and in a giant standing safe secreted behind swinging shelves in the main house's pantry.

"*Sí.*"

Hector slowed and stopped when they reached the highway. "He didn't even say thank you."

"Yes, he did. He didn't say he was going to kill us. That is thanks enough."

Chapter 41

Esteban felt he'd been holding his breath for an hour. He released it in one long whoosh and reloaded the Scorpion he'd taken from Alejandro's truck. It was the perfect weapon, and he knew from the moment he saw it in the back seat that the little death machine would be his. He'd lifted it before meeting with the Ranger, knowing that Alejandro would be dead by Fosfora's hand minutes later.

It was the way of their world.

He was forced to set up the assassination of the Ciudad Acuna police officer to keep his own cover secure. As he'd told Hawke, he committed certain crimes for the greater good. Though Alejandro struggled to honor the badge he wore, he'd taken bribes from the cartel to look the other way a number of times.

But when Fosfora came into the picture with him, Esteban was forced to assume she'd told him about their association, and how she was a go-between linking him with the handler who communicated through her brother's bar. He couldn't afford to let the officer live, unlike the Ranger he'd knocked out earlier that night.

The Ranger was on his side, working toward plugging the Devil Woman's pipeline. His sudden arrival and highly illegal investigation just might be the unexpected move to force her into the states where she wouldn't have as much heavily armed protection and could either be taken into custody or eliminated.

And here he was, staring down at the bodies of the Americans he'd been working with only hours earlier, lying in still another dry arroyo where they'd finally made their stand. He'd used the team for his own gain, but it backfired when he realized they'd lied to him days earlier. The Black Ops members were charged with killing the Devil Woman, and they were funded by a dark company back in the states, but when Fosfora accidentally mentioned the vast amount of money that was supposedly hidden in the house after she and the Ranger arrived that night, the mercenaries changed their plan.

It changed again when Ranger Hawke talked them into taking him along. Fosfora used her own SAT phone hidden in the purse she seldom took off her shoulder and relayed the Black Op team's new plan to her brother back at the *Caballo Diablo* bar in Ciudad Acuna. He called Esteban who contacted a Mexican officer named Perez.

The running gun battle away from the *rancherio* became a slaughter when more than two dozen soldiers from the Mexican army joined in with *La Reina del Diablo*'s men and forced Judge's team into a well-planned ambush.

And now it was over, and Esteban had even more blood on his hands. He wondered if his own soul was as bloody.

Incencio slapped Captain Perez on the shoulder. "They were very good."

Half a dozen surviving cartel *soldados* stood alongside twenty Mexican soldiers playing their lights over the bloody bodies of the American mercenaries lying in a shallow arroyo where they'd tried to make a stand. With arms and legs splayed in the blood-soaked sand, the men still looked dangerous to Perez.

Perez stuck a *cigarillo* between his lips and lit it. The tiny flame was bright in the pre-dawn darkness. "Military?"

"Mercenaries, *operaciaones negras,* I think." Incencio blinked, reacting to the light. "But it makes no difference."

"How did you know they'd be here?" Esteban slung the Scorpion over his shoulder and turned toward the glow on the eastern horizon.

"Fosfora sent word they'd come this way." Captain Perez drew deeply on the cigarillo. "*Esa travesti* says they were planning on taking *La Jefa*'s money and using her as a hostage for ransom. Fosfora was going to get part of that money. She had been working with these *norteamericanos* and talking to us at the same time."

So she'd worked out a deal for herself. Esteban kept his face expressionless, though he was surprised. You never knew who was working a side deal, and you never, never spoke against anyone, no matter their social class. "That idea was suicide."

"Yes, it was, but they dreamed large. I admire them for that."

Incencio tilted his head in question. "Why do you let Fosfora live, then?"

"Because, she is like us, or worse. Every time she shows up, her hand is out, but the information we get from her is more valuable than her life." Captain Perez waved a hand. "We are done here." Reloading their weapons, his men jogged toward the Humvees parked a hundred yards away. "I assume we will be paid for our ammunition."

Incencio chuckled. "Of course. *La Jefa* always takes care of those who remain trustworthy."

As the men scattered, Esteban wondered how much longer he could play both ends toward the middle. He had the information they needed to put an end to the Devil Woman's operation on the Texas side of the border.

Maybe it was time to go. There were too many double-crosses to contend with, and it was as sure as the rising sun that his time was coming. He stifled a shiver at the thought of her garden of bodies.

Incencio wasn't finished just yet. He waved a hand at his *soldados*. "Amigos. Shoot them again to make sure no one is still breathing and we will come back with a truck to take these *pendejos* to *La Jefa* so she can add them to her garden."

Always ready to shoot their weapons, two of his men stepped forward and opened on the bodies with rifles switched to fully automatic at the same time the walkie-talkie on Incencio's belt squawked to life.

Esteban listened to the exchange with Carlos and saw his world had just changed, exactly as he predicted.

Chapter 42

An hour after Sonny's call, Perry Hale and Yolanda Rodriguez watched the dark terrain flicker below the scratched windows of a helicopter piloted by a seedy-looking character named Lance Hopkins. The chopper flew so close to the ground Perry Hale thought they would hang a runner on one of the tall chollas reaching upward.

In battle gear and a four-day beard, Perry Hale could pass for anyone in the U.S. military, but without identifying insignia for any branch. Though she wasn't wearing makeup, Yolanda could have been a model for a recruitment poster with her naturally long eyelashes and dark complexion.

Lance on the other hand was 100 percent civilian, now, wearing a faded black AC/DC sleeveless concert T-shirt and cargo shorts. Their pilot was way too chatty, and his speech patterns set Perry Hale's teeth on edge, but the man was a vet, and that made them brothers in arms. Preferring not to engage in conversation, Perry Hale had the microphone on his helmet pushed downward, hoping that Lance would get the idea.

Yolanda had no problems talking to him. She spoke into her mouthpiece. "You're scaring me to death."

"Hey man, y'all said you didn't want to be seen coming in." Lance talked like an '80s California surfer dude, though he was from the Mississippi delta. "This is called flying under the radar, man."

"Fly, yes, but I didn't know we were going to *drive*."

Lance barked a laugh. "The only people who hire me for runs like this usually don't make many comments on my technique." He angled the stick, following a deep, rocky canyon leading into the northern part of Coahuila. "This is nothing, man. I had some guys hire me last year who insisted on flying in the ungodliest weather you ever saw. Raining like hell, man, from a hurricane that came in off the Baja coast and, like, cruised all across Mexico. If that wasn't bad enough, all I had was a pair of headlights to look for when we got to the LZ. We were in and out without anyone suspecting, but I never did find out why they were dropping off. I don't mind that, like you two. It's the stuff folks want to pick up and haul *north* that I won't work with, and believe me, man, there's plenty of business to keep me busy if I wanted it.

"But this is better though, staying in-country, if you know what I mean. Grease a few greedy palms, and you can do damn near anything you want down here, as long as you don't cross the cartels or the Mexican police . . . or the military, come to think of it. Just keeping my head down, man. You won't believe how many people ask me to do just this kind of thing.

"The problem flying this close to the ground these days are drones, man. They're everywhere, even at night. Especially up around the border. The cartels are flying drugs over the river with those things all the time now. I've had those damned mechanical bugs almost tangle in the rotors, man. You don't know they're around until they whiz by. I had one just two days ago on a clear day almost punch through the canopy, man. Glanced off the plastic like an RPG. Damn! That's the scar right there." He pointed off to the co-pilot side. "Scared the piss out of me.

"And man, you know, I heard they have 'em big enough to fly *people* over the river now." He held his right hand as wide as he could in the cockpit. "Can you imagine one this big? Dude, that'll put a dent in the coyotes' business for sure if they get that technology up and running. Think of it! Swarms of giant drones hauling people? Think of the traffic flying back and forth."

He checked the instrument panel and gave a harsh bark. "Man. That brings a whole new meaning to human trafficking."

Lance came recommended by a friend Perry Hale had known while he was in Iraq. He'd called the guy from the truck only a few hours before Sonny called, and asked if he knew anyone who flew choppers in Coahuila.

The friend recommended Lance with one caveat. "He's crazy as a Bessie bug, but he can fly anything that'll get off the ground."

Lance pulled the stick back on the battered old Eurobus helicopter that was once painted a pale blue, but now was almost neutral in color. They rose above a rocky ridge, but still well below the radar. "Dude. Y'all want me to pick you up later?"

"No." Perry Hale adjusted the microphone. "I don't know where we'll cross back."

"Dude. Just keep my number handy. I'll come get you."

"Roger that."

"Hey, man, can I ask you something?"

"Sure."

"I saw those bags you loaded. They're *heavy*, and I think I know what's in 'em. How'd y'all get firearms across the river?"

This was why Perry Hale didn't want to talk at all on the trip. "Coming south is a breeze. Like you said, it's moving stuff north that's the problem."

"Man, they catch y'all with just one little .22 round in your pocket and you'll be in a Mexican prison for the next thirty years, if you live that long, and here I am hauling enough guns to start our own country. Dude, you have some kind of death wish?"

"They won't catch us."

Something in Perry Hale's tone slowed Lance's roll. He checked the instrument panel again. Several non-essential pieces of equipment were gone, leaving dark holes where the electronics had been. "All right. We're almost where you wanted to go, but man, I hope you have enough rats and water. I haven't seen a light in miles."

"We know." Perry Hale pushed the microphone back down, ending his part of the conversation.

"We're here. Chalk Canyon's that way."

"Don't land too close. Take us a couple of clicks back to the east."

"So no one hears us come in. Right, man."

Staying right above the canyon, Lance followed a

few more miles before finding a good place to land. "This is it. Honey, we're home."

The moon was still high enough for them to see a wide, flat section big enough to handle the helicopter. Lance slowed, raising the chopper's nose, and settled onto the sand, landing light as a feather, but keeping the big engine at idle.

"We're far enough away from your target area that they won't hear the rotors, whoever *they* are. Good luck, man! *Vaya con dios!*"

Perry Hale and Yolanda popped the door and were out in seconds, dragging two packs and the same number of heavy bags out onto the ground. As soon as they were clear, Lance gave them a thumbs up, and the helicopter rose barely thirty feet into the air before he turned and disappeared back the way they came.

"Won't Sonny be surprised to see us?" Perry Hale kept it light as he threw the strap of his MOLLEE pack over one shoulder and shrugged into the other.

"He will after he gets through chewing our butts." Yolanda settled her gear, patting the pockets of her tactical vest that would blend into the desert come daylight. By the way, *man*, how much did that little trip just cost us?"

Perry Hale laughed at her impersonation. "Well, *man*, it was a freebie. An old pal owed me one and footed the bill."

Standing on the rocky desert floor, Perry Hale and Yolanda pulled their weapons from the black bags and slipped the straps over their shoulders. Leaving the bags behind, they saddled up and headed across the desert toward a canyon highway leading to Texas.

Chapter 43

Conversation between me and Devil Woman Tish kinda dried up for a little while. I had the foot-feed almost all the way down to the floorboard and we were booking it as the sun peeked over the horizon on our right. At that hour, there was very little traffic, but each time we rounded a corner I expected to see a roadblock manned by cartel members or the military.

We passed a couple of old trucks going the opposite direction, and caught up to a late-model Mercedes that saw us in their rearview mirror and immediately pulled onto the shoulder to let us pass.

They'd likely recognized something in the style of the SUV I was piloting or from the way we roared up on them so fast. In that country, citizens probably didn't want to take the chance of pissing off the wrong person who might kill them with as little thought as running over one of the many terrapins crossing the highway in the pre-dawn cool.

We'd been driving with all four windows up, because the desert air was chilly and I couldn't think with the wind roaring in my ears. I was glad we were, because dry dust boiled up from under the car slowing on the shoulder as soon as their tires were off the pavement. We punched through the cloud as our own tires ate up the miles.

My eyes kept flicking from the highway ahead to the rearview and side mirrors. I couldn't believe we weren't being followed and after a while, began to think that my luck had held for once and we'd gotten away clean.

The intersecting road I was looking for appeared on the map in the dash and I slowed. My spirits sagged a little when I got a good look at the rough track's diagonal path off the highway. I took it anyway and the tires sang a different song on the caliche as rocks rattled against the undercarriage. They were much more muffled than I would have expected.

Steering felt a little squirrely, and we rocked side to side. Like I said, I'd learned to drive on dirt and gravel roads, and something wasn't right. It finally dawned on me that the Expedition didn't feel the same as other SUVs I've driven in the past. "You had this thing upgraded, didn't you?"

My new little friend glared a hole through the windshield.

"Beefed up suspension, heavier doors. We're in an armored vehicle. Did you have them install steel plates? Nah, that'd be too heavy, Kevlar, I bet." Using a knuckle, I reached out and tapped the windshield. "Bulletproof?"

"I've already told you that if you release me, I will let you live. I see blood running from your hair and onto the side of your face. Have you been shot? Let me go and you won't be hurt any worse."

"Cut myself shaving this morning."

"Turn around and get back on the highway so you can drive us east to Piedras Negra and you can get out and disappear."

"Well, that's a fine offer, but you've already shown me your stripes, so I'll pass. And besides, now that we're off, I'm not getting back on Highway 53. I 'magine it's about to be working alive with your people and likely the police or military."

"People get lost and die out here. I don't intend to die with you."

Long morning shadows from desert vegetation stretched across the dry landscape. "They do, but I don't think we're gonna get lost." I checked the map on the screen and zoomed out to be sure I was still going the right direction. It was dangerous business not giving the road my full attention, but I had to be sure.

"Do you know where you are going?"

"I do." Now that I'd figured out we were in an armored vehicle, I felt a little better. I've worked security when dignitaries come to my part of the state, along with other experienced Rangers. Some of the vehicles supplied by the feds were outfitted with everything from military grade run-flat tires, Kevlar wrapped gas tanks and radiators, and underbody panels. The electronics in those things are mind-boggling.

Over the years we'd heard about cartel leaders buying tricked out SUVs. We suspected three had crossed the river into El Paso five years earlier and engaged in a rolling gun battle with a rival cartel down the streets bordering the river. Apparently, the bad guys from across Mexico were better shots than the bad guys on our side, because after they killed a car full of the opposition, and since there were no bullet holes in the

SUVs, they simply drove across into New Mexico and then back home without being stopped.

"What other upgrades does this have?"

She turned dead eyes on me. "My hands are going to sleep."

"If you think I'm gonna give you any slack, in any sense, you're wrong."

Something in the rearview mirror caught my attention and the thing I'd been dreading was about to happen.

A similar dark SUV was gaining fast, followed by the rooster tail plume of dust, golden and oddly pretty in the morning light.

Chapter 44

With the rising sun peeking over the ridge of mountains at their backs, Perry Hale and Yolanda pushed hard, alternately jogging and walking through the chilly desert air. Not one to completely trust technology, Perry Hale double-checked the position with a map and compass.

The dark purple sky lightened to a pale blue. Muted grays only minutes earlier burst with color. Deep browns and ochre stones mixed with gold and green leaves of sage plants. The colors would wash out as the sun rose high overhead only to regain their rich hues at sundown.

He sucked water from his camelback, satisfied they'd made good time from where Lance dropped them off. "We're about a mile away."

Figuring they were on one of the expansive, remote ranches in that dead zone of the Coahuila state, he was looking for a packed dirt and caliche road that wound around arroyos, deep canyons, and low mountains. Their decision to try and intersect Sonny Hawke's escape route seemed insane, but they'd been with him enough to know how his mind worked.

It was like no one else's.

Most of the ranch roads followed the terrain sculpted by erosion. Some were short and winding two-track lanes that most often dead ended at a canyon or defunct windmill. Others led through dry washes to huge ranges and pastures, but the one he was looking for was wider than most, and ran truer than the others toward the border.

It was a natural route used for hundreds of years, first by raiding Comanches. The Mexican people followed the route as well, and once the Indians no longer harassed those living in the territory, traders and travelers kept it wide and clear with millions of footsteps, both human and animal.

Now hardened almost to the consistency of cement, it was made wider by vehicles that came through several times a week, coyotes moving people and goods north to Chalk Canyon. Due to the lack of intersecting highways, habitat, or settlements, the frontier was seldom patrolled on the Mexican side by police or the military.

That's where Sonny would go.

Chapter 45

My passenger must have sensed my body tighten. The SUV was quite a ways behind, but he was catching up. The road curved back there, and when it did, I saw a second SUV following with just enough distance to avoid the first one's plume of dust.

A flashback to the movie set. Two vehicles, driving with the same amount of distance between them. These were the same people.

Instead of following the canyon's edge on our left, as we'd been doing, the road straightened, angling away. I punched the accelerator and we gained a little distance, but it wasn't enough.

The navigation system didn't show any road going directly to Langtry. My intention was to drive as far as possible, and that hopefully meant to the road's terminus, then get out and hump it along the edge of the canyon to the river. I knew Villarreal would intentionally slow me down, but she didn't weigh a hundred pounds soaking wet and full of bananas. I'd knock her out and carry her if I had to.

The knowledge that I was likely spinning my wheels weighed at the back of my mind too. There was the chance that I'd already created an international incident by taking the woman. The Mexican government didn't much like the idea of Americans dragging their citizens north against their will. Soldiers could at that moment be cutting cross country, ready to intercept me.

Major Parker had given me free reign to step outside the Ranger's traditional legal boundaries to get the job done, but he might have the same issue as the Mexican government, taking Villarreal without an arrest warrant. Then again, my charge was to handle things the same way those old Rangers did in the 1800s and the early part of the twentieth century, driven by instinct, gut reaction, and right vs. wrong. Maybe this time I'd gone too far.

Lessons from my high school civics class kept popping into my mind. The job of the U.S. government was to maintain foreign diplomacy, second was military defense, third was maintenance of domestic order, fourth was administration of justice, and I couldn't recall the rest.

That was enough. Maintenance of domestic order and administration of justice kept running over and over in a continuous loop. I was bringing a cartel leader to justice, a woman who ordered the deaths of countless individuals, many innocent. I was putting a stop to a cruel woman who was bringing her addictive crap into my country through a pipeline that would potentially impact hundreds of thousands of people in unimaginable ways.

I'd seen videos shot by hidden cameras the Border

Patrol had set up south of Big Bend, and eastward to where I was headed in Langtry. Teams of camouflaged men carrying huge packs on their backs walked in line through the desert, bearing automatic weapons. They were hardened, disciplined mules loaded down with drugs, and the rifles proved they would kill anyone who got in their way.

It wasn't just there. I'd also viewed similar footage taken by hidden cameras on private ranches of gangsters on horseback in Arizona, armed with AR-style rifles. One of the horses also had an AK-47 strapped to the saddle. These were the same kind of people who worked for the small Latino woman riding beside me.

And now they were on my tail.

A bend in the road yanked me back to the job at hand. I tapped the brakes and power-slid around the wide curve.

Chapter 46

Sonny Hawke's Shadow Response Team, Perry Hale and Yolanda, broke into a trot, afraid they'd reach the road too late. Coming around a particularly lush stand of cactus in the morning light, they emerged on a ridge overlooking their destination. According to the information they'd gotten from Sonny, it was the logical place to intercept the fleeing Ranger.

Breathing hard, Perry Hale was pleased that he'd led them to Chalk Canyon and the wide track following the rim. "Now where to?"

"Up yonder." Holding a small pair of binoculars to her eyes with both hands, Yolanda pointed with a little finger. "See how the road bends to the right? It curves away from the canyon, but see that?"

Perry Hale dug from a pocket on his cammies and came out with a pair of compact Zeiss binoculars. He squinted in the direction she'd pointed. "I got it. That looks like a wide pull off." He spoke without taking his eyes from the glasses. "It is, but it's a helluva turn-around."

"That's what I saw on Google maps." She glanced

southward, where they expected Sonny to appear. "The road bends to follow the river to the east, but that swirl in the sand told me that's where the traffickers drop people off to be picked up by the coyotes."

"This road's damn near a highway. I bet buses come through here."

"I've heard they pack them full at two or three thousand dollars a head. That's why the turnaround's so big. Look, the road that branches off over there and crosses the river is half as wide as it is before it gets to the turnaround. We found it."

Perry Hale lowered the glasses. "So what do you think?"

"If Sonny has enough of a lead, he'll leave his car right there and run for the border on foot. I don't think a regular vehicle can drive far through all that. He might intend to follow the edge of the canyon, or drop down like everyone else has done and walk the canyon trail. That way he'll be less likely to be seen from the air.

"There might be trails or roads up here on the surface, and staying up topside might not be a good idea. One thing's for sure, if he follows the coyote's path, he won't get lost. Remember that trail out of El Paso where we practiced tracking? There was no way to get lost more than half the time because of everything they drop on the way."

Months earlier, the class members that day had all been stunned at the amount of refuse left behind by illegal aliens crossing the ranches west of El Paso. The Border Patrol agents led the group of ten people, along with an environmentalist who told them that since the turn of the twenty-first century, a more than forty percent increase in illegal immigration on the southwestern border severely impacted the desert ecology.

It was the first time any of them had heard the term "nesting" in reference to the people marching northward across the harsh desert. During one rest stop in the heat of the day, the environmentalist named Curt Caldwell pointed to what looked like a giant trash dump in the shade of several spreading mesquite trees.

He explained that nesting occurs in the desert under native plants that provide scant cover from the blistering sun. It's when the immigrants stop in the same shade over and over again, like family groups, killing the ecology with their refuse and waste. It's not uncommon for agents on the Texas side of the border to discover and take into custody large groups of exhausted and dispirited illegal immigrants gathered together to rest and stay out of sight.

Like nomads, they leave behind what is no longer useful, such as used needles and drug paraphernalia, empty water containers, plastic bags, clothing, food containers, and hundreds if not thousands of used diapers. They also drop whatever is too troublesome to carry.

"All he'll have to do is follow the trash they leave." Yolanda put her binoculars away. "There's no way he can get lost, and he'll find where they cross. So, we hoof it for the river?"

"I don't think so." Perry Hale squinted toward the south, looking for a dust plume or people walking the road. "If they're close on his tail, this'll be where it's most dangerous. He won't follow the road's bend over that dry wash. That'll take him away from the border. He has to take the canyon, so he'll follow the road until it runs out and leave his vehicle.

"Let's move down there where the road necks down between the canyon and that steep slope. We might be able to catch anyone following Sonny in a crossfire and hold them long enough for him to get gone. One of us can stay here, and the other head for the river. It'll double our chances of being right, and we can cover him when they cross."

She considered the idea. "You're right. How far is the border?"

"About ten miles."

"You think one of us can make it that far before he gets here?"

"Won't make any difference. Say I stay here. If I engage, it'll buy Sonny time. If I don't, and he has time, I can pitch in with them and you'll be our insurance for later. You'll get there well before he does."

She bit her lip, thinking. "You don't think he'll try and drive up here."

"No." Perry Hale pointed. "Look off down yonder. That's a deep canyon that leads into country too rough from here on out for anything other than a Humvee, and I doubt that's what he's driving."

"Fine then. I'll be waiting for you."

He gave her a wide grin. "Follow the trash, like you said, but be careful, there may be coyotes coming back this way after dropping people off last night. You don't want to tangle with them if you don't have to."

"I hope he hasn't already passed."

"I doubt it. From what he described, we got here in time."

She nodded and settled the pack on her shoulders. "All right, buddy. Be safe. I'll see y'all on the river." She turned and broke into a jog.

"Right. Hey, Yoli!"

Irritated, she whirled. "I told you about that nickname . . ."

"I love you. Be careful."

Speechless, she turned and took off, but she was smiling into the morning light.

Chapter 47

We drove along the edge of what I hoped was Chalk Canyon. It could have been an unnamed gash, a different canyon for all I knew, but I thought we were in the general direction.

Didn't matter. The road split once again, this time a branch angled to the left and downward into a low-water crossing. I slowed and stopped, studying the fork. Another look into the rearview mirror. The terrain hid the oncoming vehicle, but I was sure he wasn't more than two miles behind.

The road emerged from the now-dry wash and angled up a shallow slope on the other side. It became a two-track path that disappeared toward the northwest. Bad guys could pop up behind us at any moment, but I sat there and adjusted the map view in the dash, thinking that maybe the road widened or turned north, but I finally saw that it ended only a mile farther.

That's when I saw another map feature I hadn't noticed. I punched the icon that looked like Sputnik and the view suddenly changed to a 3-D satellite picture of everything between me and Langtry. It was like staring down from an airplane, and I was shocked at how rugged the country looked.

It gave me an exact view of where we needed to go.

Villarreal twitched, and a quick glance told me she was mad as a sore-tail tomcat that I'd found that feature she'd likely installed just for herself.

I knew we'd eventually have to dump the SUV and walk the rest of the way, but the road ended way faster than I expected. It looked longer on the screen, and terminated at a wide turnaround. Beyond that was nothing but rolling, rocky country slashed with deep ravines and shallow runoffs. It looked like God had finally gotten frustrated and hacked at the land with a sword until he burned off some irritation. Then he scorched it.

We'd have to leave the SUV at the turnaround and take the canyon. Satisfied that we were still on the right road, I adjusted the rifle still laying in my lap and we took off again. Down the road a piece, it curved into a sharp drop on our left, and a steep-layered shale cliff on the right.

The terrain and that satellite view gave me an idea.

I stopped again and wasted a few more seconds on the map. There it was, the terminus of my dirt road half a mile farther. Based on what I was seeing, the river was around ten miles away. The wide turnaround told me that's where we'd drop off into the canyon on foot, but we didn't have to drive all the way.

"This is where we get out."

Villarreal looked around. "Here?"

"You ever hear of The Three Hundred?"

She frowned. "Are you talking about that movie?"

"In a sense."

I didn't have time to explain the battle of Thermopylae and the three hundred Spartans who held off the entire 20,000-man Persian army for three days. The Spartans stalled the invading army by using a natural choke point, a narrow pass bordered by a steep mountain wall on one side and a cliff falling off to the sea on the other.

Of course, they lost in the long run, but I had no intention of staying there in an extended gun battle. The men coming up on our tail would simply drop down into the dry canyon or send me around the low ridge and come in from the back, catching me in a crossfire, which was exactly what happened to the Spartans.

What I intended to do was get them out of those mobile battleships of theirs and stall them as long as I could. We'd all be walking, or running, pretty soon anyway.

I detrucked and circled around the hood, yanking the passenger door open when I got there. I knew then why they called Villarreal the Devil Woman, because she went insane, kicking and screaming and fighting as I unbuckled the seatbelt. The top of her head caught my cheekbone. I saw stars for a moment.

With all that black hair flying around, I grabbed a handful and hauled her out onto the ground. She landed with a thump and spun around on her butt, trying to kick me. Getting a better hold on her hair, I pulled her backward as fast as I could, dragging her across the sharp rocks and hardpan.

Squealing at the pain in her scalp and bound hands, she twisted sideways. I bore down until pain changed the shape of her mouth. "All right! Cut me free and I'll walk."

"You fight, and I'll drag you some more."

"I won't."

I stepped back, throwing another glance back where we'd come from. "Your hands are going to stay tied for the time being. Stay right here. If you try to run, I'm gonna yank your pants down around your ankles and you'll have to shuffle along like you're in shackles. You get me."

"I'm not wearing anything under them." Sullen, she stared at the ground. "I bet you'd like to see that, wouldn't you?"

"Not hardly."

But I'd peek, anyway.

I hurried back to the car and started the engine again and grabbed up a disposable lighter I'd seen in one of the cup holders between the seats, then popped the hood. It took me a minute to find what I was looking for under there. Back in the old days, engines took up only three-quarters of the space under the hood. The Expedition's power plant was packed in so tight I could barely see.

I cut the gas line. Under pressure, it spewed like a tiny firehose while the hot engine coughed and sputtered. If the line hadn't been held in place by clips, it probably would have flailed around and soaked me. I didn't want that to happen. Once while working on an RV in Quanah, Texas, I got a face and nose full of gas and it like to've killed me. I didn't want that experience ever again.

I jerked the gas line free of its clamps, getting enough slack to direct as much as possible across the engine until it died and the pressure lessened.

Then I lit it. The gasoline caught with a whoosh, startling me even though I'd been expecting it.

That'll give 'em something to think about. The Old Man's lessons came back like the reruns of an old TV show. *Now you're using your noodle. They can't get out and push a burning car out of the way, so if they keep chasing you, they'll be on foot, too.*

I needed every edge I could get to make it out alive.

Villarreal was standing when I backed away from the fire. "Thanks for armoring this monster. It'll make it harder for them to get around." I reached for her hair again and she stumbled back, almost falling. "Let's go."

"All right. I'm coming."

She shoved past me and I put a hand on her shoulder, pressing her to move faster. "We're jogging."

"Not in this heat."

"It's not hot yet. Get going." I glanced over my shoulder at the fire and boiling black smoke and pushed her again. She shifted into a stumbling jog and I followed.

A gray, crumbling rock on the layer-cake cliff ten feet overhead vaporized. Then the dirt in front of us exploded in a line of mini detonations. I whirled at the same time the gunshots echoed down across the canyon and saw a man standing in the middle of the road fifty or sixty yards behind the burning SUV.

They caught us faster than I expected. I shouldered Victim's AR-15 and cut down on the guy, but at the last moment, I shifted my aim.

It was Esteban.

Chapter 48

Esteban and two *soldados* rode in the back seat of the SUV driven by Incencio. Geronimo rode shotgun.

Geronimo pointed. "There they are!"

Incencio sped up, but they lost sight of the Devil Woman's black Expedition as a curve took it from sight. "This road dead ends not far from here."

"Then we have them." Geronimo unconsciously rubbed the machine pistol in his hand. "I will blow that man's knees out."

"When we catch him."

The second SUV behind them stayed as close as possible. The air-conditioned atmosphere inside the Expedition thickened with tense anticipation. It had been an extraordinary night that elevated their blood-lust to an almost fanatical height.

Esteban bit his lip. "It won't be that easy."

Geronimo twisted to look over his shoulder. "Why not?"

"Because this man is more dangerous than you give him credit for. He created a diversion with that team of mercenaries so that he could get in and kidnap *La Jefa*.

Don't you think he's planning something for up ahead? He's not simply running in fear."

The engine slowed as Incencio and Geronimo exchanged glances. Incencio looked into the rearview mirror to see Esteban. "What do you think he has in mind?"

"We all know this road dead ends. It is where the Devil Woman's cargo is unloaded to walk the rest of the way. He will plan a trap in which he ambushes us somehow."

Suddenly uncertain, Incencio slowed even more. "Where is Perez and those useless soldiers of his?"

Geronimo picked up the walkie-talkie from the floor. "Captain Perez."

The man's voice came back as soon as he took his finger off the button. "Yes."

"We have the *camionita deportiva* in sight. Where are you?"

Perez described his location. He was ten miles behind. Geronimo gave them their position. "We have him trapped. Come join us and we will allow you to be the one to take this man's life."

"I will be there in five minutes."

The Expedition slowed again, and Incencio pulled onto an open, flat area cut on the inside of the road and cradled by the steep mountain to their right. The other SUV pulled up beside them, and the passenger-side glass rolled down. A shave-headed *cholo* with the number 1518 tattooed across his forehead stuck his elbow out of the window. His entire face was a mass of tattooed words and art. "What are we doing?"

Incencio pointed down the road. "They are close. We are waiting for Perez."

"We don't need that *pendejo*."

"No, we don't need him, but we want him. Let those fools take the lead. There may be an ambush. They can fight. I just want *La Jefa*."

The *cholo* relayed the information to those inside the vehicle with him. He nodded and turned back to Incencio's Expedition. "We want to do the blood work. Let us go ahead."

Esteban had an idea. "Let them. I will ride up there and see what happens. You can come up with Perez."

"Bien."

Esteban opened his door and spoke through the open passenger window at Enrique Ybarra. "I will ride with you."

The two men in the back seat made room, pleased that he was joining them. One of the *soldados*, Alfredo Gutierrez, waved in excitement. *"Venga! Vamonos!"*

Esteban slid inside. "Go.

The driver, Enrique Ybarra punched the accelerator, and they sped down the road.

Only a mile farther, they came around a curve to find the burning Expedition parked in the middle of a narrow choke point, effectively blocking the road. Expecting an ambush, they flinched as the SUV slid to a stop in a cloud of dust.

Not wanting to be trapped inside the vehicle, despite the armor upgrades, their bloodlust took over and all five rolled out, guns raised. When no one fired at them, they relaxed and advanced.

"I'm going to check ahead. Stay here and keep me covered." Esteban jogged forward, feeling the heat from the burning vehicle as he squeezed past the open doors. His arms sizzled with the nauseating smell of burning hair. "Shit! Don't try to follow me. Get this car out of the way."

Ybarra climbed back under the wheel while the others stepped back, ready for anyone to appear in front of the dead Expedition. Esteban hurried around the corner, his Scorpion shouldered and ready to fire.

He had one hope, that Ranger Hawke would recognize him and not shoot.

Sixty yards around the curve and out of sight from the others, he saw Hawke pushing the Devil Woman ahead. Taking a deep breath, he fired over their heads into the steep slope on their right, then stood in the open with both arms open wide, hoping Hawke would understand his meaning.

Hawke whirled, raised the AR and fired also. Esteban expected to feel the impact of the bullets, but they whined off the rocks five feet to his left.

His idea was working.

Chapter 49

Behind several large boulders perched on the ridge overlooking the road, Perry Hale peered through the binoculars. A tidal wave of relief washed over him when the saw a black Expedition come around the bend. It had to be Sonny. Who else would be driving such a vehicle at a high rate of speed this far off the main highway?

The image was crystal clear in the German glass, and he barked a quiet laugh when the big SUV stopped and Sonny stepped out from behind the wheel. With two fingers, he pressed the microphone clipped on the collar of his tactical vest, hoping the signal would get through. "Yoli."

"I told you never to call me that."

"Sonny's here."

"Thank God."

"He still has his prisoner. Stop where you are and find a place to cover us. I'll make contact and help him push her along."

"Roger that."

"You gonna be easy to find on that trail?"

"Just follow the tracks and trash."

He reacquired Sonny again through the binoculars. By that time, Sonny had forcefully dragged a woman from the vehicle by the hair of her head.

Must have made him mad about something.

They had a long exchange, and she hung her head. A few seconds later, he watched as Sonny left her standing on the road and popped the hood. Moments later, black smoke rose in the sky, blowing in Perry Hale's direction.

What'n hell?

Then he got it. Hawke was using the burning SUV to block the narrow road, making it impossible for another vehicle to follow. Perry Hale grinned as he watched them jog in his direction. The grin disappeared at the sound of machine-gun fire.

Dropping the binoculars, he shouldered the AR-15 and squinted through the scope. Sonny spun and returned fire, but from Perry Hale's elevation, the smoke hid the shooter. Frustrated that he didn't have a clear target and growling deep in his throat, Perry Hale waited with his finger on the trigger, praying that the gunman would step to the side or the smoke would shift.

And it happened. A gust of wind took the smoke away to reveal a man standing in the road, arms out and hands by his side. Perry Hale hesitated. With his arms wide, the man was not an immediate threat, and he wasn't sure the *soldado* he was looking at was the one who'd fired in the first place.

Sonny had a weapon, and the distance was short. He could take care of himself.

Probably best to wait and see what happens.

Chapter 50

Knees suddenly weak with relief, Esteban lowered his arms. Sonny had recognized him. The *sicario* twisted around to make sure his *compadres* hadn't seen what happened, but the curve and smoke covered his actions. The rising pitch of an engine told him they had a plan. They were either leaving and abandoning Esteban or had another idea.

Turning back, Esteban waved Sonny onward and gave him a thumbs up signal. He'd bought them a few minutes at least. The Ranger had the woman in custody and seemed competent enough to get her to the U.S. authorities. It was time to come in and leave this life of murder and blood before his luck ran out.

I'll make sure Hawke gets her across the river, and then I can contact my handler and give them all the evidence we need.

He wasn't sure about how everything was going to work out, but he was finished.

The burning car *whumped* somewhere inside, sending up an even thicker boil of black smoke. Close enough to feel the pressure wave, Esteban staggered forward, away from the intensified heat.

La Jefa took that moment to bolt. Arms tied behind her back, she sprinted down the road, but the Ranger didn't notice. He seemed stunned at seeing Esteban, and at the muffled explosion that almost sent the undercover agent to his knees.

Too close to his men to shout instructions at the Ranger, Esteban waved his arms, pointing behind Hawke, but Hawke's attention was on the action around the SUV. The only thing Esteban could do was shoulder the Scorpion, take careful aim, and send a string of bullets in front of the fleeing woman only half a second before the wind shifted again, enveloping him in smoke.

A second weapon chattered from somewhere up ahead, and bullets stitched the ground only inches from where he stood. He jumped back at the same time the burning car suddenly *moved*.

Esteban realized Incencio intended to push it out of the way. He glanced at the front tires that were burning fiercely, but the Ranger had turned them to the right, toward the wall of rock He grinned and moved even farther back from the blistering heat to crouch behind the cover of a thick growth of desert scrub growing at the edge of the road. He figured that the shooter on the ridge wouldn't be able to find him in the prickly vegetation covering the canyon's slope.

Wondering who was up there in the first place, he waited to watch and see what would happen next.

Chapter 51

That was the damnedest thing I'd ever seen. The guy shooting at us was Esteban, but the shots were only to get my attention. Seeing him standing there with his arms wide almost made me laugh, until the car exploded behind him.

Esteban staggered and almost fell, but the next thing he did stunned me for a moment. He shouldered his weapon and fired again. The rounds whizzed past fifteen feet to my right.

"What is he *doing*!" I whirled, looking for cover and saw the Devil Woman on the ground, twenty yards away. She'd been trying to run, and I wanted to slap my head. I should have expected that.

To make things even more interesting, someone in the ridge above cut loose with a string of rifle shots directed at the burning car and Esteban. I looked up to see the shape of a man high above, and knew immediately who it was.

I waved my arms. "No! Perry Hale! He's with me!" For a moment, I couldn't process everything fast enough. Perry Hale was here! Had Esteban shot at me again, this time hitting the Devil Woman?

There was no time to stand around and think. Knowing now that I had cover from above, I rushed to Villarreal lying on the ground, expecting to find her leaking from several holes.

She didn't have a scratch on her and was not pleased at all. Sitting up, she shook the sand off her face and out of her black hair. She cut loose with a string of Spanish cussing that went on longer than Lincoln's Gettysburg address and finally ended in English. "That's Esteban! He is one of my best *sicarios*. Why didn't he kill you, and why was he shooting at me?"

A light bulb glowed over my head. It was time to knock her off her high horse and put a little doubt in her mind. "It looks to me like that guy's trying to kill *you*. If he'd been a better shot through all that smoke, he'd'a done it."

Her eyes narrowed as I put both hands under her arms and stood her upright. She threw the hair out of her face and twisted her torso to the side, likely thinking I was going to make good on my promise to drop her britches around her ankles. "You're wrong. My people are loyal to me. He's been with me for years."

"Yeah, but you weren't under arrest then and headin' back to stand trial. Looks to me like he wants to take you out so you won't talk, or maybe your whole gang's in on it. I bet one of 'em intends to take over. With you out of the way, somebody'll want to take your place, and all that money."

An engine roared just around the bend, and I knew something was up. "There's more of 'em. They're gonna do their best to run through me and get to you. I've opened a can of worms I didn't expect. Lady, they're after both of us. Run!"

Chapter 52

Enrique Ybarra, the youngest of the Devil Woman's *soldados*, was behind the wheel. Following Incencio's orders to push the burning Expedition over the edge, he'd only managed to set his own vehicle on fire. The burning SUV now sitting crossways on the narrow road ignited the sun-dried brush growing on the steep slope. Flames flickered and climbed upward. At the same time, long grasses swaying up over the drop-off had ignited, and the fire spread quickly along the edge.

Ybarra hadn't considered his tires would catch fire from the brush as he pushed the uncooperative SUV that refused to drop over the edge. Instead, it veered up against the upward slope.

More black smoke billowed from his tires. Ybarra threw the transmission into reverse and backed away. Two of the gangsters in the SUV with him jumped out to stomp out the flames, but it was too little, too late. They backed away, watching both vehicles quickly become engulfed.

Not knowing what to do, they waited on Incencio.

Five minutes later, the two military Humvees with

Incencio's Expedition following behind pulled up to the curve. The lead Hummer stopped. Behind it, Captain Perez stepped out of the second Humvee's passenger side and glared at the Expedition. He stalked around the first vehicle and stopped with both hands on his hips.

"You idiots! What have you done?"

Angry for what had happened, Ybarra pointed with the rifle in his hand. "I was trying to clear the road."

"And you succeeded in blocking it even more." Perez stepped to the side and waved at the driver in the lead Humvee. "Push this mess over the edge."

The young, wide-eyed soldier nodded and shifted into gear.

"Do not be too slow, or you will catch on fire, too!"

The big 7,700-pound military vehicle crunched into the back of the nearest SUV. The Humvee's engine roared as it pressed forward, shoving both vehicles down the curve until they went over the sharp edge with a furious crackle of branches. The fireballs rolled thirty feet to the canyon floor full of dry vegetation, strewing flames along the way.

Perez nodded. "That is how it is done." He stalked past the young soldier behind the wheel. "Good work! Now, go! Lead the way." Glaring at Ybarra and the others, he was back in his Humvee by the time the lead vehicle accelerated around the curve, gaining speed in an effort to catch their fleeing prey.

Perez slammed the door. "Stay on his bumper!"

The driver stepped on the gas as the same time an automatic weapon opened up on the lead Hummer. Perez's vehicle cleared the fiercely burning curve just in time to see the lead Humvee jerk sharply to the left and tip over the edge.

Perez's driver slammed the brakes. *"Hijo de puta! Ninguna arma de calibre ligero puede penetrar este vidrio!"*

"He didn't shoot through the glass, it is bulletproof. That idiot got scared and went over the edge by accident."

Chapter 53

Villarreal was running faster than she wanted. I don't know if it was because I kept shoving her to gain more speed, or the idea that I'd planted that her own men were trying to kill her. Either way, we were hoofing it along pretty good to the wide turnaround at the end of the road.

That doesn't mean we were making good time. It's hard to run with your hands tied behind your back, but she was inspired enough to settle into a fairly fast pace.

I kept throwing glances over my shoulder, terrified that someone would get a clear shot at us. My back tensed at the thought of a bullet finding its way under the bottom edge of my tactical vest or above. The unprotected hairs on my neck prickled.

Tire tracks underfoot circled the turnaround where heavy vehicles had dropped off their passengers then departed. Brush grew around the edges, but a clear space beaten down by thousands of northbound feet showed me where the immigrant trail dropped into the canyon.

"There! Get below the rim and they can't see us."

She thought that was a good idea and pitched over the drop-off and down the path that descended at a comfortable angle. It was a wide packed thoroughfare, making it easy to maintain her balance.

I relaxed a little once we reached the canyon floor and put some distance between us and them. You'd think it'd be bare, and some are, but this one was grown up more than most. The route led through scraggly bushes scattered as far as we could see, along with clumps of desert grasses, thick growths of ever-present prickly pear cactus, bunch grasses, and other scrub I couldn't identify on a bet.

All we could hear was the thud of our feet on the hardpack and our own heavy breathing. We'd gone a good long ways before Villarreal finally whirled, hair plastered across her sweaty face. "Cut this damn cord off my wrists. I can't run like this."

"You did a great job, and no, I'm not gonna give you one single chance that don't involve your feet."

"I'm barefoot! I can't go much further. The bottom of one foot is already cut." She stood on one leg and showed me her wound that welled blood.

I hadn't really thought of that part, and in a way I felt sorry for her. I'd been on the run through the desert in bare feet once and still had the scars to prove it. "Sorry, but this trail's wide. Stay in the middle and watch your step."

"You bastard!"

"You may be right, but there's nothing I can do about it right now." I pushed her shoulder. "Get going."

Cussing under her breath, she turned and led the way, stepping carefully in the widest, sandiest places she could find. I took a quick look over my shoulder to make sure no one was within shooting distance, and then followed, pushing her again to pick up the pace.

Somewhere behind us and high above, a rifle cracked three quick times. That would be Perry Hale. He liked triple taps. He'd cover for us a little while longer, and be along after that.

There was little air movement in the canyon, and it got hot pretty damn quick. The wide path full of footprints would have been easy to follow, even if it hadn't been strewn with trash. Plastic water bottles, empty gallon plastic jugs, and all sorts of food wrappings were scattered where they'd been dropped. Some of the trash was half buried in the sand. A lot was fresh, lying loose, or blown against the brush.

Resigned, Villarreal plodded ahead despite her bare feet.

More shots echoed behind us, and then quiet.

Chapter 54

Downstream in Chalk Canyon, Yolanda Rodriguez kept up a fast, steady pace northward until Perry Hale radioed that he'd found Sonny. Now she was looking for a good place to set up and wait for them. It wasn't easy. A clear field of fire was foremost, but with so much scrub and brush growing in the canyon bottom of varying widths, she had to keep looking.

She passed a pile of cast-off garbage under the thin shade of a very old mesquite. The area was beaten clear, and the smell of human feces that followed her everywhere was too much. She jogged past cast-off clothing and used diapers ripped open by scavengers. Clouds of flies made a steady, audible hum.

A coat draped over a sun-bleached log.

Dead trees high overhead.

Scattered bones of some large animal.

The canyon rose steep on both sides, offering no place for concealment.

Finally, when she was about to give up and make do with what she found, Yolanda found what she was looking for. Waving the flies out of her face, she peered upward. The canyon bent, and ahead was a tumbledown of boulders and long-dead, silver-gray tree trunks washed into a tangle by a long-past flood. A similar tangle almost fifteen feet above her head defined the high-water mark of a massive flood.

Relieved that she didn't have to go any farther, she scrambled up the slope, starting crumbling rivers of sand and loose stones with each footstep. The sun-bleached detritus provided better footholds and with the crackling and popping of dry branches beneath her shoes, she wriggled into a natural lookout resembling the ragged nest of a giant, mythical eagle.

From that vantage point free of flies, she could see down the canyon and cover Perry Hale and Sonny as they came through. If the pressure became too much, the slope behind the position was swept clear, offering a quick retreat back to the canyon floor.

She settled in, moving smaller branches to make her position more comfortable. A thick, twisted cedar log was the perfect place to rest her AR-15.

Her side of the canyon was still in shade, making it harder for those down on the floor to see her. The sun wouldn't get high enough to throw light on the tangle for another hour or more.

Satisfied, she keyed her radio. "I'm in position."

Perry Hale answered, breathing hard. "Moving."

Yolanda swept the scope from side to side, familiar-izing herself with the floor. Satisfied that she had a fairly clear field of fire despite the dried grasses and sun-scorched plants, she relaxed.

A faint odor of wood smoke reached her, and she wondered how close the people were who'd built a campfire.

Chapter 55

Eyes fixed on the hard ground so that she could avoid as many sharp rocks and cactus as possible, Tish Villarreal, the Devil Woman of Coahuila, trudged forward in the now-stifling canyon, furious at the indignity of being taken from her home against her will and tied up with lamp cord, and now chased by her own men who intended to kill her.

Sweat trickled down the sides of her face, making her angrier still. Usually calm and calculating, her head was buzzing enough that she couldn't concentrate clearly. She was the leader of one of the most powerful cartels in Mexico, and the only woman who'd reached such a position of power. Not bad for a middle-class girl who grew up in the U.S.

Up until the moment Esteban shot at her, she'd been confident a massive machine was gearing up to get her back from the Ranger who had simply walked into her *ranchero* and took her without a warrant or any legal documents at all.

Law enforcement officers from the U.S. couldn't do that! They *had* to obey the strict laws that, up to then, kept their hands tied. With every step down that hot, still canyon, she fumed because this man yelled and threatened her! He'd threatened to take her pants down like a spanked child.

No one threatened the Devil Woman of Coahuila.

Though no one would dare use the name in her presence, she knew that's how they often referred to her, and she liked it. Villarreal carefully cultivated that persona to ensure that everyone feared her and obeyed without question. Those who hadn't wound up in her garden.

She rolled it over and over in her mind. It must have been one of her men who'd turned her over to this *rinche*. The security system she'd paid hundreds of thousands to install should have picked him up, especially after the original assault by the American team triggered all her alarms.

The drones, her extended eyes and ears had failed also. It had to be an inside job, and that's why she could so easily believe that an organized coup was taking place, possibly with Esteban at the helm. Once she was free, those two *idiotas* who were in charge of security would soon be rotting in the ground with the handles twisted around their spines growing hot in the summer sun.

Esteban would be a special treat. She wouldn't kill him. She'd personally bury him alive with his own handle protruding above the ground. She'd make sure he'd have access to air in some way to prolong his suffering. Maybe she'd stop by every hour or so to make sure he was suffering enough.

Could she hear him scream from below the ground?

That maddening shove on her shoulder by that

damned *rinche* brought her back to the present, making her realize she'd unconsciously slowed, walking along *empanado,* slow and absent-minded.

This was her country! He had no right to be there, dragging her along with people shooting at them. He'd gotten in so easily that her mind went down another rabbit hole at the thought that it might be someone else. Someone closer.

It could be Incencio, too! Up until then he'd been her right hand, her primary *sicario*. Could it be that he'd designed the aborted hit on the Nelson women from the start? He'd never failed before, but two little old ladies with *revolveres* shouldn't have killed three of her best men. He must have done it, laying the groundwork to take out those who were loyal to her, to shave the odds in his favor.

If it was him, she would watch as Geronimo ran the wires through his partner's living back while he screamed for mercy until his voice tore.

Her nose ran and she sniffed, then regretted the sound. The Ranger would think she was weak and crying like those pampered, soft women from across the border. The *Mujer Malvada* never cried. She never wept. She was as strong as any man.

In her mind's eye, Geronimo held Incencio to the ground while she personally worked the wire around his spine . . . wait! Could it be Geronimo who'd orchestrated this whole disaster? Was he alone? Maybe Incencio and Geronimo *together*?

It made sense. They'd been gone far too long, and the two spent so much time together that they could have planned the entire operation to take the cartel for their own. She was in the way, and a woman to boot.

Most would wait until the leader was arrested or dead. It would happen. It happened all the time, but she was smarter than the other cartel leaders.

No one could take her down. Not the Mexican government who wasn't on her payroll. Not the Americans, and for sure not the other cartel leaders who stayed in their own territories.

And those three, Incencio, Geronimo, and Esteban, knew it, so they planned everything down to the last detail to assume her position. After all, she was a woman wielding power in a world of *machismo*.

That was it. The three of them had arranged for her murder by the team of American operatives who failed, so now they were forced in the open, running her to ground like a dog.

But she couldn't figure how this infuriating man behind her fit in. He sounded like the Texas Rangers she'd studied back in her El Paso middle school, men who relished in following the law and couldn't be bought. Maybe this was the one odd man out, one who went out on his own, a renegade like Lone Wolf McQuade, but she hadn't seen the distinctly recognizable badge, either.

And then there was that loud Hawaiian shirt under his vest.

No matter. She had an idea. She'd use him to get to the river and across. She knew all the major smuggling routes along the fourteen contiguous Texas counties bordering the 1,254-mile-long Rio Grande. One came in near Laredo, and another south of Del Rio. Farther to the northwest, the routes entered Texas in the Big Bend Region and the last, El Paso.

All those routes were familiar, because she used

them to move drugs and people. The newest route, and one that was only becoming familiar to those outside law enforcement was where they were headed. For the past couple of years, the weather had been wet enough to pump the Rio Grande to near historic levels. Reports coming back from her *coyotes* said the crossing was difficult.

There the game would change. He'd have to free her hands so she wouldn't drown. When he did, she'd slip underwater and swim downstream for all she was worth. The Ranger couldn't have known she was a competitive swimmer in high school, and that she swam laps every morning in the *ranchero*'s Olympic-size pool.

It would be easy to evade capture in the water, and by that time her rescuers would be on the way. At the moment she set foot on American soil, she'd slip away and call people whose loyalty she could absolutely count on.

Her family.

All she needed to do was activate the tiny locator taped under her breast. The brainchild of Carlos, who was in charge of the drones, it was a last, desperate homing device in the event she was ever taken by a rival cartel. None of them ever expected that she'd be *arrested* by *anyone*.

Once activated by squeezing the thin device that looked similar to a tiny allergy pill in a blister pack, the locator would send a powerful signal to those who would be waiting on the other side. One was a half-brother Miguel Villarreal, who worked for the Texas Border Patrol. The other was his partner, who would help, because he was the first one they turned nearly eighteen months ago.

It was that partnership that gave her the idea to create even more teams under her control so that she could eventually run most of the drug and human trafficking into her home state.

"Faster!" That damned Ranger pushed her again. She picked up the pace and focused on following the trail to the river. The sooner, the better.

Chapter 56

The canyon was stifling, another reason *coyotes* moved their people at night. Sweat ran in a steady stream under my tactical vest, soaking the back waistband of my jeans. People voluntarily hike through canyons like that in the Big Bend, admiring the rough, dangerous country that could injure or kill you in a variety of ways, but right at that moment, I couldn't figure out why.

The rising sun still shaded the steep wall on our right, but it was growing thinner by the minute. I glanced up to see the sky was quickly changing from blue to white, bringing blistering heat to the canyon floor.

The idea that her own people were after her inspired Villarreal to move as fast as possible. Not used to that much exercise, she was sucking wind and I knew we'd have to stop soon. We both needed water.

Not that we were really running. No one can operate at maximum speed with both hands tied behind their backs, but she was game. The ground under our feet changed from hardpan, to soft sand for a good long while, giving her bare feet some relief, and then back to hardpan.

Every so often I'd swing around, checking our back trail, but it stayed empty. There was no more gunfire behind us. Perry Hale either had 'em pinned down, or maybe even killed them all. Now we were far enough away I didn't hear anything except the rustle of my clothing and our feet pounding on the ground.

It was an easy trail to keep up with. I felt like we were following a trash truck distributing its contents like a fertilizer spreader. The people who'd traipsed the canyon floor before us must have carried way more than they needed or figured everything on them was disposable.

I would have laughed at some point, despite the pain in my bruised chest or the pain in my head. Fate dropped doubt in Villarreal's mind at just the right moment, and those figurative dominoes were now falling in *her* mind. At least I didn't have to drag her along.

I finally took pity on her bare feet. "Hold up there in the shade. We need water, and you need something on those hooves of yours."

Hair damp against her face, the Devil Queen looked much less regal than when I found her back at the ranch. She slowed and finally stopped in what sparse shade she could find. "Yes. Water, please."

For the first time I noticed the swarms of flies buzzing in and out of the shade. Waving them out of my face, I angled myself to see back from where we came from. Satisfied that no one was close, I dropped a man's shoe and a carpet remnant on the ground. We'd passed a ton of broken flip flops and blown out sneakers along the way and I'd wondered how anyone on a trail would abandon *shoes*. "I'm gonna put these on you."

"That one's too big, and I'm not a drug mule. I'm not going to wear carpet shoes."

The cheap shoes are a simple, ingenious trick that cartel members came up with over in Arizona, but we hadn't seen it much in Texas. The soft rug soles from carpet remnants leave few scuffs for Border Patrol agents to use when they're tracking. They can't figure out which way the drug runners are traveling or even which way they're going.

We'd long ago figured out that the drug runners were using the low-tech footwear to move drugs. That was a given and confirmed by a rancher in Arizona who'd found dozens of pairs of multi-colored carpet shoes. He even took photos on his game camera of the drug mules passing with backpacks full of what we knew were narcotics.

The mystery wasn't that they used carpet shoes to cover their tracks, but why they leave them in random piles, or scattered behind?

She kept giving her alibis away, not that I'd bought it in the first place. "Ninety-nine point nine percent of the people in my country would have no idea how this piece of carpet is used by drug runners. I have no doubt about who you are, and at this point, I really don't care if you strip all the skin off those feet because of what you've done. But we can't move fast if you're completely hobbled. Neither one of us wants to die here in this godforsaken place."

I twirled a finger. "Turn around and let me check to make sure that cord hasn't gotten too tight."

She was too tired to fight, and we were far too deep

into the canyon for her to try and run away. Even if she got past me and went back the way we'd come, Perry Hale was back there somewhere, and he'd be along pretty quick.

Without a word, she turned around. The wrap around her wrists hadn't been so tight it cut off the circulation. "Looks good. I'm gonna kneel down and put these on you. If you try to kick me, I'll bust your nose. Understood?"

She nodded because she believed me.

Her feet were bleeding from a dozen small cuts, but only one looked bad. We'd stopped in time. She could still walk. The sneaker was only a couple of sizes too large. I pulled the laces tight and double knotted them so they wouldn't come loose. Crude laces on two sides of the carpet allowed me to wrap it around the other foot and I pulled it tight.

"This will probably be better. It won't wear a blister like that tenny shoe will. You're lucky we don't have much futher to go."

I swung Victim's pack off my shoulder and dug around inside and came out with three bottles of water. I twisted the cap off one and held it so she could drink. She sucked down the contents in a series of long swallows. I drank one, and then we shared the third.

Feeling a little better, I fired up the Sat phone, but the canyon walls blocked the signal. I put it back and crushed the bottles to cap and put back in my pack. A slight breeze brought the faint scent of a campfire.

She snorted. "You're carrying those out? With all this around us."

"I'm not adding to the trash here." We'd been there

way too long and now I was worried that people were too close. "All right. Let's go."

"One more minute."

"We don . . ." I stopped when I heard the distinct sound of a crying child. The rifle instinctively came to my shoulder, and I swept the area with the muzzle, searching for the source.

Villarreal heard the same thing. Her head snapped around, and she peered into a tangle of tall desert scrub and grass on the shady side of the canyon. Near the edge of the wall, something moved. Someone was crouched under a scrub bush.

I looked down the barrel of my rifle. "Come out."

The thin cry came again. Still tense and with the rifle ready in case they tried something, I edged closer. Movement.

I switched to Spanish. I'm not fluent for casual conversations, but any law enforcement officer who works the border knows common phrases that come in handy through the years. *"Salir ahora!"*

An adult hand stuck up, then its mate.

"Ahora!"

A woman in a torn T-shirt and gray sweat pants crawled out of the jumble. *"No me despares."*

Villarreal translated. "She said don't shoot her."

"I got that part." I switched to Spanish. *"Yo hablo Engles?"*

She shook her head. The woman's face was bruised, and her clothes were dirty and torn. *"Tengo una nina pequena. Ella esta enferma."*

"She says . . ."

"She has a little girl who's sick."

"You *do* speak Spanish."

"I understand *some* words."

The mom turned and motioned for the little girl to come out of hiding. Hesitant, she stepped out and coughed deep and wet. She couldn't have been more than three years old, but the tiny, skinny little thing was poor as a snake and looked like she hadn't eaten in a month.

As tired and scared as I was, I worked up a smile and waved them forward.

"All right, Villarreal. Try to redeem yourself a little and find out why they're here alone."

Face impassive, she asked if they were all right. I understood that much, but then they launched into a stream of rapid-fire Spanish that completely lost me. It went on longer than I wanted before Villarreal shrugged. "She wants to know why I am tied up, and if you are going to do the same to her."

"Tell her that I'm a Texas Ranger and you're under arrest, my prisoner. Tell her I'm taking her with us until we get to the river and she is free to go, or I'll contact someone on the other side and get them both some help."

They talked some more. "She says she's an immigrant from Honduras. Her name is Jacinta. They were with a *coyote* who raped her. She fought back and he beat her, then said he would beat the child if she didn't submit to another *coyote*. She did what she had to do, but in the night they slipped away. They didn't look for her when they took the rest of the immigrants to the river last night. Jacinta and the child have been waiting for the next group. She hopes they'll take her with them."

I felt my face harden. The image quickly played out in my mind, because I'd heard it before. Coyotes raping women while the others they were leading across the border did nothing but turn their heads and pretend it wasn't happening. Men like that had no right to live.

Now with her and the little girl, I was between a rock and hard place. I couldn't leave them in the canyon, because they'd surely die, or those guys would come back and probably rape and kill her and the little girl on their way out. The next group that was sure to come through after dark wouldn't let her join them, because they hadn't paid *that* coyote.

I wondered if those guys retraced this path back to the turnaround once they'd delivered their people to the river.

"Were the coyotes armed?"

Another long exchange.

"Yes."

"What with?"

"Automatic weapons."

"Figures. How many?"

"Three."

We were low on water, but I dug my last two bottles from the pack and gave them to the woman. She opened the first and gave it to the little girl who drank like she hadn't had any water in a week. Once the mom had taken care of her daughter, she opened the other. There were a couple of energy bars in my pack and they were glad to see 'em.

While they drank, I studied on our problem. The

woman looked like she was in good enough shape to travel, despite the attack. I could carry the little girl. Or we could stay right there and wait for Perry Hale, but his exfil might have been along another route. There was no guarantee he was coming along behind us.

And where was Yolanda? Those two were virtually inseparable. If he was up on that ridge alone, then they had a plan, but what was it?

Without any more information, the only thing we could do was continue down the canyon, working our way northward to the Rio. I'd deal with everything once we got to the border.

"We have to go. Tell her there are bad people after us. She has to come with us. I'll carry her baby."

Villarreal translated and I reached out for the little girl who shrieked and held tight to her mama's neck. The woman recoiled also, and I stepped back, fighting down a growl of frustration even though I understood her fears.

We were at an impasse when a gust of hot wind came up the canyon, bringing the thick odor of burning wood. I looked back the way we'd come and was stunned to see a roiling column of dark gray smoke rising up from the canyon. We were in a dry tinderbox facing what amounted to a flash flood of roaring fire rushing in our direction.

I checked the steep shale walls around us, looking for a way up. If I didn't have any bad luck, I wouldn't have any luck at all. We were in a narrow section of the canyon that was shaped like a taco, with the high, steep walls offering no way to get out.

"We're going to have to run. Villarreal, turn around so I can cut you loose."

The woman gasped when I took the knife from its sheath. Villarreal said something to calm her and turned. I cut the lamp cord, letting it fall at our feet.

"Run as fast as you can until we can find a way out of this death trap."

I grabbed up the screaming little girl, and we took off like scalded cats.

Chapter 57

The smoke was still thin enough at times for Perry Hale to see a man in a military uniform creeping through the brush lining the canyon's edge. With the calm deliberation of a deer hunter at the target range, he looked through the rifle scope with both eyes open and slowly pulled the trigger. He saw the impact in the man's shirt. Legs stiff, he toppled sideways and landed like a felled tree.

At the accurately placed shot, others retreated back around the bend in the road where Perry Hale couldn't see them, and all went quiet. He waited several minutes and decided they'd likely retreated, or worse, found another way into the canyon.

He swept the area with the rifle scope, looking for more targets. Smoke was making it impossible to see. The fire climbed the steep wall, jumping from one struggling bush or clump of grass to the other, and was burning toward the ridge. Down below where the cars had gone over, it was an inferno.

The crackling and popping fire was clearly audible as

yellow and white smoke roiled into the air and drifted overhead, northward. Several minutes later, a twisting column of hell's fire rose into the air telling him it was time to move.

Now he had to find another position, but the question was where.

Chapter 58

Incencio and Geronimo held back around the corner, letting Perez's men draw the sniper's fire. They had no idea how many were on the ridge above, but they had no intention of showing themselves.

"Should we send someone up back there to come around behind him?" Geronimo was so wound up and angry he paced back and forth on the road.

"No. They will retreat soon. Either they will kill all those *soldados* and maybe even Perez, or they will retreat. No matter. We will wait for a few more minutes while the fire builds. The smoke will conceal us."

"Are we going into the canyon to follow?"

"No. That will be suicide. The wind is coming from the south. The canyon will become an *infierno*. They are fools if they go in there."

"I think some of them already have."

"Like I said. Fools."

Rifle slung over his shoulder, Geronimo studied the rising smoke column. "They are getting away with *La Jefa*."

"No."

From the smoke boiling over the road, a figure emerged coming in their direction. Both men readied themselves to fire, but it was Esteban. "I am glad you weren't in those *vehiculos deportivos*, or that Humvee."

"So are we."

He flicked his hand southward. "We can go now. The sniper is gone."

"Did you kill him?"

"No. He did what he wanted and left. We cannot go down into the canyon now. Perez sent three of his men in before the fire got out of control, but they will burn. We are not obsessed with staying hidden. We can go cross country and follow the same path. I know the way, so we can get ahead of them before they reach the border. Going in a straight line will be much shorter than following that damn canyon."

Incencio grinned. "I have a better idea."

"What's that?"

"Perez and only one man are over there, guarding his Humvee. We will kill them and drive to the border in their military vehicle."

Esteban's eyes widened. It was obvious he hadn't thought of such a savage solution.

Geronimo nodded at the suggestion and walked back to the soldier who was standing beside the left front tire, smoking a cigarette. His rifle lay across the hood. Perez was leaning against the door, talking into a microphone threaded through the open window.

The *sicaro* walked with a big smile on his face. "I have a question."

The man raised an eyebrow in question and Geronimo nearly cut him in half with a burst of automatic gunfire. Shocked at the unprovoked attack, Perez dropped the microphone and held out both hands, as if the gesture could stop a 5.56mm bullet or make the man change his mind.

Geronimo emptied the magazine into the captain's chest and as Perez crumpled, he turned and waved. "Get in. I will drive."

Chapter 59

Running parallel to the canyon, Perry Hale moved through the desert with ease, occasionally checking over his shoulder. He was confident that he'd slowed, if not stopped, Sonny's pursuers. In addition to hopefully killing those in the Humvee, he'd managed to nail two others, one wore a uniform, the other likely a cartel member.

Barely slowed by the water and wind-scorched desert floor, he wove his way around the scattered plants, trees, and cactus. Dry washes were shallow wrinkles that barely slowed his progress.

Slowing to a jog, he keyed his microphone. "Yoli."

"Asshole."

It was their way of making sure they had radio contact. "You still there?"

"Yeah, but I see a lot of smoke."

"See Sonny yet?"

"Nope."

Perry Hale's heart was beating fast, both from exertion and dread. That fire down below could be a death sentence for Sonny and his captive. "Are you where you can get out fast?"

"Yeah, it'll be a bitch, but I can climb out right here. I hope Sonny's already out."

"You'll be on my side when you pop up?"

"Affirmative."

"I'm hoofin' it cross country up top. I'll be at your position in about ten minutes . . ." A sound he wasn't expecting reached his ears. "Dammit!"

"What?"

"There's a car coming."

"Out in the middle of the desert? There aren't any roads out here. I checked on the satellite map."

"Well, it's not on the road. I'll get back to you."

Perry Hale knew exactly what happened. Once he'd abandoned his position, they simply drove through the smoke and across the turnaround. It had to be a Hummer.

To his right was still another shallow wash, no more than knee deep. Thick, low growing creosote bushes offered shelter. He cut sharply to the right, away from the Hummer's path and dropped behind a bleached mesquite log, depending on his camouflaged clothing to hide him.

The big military vehicle passed thirty yards away without slowing, weaving around larger vegetation, and rolling over anything else in its way. It dipped into a shallow wash and then reemerged back up on the other side.

Once they were out of sight, Perry Hale rose and followed their tracks in the sand.

Chapter 60

From her vantage point five feet below the canyon's rim, Yolanda Rodriguez watched smoke boiling into the air, diffusing the morning sun and looking like someone had opened the gates of hell.

She keyed her mike. "Can you talk yet?"

"Yep. It's a Hummer. Went past and kept heading north."

"The fire's getting closer. Tons of smoke. You start it?"

"*They* started it when they pushed a couple of burning cars off the road."

"Well, it's coming this way fast."

"They better be running, if they're still down here."

"They haven't come through." She checked the opposite side. The rim was close, but the wall was straight up and covered in prickly pear. "Maybe they've already found a way out. Where are you?"

"Hard to tell. What are your coordinates?"

She rattled the numbers off and he dug a GPS the size of a pack of cigarettes from a pocket on his MOLLEE pack. "I think you're half a mile away."

"You can't get down here. The walls are too steep."

"We'll work it out when I get there. By the way, you have hostiles headed your way, too. All armed."

"Do you have any *good* news?"

He was panting when he answered. "Hawke's cooking us a Wagyu steak when all this is over."

Chapter 61

With Villarreal leading the way along the canyon floor and Jacinta following with the little girl now in her arms, I brought up the rear. Our pace was far slower than I wanted, but there was nothing we could do about it.

At that point I wasn't looking to make time all the way to the border. We needed to find a way to the top. Confidence was high that there were several trails leading up, but the question was how far away.

Canyons aren't straight. Water follows the path of least resistance, and through thousands of years, it finds it way around the most difficult obstacles. Because of its winding nature, and all the vegetation around us offering way too much concealment, I was never confident that whoever was chasing us wasn't going to pop up behind us at any moment.

The sun was high overhead, flooding the canyon with light, when I finally saw what I was looking for. "Villarreal."

She paused and turned. I pointed upward toward the high-water mark. "There's the way out." We were both looking at that tangle when I saw the shape of a person holding a rifle. My own weapon came up and I was tight on the trigger when a voice stopped me cold.

"Sonny!" Yolanda rose and waved. "Get up here fast."

I lowered my weapon at the same time she shouldered hers and sent a burst over our heads. The hard echoes filled the canyon as lead stitched the ground beside me and it wasn't hers.

Everyone scattered.

Chapter 62

Perry Hale heard the chatter of automatic gunfire and sprinted toward Chalk Canyon's rim. The first reports were followed by a second weapon, then a third. They came from the exact coordinates Yolanda gave him earlier.

The fire chasing down the canyon had grown in intensity. Burning through the vegetation along the canyon's edges, it spread over the lip, consuming everything it touched. The column of smoke rose into the sky and bent over the canyon itself, pushed upward by licking flames that grew in intensity. Behind him, it jumped the dirt road and widened in its path toward the river.

The blaze spread quickly across the desert floor. Creosote bushes virtually exploded in flame, and the sun-bleached deadwood and dry vegetation burned as if soaked in gasoline.

Heart in his throat, Perry Hale finally reached the sheer brink and dropped to one knee to peer over. A burst of automatic weapon fire down below made him flinch backward. Weapon shouldered, he leaned

forward and scanned the situation, first finding Yolanda from her description of the natural sniper's nest
on his side of the canyon, fifty yards to his right. She
fired a three-round burst and someone in the brush
shrieked.

To his left was Sonny on the canyon floor, wearing a
bright yellow Hawaiian shirt covered by a tactical vest,
and backing in her direction and returning fire directed
toward men concealed by a screen of desert trees. The
straw hat on his head didn't fit the scenario at all.

Two women, one carrying a child, were running as
fast as they could away from the battle.

Growling deep in his chest, Perry Hale snugged the
stock of his AK to his shoulder and swept the canyon
floor, looking for a target. A woman screamed and he
prayed it wasn't Yolanda. Movement in a gap in the
leaves was exactly what he was looking for. Those
same leaves shuddered from the muzzle blast of a rifle
pointed toward the fleeing women and Sonny.

Perry Hale sent three controlled rounds behind that
rifle. It dropped and he searched for another target. A
swarm of hot, angry insects rose in his direction, too
far away to pose any threat. He saw where they came
from and fired again, this time seeing his target. The
rounds tracked the ground where a man had been only
a second before. He was falling back from two streams
of fire from Yolanda and Sonny.

The echoes faded from the canyon, replaced by the
crackle and roar of the oncoming wildfire.

A Mexican soldier broke into the open, running for
all he was worth away from the oncoming fire. Yolanda

double-tapped him, and when he dropped, shot him again.

Perry Hale knew why she'd fired the anchor shot. He'd killed one of the fleeing women.

More gunfire chattered from cover and his return fire silenced them.

Chapter 63

Four men in Mexican military uniforms were still on the canyon floor, and I suspected others were lying where we couldn't see them. I rose and rushed back to find Jacinta facedown in the sand. Two small holes in the back of her shirt told me that she wasn't getting back up again.

Flies were already swarming her body, drawn by the blood.

The little girl twisted out of my arm and ran to her mom, crying and tugging at her hand to pull her upright. Jacinta's limp arm twitched, but I knew that she wouldn't be getting up. To be absolutely sure, I rolled her over. Two large exit holes confirmed my fears that she'd never hold her baby again.

"Sonny! She's running!"

"Dammit! Come get this baby!" Not waiting for Yolanda's response, I charged down the canyon after my detainee. She had a fair head start, but her feet were already sore and with only one shoe and a piece of clumsy carpet, I tackled her after about a hundred yards.

She went down hard, her face slapping in the dirt. She didn't roll or struggle or cuss. I was madder'n a wet hen and wanted to slap the piss out of that stupid, evil woman, but there wasn't time. I did the next best thing. Once again, I grabbed a head full of hair and jerked her upright.

Villarreal wasn't tender-headed, that's for sure. She gasped from the sheer violence of it, and then caught her balance, her eyes shooting daggers.

I gave her head a shake. "We don't have time for this! Don't you know that fire's gonna be here in a few minutes and we don't have time to play grab-ass. Get back there. We're gonna climb out before it catches us."

No longer in her sniper's nest, Yolanda was holding the little girl by the time we got back. The baby was down to sobbing hiccups. Yolanda wiped the little girl's nose with her hand and rubbed the results on her pant leg.

I could tell she took an immediate dislike to Villarreal. "You should have shot her and saved us the trouble."

"I will, but if she runs again, I'm gonna let her own people kill her."

Yolanda's brow knit at the comment. Holding her rifle in her right hand, she shifted the little girl to rest on her left hip, a natural move that I'd seen thousands of times. My bride Kelly calls 'em hip babies, and I always love to see her standing hipshot with a little one saddled securely with one arm around them.

I explained. "They've all turned on her. Afraid she'll sell 'em all out." I pointed up to where Yolanda'd been covering us. "Is that a way out?"

"Yeah, but the last five or six feet is straight up and crumbly."

"Perry Hale will take care of that for us."

"That's my guy."

I pointed upward. "Villarreal, climb up there."

She looked upward, at me, and without a word started up the incline toward what had been Yolanda's sniper position.

Yolanda was still holding the baby and I took stock of her slender frame and studied the grade. Keeping an eye on the smoke that was blotting the sky, I shrugged off my pack. Opening it up, I dumped the contents, including the extra magazines for the AR. I still had three in my vest pockets.

"She may not like this, but we're gonna need both hands." I held the MOLLEE pack open and knowing what I wanted, Yolanda gently lifted the baby with both hands and whispered to the little one as she put her feet into the empty pack.

She started wailing and struggling, but I'd seen worse trying to strap my own kids into car seats when they were little. The two of us worked her down inside, and I pulled the pack tight over her shoulders, leaving only her head sticking out.

I turned and with Yolanda's help, shrugged the straps over my shoulders.

That little head behind mine tuned up loud and long. I was dang glad she was facing the opposite direction. My hearing was about gone as it was.

"This won't be pretty." I led the way and started up the incline. "Keep an eye on this kid."

Yolanda followed.

Each time the little one shifted her weight, it pulled me off balance, but we had to get out right then, and there was no time to waste. A couple of times Yolanda had to reach out and steady me, but the little girl struggled for less than a minute before exhaustion and the past few days took its toll and she quieted.

"She breathing back there?"

"Poor little thing's asleep or passed out."

"Thank the lord."

Villarreal was already at the high-water mark by the time I picked my way up to within six feet of the top. I was wringing wet with sweat. Something in the flames popped not far away.

"What took y'all so long?" I looked up to see Perry Hale on one knee and peering over the edge.

"Picked up a passenger."

"Hurry up. It's gonna catch you."

The weight on my back lifted when Yolanda took hold of the pack. I slid out of the straps and took it from her, lifting it high. "There's a baby in here."

Perry Hale didn't change expression. "Of course there is." He reached down and I handed up the sleeping girl. He grabbed a strap and disappeared from view. He was back a second later. "Next."

"Yolanda." I knelt and laced my fingers. She put one boot in the stirrup made by both hands and jumped at the same time I lifted. She virtually flew over the rim.

All the while I made sure Villarreal was behaving herself. The only thing she did was adjust her boobs, and I figured she was sweating as bad as I was under the tactical vest I couldn't wait to take off.

"You saw how she did it. You're up."

She put both hands on my shoulders, her foot in my hands, and I lifted.

The firestorm made the turn up-canyon, pushed hard by the weather it created.

"Sonny."

I took his hand, dug my foot into the dirt wall, and Perry Hale pulled me up and over.

Chapter 64

It wasn't a whole lot better up topside. There was a fire up there, too, but it wasn't burning nearly as fast as the one in the canyon pushed by a venturi effect. Perry Hale lifted my pack by the straps and I put the sleeping little girl on again.

Yolanda stood facing outward, covering for us. I rested a hand on her shoulder. "Thanks, kiddo."

"Hug me later. We're still in hostile territory."

"That's the truth." Swiveling back around, I slapped Perry Hale on the shoulder.

He surveyed the terrain around us. "What next, Kemosabe?"

I grinned. "Oh, I get it. The Lone Ranger and all."

"It really hadn't occurred to me, but now that you mention it, it kinda fits."

Yolanda broke up the boys' club conversation. "How far is the river?"

"About two miles." Perry Hale took a reading with his compass. "It wouldn't be so bad if it wasn't for this damn fire and a Hummer full of bad guys up here looking for us."

I wanted to keep the pressure on Villarreal, so she'd continue to cooperate. "They're after her, too."

"What? Ain't she their boss?"

"She was. They tried to shoot her a little while ago. I figure they want to shut her up before I get her to the states and take over the operation down here."

Her eyes met mine and wouldn't let go.

He gave her the once-over. "Well, let's all stay healthy. You want me to tie her up?"

"Villarreal, that's up to you."

"I won't try to run."

"There's your answer. But if she does, you both have orders to shoot her in the legs. We can carry her two miles between the three of us."

Perry Hale gave her a sinister little grin and raised an eyebrow. "Fine then. Let's go."

We took off under a smoke cloud as the firestorm down below scoured Chalk Canyon clean.

Chapter 65

With no road to follow, Geronimo steered the Humvee with care around whatever obstacle came in their path. As they rolled away from the canyon and the steep, rocky ridge, the vegetation thinned out to nothing more than scattered scrub growing barely three feet high.

Esteban rode shotgun, as he'd called the passenger seat when he was a kid. He didn't want to be there, preferring to have Incencio in front. If that had happened, he could have easily shot them both in the back of the head and driven himself to the border.

However, for the first time since he'd known them, Incencio insisted on riding in the seat behind Esteban. There was no way he could shoot them both without endangering himself. The best thing to do was continue the search until he could take advantage of their situation.

From their vantage point in the military vehicle, the three in the Humvee could see for long distances. However, the eroded country cut and slashed by wind and water provided millions of hiding places for anyone, or anything, unwilling to be seen.

Unable to find their prey, Incencio became increasingly frustrated, making sounds deep in his throat as if the man were an animal. He pointed to the left. "That way. Closer to the canyon. The fire is going to force them out."

Geronimo veered as directed. "They may come out on the other side."

"They will still come out. Our bullets will reach across."

Dead wood snapped and crunched under the tires as they neared the edge. Incencio tapped the back of Geronimo's seat. "Stop."

He stepped out and climbed onto the Humvee's roof. The windows were down and Esteban called out. "What do you see?"

"Nothing. Do you think the fire caught them?"

Esteban hung his elbow out the window. "They may be farther down than we thought. Let's continue."

"Wait." Geronimo tapped the steering wheel with his fingers. "We still have that sniper out here. Could we have passed him?"

Incencio jumped onto the hood, and then to the ground. He came around to Esteban's side. Instead of carrying his rifle muzzle downward, he had it cradled in his left arm, far too close to Esteban's head than he would have liked. It was as if he sensed what was in Esteban's mind.

"Maybe. I think we should go back. Maybe we passed all of them."

Geronimo shrugged. "I don't care."

The border was so close, and yet Esteban had the sense that the Ranger still might need his help. "I agree. Let's drive along the edge back as far as the fire.

If we don't see them, then we turn around and wait for them at the river. That's where they'll cross with *La Jefa*."

Incencio met his gaze far longer than was comfortable. "You are right."

He opened the back door and settled into the seat.

Esteban glanced back to see Incencio watching him. "Is something wrong?"

"You seem nervous. I've never seen you like this before."

Esteban turned forward. "That's because no one has ever taken *La Jefa* before. I want to get her back, but at the same time, I hope she understands there is no fault with the three of us. We don't want to wind up in her garden."

Incencio laughed, slapped Esteban's shoulder, and leaned back against the seat. "No worries about that. She will be very thankful and will probably bed me for it. I will give her what she wants and put in a good word for the two of you!"

They laughed at the joke as Geronimo reversed direction and headed south.

Chapter 66

Perry Hale pointed. "A Hummer passed me a little while back, heading toward the river. They're looking for me, but I figure y'all, too."

I adjusted the pack straps to settle the sleeping kid in just the right place. Yolanda took a boonie hat from her own pack and put it on the little one's head for shade. She came around me and paused, giving Villarreal the once-over.

It was a girl thing, and I could feel the claws come out on all four hands.

"I'll take the point." Yolanda directed her comments toward Villarreal. "You try and keep up. I'm not slowing down for you."

"Someday I would like for you to see my garden."

Yolanda raised an eyebrow in my direction.

"She buries people there."

"Fat chance."

She spun on her heel and led off. I jerked a thumb in her direction and Villarreal followed with me right behind. Perry Hale brought up the rear.

We were less than two miles from the river.

Chapter 67

We hadn't gone two hundred yards when a group of about thirty people popped up out of the canyon, driven up by the smoke, and we were in the wrong place at the wrong time. They couldn't go back down, so they milled around the edge while two men separated themselves from the crowd and came forward. Both carried pistols belted around their waists.

Coyotes.

"Illegals." Perry Hale's soft voice came from over my shoulder. I sensed, rather than saw him step sideways to get a better field of view. "These guys are trouble."

Villarreal spoke just as softly. "They aren't illegal yet. They're migrants."

Yolanda angled herself to keep Villarreal in sight and still keep an eye on the two men.

Rather than get into a debate over migration, I cut the conversation off. "Yolanda, you can give her your views as a Mexican-American later. We don't have time for this. Find out who they are, and tell them we aren't interested in 'em at all."

Fluent in Spanish, she called out to the two men who'd separated themselves and stopped a couple of yards from their people. The conversation went back and forth until Yolanda shrugged. "They want to know why we have weapons, and why she's with us."

"Tell 'em it's none of their damned business. We're headed north, same as them. Leave us alone, and we'll do the same."

"Sonny, I can't shoot from here if I have to. Too many people behind them." Perry Hale shifted again.

One of the men in a ragged gimme cap pointed at him and shouted for him to stop. At least my Spanish was good enough to understand that. Gimme Cap rested his hand on the butt of the semi-automatic stuck gangster style in his belt.

"Tell that son-of-a-bitch to get his hand off that weapon!" I didn't want the situation to accelerate even more, so I kept my voice low.

Yolanda translated and Gimme Cap's partner drifted in the same direction Perry Hale had moved. The crowd behind them milled around in the hot sun, not knowing what to do. One or two pointed at the fire coming across the desert in our direction.

There was one guy at the back of the group who remained stock-still, not appearing nervous like the rest of them.

He also wore a dirty foam cap that went out of style thirty years earlier. All I could see was his head and one shoulder, because others were in the way. He wore a gray sweatshirt with the sleeves cut off.

"Perry Hale. The guy in the back."

"I see him. There's a sling over his shoulder. Yoli,

these two in front are yours if it goes south. I need to concentrate on that rifle back there."

You could feel the tension heavy as the hot sunshine beating down on our heads. My heart was hammering a mile a minute and I wanted a drink of water in the worst way. I didn't want to be behind Yolanda, so I stepped forward and put my hand on Villarreal's arm.

"Don't say a word. You and I are stepping over here."

She cooperated, and we drifted a short distance to the side as casually as possible. I still had that baby on my back and for the first time in my life kept someone between me and danger. I figured, right or wrong, that if they started shooting and hit the cartel leader, even if the bullet went plumb through, there was a good chance that my vest, and ultimately, my body would protect the sleeping child.

Gimme Cap pointed and hollered again.

Yolanda spoke without turning her head. "Says to be still. He doesn't like you moving around."

"Had to get some distance. Tell him to move on."

They exchanged words again. I took stock of the rapidly deteriorating situation. Perry Hale was as tense as a wound mainspring, his eyes rock steady on the man in the back. Index finger along the trigger guard of her rifle, Yolanda continued trying to talk the man down.

I'd about had enough. "Why won't they move along?"

"Because we have what he calls a Mexican prisoner. He wants us to release her and they'll take her and go."

"That's not happening."

"I told him the same thing." Yolanda spoke again,

pointing with her left hand toward the border, then in the direction of the approaching wildfire. This time she translated it into English for my benefit. "Take your people with you and go. We're doing the same thing. Let's keep this peaceful so we can all get away from the fire."

At her command, some of the migrants started north. Mr. Out-of-Style shouted at them to stop, but they were afraid of the oncoming flames and enough had moved that Perry Hale could now see the man had an AK-47 slung muzzle-down over his shoulder. "Rifle."

I held out my left hand. "It's still down. Everyone stay cool."

The group continued to drift away and Out-of-Style grabbed a woman by the collar, jerking her still. Gimme Cap tilted his head, as if assessing the situation, and Yolanda continued to talk.

He snickered and said something that caused Yolanda to stiffen. Villarreal laughed and Perry Hale tensed. I picked out a word or two, and saw the look in his partner's eyes. These were probably the men who'd raped Jacinta, two young outlaws full of themselves and feeling indestructible.

"Perry Hale, stay cool."

"I know what they said."

"I bet you do. It's just words at this point."

"I'll bury those sons-a-bitches with those words still in their mouths."

"Maybe. Let's try to de-escalate. Everyone take two steps back. Give them room."

"The rifleman back there has his hand on the grip."

"So do you, and me, and Yolanda. Yoli, ask them nicely to let us go. We're backing up."

In my mind, if we asked permission and appeared submissive, they might let the situation pass. I read *The Art of War* by Sun Tzu, and he said that if you leave your enemies a way to escape, they'll likely take it. If they can't get away, they'll fight like wolves to protect their lives.

Wanting to give them the option of leaving our standoff, I stepped back, pulling Villarreal with me again. The others did the same in a weirdly coordinated ballet.

Gimme Cap didn't get the point. He switched to English, and I realized he'd been playing with us. "You! Cowboy, hiding behind that woman. Put your weapons down and give us your packs. We have men behind you. If you don't do as I say, we'll kill you all and take them."

"Bullshit. There's no one back there." Perry Hale's voice was even, but I could tell he was tense as I was.

I shook my head. "Not happening, and I'm getting tired of standing here in the sun, talking."

Out-of-Style said something and Gimme Cap's head snapped around to find his group headed away as if nothing were happening. They'd taken the out I'd provided. He shouted at them to stop, and when they didn't, his smiling face hardened and he broke loose in a long string of Spanish directed at everyone with him.

A grin fractured Out-of-Style's face and he sashayed to the left, following the migrants. Gimme Cap finally did the same, backing away for several feet before breaking into a trot to catch up with them.

When he reached the leader, Gimme Cap slapped the man in the head, then hit him again with his fist. The group paused as if they'd reached a stop sign. Gimme

Cap struck the man twice more until he fell, then pointed at himself.

His authority restored, he turned and led the way. They soon disappeared down into a draw and vanished, while we let out long-held breaths.

Perry Hale lowered his weapon and blew out a breath. "Just like that it's over? I was ready to kill that sonofabitch."

"You still might get your chance later, but right now the fire's getting closer." I pointed. "We need to get."

Chapter 68

Geronimo drove without any particular destination in mind. He slowed and pointed at the smoke coming from the canyon fire racing northward. "They can't be back there. I say we intersect the canyon and drive toward the fire. It will be like the rabbit killings I was a part of when we were kids."

Esteban had never heard of such a thing. "What?"

"A couple of times we were overrun with jack-rabbits in the village where I grew up. When it got really bad, the men would gather in a line and beat the bushes, driving the rabbits toward great nets they had erected between posts. When the rabbits arrived there, they couldn't pass through and ran in circles. Our people were there waiting and beat them to death with clubs. It was great fun. This is the same. We strike the canyon and drive toward the smoke. The fire will chase those who have *La Jefa* into our guns."

Esteban glanced northward. In addition to the canyon fire, the desert was also burning toward them. "I say we give this up and wait for them at the river.

These fires are coming too close. We will burn if we stay here."

Even as he spoke, a jackrabbit bounded by, away from the fire coming toward them.

Incencio studied on the problem. "Why drive. We wait right here until it is too dangerous. If they don't come, then they are burned to death or they have gotten past. Either way, after that, we go to the river."

"I like that idea better." Esteban relaxed, as much as he could.

Chapter 69

There was no time to wait. The wildfire was moving fast, heading straight for us and driving wildlife before it. Deer, rabbits, and javelina ran south, away from sure death.

We needed to do the same.

This time Perry Hale took the lead. "I hope those people are moving fast, 'cause this is the only way we can go, and I don't want to run up on them." He gave a strange little grunt. "Or maybe I'd like to catch up with those three."

Yolanda fell back to cover our rear. "Temper, dear." She stopped behind me to check on the little one in my pack who'd slept through the whole thing. "She must be burning up in there, but the poor little thing's sleeping hard."

"It's all been too much for her." I told Villarreal to get going with a nod of my head and fell in behind her. "Perry Hale, this fire's moving fast."

He waved two fingers and set a pace that ate up the ground trampled by many feet. After a few minutes he slowed, then stopped. "I got a bad feeling about this. Yoli, I think you and I need to go on ahead. I'll bet a dollar to a donut that they're waiting for us in the next draw deep enough to hide everyone."

"Better idea." She pointed. "They keep on this way and we make a wide swing. Get behind them, or at least come in from the side."

"Let's all go around." I liked that idea better. "Perry Hale, lead the way and we'll sweep around them double time. I don't want to get in a fight with this baby on my back."

He bit off a response, and I was sure he was spoiling for a fight. "Fine then. You, lady, keep up."

Villarreal frosted him with her eyes and we ran northeast, the shortest way around the threat that might have been waiting for us.

We pounded along, and I couldn't believe that baby stayed asleep back there. It might have been a rougher version of when parents strap infants into their car seats and they drop off and stay asleep for an entire road trip, at least until the driver stops in front of the house.

Keeping in stride behind Villarreal, I tightened the straps so the pack wouldn't bounce as much. That little sleeping body was pounding a mud hole in the middle of my aching back.

The terrain sloped down, helping a little and we reached a dry wash leading toward Chalk Canyon. The slope on the opposite side wasn't bad, and we were making tolerable time until I heard Perry Hale shout.

"*Baja esa arma!* Put down that weapon!"

I came up on level land once again to see Out-of-Style standing there with the AK shouldered and pointed in our general direction. Perry Hale and Yolanda separated, advancing with their own weapons ready to fire.

A quick glance to my left showed me Gimme Cap standing there with a pistol raised. They'd outsmarted us, likely leaving their group to make their way north all alone for a while, so they could ambush us.

I snapped the AR to bear and pulled the trigger on Gimme Cap faster than conscious thought. My three-round burst caught him dead in the chest and he fell at the same time all hell broke loose up front.

The third *coyote* had been lying behind a creosote bush and opened fire at the same time everyone else started shooting. Bursts of sand exploded around him as Yolanda's rifle chattered nonstop. His body jerked at the impacts and the gun fell from his fingers.

Gimme Cap dropped like a rock, dead from Perry Hale's extremely accurate fire. He paused, and shot once more, taking Gimme Cap directly under the rolled bill.

Yolanda lowered her weapon. "Get your point made?"

"Told that bastard I'd bury him."

I checked the area around us. "No time for that."

Perry Hale lowered his rifle. "Look."

We followed the point of his finger to see the migrants running nearly two hundred yards away, free, but on their own.

"They're going to the river, but whoever's waiting on the other side won't let them cross. Not without these three."

"They've wasted their money." Villarreal laughed. "They'd just as well walk back into the fire."

I gave her a hard shove. "Get going. We're traveling with them now."

"I don't travel with such trash."

Yolanda gave her a thin smile. "I felt the same when I met you, but then again, here I am."

Chapter 70

"Incencio."

A grunt from the back seat told Esteban the *sicario* was listening.

"What if *La Jefa* is already dead."

"That may be so."

"And if she is, what do we do?"

Esteban was quiet with the thought, as was Geronimo.

Even though Esteban fought the urge to continue with that line of thinking, he waited, just as his grandfather had taught him how to fish.

First throw the lure onto the water and wait. Let the ripples still so the fish underneath can ponder the meal above. Wait some more. Now the fish thinks the meal is his and moves up to eat. Give the lure a tiny twitch, signifying life. Maybe enough life for the meal to swim away, and the fish rises to swallow the bait. Unfortunately for the fish, there is a hook inside and he is caught.

Incencio finally spoke. "If she is dead, then there will be a new *jefe*."

Esteban waited, and waited some more while flies buzzed in and out of the Humvee. The time was right. "Then who will that be?"

The figurative ripples radiated from the center of the question.

Instead of Incencio, it was Geronimo who spoke. "Maybe the three of us could work together."

Incencio breathed through his nose. "If she is *muerte*."

"*Sí,* if she is *muerte*."

"We will try and get her back, of course." Esteban gave the lure one final twitch. "Maybe at the river we'll find out."

Formulating an answer, Incencio took a long, deep breath through his nose and opened his mouth to speak at the same time distant gunfire took his thoughts. He pointed to the north. "There. They were further than we thought."

Geronimo slammed the Humvee into gear, rolled over a small mesquite, and accelerated toward the spot where he figured the gunfire was coming from, only a mile from the Rio Grande.

Chapter 71

We caught up with the group of migrants who stopped at our arrival. Casting frightened glances around, they waited, most kneeling on the ground. One young man with eyes full of life stepped forward and spoke.

As usual, I didn't understand what he was saying, but Yolanda talked, patting the air with her hand, letting them know we didn't intend any harm. You could see the people visibly relax as if they'd been tensed up for days.

While they spoke, I glanced toward the south, seeing smoke rising high above the fire incessantly moving in our direction. A real, four-legged coyote ran past only a few feet away, most of the hair on his tail burned off.

I was pondering the poor animal when I saw smoke coming from a different place, to the east, and much closer. It took a moment to put two and two together and I realized the fire had jumped, not from the wind or sparks, but likely from a burning animal.

It's the hard truth about wildfires, especially forest fires. Sure, sparks and the advancing firestorm moves the conflagration forward, but burning animals run-

ning in panic also spread the flames, and that's what
was happening here.

Even as I watched, two more scrub bushes exploded
into flame fifty yards away. "Yolanda, wrap this up.
We gotta move!"

"What'n hell?" Perry Hale's eyes narrowed.

"You're from East Texas. You know how wildfires
spread."

He looked in the direction that the coyote disappeared. "Burning animals. We gotta move. Yoli, tell them
to *adelante*!"

"Already have, and you two quit calling me Yoli!"

"Villarreal, get moving. The river's less than a mile
away. Once we're across, we're safe. There ain't much
around there except rocks and sand."

She took off after Yolanda, who led thirty migrants
toward the Rio Grande, and I wondered why the Devil
Woman's eyes crinkled in the corners.

Chapter 72

The Humvee driven by Geronimo seemed to hit every rock and pothole in the desert, bouncing them like ping-pong balls. Esteban was the first to see the tracks of several people in the soft sand of a dry wash, but he pretended to be looking ahead.

It was Incencio who finally looked down through the open back seat window. "Look! Tracks. Follow them."

"I don't have to. They are going where we want."

Half a minute later, they came to still another wash and the bodies of three men. Geronimo slammed the breaks, and the big vehicle slid to a stop. Incencio stepped out into the roiling dust and stared down at a young man with a hole in his forehead. A semi-automatic pistol lay at his side.

"Coyote."

He cast around, looking at the tracks and working out the scenario in his head. "They waited here, probably to ambush the ones we're after."

"I hope they didn't shoot *La Jefa*." Esteban opened his door and stepped out.

"There is no other blood around here." Incencio pointed at the body of a man in a sleeveless gray sweatshirt. He was lying on an AK-47. Another body was sprawled several yards away. "These are the only ones who are hurt. They *enredada* with professionals."

Geronimo, still behind the wheel, pointed. "The tracks lead that way."

Hands on his hips, Incencio studied the smoke rising far above their heads. "Then that is the way we will go."

Chapter 73

It was well over a hundred degrees as we made our way to the river. It was odd to see the vegetation change. Where there had been scrub, cactus, and low-growing bunch grass, there were now wide spaces between the plants. With no fuel, the fire would die out behind us.

We slowed to a walk behind the people who kept talking quietly to themselves. Yolanda drifted back to join me and Perry Hale. "They say they're too open out here. They want to drop back into the canyon over yonder."

Villarreal was walking with her chin up, looking ahead. I studied her posture for a moment. "I feel the same way. Anyone on the other side of the river is bound to see all of us before we get there. That goes the same for anyone on this side. I don't want to get caught with this gal in the open."

"So what's the plan?" Perry Hale reached into a pocket on his vest and pulled out a package of chewing tobacco. Tucking a pinch into his cheek, he returned the package and spat.

"I say we all drop into the canyon. That fire has nothing to eat now. Look, the smoke's getting lighter."

The young man who was leading the migrants led them toward the canyon. Lacking any other alternative, we followed.

It was easy walking, not having to dodge so much cactus, and we made good time back to the steep canyon. Luck was with us, and we crossed an arroyo that would have fed water into Chalk Canyon, if there'd been water. As it was, we stepped down into the wash and followed it to the confluence of the canyon.

At this point, the young man stopped, putting both hands in his pockets and giving us a wry smile. Once again, I relied on Yolanda. "What's that about?"

After talking for a minute, she grinned and turned back toward me. "He says the coyotes told them there's a grove of mesquites not far away. They are to wait there until dark to cross. Someone will be waiting on the other side. He says *we* can pass for coyotes in the dark to get them across. Those over there won't know who we are."

I turned my back on the group so they wouldn't see my expression. "He wants us to help get them into the country?"

"That's his thought. He's a pretty sharp guy, and he has no idea who we are. You two gringos traveling with two Mexican women makes him think we're some kind of new coyotes who carry more power this close to the river, moving people, tied up or not."

I couldn't put my finger on it, but I was beginning to suspect Villarreal had something up her sleeve. She hadn't said a word to the migrants, and was uncharacteristically cooperative.

My watch said it was barely noon, and I was almost at the point of exhaustion. Like the young man and the migrants, I didn't really want to cross in the daylight. Because so many came through Chalk Canyon, it was too well known to those over in Texas. There was too much of a chance the Border Patrol would be there, and I wanted Ethan and Agent McDowell close by when we came out of the water.

"Tell that guy we'll wait with them, but I'm not helping anyone cross but us and my prisoner, and that's a fact."

I would have said more, but the little girl on my back woke up and was telling it. None of the immigrants knew she'd been in the pack until that moment, and I almost laughed at the looks on some of the women's faces at the little girl's cries.

Yolanda quickly told them what had happened as she came around back and took the straps so I could slip out of the pack. Seconds later, two of the women lifted the little girl out and carried her away, hugging her and talking in soothing voices.

"You did good." Yolanda smiled at me. "They think you're one of them now."

"I'm not sure I'm even one of me."

It wasn't much farther to the waiting point the young man I knew now as Leon Gutierrez had told us about. A natural-born leader, Leon took his people to the least filthy shade where they waited for the sun to go down.

Again, flies were everywhere, especially near a section I soon thought of as the latrine. No one wanted to go over there, but those in need did just the same, breathing through their mouths until they were finished with their business.

One of these days a good, hard rain would wash down the canyon, flushing all that filth into the Rio Grande, where people swam to get to the other side, and fished downstream. I didn't want to think about it further than that.

The three of us, along with our prisoner, squatted in the shade of a twig. I was glad to have my hat on. Yolanda and Perry Hale had their caps, but Villarreal was bare-headed. For once, I didn't care. She could pop and sizzle in the sun like a slice of bacon for all I cared.

Expressionless, she sat with her back against the canyon wall, waiting for the sun to slide farther west and give her some shade. Yolanda and Perry Hale had water that we shared, but I felt guilty that there wasn't enough for the other people. We made sure the baby got some, though.

We'd gotten loggy in the heat when Yolanda suddenly perked up. "Oh! I forgot." She rummaged around in her pack and came out with something I didn't expect.

It was my .45 with the Sweetheart Grips in my holster.

"Here."

"Where'd you get that? I left it in the truck in Del Rio."

"Well, we knew the most likely place for you to park your truck."

"But it was locked up."

Perry Hale grinned from under the cap pulled low over his eyes. "I have a set of keys, remember?"

I stood and buckled the belt around my Wranglers, setting it just right on my hips. I must have looked a sight, wearing a cowboy hat, a neon flowered shirt, tactical military vest, jeans, and boots.

Already feeling almost normal, I reached into the inside of the vest Judge gave me and took out my Ranger badge and pinned it to the vest. Suddenly I felt like a lawman again, instead of a felon on the run, and my spirits lifted.

Watching me through lidded eyes, Villarreal's face went hard. I guess she hadn't believed that I was really a Texas Ranger, but now she knew better.

"My people are going to kill you and those dogs with you."

"You can't sweet talk *me*."

"I'm going to roast your tongue and eat it while I remember how it flapped in your mouth."

"You're a charmer."

She clammed up, and I again wondered what she was trying to hatch in that evil little brain of hers.

Chapter 74

The shadows crawled across the canyon, finally giving us some relief. The girl was crying, and I figured it was hunger and partly dehydration. One or two of the adults still carried water in plastic water jugs, and one of the women finally stalked over to a man lying on the ground and snatched up the half-empty jug beside him.

He came off the ground like a shot and was about to advance on the woman when Leon stood and spoke sharply. They squared off for a moment, but he pointed at the little girl drinking from the jug and the man bit off a reply. When the little girl was finished, the woman carried it back to him and put it on the ground at his feet.

Still glaring, he picked up the jug, flipped off the cap, and tilted it up, drinking every last drop. Finished, he pitched it on the ground.

I know the next thing that happened was stupid, but I couldn't help myself. I was tired, thirsty, hungry as a horse, and irritated by everything around me. "Pick that up."

"Sonny." Perry Hale's voice was low.

I knew he was trying to cool me down, but I wasn't having any of it. "I said pick it up!" Knowing he likely couldn't understand me, I pointed at the jug lying on the ground with everything else that had been dropped for months.

It was ludicrous, but my mind was in a different place. "That baby was thirsty, and you've been hoarding water. I don't care if it was yours, but I'm tired of seeing all this. Pick up the damn jug and at least put it over there on top of that big pile of trash."

Kelly's voice came to mind, soft and sweet as only my wife can speak. *Is this the battle you want to pick?*

You'd have done the same thing. That baby was thirsty, and she's hungry, too. I bet he has food stashed away.

But you don't know his life story or theirs. Let it go.

Her hand quietly slipped into mine, bringing me back into the real world. It wasn't Kelly's hand, though. It was Yolanda's.

Once she knew I was back, she let go and stepped forward to talk with the angry man. At one point she turned and pointed at the badge on my vest, then at her own chest. Half a second later, she produced her own badge that Major Parker had given her for emergencies and pinned it to her vest.

As if they'd received an electric shock, the others stood, talking quietly among themselves. They milled for a moment before a couple of the other men stepped in and talked to the guy with the water.

Yolanda came back and grinned. "Kelly's right. You need an anger-management course."

Deflated, I glanced up overhead at the gathering darkness. "Maybe, but I'm done with this place. Villarreal, stand up."

She'd been sitting against the rock with her eyes closed. Gathering her feet under her, she stood like I told her. I grabbed her shoulder, turning her toward the river. "Walk."

It was nearly full dark when we stepped out of the canyon and onto the carrizo cane-choked bank of the Rio Grande. As far as I could see on our side of the bank, there was nothing in both directions, except for a two-track caliche car path. The tall green cane rose high overhead, pushing through the swirling water that chuckled around the thick stalks.

The greenery provided perfect cover for anyone moving on our side of the river. An opening forced through the cane provided access to the river that was still silver from the last of the day's light. Perry Hale and Yolanda gathered beside me, and I heard the migrants several yards back.

"I told them to wait for their contact." Yolanda's voice was husky. She swallowed. "We'll go first, and someone should be along soon to get them." She was looking through the opening toward the Texas side. "They've come a long way on lies and promises. I feel for them."

I looked over at Villarreal who was staring, studying the gap through the long green leaves. "So do I, but I need to get this woman across first. Then I can tell the agents over there that there's a little girl on this side that needs help. They can contact some of the honest police over there who can come and take these people back to safety."

"What if they don't?"

My mind was reeling with guilt, compassion, and frustration. "Yolanda, I have one job, and that's to stop the murders on our side. Maybe once I've turned her over to someone else, we can see about helping them. Okay?"

She patted my arm. "If we can."

The sun was finally down when Perry Hale, who'd been watching not the river but the canyon behind us and the riverbank on our side, stiffened. "Vehicle approaching."

"There's no road." I squinted downriver, where he was looking.

"I hear an engine."

"Maybe it's coming from the Texas side."

"Uh, uh. There."

I swung the pack off my shoulder one last time and dug inside for the NVGs. Slipping them over my eyes, I looked to the east to see a large vehicle approaching on the dirt track. "That's a Hummer. No headlights."

"It's likely the one that chased me off the mountain."

I saw that he'd put on NVGs, too. Yolanda had done the same thing. They'd come prepared.

The sound of an oar thumping the side of a boat came to us. I spun to see a man floating past in an old vee-hull. He flicked a flashlight twice, and kept floating downstream.

The migrants rushed down to the water and waited.

"This ain't right." Perry Hale stepped away from us. "Something's up."

"You're damned right. Those people have found us." I waved the migrants back from the riverbank. "Yolanda. Tell these people to get back."

She translated, but was cut off when a barrage of gunshots came from the direction of the Humvee.

I heard a splash and turned to find Villarreal gone, leaving nothing but a dark swirl in the current.

"Goddamnit!"

Yolanda spun and shouted at the man in the boat in Spanish. "I have one thousand dollars for you to come get three of us!"

Chapter 75

The Humvee driven by Geronimo intersected the Rio Grande just east of where Chalk Canyon emerged into that same river. Across the river, a highway paralleled its winding course. Headlights lit the Texas side as a farm truck drove on, oblivious to what was about to happen on the other bank.

Geronimo had little to avoid other than rocks and deep rivulets winding down to the river. Sparse vegetation grew in the hardpack, but across the river, as if in an entirely different world, vegetation both voluntary and planted, greened up the landscape.

They drove as far as they could, until a protruding point narrowed the bank too much for the vehicle to continue. As soon as he stopped, Incencio stepped out with an automatic weapon in his hand.

"Finish this now!"

With a determined set to his jaw, he rushed upriver. Esteban stepped out and waited for Geronimo to follow, but the *sicario* waited. "It is his kill. Let him have the first shots."

Frustrated beyond measure, Esteban talked himself

out of shooting Geronimo, who was partially protected by the Hummer. Even if he did kill him, that would put him in a direct shootout with Incencio, and though Esteban was a professional himself, he was too close to freedom. And besides, he didn't think he could survive against the much more experienced killer.

Incencio's weapon opened up, flashing in the darkness, followed by a return barrage.

At that moment, a splash far from the bank caught Esteban's attention. The cane was much shorter there, and he jumped onto the Humvee's hood to get a better angle. A flash of white rose from the depths and submerged again. It was someone in the water. He waited, and the figure rose once more, this time swimming on the surface with a familiar rhythm.

Many of *La Jefa*'s men had watched in the past as she swam each evening, reveling in the water and the knowledge that her men were watching her sleek body slide through the water, clad only in the tiniest of bathing suits.

Esteban knew the body of that swimmer. It was *La Jefa,* pulling strongly for the Texas side.

His decision was made. He jumped to the ground. "Geronimo! *La Jefa* is in the river!"

The *sicario* rounded the front of the vehicle to look where Esteban was pointing. He stepped up around Esteban to get a clear look. His attention was on the woman when he twisted from a searing hot pain that lanced through his kidneys at the thrust of a razor-sharp knife.

Esteban grabbed Geronimo's gun hand to prevent him from drawing the pistol at his side, and stabbed again, cutting deep and outward, just below the man's vest. Geronimo's knees gave as Esteban withdrew the blade and this time cut the man's throat in a spray of dark blood.

Geronimo dropped, rolling down the riverbank and into the water where he sank in an instant.

Esteban quickly dropped all of his gear and kicked off his boots. He wasn't a great swimmer, and the current looked strong, but he was determined to get across and intercept *La Jefa*. He could keep her beside him, acting as her guardian until the authorities found them, then he would turn her over and explain who he was.

With nothing more than the knife in the belt of his pants, Esteban threw one last look over his shoulder and pushed and stumbled through the cane and into the swift river. The current immediately melted the gravel beneath his feet and sucked him under, and he began swimming, pushing hard for the Texas side.

Chapter 76

I happened to be facing downriver when a man carrying an automatic weapon suddenly appeared on the riverbank. I figured there were others behind him, but right at that moment, he was my primary target.

"Stop! *Alto!*"

Women screamed behind me, and the sound of running feet and splashing water told me the migrants were in panic mode. I hoped the women with the little girl would have the sense to simply drop to the ground until whatever was about to happen was over.

The man shouldered his weapon and pulled the trigger at the same time I did. Strobes of flashing light lit our world as I fired, aiming for center mass. The guy stumbled backward, screaming something I couldn't understand.

Flashes of light from both sides of me came from Yolanda's and Perry Hale's weapons.

The guy hit the ground, still shooting. I couldn't figure out how he was still sucking air with all the lead he'd absorbed, but he wasn't through. When his rifle went silent, he reached to his waist and came up with a handgun.

It flashed several times and Yolanda fell backward, gasping in pain.

My brain shifted gears and muscle memory kicked in. I drew the .45 from its holster and it came up smooth as silk, familiar in my hand. Perry Hale's rifle went silent, and at the same time I cranked off my first shot, he joined in with his own pistol, a Beretta M9.

Advancing on the fallen man, we continued firing until we were so close there was no chance of missing. Our last few rounds struck his neck and head. His arm fell and it was over. Perry Hale whirled and ran back to Yolanda. I kicked the man's weapon away and knelt to look at him through the green lenses.

He wore a tactical vest, and most of our rounds had impacted the plates. I'd never seen the guy before, and unlike most of the cartel members I'd encountered, he didn't have one visible tattoo on his face, throat, or hands.

That wasn't right. I ripped the Velcro loose on the vest and yanked it to the sides, then tore his shirt open. There they were. His torso that you couldn't see was covered in gang tats, including the year 1518 and the word Hidalgo. Under that, the name Incencio.

I pitched his weapons into the river and hurried back to find Yolanda sitting up. Perry Hale was running his hand inside her tactical vest, but other than a grimace, she looked unhurt.

I knelt beside them. "A little forward, ain't it."

She pulled off her NVGs. "You could have kissed me first, buddy."

He grinned at us both. "No penetration. The bullet didn't go through."

Yolanda took a deep breath, likely to confirm that she still could. "Well, *that* hurts."

Chapter 77

Tish Villarreal reached the Texas side of the river and pulled herself onto the bank. The cane was thinner there and much shorter. She crawled on her hands and knees to the top and sat there, shivering. It took a few moments to get ahold of herself, and when she did, she realized a two-lane highway was only a few short yards away.

She regretted the white blouse, now stained with muddy river water. There was no way to hide on the barren highway, so she practiced a quick alibi in case some good Samaritan saw her and slowed.

I was out with my boyfriend and he wanted more than I was willing to give. I made him stop, and I got out of the car, but he chased me. I ran to the river, but fell in, and he drove off and left me.

Delivered without any accent at all, it would pass muster with most people who only wanted to do good deeds, and didn't expect to find themselves with a cartel leader asking for a ride on the side of the highway.

Pulling her hair from her face, she felt underneath her left breast. The transmitter was still there, sending out its signal. She would wait right where she was, until her half-brother arrived to pick her up.

"La Jefa!"

Shocked by the familiar voice in the darkness, she whirled to see a shirtless figure coming close. "Esteban?" She recoiled, backing away. He'd tried to kill her earlier in the day, and now here he was with a knife in his belt.

"Yes. It's me. I saw you go into the water and jumped in to help. It's a good thing I did. The Texas Ranger who had you killed both Geronimo and Incencio."

"Both of them?" She'd heard the machine-gun fire while she was in the water, glad that none of it was directed at her, though she fully expected the Ranger to keep his word and shoot her at the first opportunity.

"Sí. They are both gone. It is just the two of us until I can get you somewhere safe."

"You tried to kill me. You shot at me when I was with the Ranger." She backed away even farther. "He said you wanted to take over after I was dead."

Esteban's eyes widened in innocence. "Señorita, *jefa,* I would do no such thing. He lied to you, as all Americans lie. I wasn't shooting at you. The smoke was in my eyes and I was shooting at him. I am sorry if I scared you, but here I am." He held his hands wide.

The truth was that he could have killed her with the knife as soon as he emerged from the water. Esteban *hadn't* been shooting at her. The Ranger had put worms in her head, trying to confuse her in order to get her across the river.

Her jaw clamped. What she'd told him would come about. She would make the Ranger pay by killing his entire family, anyone who bore his last name. Her wet shoulders squared in the darkness. She would wipe out his friends, also. Her wrath would be demonic! People on both sides of the river would talk about the cleansing for generations to come, ensuring the respect that she deserved as the Devil Woman.

She laughed and clapped her hands like a child as Esteban crossed his arms and watched with interest.

Her original alibi out the window, she thought quickly. "We have to get off the road. If the police come by, they will know we swam the river. Without documentation, they'll take us to a detention center."

"I'm not sure what we should do now."

"We look for headlights and hope they aren't police. I have people coming to get me."

Esteban hesitated for a second and then nodded. "*Bien*. I will wait, but my job is to protect you, señorita."

"I know. You will be there when I need you. Now, go hide until a car slows."

She watched him slip back down the riverbank, thankful that one of her faithful men was there for her, but angry that he might ruin her escape.

Chapter 78

The man in the boat smelled like he'd never bathed in his whole life. He pulled up close to the shore, as far as the cane would allow, and shipped the oars he used to float downstream. Now the small 7.5-horse engine on the back was idling just enough to maintain his position in the strong current. The little motor was unnaturally quiet, and I realized he'd used some kind of upgraded muffler to silence the noise.

He didn't come all the way in, because several of the migrants were waving for him to come closer and I suspected he was afraid they'd all try to jump in at the same time.

He shook his head and ordered them back in Spanish. With Yolanda between us, we pushed forward and she took over. The boatman almost twisted the throttle at the sight of our NVGs, but her soft voice held him steady.

When she finished talking, he nodded and held out his hand. Jaw set, Perry Hale reached into a pocket on the leg of his pants and waded out thigh deep through the cane, setting his legs against the current. He pulled out a packet of bills that he counted into the man's palm.

"*Bien*. Get in."

I waded out and climbed in. Yolanda turned to the others, explaining that we had to get across to catch the Devil Woman. At her name, several of the migrants crossed themselves. Assisted by Perry Hale, she pulled herself over the side near the bow and stepped into the middle seat. Perry Hale followed and settled into the bow, adjusting his rifle so he could swing it easily into position.

A squatty woman pushed through, talking quickly and carrying the little girl I'd toted in my pack for so long. She charged forward and was waist deep before any of us reacted, and in a moment of incredible strength, she literally threw the child into Perry Hale's arms. Startled, he let go of the AR and caught the wailing little girl at the same time the boatman twisted the throttle and turned us away from the Mexican shore.

The now dark water grabbed the boat, trying to spin it downstream. The Rio Grande, like all rivers, have their own personalities. The stretch of the lower Rio Grande usually looked deceptively calm at first glance, but under the surface, it moved with great power, especially around bends in the river where it doubled its strength. Right then, we were between two bends and the water pulled at the boat like it wanted to slam it into the nearest bank.

We were chugging across the water when a flashlight on the Texas side flickered three times. Perry Hale held the crying little girl in the bow. "Uh oh, that ain't good."

Chapter 79

Good or not, someone was waiting on the far side of the river. Small clicks from my SRT members told me they were doing the same thing as me, reloading their weapons. The boatman in the stern leaned around me and spoke to Yolanda, who twisted to straddle the seat so she could see both of us.

"He says those lights are the men who pick up the migrants and take them to the safe houses."

Perry Hale growled. "They aren't gonna like finding it's us."

My mind raced. It was damned dark, and the moon wouldn't be up for a couple of hours. With the night vision goggles, we had the edge on those guys, but we were easy targets if they lit us up. "With the baby crying, they won't know who we are until we push up on the shore. When we do, you jump out quick and we'll cover you. Hand the girl back here."

Perry Hale passed her over his shoulder to Yolanda like a sack of potatoes, who handed her on to me. I sat the little girl on the seat and snuggled her up to my side. "It's all right."

I'm not sure what the boatman was thinking, taking money from us and leaving paid customers on the other side, but he steered us across the river. Instead of nosing the boat up against the bank like he did on the other side, he turned it and drifted the left gunnel up against the bank overgrown with willows and a thin screen of carrizo cane. I realized the Mexican side of the river was shallow, while the Texas side dropped off sharp and deep.

Somebody was waiting for us, but I couldn't tell through the green water of the NVGs.

Hands reached down from the shore and I handed the little girl up to a man with a hat brim hiding his face. The boat rocked, and I grabbed the gunnel. She disappeared and the same strong hand took mine and pulled me out of the boat. The others were virtually lifted out by two other men with hats pulled low on their foreheads.

Perry Hale and Yolanda must have read my mind, because as we were on solid ground, our weapons came up and we forced the strangers back toward the road. "Hands up! Back up and let me see those hands!"

All three of us were shouting when I heard a laugh I'd known since high school. "Ethan?"

Sheriff Ethan Armstrong tilted the hat off his face and flicked on a flashlight. "Y'all take it easy. It's me, McDowell, and Officer Rene Rodriguez, highway patrol."

"What are *you* doing here standing around in the dark?" Laredo is well out of Ethan's jurisdiction.

"We needed to play this close to the vest for a while, at least until we were sure it was you we were picking up. Nice shirt, by the way."

I wanted to give him a smart-ass answer, but I was too tired. Rodriguez stuck out his hand. "Welcome back."

I couldn't figure out why the highway patrol deputy was there. "How'd you get tied up with these guys today?"

DPS officers cover a lot of territory in that part of Texas. It was nothing when I worked for the highway patrol to get a call about a car wreck and have to drive well over an hour to get to the accident scene, but it was a strange coincidence to find him with the other guys.

"I was here when they showed up, untangling a car wreck, and saw Sheriff Armstrong sittin' on the side of the road with an FBI agent. There's no way I was going to pass up *that* story."

I nodded, studying on Rodriguez's strange explanation. "You any kin to this gal, Yolanda? Same last name."

"Naw, there are more Rodriguezes than Chins in a Chinese phone book."

Relieved to be back in the states, I laughed at that tired old dried-up joke like it was the funniest thing I'd heard in years. "I get it."

FBI Agent McDowell spoke up. "Where's that prisoner I've heard about. I have the papers you asked for. They cost me a lot more skin than you can imagine."

My heart sank. "She jumped into the river when we had that little altercation over there y'all probably heard. I don't know if she swam over to this side during all the shootin' or went back into Mexico. I had her, and now she's gone."

Chapter 80

Their cars were parked half a mile down the road, at a crumbling cinderblock station that hadn't pumped a drop of gas in over a decade. While we waited in the darkness by the river, Rodriguez hurried back down the road to get his truck so we could all ride back instead of walking.

A couple of minutes later, a Border Patrol SUV came around the bend from the opposite direction. Its headlights caught us standing there, dripping with automatic rifles. It squalled to a stop in the middle of the lane, fifty yards away.

Both doors flew open and the agents knelt behind the doors, shouting orders. "Border Patrol! Put your weapons down! Hands in the air! Hands in the air!"

We complied.

"Easy boys! Badges here! I'm Sheriff Ethan Armstrong." He pointed at the vehicle approaching with its bar lights flashing. "That's Officer Rene Rodriguez coming back with his truck. Don't shoot him, neither."

A badge magically appeared in McDowell's hand, glinting in the headlights. "FBI Agent Landon McDowell."

I pointed down with one finger to my vest. "Sonny Hawke. These other two with me are also special Rangers, Perry Hale and Yolanda Rodriguez."

Rodriguez's DPS Ford pickup rolled up with his emergency lights on. The door opened and he stepped out. "What are you doing pointing weapons at these officers? Bill Tyler! Diego Morales! It's me, Rodriguez. Highway patrol. Holster your weapons!"

The agent on the driver's side of the vehicle was Tyler. He recognized Rodriguez's voice and rose. "We saw all those guns and a bunch of people standing around in the dark. What else were we supposed to think?" He dropped down behind the wheel and they pulled up, parking sideways with their lights on to block the empty road. "Nobody told us y'all were here."

Now that we could lower our hands, we relaxed and Ethan explained what was going on. His story covered most of the details but not all of them. He paused when the little girl in Yolanda's arms tuned up again.

"They had to bring this kid across, because she's in danger." I had to raise my voice over her wails. "We need to get her medical attention and food and water right now."

Agent Tyler leaned inside and spoke with someone on his radio. "We'll have another car here in a minute. There's one just a couple of miles down the road that can take her to a processing station. You want to put her in our back seat while we wait?"

Yolanda walked past. "Only if I can sit in there with her."

"Go ahead, ma'am."

She opened the back door and sat with one foot on the ground.

Chapter 81

Tish Villarreal was standing on the side of the dark highway when a Border Patrol car appeared in the distance with its lights flashing. She unconsciously touched the tiny transmitter under her breast and smiled.

It had worked.

She waited there in full view as it drove much too slowly down the road. She was frustrated enough to chew nails by the time they picked her up in the headlights. Seeing her, the car accelerated and pulled up quickly, keeping her in the headlights, but still not getting too close.

The officer in the passenger seat stepped out. "Tish?"

"Miguel, it's really me."

Relief was clear in her brother's voice. "I thought it was, but your hair doesn't look anything like you."

She came around on his side and gave him a quick hug, wetting his uniform shirt. Her face hardened when she glanced inside and saw the second agent still sitting behind the wheel. "He is our first *agende trans*?"

Miguel laughed at the newly minted phrase, "trans agent." "Yes. Relax little sister. He's one of us."

"Does he know who I am?"

"Of course."

"Then he should show some respect and get out of that damned seat!"

Raul Lopez quickly unsnapped his seatbelt and stepped out of the car. "I'm so sorry, *Jefa*. I did not know what to do. My apologies."

The fire in her eyes went out and was replaced by those dimples that melted men's hearts. "It is okay, *mi vida*. I understand, and now you do, too."

At the edge of his flashing lights, Miguel saw a dark figure rise from the riverbank and drew his service weapon in a flash, shouting in Spanish, "Do not move!"

Tish recognized the figure when he stepped further into the light. She held out a hand and gently pushed her brother's gun hand down. "His name is Esteban."

Miguel relaxed. "I have heard about you. You're famous."

"I shouldn't be." Esteban shrugged. "I simply do what *La Jefa* orders. That is all."

Miguel opened the back door. "Both of you get in, but Esteban I need to cuff you."

"Why?"

"In case someone sees us. It is procedure, but I can't cuff my own sister, can I?"

Esteban shrugged. *"Bien."*

He was cuffed, and they climbed in the back seat. Raul Lopez dropped down behind the wheel at the same time their radio squawked. He picked up the microphone. "Lopez."

"This is Bill Tyler."

"Hey, Bill. What's up?"

He told them where to meet him, only two miles

westward. "I need you to pick up an individual for transport."

"I already have two in the back now. Why can't you do it?"

"We're tied up with something else. This one won't take up much room. I need you now."

"Roger that." Lopez replaced the microphone on the hanger. "Señorita, I have to do this. Please sit with your head down and your hands behind your back, as if you're cuffed like Esteban."

The Devil Woman's eyes flashed. "No. You cannot let anyone see me."

Her brother turned in the seat. Miguel grinned. "It's okay. You are just another illegal to them. We see dozens a night. Don't worry. More of *our* people are there."

Chapter 82

Yolanda was still seated in the back of the agent's car when another just like it approached from the opposite direction. It pulled up and stopped in the middle of the lane and the two agents got out.

I was standing beside Ethan when they approached. The tallest of the two gave us a good going-over before he spoke. The name on his shirt was Miguel Villarreal. "What's this?"

State Trooper Rodriguez waved a hand. "Something a helluva lot above your pay grade, starting with this FBI agent here. We have a kid you need to take to processing. Ranger Hawke, these are agents Lopez and Villarreal."

Rodriguez sure was ordering those guys around. All Rangers had served the DPS as highway patrol officers, and at no time did I ever issue *orders* to Border Patrol.

My head spun at the name. Of course, Villarreal was like Rodriguez or Gomez or Smith on our side of the river.

That sixth sense of mine kicked in, telling me something wasn't right. I didn't like that feeling, especially when Rodriguez held Villarreal's gaze way too long.

Border agent Villarreal's partner, Lopez, came forward. "Like he said, we have . . ."

"Two in custody." Rodriguez sure did act like he was in charge all of a sudden. "I know, but this one's no bigger'n a minute, Villarreal. Break the rules and put her in your lap if you want to."

Rodriguez sure was using Villarreal's name a lot. Something was out of place, but I figured it was probably because I was worn to a frazzle, hungry and damned thirsty.

"Yolanda. You want to bring the baby over?"

She rose with the sleeping three-year-old in her arms and my heart ached watching the little one, so limp and innocent. Yolanda walked to the driver's side, waiting for one of the agents to open the back door. It was an odd sight, because she still had her rifle slung under her shoulder.

The dome light had been deactivated to eliminate issues in the dark, but when the back door came open, a young man slid out of the seat. It was probably to make room, but we all reacted like any other officer when someone in cuffs and presumably under arrest pops out of the back of a police car.

Voices rose in unison, speaking a mix of languages.

"Whoa!"

"Get back in there now!"

"Alto!"

My hand was on the butt of my .45 when I recognized Esteban in the flashing lights. "Hang on a minute. Everybody stand down. Bring that man to me, would you?"

Villarreal and Lopez, the border agents who brought him didn't like that one bit. Villarreal waved his hands. "Wait a minute. This is *our* prisoner."

"I want to speak to him for a minute. Rodriguez, I believe I might be above your pay grade, right? We can hash this out later, but right now I'm talking to that man, and I'm not asking permission. I'm telling you."

A look passed between the agents that almost made me draw my weapon right then. Something was wrong, but I couldn't put my finger on it. I crooked a finger at Esteban. "You. Come here."

Still holding the sleeping child, Yolanda must have felt what was going on. She slowly backed away from the vehicle, keeping an eye on the situation. Always watching her, Perry Hale saw her body language and lowered his hand to the rifle he'd re-slung over his shoulder.

Highway patrol officer Rodriguez didn't like the sudden tension in the air, either. "What's going on here?"

"I just want to get a good look at this guy. I might have seen paper on him at some point."

"He's nothing but an illegal. We get them all the time. Hey you in the camo, take your hand off that rifle! Get your hand off that weapon, Hawke!"

Who'n hell was he telling me what to do? To my left, Ethan matched my stance and the air became thick as syrup. I held out my left hand to calm things down. All of a damn sudden we were in the middle of a Mexican standoff and for no reason I could identify. "Easy boys."

Esteban smiled like he didn't understand a word we were saying and stepped forward. I wasn't sure what was going on, but I intended to get to the bottom of it.

It was that nest of snakes thing that had been haunting me from the outset. Was he really still one of us or a true *sicaro* who was playing all the angles?

"Stop right there, Esteban."

He did. His eyes flicked to his side. Seeing that I'd noticed, they also flicked up and back, as if jerking a thumb over his shoulder.

He hadn't done me wrong one time, and suddenly that first domino fell and I knew what was happening. The sudden thought that the other shadowy person in the back seat might be Tish Villarreal made the hair on the back of my neck rise. Had these two agents arrested them after they swam the river?

My eyes flicked to the agents. Border Patrol agent Miguel Villarreal's shirt was wet. Maybe from a hug, Villarreal to Villarreal.

The dominos clicked faster as they fell. Rodriguez was on the cartel payroll, as were Villarreal and Lopez. I was staring at the Devil Woman's work, law enforcement agents who worked for the Hidalgo cartel. This was the thing I'd been chasing from the outset, officers forced to protect their families by submitting to the cartel.

Men protecting their families are the most dangerous animals in the world. The Villarreals were related.

My .45 came out smooth and fast. Seeing the movement, Perry Hale's rifle rose and he crouched with the stock against his shoulder. He had no idea what was going on, but like Ethan and Agent McDowell, he was backing my play.

Keeping my voice even, I tried one more time to

defuse the ticking bomb. "I want everyone to stand right where they are, hands in plain sight."

Esteban's knees bent, and he knelt in front of me, intentionally twisting to reveal the butt of a knife in his belt. His actions spoke volumes.

"You two didn't pat this man down? Villarreal, you and Lopez stay right where you are. None of this smells right!"

At my order directed at the two officers, Rodriguez swelled with anger. There was no reason for the DPS officer to get mad about the same thing he'd been doing only a minute earlier. "What in hell is this all about? *You* men stand *down*!"

All the air was suddenly sucked out of the night. You could feel men tense and I felt, rather than saw Ethan's weapon come up. McDowell's Glock materialized in his fist and the Border Patrol agents Bill Tyler and Diego Morales froze, looking left and right, not understanding what was going down.

It was one of those *oh shit* moments and I knew in about half a second the dance none of us wanted was going to start. I registered the vehicle's emergency lights flashing in the darkness. Border Patrol Agent Villarreal moved his gun hand as slow as molasses, not taking his eyes off of me. It was that thing I've seen in the past, with men thinking that if they gently continued what they were doing, they might get away with it.

My voice snapped loud and sharp. "I said everyone freeze!"

He paused.

I ignored him for the moment. "Prisoner in the back. Slide across and come out the open door."

Agent Villarreal, with his hand now on his own holstered weapon shook his head. "She's cuffed. Leave her in there. What are you *doing*?"

"My job. Prisoner, come out."

Yolanda's voice repeated my order in Spanish.

Head down, a soaked woman with wet hair slid across the seat, and when she did, I recognized her, as well. "Tish Villarreal, on the ground now!"

Perry Hale's weapon swept to the side to cover her.

The Devil Woman's voice barked harsh and loud as she rolled out of the car seat, "Kill them all!"

At the same time the Border Patrol Agent Villarreal finished drawing his service weapon and leveled it at me.

I was half a second ahead of him, but because I was near exhaustion, my reactions were slow.

With a terrified look on his face, Villarreal's partner Raul Lopez snatched his own weapon from its holster and opened fire a split second before Rodriguez drew his Glock and shot me square in the left chest.

It was like being hit with a sledge hammer from that range. My whole left side again went numb and I folded sideways from the pain and reaction while at the same time shooting Rodriguez over and over as I fell.

At least two bullets caught him in the vest, knocking him backward as a third big .45 round went high and caught him under his right eye. Something flew from the back of his head and disappeared into the darkness as I hit the ground hard.

Weapons exploded over me and the world strobed like a disco from automatic weapon fire.

On the ground, and half-blinded by the flashes overhead, I saw Tish Villarreal on her knees, picking up a pistol lying beside a still body. An encyclopedia of thoughts flashed through my pain.

She buried people in her garden.

She hung body parts from her tree.

She ordered the deaths of innocent people.

She ran drugs and humans across the river.

She'd threatened my family.

No one threatens my family.

On her knees, Tish Villarreal swung the pistol toward the nearest target, Yolanda and the baby in her arms. I saw the look of fear in Yolanda's eyes as she twisted her body to place it between the Devil Woman and the child.

Headlights illuminated the eight feet between us. Lying on the ground, I extended my arm and shot the Devil Woman in the chest four times before she quit moving.

By the time I rolled over to suck air in my lungs, it was over. The rest of our people were still upright, along with Bill Tyler and Diego Morales, who stood tall, wide, and white-faced with their hands high in the air. FBI Agent McDowell had his weapon trained on the two officers who were rooted to the ground in shock. Neither had a weapon in his hand, and that fact alone saved their lives.

Border Agent Villarreal, who'd betrayed every honest law enforcement officer in the country, lay dead beside his partner, the late Agent Lopez. Rodriguez was on his back a few feet away, the pistol he'd shot me with lying under his right arm.

Struggling to my feet, I gasped as the pain in my chest from the bullet that hit exactly where the other one struck me back at the *ranchero*. "Dammit! I wish people would quit *shooting* me there."

"They were probably aiming for that shirt." McDowell helped me up with one hand under my arm, his pistol in the other. "What'n hell just happened?"

I looked around, finding everyone but Yolanda. Perry Hale saw the concern on my face. His rifle was still tucked against his shoulder, low, ready. He answered my unvoiced question. "She's over there with a kid in one arm, a knee on the back of your little dead friend Tish's neck, with an automatic to the back of her head. Just to make sure she's gone."

It was only then that the sound of a crying child penetrated the ringing in my ears.

Esteban's voice came from the ground where he'd dropped. He hadn't moved during the fight. "Can I get up now?"

"I think it's safe, for the time being."

Despite the cuffs, he got his knees under him and rose in one smooth move. He turned to McDowell. "Sir, my name is special agent Jacob Delgado. Over there they call me Esteban Barrera. I've been working undercover in Mexico for the Hidalgo cartel for the past three years. I can identify Tish Villarreal there as the leader of that cartel, and will provide eyewitness accounts, along with physical documentation of her crimes during that time."

No one made a sound as he continued, sounding like he'd rehearsed a speech for class.

"These men lying here are dirty. That one is the Devil Woman of Coahuila's brother. The other, Lopez, has been blackmailed to work for her." He pointed with his head. "Rodriguez there's been on her payroll for years."

I winced and straightened up. "My God. He wanted to be a Texas Ranger. No telling what would have happened if he'd gotten in."

Esteban nodded. "For your information. I watched Tish Villarreal voluntarily swim across the border and illegally enter the United States and will testify that she tried to shoot that woman over there with the little girl. I wish to turn myself over to *your* custody and to contact my handler. He'll explain everything else."

McDowell holstered his weapon. "I'll be damned."

Esteban, whose real name was Jacob, continued. I knew why, the cameras on the cars were running, as well as those worn by agents Bill Tyler and Diego Morales.

"The police chief in Del Rio has been taking money and turning his head to what's going on here since he was elected. That's why Chalk Canyon has been a highway into the states. This woman has killed dozens if not hundreds of people and the proof is hanging from a tree in her *ranchero* in Coahuila. There's only one honest policeman I know across the border and that's Maximilian Zapata. He has photos and video that I left with him. Contact him with my name and he'll do the rest. He's been waiting a long time for this."

The two stunned Border Patrol agents finally moved. Bill Tyler looked at me through the flashing lights. "Is all this for real?"

Feeling inside my vest to make sure there was no blood, I raised an eyebrow at Esteban. "Fosfora?"

He shrugged. "She's a chameleon. Who knows."

I drew a deep, painful breath and finally answered Tyler. "It is. Every bit of it."

Bill Tyler still had his hands halfway in the air and finally lowered them. "Just for the record. What's *your* name again?"

"Sonny Hawke. Texas Ranger."

ACKNOWLEDGMENTS

This author wouldn't be where he is without the support of readers. Thanks to everyone who has become a fan of my work. I also want to thank every teacher who in some way influenced my dream of writing.

This novel wouldn't have been what it is without the insight provided from retired Border Patrol agent Billy Kring (he also writes great novels), who told me of what he'd seen on the Rio Grande throughout his career. A couple of the twists came from some of the all-too-brief conversations we've had down in Austin. Precinct 4 Lamar County Constable Rick Easterwood is always there for questions and provided input that proved valuable to the plot.

It's a pleasure to work with my editor at Kensington Publishing, Michaela Hamilton, who has championed my writing career since the day we met. She has always been a believer in Texas Ranger Sonny Hawke, and now we share the Spurs to prove it. None of this would work without her great team at Kensington, and I appreciate everyone who is a part of this process.

To my agent, Anne Hawkins, who is always only a phone call away—thanks for seeing value in my work.

My runnin' buddies are bestselling author John

Gilstrap—you know where you stand with me—and Steve Knagg, who was there through the years while I tried to figure all this out.

And of course, my bride, Shana, the love of my life, is always by my side.

In case you missed the Spur Award–winning thriller
Hawke's War,
keep reading to enjoy the excitement of the first chapter.
All the Sonny Hawke thrillers are available from
Pinnacle Books,
an imprint of Kensington Publishing Corp.

Thunderheads boiled over the high desert peaks in Big Bend National Park as four hikers stretched out along the winding Devil's Den Trail. The experienced thirty-somethings filled the dry, cool morning air with comments and good-natured ribbing.

Trailing last as usual in the group's fifteen-year relationship, Harmony Cartwright stopped to tighten the faded Texas flag bandana she used as a headband to keep her blond hair under control. She adjusted the pack straps and, seeing that she wasn't falling too far behind, bent to pick up a 520-million-year-old chunk of quartz from the well-traveled trail.

She scratched away a few grains of sand with a chewed, unpainted thumbnail and angled it toward the sun. After a short examination, Harmony blessed it with a quick smile and tucked the rock into the pocket of her cargo shorts, where it clacked against half a dozen similar stones. The others continued at a steady pace and she hurried to catch up with her husband, Blue. He trailed behind Chloe Hutchins, who followed *her* husband, and the troop's leader Vince.

The veteran Marine stopped to take a long, deep sip of water from his bright yellow CamelBak pack. Solid as the trail under their feet, Vince was fearless, and had been all his life. After two tours in Afghanistan, he wrapped up his time in the Marine Corps and came home to sell real estate. Such a sedentary life caught up with him after months of inactivity, and he cast around for something adventurous.

Over half a dozen Friday nights and many cans of Coors, the four of them decided to hike the Devil's Den trail in some of the most rugged backcountry of the national park. The trail was off the beaten path for most hikers, who preferred to drive deeper into the park. Rated as a moderate five-and-a-half-mile hike, the trip would at least help them burn up some Yellow Belly calories and maybe lead to even more outdoor activities in the Rockies, a place he loved to visit, a few months down the road.

He swiveled to see Chloe hoofing along at a pace as quick as her wit. "Hey, Spousal Unit, how about you walk point? The view of this trail is getting boring, and that way I can watch your transmission twitch."

Chloe gave Vince a wink and pinched the blue nylon shirt from her damp skin, pumping it like a bellows to cool herself. The brunette wore a wide-brimmed straw hat exactly like the one shading her husband's head. "You wouldn't be able to concentrate then, Sergeant Hutchins. You'd probably trip on something and break a leg, and none of us can carry you out of here, so behave yourself and keep an eye out for marauding Indians."

Blue caught up with the sparring couple and tilted his Tilley hat upward. Built like a fireplug, he wore khaki shorts that revealed thick legs built for walking. "Y'all drinking enough water? This dry air's suckin' it out as fast as I can pour it in."

Chloe rolled her eyes in fun. "Not as much as Big Guy here, but he's working harder than I am."

"I'm still fresh enough out of the Sandbox to think this is chilly." Vince frowned in mock anger. "You're right though, Little Bit, y'all need to make sure you're staying hydrated. I don't want anyone on this team to be falling out."

"You should be sweating out all that beer y'all poured down last night." Chloe poked his flat stomach with a finger.

He raised an eyebrow at the petite brown-haired woman who weighed less than a hundred pounds. "Twelve little ol' cans ain't that much, besides, I run a bigger machine, so I can handle it."

Blue watched the clouds in the distance. "I wish I had one of those Yellow Bellies right now."

The quartet had formed in college, and Blue was used to the same good-natured arguments he'd been hearing in the years since. He waved a hand at the scattered scrub below the ridge above them. "Couldn't you guys find somewhere in the shade to stop?"

Vince spread both hands. "We're a little short on trees around here."

Blue scanned the sun-blasted landscape. The only sign of active life was a lazy buzzard drifting on the thermals high overhead. "Yeah, which is exactly why we should be hiking in Colorado, where there's trees, instead of this godforsaken desert. I get to pick next year, and it's gonna be a hike in Hawaii . . . from the condo to the beach."

Harmony caught up with them and tugged a bottle of water from her pack. "This is beautiful! I love all this space! Look." She picked up a twisted piece of wood. "This will look good in a flower arrangement." She brightened. "You know, I'm gonna use it to make one for Kelly Hawke. I tried to get them to come with us, but she said Sonny couldn't get loose this week."

"Honey, that'll just add weight to your pack." Blue watched the love of his life tuck the wood into a side pocket. "I've already seen you put three pounds of rocks in your britches, and besides, it's *illegal* to take anything from a national park."

Harmony winked at Chloe. "They have plenty of rocks around here. I doubt they'll miss a handful."

Chloe tore open a packet of powdered electrolytes and was pouring the contents into her high-tech BPA-free water bottle when Vince grunted, staggered, and folded in half. The sharp whip-crack report of a rifle shot reached them half a second later and echoed off the bare rocks and cliffs bracketing the trail. Shocked, her hand moved and the remainder of the powder drifted on the slight breeze in a tiny orange cloud.

Unable to grasp what was happening, Chloe sat the bottle on the ground and knelt beside her husband as he dropped to one knee. "Vince. Vince?"

The look in his eyes from under his hat brim was one of pain and confusion. He took his hand from his chest and stared at the blood-covered palm. "Oh hell. I've been shot."

Blue's head whipped toward the ridge. "Some idiot

isn't paying attention to where he's shooting! Y'all, get . . ."

A second shot hit Vince above his left ear. The soft-nosed round expanded, blowing out the side of his head. His gore-splattered hat flipped off to land in a clump of bunch grass. The man who'd survived two tours of duty in Afghanistan dropped without a sound onto the American soil he'd sworn to protect.

Recovering faster than he would have ever imagined, Blue slammed Harmony onto the dry trail in a full-body tackle. They hit the hard ground at the same instant a third round punched through Blue's pack with a *thock*. Digging in with his hiking boots, he yanked his confused wife against the rocky arroyo wall and waved at Chloe, who was petrified with shock. "Chloe! Get down!! Get over here with us!"

Still not grasping that she was also in danger, she grabbed the straps on Vince's pack to drag him out of the line of fire coming from above. His dead weight and the heavy pack proved too much for her slight frame. She grunted, and jerked back on her heels. Vince's body moved an inch.

The shooter's next round plucked at the top of her shoulder. The ripstop fluttered and blood wet the nylon. Chloe gasped, lost her grip, and fell out of sight from above.

Blue and Harmony squeezed against the shoulder-high rise between them and the shooter on the ridge above. Keeping one eye on Chloe's struggle with her husband's body, Blue shrugged out of his backpack and dug into its contents. "Dammit, girl, get under cover!"

Eyes wide with fear, Harmony crouched low, her

shoulder against the bank of rocks, dirt, and scrub. "What are you *doing*?"

"That's no accident. Somebody's shooting at us on purpose!" Elbow deep in the pack's contents, Blue fished around for a long moment before pulling out a Glock 19. He would probably have left the heavy weapon home had they not planned on camping overnight in the back-country.

Vince had a Glock 40 in a Kydex waistband holster tucked under his shirt, but neither expected a sniper attack in the middle of a national park. The night before, they'd discussed their concern over illegal aliens who often crossed into the U.S. from Mexico. Though most of them only came looking for a better life, there were always a few with bad intentions.

The guy above seemed to be something completely different. Blue jerked the slide back to chamber a round. He didn't intend to let him murder them all.

Feeling a little better now that he could shoot back, Blue took several deep breaths to settle his nerves. Another chunk of lead slapped into a rock near Chloe, showering her with rock fragments and sand. It whirred away with a low, vibrating buzz.

Assuming the shooter was using a bolt-action rifle for accuracy, Blue figured it would take a few seconds for the sniper to rack a fresh round and reacquire a new target. He rose enough to peek through a scrubby honey mesquite growing at eye level on the arroyo's edge and squinted upward to locate the shooter. The ground exploded only inches away, spraying the side of his face with sand and pebbles, the echo of the shot coming half a second later.

"Shit!" Skin hot and stinging from the tiny bits of shrapnel, Blue fell hard onto the trail and gasped when he realized he was fully exposed. A round punched through his left shoulder and shattered rocks on the hard trail underneath his body. His arm went numb.

Grunting, he flipped onto his good shoulder and squirmed back to the rise, far enough away from Harmony to draw the fire and keep her safe. She screamed at the sight of blood welling from his wound.

Panting and in shock from the wound, he thought only of keeping her out of the maniac's sights. "Stay there!" He held out the hand with the Glock, muzzle pointed at the sky. She rose in a crouch, as if to race out and help. "No! I said stay down!"

Only yards away, Chloe gave up on pulling Vince's body to cover. She sat against the sheltering rise. Blood soaked the front of her shirt from her shoulder wound, but the shocked woman's soft voice floated over the bare ground with the inflection of a worried child. "Blue, Vince's been shot!"

"So have I!" He groaned and used his feet to push away and gain more distance from the women. "Stay down!" He crawled ten feet to the lowest part of the bank's taper.

Another round hit Vince in the chest. Echoes bounced from one hard ridge to the next. His shirt fluttered from the impact, but he was already beyond hurting or responding. Chloe shrieked and covered her face with both hands. "They shot him again!"

Blue reached the rise's downward slope that tapered

to a dangerously low level, ending his cover. He wondered why the sniper was shooting at the motionless body. Then the realization struck him. "Stay down, Chloe! He's trying to draw you out! Harmony, don't move, baby!"

"Why is he *shooting* at us?"

Blue ignored Chloe's question that didn't need an answer. It didn't matter *why* they were under fire. Someone was trying to kill them and that was the hard, simple truth. It was unbelievable that four people on a hike in a U.S. national park were the targets of a madman with a rifle.

The numbness of the shot was already wearing off. His arm hung limp and useless. He'd never felt such intense pain before and was swimmy-headed. Afraid he'd pass out from either the pain or shock, he gritted his teeth to keep from puking and focused on a piece of quartz to get hold of himself.

Harmony stripped the pack from her shoulders and crawled toward Chloe at the same time Blue rose just enough to peek through a different cluster of honey mesquite. Movement from above caught his eye and he saw the upper half of a man's body shift and twist in her direction.

"There you are." Drawing on hours on the shooting range back home in Dallas, he aimed the 9mm and adjusted for the elevation, hoping that the new technology in Parabellum ammo was true to the manufacturer's hype. He'd never shot uphill before, and the shooter looked to be at least a hundred yards away, but the trigonometry in his head worked out the angle for the trajectory he'd read about. He cranked off six fast shots from the 15-round magazine, thinking it was odd that his mind would register the empty brass tinkle off the rocks in such an intense situation.

The man on the ridge above threw his hands into the air and a rifle flipped end over end. "Got you, you son-of-a bitch!" Blue started to rise, but his response drew a stunning fusillade from above. The world erupted in mind-numbing noise as more than one fully automatic weapon hosed the area below the ridge.

The tiny geysers of dirt and rock exploding around Blue looked like hailstones falling onto still water. Rounds shredded the leaves off his covering brush and punched through the scant branches and lacy leaves to find flesh. His legs folded and he went down hard.

Harmony screamed over the rolling man-made thunder and reversed her direction, belly-crawling toward her husband.

Startled by the sudden continuous gunfire, Chloe spun toward Blue's body and became the next target when she involuntarily straightened into view. The rifle spoke again and Chloe's hair flew from the round's impact. Dead before she landed, she fell across Vince's legs and stilled.

Harmony's tan shirt and shorts blended well with the landscape. Knowing what would happen if she presented any part of her body above the rise, she kept her head low, grabbed Blue's shoulder, and rolled him out of sight from the rifle above.

Her husband was already gone. A single tear ran from the corner of his eye. The sight of that clear drop of liquid defined the moment, and Harmony cradled her husband's body. Trembling with fear and horror, she wept with deep, wracking sobs.

The high desert grew silent. The buzzard narrowed its spiral and circled overhead, waiting.

The day's heat rose as the sun reached its peak in the blue-white sky. Dark thunderheads to the west built to 50,000 feet, but refused to bring relief to the only survivor of the ambush. Flies buzzed the corpses and clotted pools of blood. Beyond those insects, there was no movement other than a kettle of buzzards circling in an airborne funeral procession.

No one came down to inspect the carnage. Throughout the day, Harmony had expected the shooters to come check on their victims. She worried that other hikers would stumble onto the massacre and become victims themselves, but she remained the only living human on the sun-blasted trail. The buzzards dropped lower, but wouldn't approach with one of the figures still moving.

They call them a kettle when they're flying, she thought, her shocked mind working to overcome the horror of what had happened. *They're a wake when they're feeding.*

She covered her mouth and gagged at the thought of what would soon happen if help didn't come.

Dusk arrived, bringing relief from the blazing springtime sun that slipped first behind a collapsing thunderstorm, then reappeared momentarily before settling below the bluish mountains in the distance.

Stiff and dehydrated, she released her husband's

body and risked a quick peek at the ridge above. It was as empty as the rest of the park around her. When there was no more gunfire, she gained even more confidence and knew what she had to do. She kissed Blue's cold forehead and ran a finger along the thin white line of the dried tear.

With a deep, shuddering sigh, she hooked two fingers through her backpack and swung it over one shoulder. Hesitating for a moment, she picked up his Glock that was familiar from shooting at the local outdoor range not far from their house.

A house that'll be lonely and still from now on.

She gasped at the thought and gagged, but nothing came up but bile.

With an effort, Harmony gritted her teeth until the feelings passed. She didn't need distractions right then. She needed to escape, to bring help, and tell the authorities what had happened.

Still cautious, she belly-crawled along the edge of the low rise. It was slow, painful work as rocks gouged every part of her body that scraped along the trail. Her elbows, thighs, and knees took the brunt of the abuse and were soon as raw as hamburger. After a hundred yards, her shirt and shorts were cut and torn in a dozen places, her waistband full of sand and pebbles. She paused to dig the rock samples from her pockets and drop them on the trail.

Her crawl resumed, and when her bare legs couldn't take any more, she decided she'd had enough. Hoping she was finally out of range, Harmony rose and ran in a crouch for another hundred yards without drawing gunfire. There was nothing but a brilliant orange glow over a ragged line of mountains behind her as Harmony straightened, slipped the second pack strap over her other shoulder. Grasping the Glock in a white-knuckled death grip, the only survivor of the attack jogged through the dusk to get help.

Backlit from her angle against the orange horizon and pinkish clouds, the sniper wearing a *shemagh* head scarf rose and watched the blond woman's escape. Acquiring her dim image through the scope, he grunted and asked Allah for the strength not to shoot the fleeing target.

Though the gathering darkness and her bobbing figure would have made it a challenge, he was confident it would have been an easy shot to bring her down. But then there wouldn't be anyone left alive to tell the story.